The Mutiny of the American Foreign Legion

The Mutiny of the American Foreign Legion

A novel set in the near future

Neal Alexander

Extraliminal Producciones
Cali, Colombia

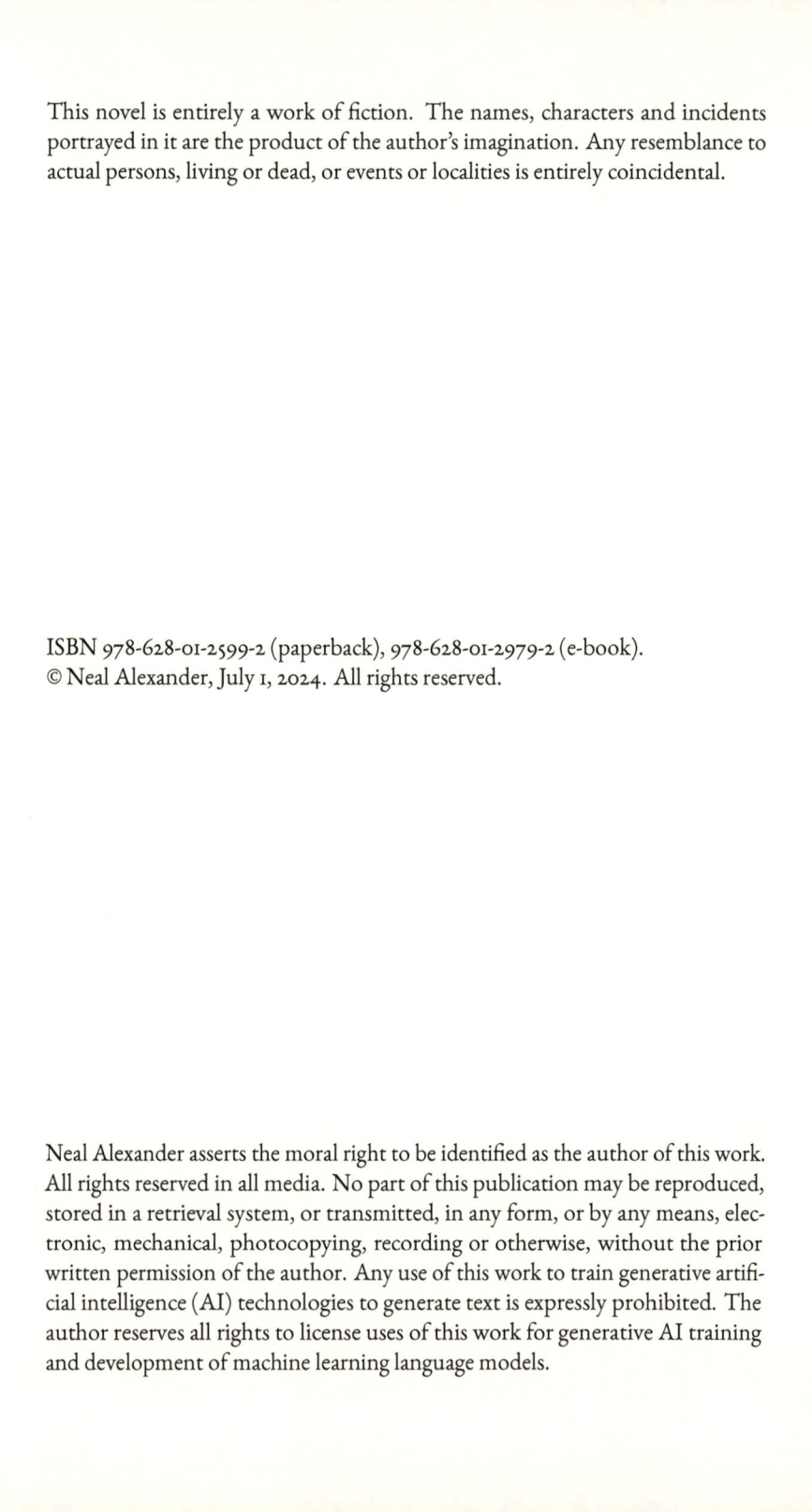

This novel is entirely a work of fiction. The names, characters and incidents portrayed in it are the product of the author's imagination. Any resemblance to actual persons, living or dead, or events or localities is entirely coincidental.

ISBN 978-628-01-2599-2 (paperback), 978-628-01-2979-2 (e-book).
© Neal Alexander, July 1, 2024. All rights reserved.

Neal Alexander asserts the moral right to be identified as the author of this work. All rights reserved in all media. No part of this publication may be reproduced, stored in a retrieval system, or transmitted, in any form, or by any means, electronic, mechanical, photocopying, recording or otherwise, without the prior written permission of the author. Any use of this work to train generative artificial intelligence (AI) technologies to generate text is expressly prohibited. The author reserves all rights to license uses of this work for generative AI training and development of machine learning language models.

> The surest way to prevent seditions is to take away the matter of them.
>
> — Francis Bacon

Abbreviations

A-Number	Alien Registration Number
ADM	automated dispensing machine
AFL	American Foreign Legion
AG	Attorney General
BLS	Basic Life Support
CAT	counterassault team
CBP	Customs and Border Protection
CO	Correctional Officer
CRV	California Redemption Value
CSP	California State Police
DHS	Department of Homeland Security
DoD ID	Department of Defense Identification
EMT	emergency medical technician
ERO	Enforcement and Removal Operations
EVOC	Emergency Vehicle Operator Course
FCC	Federal Communications Commission
HAE	hereditary angioedema
ICE	Immigration and Customs Enforcement
IED	improvised explosive device
IFAK	individual first aid kit
IFF	identification, friend or foe
LRV	light reconnaissance vehicle
MANPADS	man-portable air-defense systems
MRAP	mine-resistant ambush protected vehicle
NCLEX	National Council Licensure Examination
NDA	non-disclosure agreement
NTA	Notice to Appear
OIC	officer in charge
OPR	Office of Professional Responsibility

PSD	personal security detail
SJW	social justice warrior
TCN	third country national

Prologue

Atrato River, Colombia

As payback, they'd put Hugo on point. Again. This time, his squad had to search a boat that transported vehicles up and down the Atrato River. It was built like a landing craft with an open deck, and two floors of cabins under the bridge at the stern. Beached on the riverbank, its open loading door was down flat on the sand. His squad had boarded, and walked the length of the empty cargo deck, as far as the passenger door into the lower cabin. He had to go in first.

In the darkness, at first he could only sense the smell of rotting fish. The only light was from a single porthole to the outside. When his eyes had adjusted, he prepared to go up the metal steps to the next level. By now the rest of the squad should've followed him, but he'd known they'd leave him on his own. He raised his rifle and carried on up the steps. At the top there was a metal door with a wheel lock, a few centimeters' gap between the door and its rounded frame.

He needed the weight of fire from his team to protect him from any waiting hostile. But it was just him. He counted to ten, kicked open the door, and immediately crouched back into the corner of the stairwell. That was when the bullet ricocheted off the door and through his arm. He stopped himself from shouting out and drawing more fire. He edged back down the steps into the deeper darkness, keeping his eyes on the dark gray open doorway, above in the black wall. Only then did he shout, "Man down!" He waited silently in the darkness, hoping that this had been enough for Lieutenant Lleras. Finally Hugo heard the order to enter the cabin.

Hugo was surprised to see Lleras first up the stairs. Lleras called out "It's done," then stepped through the door. Then there were some words that Hugo couldn't catch, a single shot, then Lleras came out again and called the all clear.

The bullet had broken both the bones in Hugo's left forearm. He found a poly burlap sack on the boat, and got a squad mate to cut him a sling out of it. Then he stuck himself with a morphine auto-injector from the first aid kit. That got him through the jolts on the journey upriver in their Naval Infantry motorboat. He should've been medevacked by helicopter to Bogotá that day, but they made him wait for an officer from another unit who was going on leave.

Hugo reached the Military Hospital a day and half after getting shot. At the orthopedic ward, the receiving nurse frowned at the necrosis on his wound margins. She took issue with the only person around with any responsibility for his prior care: Hugo.

"Injuries like this have already got a high risk of infection. Not treating them with the right first aid just worsens the prognosis."

Hugo's smile was not received well.

"Don't you want to use your left hand again?"

"Sorry, I just like people taking their work seriously. I'll do whatever you say."

She seemed placated.

Hugo learned that the nurse was called Valentina Díaz. The next day he had surgery on his arm, and stayed on the ward for a week. Before getting discharged, he asked Valentina for her number, and she agreed. Then he tried to time his physical therapy sessions to finish before she got off shift. The bones knitted back together, and he was an exemplary patient. Although, after a few weeks, when his superiors started angling to send Hugo back to active duty, both he and Valentina enjoyed imagining how to evade the system for a while and spend more time together.

1

South Bogotá, Colombia, six months later

VALENTINA HAD felt something wrong in Hugo's voice when he called. He'd returned to Bogotá ahead of schedule, but he was holding something back. Gradually she got the story out of him. He'd been medevacked again. He'd been knocked unconscious, saving his squad from being blown to pieces. She was proud of Hugo, but felt like it was always him carrying the can.

Now she was driving him back to her flat, after picking him up from Military District 52 in the south of the city. On one side of the road was Tunal Park with its lake and skateboard track, and on the other were two-story, utilitarian concrete houses and the occasional neighborhood store.

Hugo looked out of the window as he described what'd happened.

"It was peaceful on the way up. Yeah, there were a couple of bodies in the water, but they were from upstream, beyond the village. You could tell, from the state of them."

Hugo looked out the passenger window. The car was stopped at lights, and a street vendor approached, hefting a string bag of oranges. Hugo was still thinking of the bodies in the river— hands and feet gone, torso bloated and puffy. The vendor recoiled from Hugo's look.

"Downstream, where the river widens, the bodies get washed up and the people there take pity on them. They give the bodies names and bury them. May God bless them." Hugo turned to look through the windshield.

"When we got to the village, we started clearing the mines. Bending over the ground in an apron, like a campesino, as if there was something useful in there. But it's just bits of rubbish."

Hugo exhaled scornfully through his nose.

"And the odd mine that can blow your arm off. You know that I never liked our first corporal, Vázquez. Yeah, maybe sometimes it helps to be a bullshitter. But, clearing mines, you need to concentrate. You don't need someone standing over you, jerking you around. Whenever your prodder turns up something, he comes out with the shit talk. 'Your number's up this time.' 'Your balls are going to get blown off, but don't worry, we'll keep them in a ziplock bag.' All that."

Hugo looked out the side window again. They were stopped at a light going north on the Avenida Boyaca, with a car dealership on one side of the road and a cluster of cheap midrise apartment buildings on the other.

For once Valentina didn't mind being stuck in the traffic. Hugo didn't often talk about his active duty, and she wanted to hear, no matter how gory.

"Then the village head came and had a word with the corporal, and he said we all needed to go to the school for a meeting.

"We thought it was some of the usual nonsense about someone stealing a chicken, or bugging a girl.

"When we got to the schoolroom, the village head said he'd forgotten something, so we went in by ourselves. Most of the guys sat down on those miniature chairs, but for me it was a relief to stand up straight for a while.

"After a minute the chat faded and we started wondering what was going on with the village head. I turned to ask the corporal, but he looked past me like he'd seen the bloody *cuco*.

"I turned back to see what it was, and I heard him scatter chairs on his way out through the door behind me, the chickenshit.

"So I saw the grenade land on the floor in the middle of the classroom. Someone had lobbed it in through the window. I saw the other guys staring like idiots. I threw myself on top of the grenade, trying to smother it with the demining apron. It seemed like forever before it went off. I started to think again, and wanted to panic. So I told myself that the grenade was the corporal's head, and I was crushing it. That's the last I remember. They told me I was knocked unconscious on the ceiling of the schoolroom."

Valentina turned to Hugo, who was smiling grimly to himself.

The two of them were silent for the remaining half hour, till they got to Valentina's apartment near the military hospital.

Hugo went into the bedroom and drew the beige polyester curtain across the small window. Then he shuffled along the narrow gap between the closet and the bed, and lay down. When Valentina finished cooking lunch, she found him asleep, still dressed. An hour later, he hadn't moved, and she left a plate of chicken and rice under a bowl on the kitchen table, with a note that she was leaving for her shift.

She walked over to the hospital. To cross the Avenida Caracas, she had to wait for a couple of Transmilenio buses to blow past nose to tail. Their articulated carriages seemed to bulge out with people squeezed up against the windows.

Once inside the hospital grounds, Valentina walked past the helipad and prayed that Hugo would never land on it again.

2

Central Bogotá

AFTER HER shift, back in her flat, Valentina saw Hugo's empty lunch plate in the kitchen sink. She went to the bedroom door and called his name before going in. He was sitting up in bed, bare-chested, watching the screen on the opposite wall. American soldiers were fighting in Iraq. He turned it off with the remote and looked Valentina up and down.

"Why aren't you wearing your uniform?" he challenged.

"Because I'm not in the hospital," she replied archly.

The bed was just one step from the door. She kicked off her shoes, upped her knees onto the bed, and straddled him.

Hugo pulled her embroidered white blouse out of her dark blue pants.

While he unbuttoned her blouse with his right hand, she caressed the scars on his left forearm.

She shrugged off her blouse and lay down alongside him. She squeezed one arm under his back and laid her head on his chest, while her other hand caressed the flat of his stomach before working gradually down.

When she woke up, she was lying on her side with her cheek against Hugo's midriff and one arm across his thighs. He was watching the movie again.

One of the actors, a Latino, was holed up in a firefight, in a jeep with its wheels shot off. All his squadmates were dead around him, and no matter how many Iraqi attackers he picked off with his pistol, more kept closing in.

Cut to a windowless meeting room, with a framed photo of a general in the middle of one wall. The Latino soldier's recollections of the firefight are being questioned by a uniformed military investigator.

Valentina rolled over, felt Hugo caressing her back, and fell back asleep.

When she woke again, the investigator was in the passenger seat of the Latino's car. They were in America, in civilian clothes. The officer kept questioning him about the firefight in Iraq, riling the soldier till he braked sharply, pulled out a gun, and forced the officer out of the car. The soldier drove on but stopped on a crossing up ahead.

An oncoming train appeared instantaneously, crushed the car, and jolted Valentina awake again.

Hugo stroked her back again, as if to say there was nothing to worry about.

"They'd never make a film about the Colombian military police. Who'd want to see it?"

Valentina didn't answer directly. As long as Hugo was in the military, what was the point of knocking it?

"People can think what they want. I know you do what's right."

Hugo was still sitting up against a pillow. Valentina wormed an arm between the pillow and his back, laid her cheek against the crest of his hip, and with the other hand caressed Hugo's inner thigh till he got the message and clicked the film off again.

3

José María Córdova Military School, Bogotá

THE NEXT day, Hugo was in his dress uniform, sitting on one of the plastic chairs that lined the concrete terraces overlooking the parade ground.

He looked across to the three giant flags on the other side of the parade ground: the school's, the Naval Infantry's, and the biggest one, the Colombian tricolor, the size of a tennis court. Its flagpole was twice as high as Valentina's five-floor apartment building.

Hugo was waiting for his turn to go to the lectern and get his medal. He looked down and saw that Colonel Lleras was doing the honors. Hugo was transported back to the boat on the Atrato River where he'd gotten shot. He tried to tell himself that it'd be one in the eye for Lleras to have to pin a medal on him, but really he knew that Lleras couldn't care less.

Hugo looked back up at the Colombian flag. When the fractures in Hugo's arm had healed and he was back on active service, Lleras and the others seemed to let it lie. Although Hugo wondered whether Vázquez had been tasked with keeping an eye on him. And to ride him, keep him on edge. Yeah, you can joke about someone's injury, but you lay off if they don't buy into it. But as far as Vázquez was concerned, if Hugo wasn't down with it, then so much the better.

Hugo heard Vázquez's voice.

"I said: when he shakes your hand, careful it doesn't come off."

It took Hugo a few seconds to realize that it wasn't part of his daydream. He stood up, turned around to see Vázquez, and snapped to attention.

"Surprised to see me here?" asked Vázquez.

Hugo wasn't going to wordplay with him.

Vázquez saw Hugo looking at his dress uniform.

"Other people can get medals as well. It's not like you saved the squad all by yourself."

Yes, I did, thought Hugo.

"You didn't see what happened outside the room."

Because I didn't run away.

Hugo tried to keep the scorn out of his face. Vázquez saw that he wasn't going to get a rise out of Hugo this time. He nodded to Hugo that he could stand at ease and walked off, looking for a senior officer to brown-nose.

Soon it was Hugo's turn to walk down the steps towards the lectern. He waited while a minor politician read out his citation in schooled cadences. Then Hugo stood to attention while Lleras pinned on his medal, looking at him inquisitorially. Hugo just kept the regulation thousand-yard stare.

4

Bogotá, Restaurante Los Gallegos

IT DIDN'T feel like a celebration to Hugo. That'd been the idea when he'd booked the restaurant for the night of the medal ceremony. To give something back to Valentina, so that they could relax and enjoy themselves going out somewhere that wasn't a mall food court.

The hostess had made them as a couple who were spending more than they could afford. Hugo was self-conscious in the ill-fitting sports jacket that he'd borrowed from his brother-in-law. On getting to their table, he'd taken it off and put it on the chair back. He thought he should've kept to his usual utilitarian civilian clothes, putting the staff on edge as he sized up the place, giving off armed bodyguard vibes.

"Don't let Vázquez spoil it for you," said Valentina as Hugo scrutinized the seafood menu. He'd chosen the restaurant thinking of the coconut fish stew of the Pacific coast, but now it seemed like an effete imitation.

He put the menu down precisely in the middle of the placemat and looked her in the eye.

"You're right, he doesn't matter to me." But his expression didn't change. His mind flicked to Lleras, but he didn't want Valentina to know that his supposed comrades had put him in harm's way. "What matters is that liars and cowards take credit for the good things we do, devaluing them."

Hugo took a swig of red wine and looked out the window. The restaurant was on the eastern edge of Bogotá, on the lower slopes of an escarpment whose higher forests marked the edge of the city. It was dark, but he could still see the flags of the military school against the sky. He looked further west, over the streetlights of the low-rise buildings of Gaitan, a working-class area, and then over the patch of darkness that was the botanical garden.

"You're on the right side." replied Valentina, "But they're human. When you took your pledge of allegiance, you said you'd stand by all your comrades, not just—"

"Haven't I done that?" interrupted Hugo. "But I've had enough. I don't want to make that pledge again."

Valentina stared at him. Even though she was in turmoil every day that Hugo was on active service, the military was what he lived for, and she was dismayed by the idea of him just quitting. Their plan was that he'd stay in the Naval Infantry for at least two years more, till they could afford a bigger place, although what they needed a bigger place for, and what Hugo would do then, had been left unsaid.

Finally she said, "So what do you want to do?"

"If I looked for a job here now, if I was lucky, I'd end up as a bodyguard to any old businessman or politician. Could be someone OK, or could be some corrupt bastard. Either way I'd have to spend my time standing around while he was in his meetings in offices for business, or motels with girlfriends."

Hugo paused.

"How do you think I'd be coming home after a day or night of that?"

Valentina didn't answer.

"I don't have enough to set up my own business yet. I need more money, more skills, more contacts, better English.

"What I've got isn't valued here."

This was a familiar refrain to Valentina.

"But it is abroad."

This wasn't. She tensed back. Hugo leaned forward, trying to convince her.

"In a year as a military contractor with the Americans I'd earn ten times more than I would in the infantry here."

"Where would you have to go?"

Hugo ignored the question.

"I'd have to learn proper English and I'd see how the business works."

"Some country we couldn't find on a map," said Valentina, answering her own question.

"It'd be a career path away from the front line."

Valentina knew there'd be no changing his mind, but she had to try, if only so he couldn't say that she'd agreed.

"So you'll be in some godforsaken badland town where everyone hates you. At least here you can speak to people."

"Who knows whether it'll be in the desert town, the jungle in Africa, some island somewhere?" Hugo turned to look out the window again, then back to Valentina and gestured with his eyebrows to where he was looking. Beyond the botanic garden, a plane was coming in to land at the airport, its light flashing metronomically.

"Every time I come in to the hangar on the military side, shaken around in a worn-out plane. Every time I look over to the civilian airport with the big glass walls for people to look out and think about where they're going. If I stay in the infantry, when do you think we'll get to fly out of Colombia on vacation?"

"Well, sounds like you're going and you're going without me," replied Valentina. "Most likely you won't even meet people like you do now, you'll be fenced in on your base. How would you like that, just waiting for terrorists to attack you in some way you never thought of?"

"Do you think we have a great time in the barracks here?"

Their food came while they were arguing. Finally they looked down at their cold plates, then at each other, tacitly agreeing to a truce. They ate up in silence and headed out without dessert. Hugo left his brother-in-law's jacket behind on the chair.

5

Saada, Yemen

THREE MONTHS later, Hugo was sitting behind the tinted armored windshield of a Toyota Land Cruiser. In the passenger seat behind him was the governor of Saada, the biggest city in northern Yemen. They were just outside the old town, and Hugo glanced up at the traditional-style houses towering over them: forty feet high, made of dozens of layers of mud, rising at the corners so that the top of each building seemed to have horns.

Saada was near the border with the former Saudi Arabia. Ansar Allah—known as "the Houthis" on foreign TV—had its roots in the north. In response to the killing of their leader, they'd brought down the government that had been in power since the unification with South Yemen decades earlier. Since then, Saada had been key to any new regime for the country.

Hugo looked down the road behind them via the wing mirror. He gave the all clear into his mic, even though the man he was speaking to, his team leader, was in the seat next to him. That was Carl Mack, an American. The third member of the team, seated in the luggage space behind the rear passenger seat, was Bastian, a Chilean. Hugo and Bastian were armed with M4 carbines, Carl with just a pistol. The three of them were security contractors working for the Parthian Corporation. The governor's head was covered by a white turban with strips of green, and he had a dark suit jacket over a white ankle-length traditional thoob robe. He'd been chosen by the former Saudi Arabia because his extended family straddled the porous border between the two countries, which hadn't been mapped before 2000.

On Carl's side of the car was a bombed-out market. Corrugated metal and breeze blocks were strewn on the bloodstained ground. On the roadside was a small group of young men, striped futa cloths wrapped around their waists and covering their legs as far as their shins, and AK-47s slung over their shoulders. One of them looked at the car and drew the flat of his hand across his Adam's apple. Carl fingered the pistol on his belt and cursed them under his breath.

Hugo assumed that a plane from the Arabian-led coalition had bombed the market before the town was occupied. The former crown prince had thrown Saudi Arabia into the Yemeni civil war. When the bombs and missiles hadn't had the desired effect, he'd sent his land forces into northern Yemen to support the southern-dominated coalition. Blowback in Saudi Arabia had led to the Al Saud family being overthrown, but the new government, fronted by Western-educated MBAs, was doubling down on the invasion for fear of looking weak.

Hugo looked in the side mirror for the hate truck: a backup vehicle that, should the governor's vehicle come under attack, would come in with all guns blazing and try to get him "off the X." The hate truck was a beat-up old Suzuki jeep but had a similar three-man team: another American, Nate; a Peruvian, Lucio; and a Salvadorean, Raul.

Most of the town was the color of the sand that swirled everywhere, but behind some of the compound walls there were islands of deep green. From the outside you could only see the tops of citrus trees. The old city was enclosed by a mud wall, about four stories high, which they skirted counterclockwise, squinting into the setting sun.

The governor was going to stay with his host for sunset prayers, Hugo assumed. At the north gate, they turned left into the old city and parked just inside the wall. Hugo jumped out, checking the surroundings as he stepped to the rear passenger door. Plenty of people looking suspiciously at the vehicle, but none with the attitude to make a move.

Hugo opened the door and the governor got out, followed by his right-hand man, who was dressed similarly but with a drabber turban and carried an AK-47. He was also from the former Saudi Arabia. Hugo and the others doubted that he knew how to use the gun. Bastian opened the back door of the Land Cruiser from the inside and sprang out. He and Hugo flanked the governor as they approached a two-story house. The door opened and the governor was greeted by the owner, who tried to keep his eyes on his guest and away from the glowering groups of people beyond.

Hugo looked at Raul, who jerked his head back to the Toyota to indicate that they should wait there. They walked to the driver's side of the Toyota to speak with Carl, the team leader.

"I could take up a position there" suggested Hugo, pointing up to the old city wall.

"Alright," Carl replied grudgingly. "Don't get silhouetted."

Hugo rolled his eyes behind his sunglasses but just said, "Roger." He nodded at a couple of dark-green-uniformed policemen, who grudgingly returned the gesture, then went up the steps to the top of the wall.

Hugo looked over the inner parapet and scanned the open area between the gate and the house that the governor was visiting. It was getting dark, but some of the surrounding shops and houses had lights over their doorways. Nothing suspicious. He stepped over to the outer parapet and looked west, where the sun had left red sky over the mountains. Then he looked southwest at the Zaidi graveyard outside the city walls, more than ten acres of battered sandstone gravestones engraved, as Hugo had heard, with not just Arabic calligraphy but mystic astronomical symbols.

Between Hugo and the graveyard, on the far side of a ditch opposite the north gate, was a soccer field. The water sanitation plant had been bombed out, and a pool of sewage had overspilled the ditch and spread from one corner to cover about a quarter of the field. Hugo turned again to look down at his team inside the city wall, trying to put the smell to the back of his mind.

An hour later it was dark, and no sign of the governor leaving the house. Carl would checked in periodically over the radio. Hugo was crouched down behind the parapet, but every ten minutes or so he'd stand up and check what was going on the other side of the wall before squatting down again.

Hugo had been trained by the Parthian Corporation in Tennessee and been shipped out first to Riyadh in the former Saudi Arabia, then to Khamis Mushait in the south of the country. After the overthrow of the House of Saud, Saudi Arabia had renamed itself to the Arabian Republic, but was still supported by the United States.

After dark, there wasn't much traffic in Saada. Hugo heard the groaning of a heavy truck on the road behind him, outside the city wall. Then the angrier sound of a faster vehicle coming the other way, then locked wheels scraping against the dirt road. As Hugo turned around to look over the outer parapet, he heard a glooping sound, then saw an Arabian Humvee flip over and down into a ditch full of sewage.

After a shocked split second, Hugo heard shouts from a soldier inside the Humvee. As Hugo ran down the steps to the bottom of the wall, he called over the radio that he was coming to the assistance of the Arabian soldiers. He burst past the policemen, who were edging away from the gate and towards the ditch but were unsure what to do. As he ran in front of the stalled truck, he reached down to his belt and unsheathed his knife. One Arabian soldier was standing at the edge of the ditch, covered in slurry, gazing blankly at the upturned driveshaft of the Humvee.

The head of another soldier was shat up to the surface. Hugo grabbed the arm of the dazed soldier and tried to ask "How many?" in Arabic. The soldier turned his shit-smeared face to Hugo and gradually worked out where he was and what Hugo meant. "One. Driver," he replied.

Hugo nodded and released the soldier's arm. He looked at the Humvee again: luckily it was leaning on the passenger side. Then he took a deep breath and dove into the cesspool. He thought back to his training in the Naval Infantry: imagined he was going into the same pond full of cow shit on the savanna near Bogotá. Cow shit was cleaner somehow. The effluent closed over him as he kicked his legs to swim down along the side of the Humvee. He found the handle to the driver's door. He didn't need to force it open, which meant that the inside of the vehicle was already flooded. The driver inside was struggling spastically. Hugo couldn't pay him any heed now: he had to find the harness that was holding him in. The driver started to grab onto him: his only salvation. Hugo couldn't lose the knife, so he wrestled free, heedless of the risk of cutting the driver. The struggle was using up Hugo's air, and he forced himself to stay calm. Now the driver was expiring, flailing aimlessly. Hugo found the harness, cut it, and dragged the driver out. He took a second to check that all the driver's limbs were free, then kicked back up. On breaking the surface, he snorted out the human waste from his nostrils before gasping for air.

Hugo dragged the driver around the upturned Humvee and to the edge of the ditch. He looked to the others to help him up. When they didn't, he had to crawl onshore and drag the driver up after him.

Hugo stood up and sheathed his knife. In the seconds that he'd spent underwater, another Humvee had arrived and the soldiers were disembarking. Among them was one American lieutenant. One of the policemen from the gate picked his way through the soldiers before stopping short and gaping at Hugo. He jerked his head back towards the old city.

Hugo looked at the American lieutenant, beat his fist on his chest, and pointed to the Arabian soldier on the ground, who was starting to move again.

"Breathed a lot of shit into his lungs. Better get him a doctor."

Then Hugo followed the policeman back through the gate into the old city.

Carl was furious with him.

"Are you getting paid to wallow in shit with towelheads?"

Hugo hadn't expected many thanks, but maybe some acknowledgment that he'd saved the life of a war ally. Carl continued.

"You have one job: protecting the life of the governor. Personal security detail. You know, the team you're supposedly on? And what the hell are you going to do now? Wait around so that the governor can be protected by a walking shit rag? You need to get the hell out of here and be cleaned up by the time we get back to base. The team will be one short, but that's the least bad option."

Carl turned his back on Hugo.

Hugo was pondering how to get back to the governor's house when he heard a voice behind him.

"Hey, man."

Hugo turned around to see the American lieutenant.

"You saved one of our unit. I'm Devon Reid, US Army adviser to the Third Battalion of the First Mechanized Brigade of the Arabian Army. You're in the governor's PSD, right?"

Hugo nodded.

"Need transport to his residence?"

Hugo nodded again, then followed Reid out through the gate.

6

Saada, governor's house

DEVON PULLED up outside the governor's house. Hugo was on the Humvee's running board to avoid stinking up the inside. He stepped off onto the ground, went over to the front side window, and gestured his thanks to Devon. Then he walked towards the main gate and waited for one of the Yemeni guards to recognize him.

Saada was at eighteen hundred meters of altitude and the air felt thin. No matter how hot it got during the day, at night it was cold and the evaporating sewage made Hugo shiver. Makeshift guard posts had been placed on three of the four corners of the wall around the lot, cantilevered out a couple of feet to give a line of fire on anyone outside.

One of the guards shouted a greeting. Scrabbling sounds came from inside, and a small door, inset into the big vehicular gate, opened for Hugo.

He walked into the compound, past the big house, and towards the service quarters, where he lived with the other five security contractors. The neighborhood, east of the walled city, had previously been home to some of the richest families in Saada. Presumably they were less well-off now, after years of war, although it was hard to tell from outside the tall mud walls of their compounds. There were citrus trees in the lot of the governor's house, but they were parched and neglected, with no one interested in harvesting their fruit or even letting anyone in to pick it. The house was made from modern materials and the high wall around the lot was made from concrete blocks rather than the traditional muddy clay.

The governor had three Toyota Land Cruisers of the same model, and he would jump into one of them at the last minute before the gates opened and all three rolled out onto the unpaved road. Most days he would go to the governorate office, a 1970s concrete building about fifteen minutes' drive away, and often later to the military bases at the airport to the northwest, or to Kahlan to the northeast.

The two Americans, Carl and Nate, had taken the better of the two bedrooms, leaving the other four to squeeze themselves into bunk beds in the smaller room. The Americans called the others TCNs, or third-country nationals, even though the US was already the third country here, after Arabia and Yemen.

When they weren't out with the governor, they watched DVDs and lifted weights, which they made out of metal poles and cooking oil cans. The black market cement to fill the cans cost them a fortune.

Hugo took his soiled uniform off outside the service quarters, left it on the ground, and walked inside carrying only his carbine.

The town didn't have a piped water supply anymore. If they could afford it, each house pumped water out of the ground. If they were ever somewhere away from traffic but near houses, they'd hear the thud-thud-thud of diesel water pumps. One time, Hugo had loaded a satellite map of the neighborhood and seen that one of the houses even had a dry swimming pool on the roof.

Hugo was satisfied with the trickle of lukewarm water that came out of the shower pipe.

As he scrubbed himself with a plastic brush, he thought about Valentina. Although the contractors weren't allowed their own phones, they bought time off Nayef, one of the Yemeni guards. It made them feel like kids bugging their dad to play video games, but that was the only way to chat with their girlfriends. Nayef wouldn't let them save contacts on his phone, so they had to key in the number each time.

He called when he could, not thinking about the time differences, because he didn't know what shift she'd be on. Sometimes she didn't pick up and he told himself it was for the same reason, that she was on shift. When she did pick up, she was cold, blaming him for leaving Colombia irrespective of what she thought. But she let him keep talking and he told her about his work. He imagined telling her how he'd saved the Arabian soldier and he knew she'd be proud of him.

When his body stung from the rigid plastic bristles, Hugo stepped out of the shower, dried himself, took a zolpidem, and slept.

7

Bogotá

VALENTINA WAS still shaken at the end of her shift. When a patient lost their head over their injuries, she still found it hard to keep herself straight. At the moment they had a kid who'd been paralyzed from the waist down. He'd been sedated and they'd let him come around today. His only family was his mother, whose job was to look after an elderly distant relative at the other end of the country, and they wouldn't give her the time off to go and see her son.

When the kid came around, he didn't know where he was. He wanted to know what'd happened to him and his squad, then he freaked out when he realized he couldn't move his legs. He started crying, screaming that he wasn't going to be in a wheelchair for the rest of his life, selling pencils at traffic lights. Then he wanted his mother and those were the last words he got out before it was all sobs. It was worse for Valentina because the trauma was from a grenade and it made her think of what could've happened to Hugo.

Before she changed out of uniform, she messaged her friend Leidy. They met for coffee and cake in a *repostería* a few blocks from the hospital. Leidy was a former colleague who'd left the military hospital and now was the senior orthopedic nurse at s big private clinic.

"It's best for everyone if you forget the job when you walk out of the hospital door each day."

Valentina nodded unconvincingly.

"Why do you stay there if it's getting to you?" Leidy asked.

"They almost always leave better than they came in: that's what makes it worthwhile."

"Well, they could hardly leave any worse."

Valentina raised her eyebrows to chide Leidy but still smiled.

"I think the upside of the job for you was Hugo. Whatever bad happened at the hospital, that was also where you got Hugo, so it was OK."

Valentina didn't reply.

"But he's not here now. You fix up one guy nice, but when he's out the door of the hospital it just reminds you that Hugo's gone as well."

Valentina looked at her to say that there'd better be a point to this.

"And you resent him for going off by himself. Even though you're still in the same position, it seems like he's taking advantage."

Valentina couldn't disagree.

"That isn't a healthy relationship. He's taken a step, you need to take one too."

Now Valentina was raising her eyebrows to ask: what step?

"I'm not sure you'd be good at managing a team just yet."

"Not like you do, no," said Valentina.

"You're a good nurse. I think you need to find a place that will let you get on by doing just nursing."

"But where? What I see is that, if you stick at it, it just gets harder and harder with time, doing the same thing and trying to keep up with this year's batch of new kids."

"Right, that's how it is here. People who just want to nurse are kept where they are. But it's not like that everywhere."

Valentina knew what was coming and was surprised at herself for not rejecting it out of hand.

"You mean in the US?"

"It can be an option. When they're accepting nurses, they're looking for particular skills, but you have those in orthopedics."

Valentina was thinking about it.

"Why not? What's the problem?" asked Leidy. "Your parents are still fine, right? They can get on without you?"

"Yeah, they're the ones telling me to go to the gym," Valentina replied, looking down at her cake. "But my English is bad."

"For now, you just need to pass the test, not be good at English."

They carried on talking it over. Half an hour later, Valentina walked out with some new contacts in her phone, surprised at how much she was looking forward to working not just in a different hospital but in a different country.

8

Saada, governor's house

IN HIS dreams, Hugo was in the Transmilenio bus in Bogotá with Valentina. He knew it was a special day because they had gotten two seats together in rush hour, rather than having to stand. As the bus headed further and further north, they were holding hands and watching the buildings get fancier and fancier. Then the bus veered out of its lane and bounced over the triangular separator blocks. Hugo stood up with Valentina and wanted to lead her out, but the aisle was an mass of knotted limbs. The bus jolted them again as the next axle bumped over the separators. Hugo turned round and looked past Valentina for the emergency window hammer. The last axle bumped and Hugo saw that they were falling off a bridge down towards a black lake and he woke up.

It was Carl banging on the wall between the two rooms.

"Shiteater!"

That's what Carl called him since he'd saved the Arabian soldier.

"Sir!" Hugo shouted back, as he got out of his bunk.

He stepped out of the room onto the strip of pitted grey cement that ran outside the front of the service quarters. He knocked on the door of Carl's room and went in.

Carl was sitting on the top bunk, wearing boxer shorts and a wifebeater, his legs dangling.

"Come here. Look at me," he told Hugo.

Hugo closed the door and went to stand in front of Carl. He looked straight ahead, past Carl's knees and at his midriff.

"I got a call," Carl said, lifting one hand, which held a satellite phone in a pouch.

On the bottom bunk, beyond Carl's hanging calves, Nate was lying on his side, facing the wall.

"A Parthian exec will be touching down in a few hours."

Hugo let his eyes drift to a photo taped to the wall near Carl's pillow. A couple of young blond kids in a paddling pool, one laughing as waved an inflatable Thor hammer. Carl had written a big black number 14 on the middle of the top of the photo.

"That's going to change our routes for the next few days."

"Yes, sir."

"The Governor's people should know already, but I want you to go to the house and make sure."

"Yes, sir."

9

al-Talh to Saada

THE PARTHIAN exec turned out to be Brett Kellerman, the head of the company. Despite having no military or security experience, he wore the same kind of gear as Hugo's team, including a pistol in a black ballistic nylon holster on his hip. Kellerman felt he had something to prove, relative to the executives of the other global security companies. A lot of them were ex-military types, while Kellerman had started with outsourcing payroll and hospital logistics. Kellerman had bought a few small specialized security businesses and knitted them together till they were big enough to spin off. Kellerman was still in his thirties and was more motivated by firefights in exotic locations than by cold chains for medical samples.

On the first full day of Kellerman's visit they went with him to the market in al-Talh market, about ten kilometers north of Saada, on the road to the border with Arabia. Once the biggest arms market in the country, it had been shut down after the occupation. Now the governor was there to celebrate its reopening to wholesale crops like grapes, pomegranates and citrus. At least, that was the idea, but no suppliers had signed up yet. So the Arabian Army had bought up enough produce for photo opportunities. Hugo supposed most of it would be left to rot on the ground, no matter how many malnourished kids there were in Saada. As well as the governor, there were some scions of minor lineages that the occupation government was trying to keep onside, and a few dozen Arabian Republic soldiers from the garrison at the air base.

While the dignitaries were inside the market, Hugo's vehicle was parked by a tire repair spot at the side of the road. Hugo was standing with

Raul and the repair man, under a thin green tarp which sagged between a couple of poles and a boxthorn bush. The governor was late heading back, but that wasn't unusual.

Raul saw Hugo watching Carl, who was talking with one of the Arabian Army soldiers guarding the entrance to the market. Carl patted the sidearm on his belt, then pointed at the soldier's, trying to make a joke.

"He's conflicted," said Raul.

"Huh?" asked Hugo.

"On the one hand, they're just towelheads, but, on the other, they're professional soldiers so their skillset goes beyond his."

Hugo waited.

"He used to be a cop in California," Raul continued. "He told Nate he left because no white male was ever going to get promoted there."

Hugo turned to Raul in disbelief, but, instead of explaining, Raul raised his eyebrows, telling Hugo to look back at Carl. Something was happening inside the market, and Carl was gesturing at them to get ready.

Ten minutes later they were heading back to Saada in convoy. Hugo looked out the window, through the hazy sandy air to ridge after rocky ridge. He was nervous because anyone could've seen which of the cars the governor and Kellerman had gotten into. Still, the three cars switched places in the convoy as they made their way back to Saada.

Hugo turned to look again at the road ahead. At the moment they were the last of the three Land Cruisers. Ahead of the first one was an Arabian Army Humvee. They turned a corner and saw a battered white pickup heading towards them on their side of the road. It had a squat cylindrical water tank jiggling in its bed behind the cab and was blind-overtaking an old Mercedes L-series truck that was laboring uphill. The gunner on top of the Humvee fired a warning burst from his machine gun.

The pickup driver had his nose ahead of the Mercedes truck and tried to cut back into his side of the road, but ran out of space. The rear end of the pickup clipped the Mercedes hood, and the pickup skidded sideways into the path of the Humvee. The impact flipped the pickup onto its side and threw the water tank out of its bed. The Humvee tried to snowplow the pickup off the road, but the driver stalled. Carl cursed the Humvee driver and braked the Land Cruiser. The Mercedes truck swerved into the side of the road and its front passenger-side tire blew out as the driver braked heavily. The truck's rear end fishtailed into the middle of the road and came to a halt.

The water tank was about ten feet long and had been hanging out the back of the pickup. It landed on the flatter side of its elliptical cross section, started to roll over, lingered at the tipping point, then flopped down off the road. As it settled, it crushed a pile of trash in multicolored plastic shopping bags, detonating an improvised explosive device. The tank was lifted back into the air, its bottom ripped open.

Carl braked sharply and struggled to stop his Land Cruiser skidding. Hugo flinched as shrapnel flew towards him and bit into the reinforced windshield a foot in front of his face.

The water tank flopped back to ground and split open like a paper bag. Water gushed over the desert at the side of the road and disappeared into the sand. The water spray in the air made a rainbow as Hugo assessed the damage. Two men were scrambling out of the overturned pickup. Hugo looked at Carl, who looked back grimly. They knew that the IED in the trash had surely been intended for the governor in the vehicle they were driving. Their job now was to get the governor out of this situation, but the road was blocked by the Mercedes truck and the pickup.

"Clowns!" said Kellerman in the back seat.

Without moving his head, Hugo looked at Kellerman in the rearview mirror.

The pupils of Kellerman's eyes were big, and the whites were bloody. Hugo didn't think that was just because of the explosion. One of the delays leaving al-Talh was the dignitaries' *qat*-chewing session after the speeches and eating. At first, after arriving in Yemen, Hugo had though that *qat* was no worse than coffee, but he was changing his mind. The chewing sessions took hours out of the day, and, although you got a buzz, it was followed by a real downer.

So now Kellerman was angry, humiliated, and high on *qat* because he wasn't used to it. It wasn't protocol, but he got out of the Land Cruiser. Already there was some traffic backed up on both sides of the incident. Kellerman looked around for someone to blame. Behind the governor's motorcade, one of the waiting vehicles was a small white Suzuki jeep that looked like it could've served in World War II. An old man was standing by the passenger door. He looked over the damage as calmly as an insurance adjuster. Kellerman looked at him, and he just looked calmly back, which infuriated Kellerman even more.

Kellerman gestured for Hugo to follow him and told Bastian to bring the tow rope from the back of the Toyota. Hugo looked at Carl, who nodded in acquiescence. Kellerman walked up to the old man and shouted at him in English, demanding to know who had attacked their vehicles. The man just carried on looking at Kellerman as if he'd said nothing.

Seething, Kellerman looked around and saw a run-down shop by the side of the road, with cinder block walls and a tin roof.

The other locals saw Kellerman confronting the old man. They grouped together and fingered their AKs as if they were going to try to free him, but they were faced down by the Arabian soldiers from the Humvee. Hugo saw that the Arabian officers were keen to see Kellerman and his Parthian contractors take the old man down. Hugo realized that he wasn't just anybody but didn't know how to make his boss, Kellerman, understand.

Kellerman frog-marched the old man to the old shop, kicked open the rickety wooden door, and dragged him inside. Bastian followed him, while Hugo guarded the open doorway.

From inside, Kellerman shouted that he needed an interpreter. One of the Arabian officers heard him, beckoned to one of his men, and they both approached Hugo. The officer stopped a couple of meters from Hugo and waited, sizing Hugo up. Hugo did nothing. Although the officer's intention was obvious, Hugo wanted him to explain himself.

"Interpreter," said the officer in English.

Hugo assented and stepped aside, keeping an eye on the other soldiers arrayed a couple of meters back on the roadside, and the Yemenis beyond them. Hugo was ready to let both the soldiers go in, but the officer indicated for the other to go by himself. Hugo guessed that the officer wanted deniability. How important could that threadbare old guy be? thought Hugo. But he was starting to feel sick, like the worst times in the Colombian military.

Hugo turned to watch the interpreter enter the shop, which was hot under its tin roof in the afternoon sun. The old man now had his hands tied behind his back with a zip tie. A rusty weighing scale hung from a cord looped over a wooden roof beam. Kellerman told Bastian to test whether the cord would hold his weight. Bastian threw the scale to the ground and the clang of the aluminum pan made the soldiers outside twitch. Then he hauled himself partway up the core, as if it were a training exercise, before jumping back down onto the floor and nodding to Kellerman.

Kellerman then turned to the interpreter, asked him if he was ready, and got a nod in reply.

He then stooped, putting his face up close to the old man's.

"Who did this?" he asked in English, jerking his thumb back to the road. Then he looked at the interpreter, prompting him to put the question into Arabic.

The old man looked impassively into Kellerman's eyes. Kellerman tried to repeat the Arabic that he'd heard. No reaction. Kellerman gestured to Bastian to throw him the tow rope. Then Kellerman walked around behind the motionless old man, knotted one end of the rope round his wrists on top of the zip tie, and threw the other end over the wooden roof beam.

Kellerman turned his back to the old man and walked towards the interpreter while fishing for something in one of the pockets in his military-style trousers. He brought out a smartphone, started to record video, and handed it to the interpreter, gesturing that he should continue to record the helpless captive.

Again Kellerman asked the old man who was responsible for the attack. This time there was disdain in the old man's eyes that further infuriated Kellerman, who went back to the rope hanging from the beam. The old man groaned softly as Kellerman heaved him, leaving him hanging from his wrists behind his back, a couple of feet off the ground, with all his weight on his shoulder joints twisted the wrong way. Kellerman gestured to Bastian to take the rope with the old man's weight and then walked round to face him again, checking that the interpreter was still recording. Now Kellerman didn't have to stoop to look the old man in the eye, and he asked him the same question again. This time the old man muttered something, but not to Kellerman: it was some invocation of strength for the ordeal. His eyes sank deeper into his contorted face with the pain.

Kellerman saw a sheaf of white-and-blue-striped shopping bags lying on a sack of onions on the floor. Kellerman pinched one off and flapped it till it filled with air. He walked back to the old man, put the plastic bag over his head, and pulled it down tight over his mouth.

The bag dimpled into the old man's mouth as his lungs tried to suck air. Bastian and the interpreter watched Kellerman, seeing how long he would wait before letting the old man breathe. Finally Kellerman took the bag off, looked the old man in the face and asked again who had attacked their convoy.

Kellerman waited for the old man's striving gasps to subside. Instead, they became shallower but just as urgent. The old man's head drooped.

Kellerman hesitated, then grabbed the old man's turban and pulled his head back up, but now his eyes were aimless rather than meeting his own.

Kellerman gestured to Bastian to let up the rope. The old man sank slowly to the floor. Kellerman squatted next to him on the dusty frayed cement and felt for a pulse. He stood up again and gaped at the shuttered window.

"Jesus."

He looked at the body as if deciding whether to do anything with it. Then he turned to the interpreter, took back his phone, stopped the recording, and put the phone in his pocket.

Kellerman staggered towards the door and Hugo stepped aside to let him out. On seeing Kellerman exit without the old man, a murmur of discontent rose from the Yemenis on the far side of the cordon of troops. But then all sides became aware of a sound from further down the road: a convoy of four more Arabian Army Humvees coming from Saada. At risk of being surrounded, the Yemenis retreated back to their own run-down battered jeeps. Soldiers got out from the first Humvee and tied a rope to an axle of the overturned pickup, ready to pull it out of the road. The first Humvee pulled up, and the first out were an Arabian Army captain and an American adviser, a lieutenant with ORBACH on the name tape on his uniform.

The Arabian captain went to speak with the ranking officer, and Orbach came over to Kellerman. The interpreter had come out of the shop and rejoined his unit.

"They told me that you and your men were all OK," Orbach said to Kellerman.

"That's right, thank God." Kellerman paused. "But there's something I need to show you."

The two of them went into the shop and closed the door. A few minutes later Orbach came back out with Kellerman and addressed himself to Hugo.

"Cardiac arrest. The most respectful thing is for us not to touch the body."

Orbach was starting to get the official version out there. He turned to Kellerman.

"Some of us are going to escort you to the airport while the others salvage the remains of their comrades."

Hugo saw that Kellerman was fidgeting with his phone, turning it over and over in his hand. *Kellerman's subdued now*, thought Hugo, and he hadn't even gotten into the downer phase of the *qat*.

"Sir, is your phone secure?" Hugo asked Kellerman.

Kellerman blanched. Orbach realized that something was wrong and looked expectantly at Kellerman.

Kellerman deferentially handed the phone over to Orbach, who found the video and pressed play. He saw Kellerman bind the old man's wrists and took a deep breath.

"I just wanted to see him shit himself," pleaded Kellerman.

After a few seconds, the image swerved away from the old man and went black. But the recording didn't stop. Orbach frowned and jumped ahead: still black. He jumped forward again and again: the same.

Orbach looked relieved, but Kellerman was incredulous.

"But I saw the phone in the interpreter's hand and it was recording."

Hugo realized what'd happened.

"Sir, skip to the end," he said to Orbach.

A few seconds before the end of the clip, the blackness swirled away again, replaced by the old man dead on the dusty floor.

"Sir, the interpreter switched phones. He put yours in his pocket and used his own one to record," said Hugo.

"Why the hell would he do that?" replied Kellerman.

Hugo was going to reply, but Orbach had heard enough.

"We should stay together as far as the airport," Orbach told Kellerman and Hugo.

So Lucio and Raul took over in the governor's Land Cruiser while Hugo and Bastian rode with Orbach and Kellerman.

The overturned pickup had been pulled out of the way and the motorcade carried on towards Saada. Inside half an hour, with light still left in the sky, they were at the airport. As the Humvees pulled up, short of the terminal building, Orbach leaned forward and spoke to Hugo and Carl.

"While Mr. Kellerman gets onto his plane and out of here, I'm going to brief the governor, then you're going to escort him to his house. I'm going to recommend he sits tight there tomorrow. OK?"

The three Land Cruisers pulled up in the drop-off zone.

Hugo got out and opened the door for Kellerman and Orbach. Kellerman shook Hugo's hand. He seemed to be in a daze, and Orbach had to guide him towards the doors to the departure area. Then Orbach walked over to the governor's Land Cruiser. The governor's assistant got out and talked to Orbach for about a minute. The assistant got back inside while Orbach walked over to the Humvees and got inside one of them. Then the motorcade headed on.

At the governor's house, the gate opened and the three Land Cruisers entered, along with one of the Humvees. The governor was escorted out of his Land Cruiser, and the staff from the house gestured to Hugo and the rest of the PSD that they could stand down. They walked to the back of the compound, telling themselves to be glad that they'd made it back in one piece. They heard the Humvee leaving and the gate closing behind it. Then it took off with the other one that'd been waiting outside.

10

Saada, governor's house

Hugo was woken up by a mortar exploding. By the way it shook their quarters, it had landed between them and the governor's house. He looked at his watch: 5 a.m. He got down from the bunk and kicked the other three awake. As he pulled on his clothes, Hugo looked through the jalousie windows at the inside of the compound. No one. He stepped out, knocked on the door of the other room, and Carl opened.

"Take Raul, go to the house."

Sheltering against the inside of the compound wall, they ran till they were opposite the front wall of the governor's house. They looked along the top of the compound wall, against the dark blue predawn sky, then ran across to the front door of the house. Hugo knocked while Raul stood with his back to the house, eyes open for any intruders.

As they waited, they registered the sound of gunfire coming from the west, the direction of the old town.

Hugo knocked again and shouted for Nayef.

Raul said what Hugo was thinking.

"Something's wrong. We need to get inside."

Hugo knew the door was secured by multiple bolts going into the floor and walls. He started to wonder how to get inside despite them. But he guessed there'd be another way.

"PSD! Entering!" he shouted. He turned the handle and the door swung open. He pushed against the friction in the unoiled hinges, and he and Raul were in.

Floor cushions were strewn around the main reception room, rugs had their corners upturned.

"*Hijueputa.*"

Hugo realized what'd happened. Orbach and the governor's people knew that the murder committed by Kellerman was going to set off a riot, or worse. When they got to the house last night, the governor had sneaked back out again in the Humvee, and his local staff cleared out as best they could. But as far as the Yemeni forces knew, the governor was still here, and now they were assaulting the building to kill him.

Carl came over the radio, wanting to know what was going on.

Before Hugo and Raul could reply, they heard a boom from the far side of the front wall. They hit the floor, covering their heads with their arms, and the RPG exploded against the front wall of the house's second story. They looked at each other, making sure they were OK, then got up. As they headed back towards the front door, Hugo replied to Carl over the radio.

"Sir, there's no one here. They must've evacuated with Orbach and the Arabian soldiers last night."

Hugo heard Carl swear and kick his metal bed.

Finally Carl spoke again.

"Roger. I'll send Nate and Lucio. Secure the compound wall."

Hugo sighed. But Carl was right. If the enemy realized no one was guarding the wall, they'd be inside within a couple of minutes.

Nate came over the radio, saying that they were heading for the front wall of the compound. Hugo looked at Raul and pointed to the ceiling. Raul nodded and they went up the stairs and cleared the floor: no one. They went into the main bedroom, whose window was above the front door. They approached the window from opposite sides, kicked away the rugs and cushions, not knowing whether the enemy had a line of sight. Raul opened the window, and Hugo crouched down on the floor and rested his left hand, under the barrel of his M4, on the sill.

Nothing. No incoming fire.

Hugo could see the compound walls and roofs of the houses opposite, but that was it. Then he looked down inside their own compound and saw Lucio climbing up the steps to the guard post on the left corner. Nate ran inside the wall towards the opposite corner. As soon as he started to cross the vehicle gate, it was punctured by AK fire. The enemy must've seen the shadow of his feet under the gate. The incoming fire was anticipating Nate's movement, shredding the gate around him as he ran. He staggered, injured.

"Come on!" muttered Hugo.

In the guard post, Lucio looked up over the bottom of the slit window and ducked back as some of the fire was attracted there.

Once Nate had made it past the gate he stopped and groped at his throat.

Hugo looked at Raul, who nodded back, knowing that Hugo wanted to go and help Nate.

Hugo spoke over the radio. "Nate's been hit. I'll get him back to quarters."

As Hugo ran out of the room and down the stairs, Raul pulled out an olive-colored 40mm round from a cargo pocket in his jacket. His M4 carbine had an M203 grenade launcher under the barrel. He opened the barrel and snapped in the round.

Hugo ran out the front door and approached Nate along the inside of the wall. He saw a shard of metal had been blown out of the gate and into Nate's neck. Hugo's first thought was that Nate was still holding his head up straight: there was enough left of his neck for him to have a chance. But his shirt and body armor were soaked with blood as he fingered the metal helplessly. Blood was spurting from his neck, but with less pressure each time.

Hugo put one arm around Nate.

"It's me, Hugo. Let's get you out of here and patched up."

Upstairs in the house, Raul judged the enemy's location based on the angle of fire at the gate, the street layout opposite, and what he could see of the compound walls. He judged an angle of elevation for his M4, and fired the buckshot round.

Hugo led Nate down the right side of the house, needing to support him more and more as they got closer to the back of the compound. They met Carl and Bastian coming to help.

"Jesus, how long did it take you to get a man down?" Carl said angrily to Hugo.

Hugo ignored him. He took one of Nate's shoulders and Bastian the other. They dragged him to the quarters, where Carl kicked a pile of clothes and gadgets off a plastic chair, then dragged it over to the bunk beds. Hugo and Bastian sat Nate down. Hugo tried to keep pressure on his neck as Bastian reached under the bed for an individual first aid kit.

Bastian opened the IFAK and took out a dressing. Hugo nodded for him to carry on, and he wrapped the dressing around Nate's neck, then his shoulder, then bandaged it in place. The bleeding was less, but that could've been because of so much he'd lost already. Nate was unresponsive now. Hugo and Bastian lifted him onto the bunk bed and tilted him onto his left side. They stood up and looked at each other. There wasn't much more they could do for him now.

Carl held the silence for a couple of seconds before speaking.

"I got Orbach on the sat phone. That old guy that died yesterday was some kind of Muslim priest and the whole city's in revolt."

The other two waited for Carl to say more.

"Orbach was at the airport. The governor and the Arabian Army are being evacuated and he's going with them and the other American advisers."

The other two were still looking at Carl, who gritted his teeth before continuing.

"What do you want from me? We need to secure our position before breaking out to a more secure location."

He turned on his heels and left. As Bastian followed him out the door, he glanced sheepishly at Hugo.

Hugo looked at Nate again, but the best he could do for him was to somehow fight their way out. As he headed back to the house to join Raul, he heard a phone ringing. For a second he thought it was a hallucination. Then he stepped into the other room and realized it was the sat phone, which Carl had left on one of the bunk beds.

He picked it up and pushed the green button.

"Ayala."

"Reid, US Army. I drove you back in the Humvee."

"Right."

"I can see that you're under attack. Why won't the Arabians come and help you get the governor out?"

Hugo couldn't see any reason not to be honest.

"Because he's not here. He flew out last night."

The caller laughed.

Hugo said nothing.

"Sorry, man," said Devon.

The pause was punctuated by gunfire. Hugo was about to close out the call when Reid spoke again.

"The Yemenis think he's there, though?"

"Right."

"I'm a few blocks away."

Hugo waited.

"They want the governor," Reid continued. "They'd love to shoot all of you in the PSD, but he's the one they're really after."

Reid paused to think.

"They're attacking the north wall?"

"Affirmative."

"In five minutes I'll be outside the east corner of the south wall."

"Roger."

"You should all bring Yemeni clothes."

"Roger."

"Out."

It didn't sound like much of a plan to Hugo, but it was better than what they had.

Hugo pocketed the sat phone and ran out, setting a timer on his black resin wristwatch.

Outside in the compound, Carl and Bastian had dragged one of the bunk bed mattresses over to the south wall.

"Sir!" Hugo called out as he ran over to them.

Carl looked at him impatiently.

"I spoke with a US Army lieutenant on the sat phone. He said he'd be at the east corner of this wall in five minutes."

"You must've misunderstood. Sounds like he's going to come down the chimney like Santa Claus."

Carl turned away dismissively, then gestured at Bastian to help him lift the mattress.

Hugo gritted his teeth. He needed to get back to help the others. As he ran along the inside of the east wall of the compound, he called out to Raul on the radio.

"Raul, situation?"

"Incoming fire. Me and Lucio are responding. What about Nate?"

"We patched him up, but he needs help. I'm going to go up into the east guard post and help Lucio. You go through the house and find Yemeni clothes for the six of us. And keys to one of the cars."

"Roger," said Raul skeptically.

Hugo looked at the timer on his watch. By now he was below the guard post on the opposite side of the wall to Lucio.

"When you've got the clothes, go to the east corner of the south wall."

Hugo climbed up to the guard post, using concrete blocks that had been set into the wall as steps.

"Lucio," he said over the radio, "where's the enemy?"

"Most of them are in an alley on the opposite side of the road, to my west."

"So I'm further away, but they're not expecting fire from here."

"Affirmative."

Hugo visualized the street layout opposite and made sure his M4 was set to fire on burst. He pushed up out of his squat position, aimed and fired at movements at the end of the alleyway opposite, then dropped back down.

After a couple of seconds, the enemy identified the new source of fire, and Hugo's guard post shook as AK rounds slammed against its metal walls. Hugo looked inside the compound and saw that Carl and Bastian had lifted the mattress over the top of the south wall, covering the razor wire. Carl was standing with his back to the wall, hands together on top of a bent knee, making a stirrup.

Hugo felt like shouting at them not to do it, but it wouldn't help. And Lucio had fired again, and it was back to his turn.

After squeezing off another burst, he turned and saw Bastian just ending his short run-up to Carl, putting his foot into Carl's hands, and getting hoisted up to the top of the ten-foot wall. Bastian hung on to the wall through the mattress and hooked his heel over to lever himself up. A split second after getting his head and one shoulder above the level of the wall, incoming fire ripped through the top of the mattress and hit Bastian's upper body armor. The mattress had told the enemy where to expect a target. Bastian tried to hang on, but he'd've been better off letting go. The fire continued from multiple angles, and by the time Bastian was knocked back and fell into the compound, most of his skull had been blown away.

Hugo intoned a blessing for Bastian under his breath.

"I've got the clothes, and the car keys." It was Raul on the radio.

"Roger," replied Hugo. He looked at his watch. Less than two minutes to go.

"Take them in the car to where Carl is," continued Hugo. "Back the car up against the wall. We'll meet you there."

He looked over to the opposite guard post. "Lucio, did you copy? We're going to make a break for it."

"Roger."

As Hugo scrambled down the makeshift steps to the ground, he saw Raul coming out of the house carrying a cardboard box.

Hugo ran to the back of the lot. Carl was just looking down at Bastian's body.

"Sir, we need to evacuate."

Bastian's body was in the way of the Land Cruiser that Raul was already reversing to the south wall. Hugo crossed himself and bent down to lift the shoulders. He looked at Carl expectantly. Carl gradually came around and realized what Hugo wanted. He looked back, resentful at being told what to do, but then stepped to Bastian's body and lifted the legs to drag him out of the way.

"Lucio, help me with Nate," Hugo said over the radio.

Now there was some gunfire from beyond the south wall, the same kind that'd killed Bastian. But it was answered by the deeper sound of a heavier-caliber weapon. Hugo looked at Carl, who looked away, not wanting to acknowledge that there was something to Hugo's plan.

Hugo ran to their quarters, where he and Lucio picked up Nate. Hugo carried him over his shoulder to the Land Cruiser.

They could hear a vehicle engine on the other side of the wall. Hugo put Lucio down on the hood of the Land Cruiser, took the sat phone from his pocket, and dialed.

"You made it."

"Sure did," said Devon.

"How's the enemy fire?"

"Weaker than ours."

"Roger. We're down to five, one badly injured. We're going to scale the wall now."

"How're you going to evacuate the wounded man?"

"We've got a car backed up against the wall."

"Under the mattress?"

"Roger."

"Stay clear and we'll make it easier for you. Out."

Hugo hung up and shouted at the others to step away and keep their backs to the wall.

A few feet from the top of the wall, one of the blocks exploded as a round came through it from the outside. Hugo and the others flinched. By the time Hugo recognized the sound as a fifty-caliber machine gun, a five-round burst had pulverized more of the blocks. The gunner went on, pausing for a couple of seconds between five-round bursts. As long as Hugo had his back to the wall, he could only see the cloud of fragments, not the damage to the wall itself. When a longer pause came, Hugo turned around to face the wall. The upper part, above the level of the roof of the Toyota, had been demolished. Hugo climbed on top of the car, stepping around Nate's motionless body, raised his M4 and stepped along the roof of the car till he was at the wall. Through the holes, he saw a Humvee parked about fifty yards away, with the machine gun still pointing their way.

Hugo kicked the wall and felt it flex. He kicked it again and a fragmented section fell into the alleyway below. AK fire came from one side, at too narrow an angle to do more than shower Hugo with fragments blown off the remains of the wall.

The Humvee was moving towards them now.

Hugo ducked through the hole in the wall, did his best to assess the most likely source of the enemy fire, and squeezed off a burst. Then he looked back into the compound and waved at Lucio and Raul to carry Nate out.

They heard an explosion tear metal apart at the front of the compound.

"They've blown open the front gate," said Hugo over the radio.

A soldier came out of the Humvee and received Nate's limp body through the hole in the wall. Hugo put out some more covering fire.

Raul went back and got the cardboard box out of the Land Cruiser.

Carl stepped to the rear end of the Land Cruiser's roof, jumped down and ran to the back door of the Humvee.

Now the gunner on top of the Humvee was returning the enemy fire with interest.

"Everyone out," Hugo called over the radio. He walked back to the front of the Land Cruiser's roof. He looked down at Bastian's body on the dusty ground. He pondered trying to jump down and drag it up and out of the compound. Without a head, it seemed that there wasn't much left to save it from. From the corner of his eye he caught a movement at the corner of the house. He dropped to a squatting position and fired off a burst from his M4, but not before a couple of AK rounds had gone past him and out through the hole in the wall behind him.

Outside the wall, Raul was into the Humvee with the box.

Lucio jumped down through the hole in the wall, but a stone twisted under his foot and he stumbled. As he tried to stand up, he took a burst of enemy gunfire. Off-balance, he was knocked back, but the round had been stopped by his body armor. He staggered to his feet again and managed to get into the Humvee.

Hugo jumped down through the hole in the wall, the last one out of the compound. He clambered into the Humvee, and it took off.

11

Saada, Yemen

Raul was in one of the two sunken rear seats of the Humvee, with Carl in the other. Hugo and Lucio crawled over Raul and squatted on the raised platform between the two seats. They pressed against Nate, who was lying motionless on the platform. Hugo looked at Raul and tipped his head at Nate. Raul shook his head, meaning that he was dead.

Hugo saw Devon in the front passenger seat. Carl should've been the one to speak first, but he seemed dazed.

"You saved our asses."

"I won't forget," Devon replied jokingly.

"What the hell is going on?" asked Hugo, jerking his chin at the city beyond.

"Your boss killed one of the most respected men in North Yemen. On video."

Hugo looked down and sighed.

"And no one here will stand for that."

"Shit, so the Arabians have pulled back to the airport?"

"And half of them have cleared out already. As soon as they knew about the video, they started evacuating."

"Can we get through in time?"

"No, man, no way through there. All the armed men in Saada and around are trying to fight their way to the air base and kill the *ajnabi*. One Humvee's not going to break through. We have to go the other way."

Hugo didn't know what that meant.

"From here we can go on the backstreets on the east of the city, to get onto the road to the northeast, through the Alfare Valley and cross over to Khbash in Arabia. I'm betting that the men from roadblocks will have decamped to lend a hand at the air base."

Devon gave Hugo a second to suggest something better before continuing.

"Although in this thing"—Reid indicated the Humvee—"word will get ahead of us. So we need to find a less conspicuous vehicle."

Now Hugo understood the plan. "And other clothes." Hugo gestured to the cardboard box in the back of the vehicle behind him.

"Right."

Carl seemed to be coming back to reality and he butted in. "But you're Army, you wouldn't want to be taken captive without your uniform."

"So we have to be creative. Keep our fatigues but add a futa, headdress—"

"Sir." The driver, who had HETTRICK on his uniform, turned towards Devon and interrupted him. "It's around the corner."

The Humvee slowed down and stopped.

Devon called out "Tamura!" and the man in the turret climbed down, over Nate's body, and out the side door. Gripping his carbine, he walked cautiously to the corner and looked around to what was beyond.

"This is a black market gasoline spot," Devon explained. "We're betting that anyone buying here today will be coming from the west and then head out west again, towards the airport."

Devon saw that Hugo was skeptical.

"And that everyone else except the driver has already joined the fighting."

Hugo nodded.

The soldier on the corner was still watching and waiting.

"That video's raising hell in half the world," Devon told Hugo.

Devon looked for a reaction in Carl's face but got none.

"And it's blowing back on the Arabian government as well. Maybe the Arabian soldier who shot the video had is happy about that as well."

Devon's eyes lost their focus on as he listened to a radio message.

"A likely customer for their gas," Devon explained to Hugo. "Someone's driven across the next intersection towards them."

"Let's go," said Devon to his unit. He opened the door and stepped out.

Tamura crossed the intersection, turned left and ran along the wall on the far side.

Hettrick drove the Humvee, slowly following Devon, along the unpaved road between the mud walls of two compounds. It stopped before the next intersection, so as not to be visible from the gasoline sales point to the right. Tamura could see it now, from his crouching position in the ditch on the corner.

Although inaudible to Hugo, a call from Tamura caused the driver to launch the Humvee forward, just in time to block the way of a pickup that was barreling towards it. The driver of the pickup piled on his brakes but still collided with the side of the Humvee. He cursed in Arabic, reached for the AK on the seat beside him, then leaned out the window. But before he could pull the trigger, his brains were blown out by Tamura, who'd crept up from the ditch towards him.

Tamura holstered his pistol, then opened the door of the pickup, so that the window dragged the dead man's torso out by the shoulder. Tamura let the dead man fall to the ground, jumped into the driver's seat, and closed the door behind him.

The two gasoline sellers reached for their own guns, but Devon shouted at them in Arabic. They came to their senses, realizing that they were outgunned and with only barrels of gasoline to hide behind.

In the Humvee, Hettrick relayed what Devon was saying over the army radio.

"Hold your fire."

The gasoline sellers lowered their weapons and walked away.

"Get your Yemeni clothes on," Hettrick told Hugo and the other PSD members.

Tamura drove the pickup to the gasoline sales point and got out. Hugo helped him lift a half-full barrel of gas into the bed. Tamura stayed in the back, holding the barrel steady while Hugo got behind the wheel. The Humvee took off and Hugo followed it.

Inside the Humvee, Hugo and his men were already donning the Yemeni clothes from the governor's house. Hettrick found his way onto a narrow road headed north. When they had passed the last of the walled city to their left, they turned right into another group of compounds, then right again, and carried on till the road petered out, parallel to a dry river bed.

Both the vehicles stopped. Hugo jumped out of the pickup truck and fetched a can of water from the Humvee. Sparingly, he used it to wash the brains and skull fragments off the dash and inside of the windshield.

The four others got out of the Humvee and approached Devon.

"We're heading for the border. I don't see a way to do it with the casualty. My suggestion is we cremate him in the Humvee."

"We should bury him," said Carl, trying to assert himself.

"Even if we were left in peace long enough to bury him, do you think he'd stay buried?"

Carl had no reply.

"Get everything you need out of the Humvee," continued Devon.

Then he went back to the pickup and used the hand pump on top of the barrel to fill a jerry can, which he took over to the Humvee. He looked around at the others, waiting. They stopped what they were doing and came over to stand a few yards away.

Devon acknowledged them with a nod. Then he opened the jerry can and doused everything inside. He set fire to a strip of cardboard from the box and dropped it inside. They watched the flames take hold.

After a few seconds, Devon nodded again, and they got back to work. Tamura opened the hood of the Humvee and took a grenade from a clip on his uniform.

"Frag out!"

The others ran and sheltered behind the pickup.

Tamura dropped the grenade into the engine compartment of the Humvee. When it exploded, the hood was ripped up and off the vehicle with the sound of a howitzer.

Hettrick got back in the pickup and made a U-turn. Tamura got in the front alongside him, and the five others got up behind in the bed. Then they were off again.

As they headed north along the same road, a couple of restless teenage boys stepped forward from the closed shutters of a small shop and shouted encouragement. Devon nodded back, and after a second look at him, the boys shouted agitatedly as the pickup sped past. Not getting their attitude, Hugo looked at Devon for an explanation.

"There are millions of black people in Yemen," Devon responded.

Hugo raised his eyebrows.

"Most likely you never went where they live, huts made out of cardboard and plastic sheets, on land by rubbish dumps and where no one wants to go."

Hugo wanted to tell Devon that he got it but didn't know how.

"They call them Al-Akhdam: servants. Those kids were shocked because Al-Akhdam are just supposed to do the most unclean jobs. Maybe they were shouting that you Yemeni Arabs were shamed by having me among you." Hugo nodded seriously at the joke.

"On the other hand, some Al-Akhdam have been paid to fight, so that anyone they defeat is doubly humiliated."

Devon paused again.

"So maybe the kids were shouting at me to really waste the Arabian Army."

"Maybe it looks fake for you to be the OIC," Carl butted in.

Devon ignored him.

By now they were coming up to the main road. It was empty. The pickup slowed, then climbed up from the unpaved road to the pocked asphalt. As the engine noise eased, they heard gunfire coming from the west and they turned to look at smoke rising from around the airport a couple of kilometers away. Then the pickup got its rear wheels onto the asphalt, turned right, and sped away again.

"So, what're we supposed to be doing headed out of town when anyone with any balls is headed the other way?" Hugo asked Devon.

"We're not going to be stopping to explain ourselves."

"Yeah, but even something to shout out as we carry on past."

Devon thought for a few seconds.

"We're going to ambush any Arabian forces sent south via Khbash to relieve the air base."

Hugo nodded. It seemed feasible. Worrying, in fact.

"If they really do come into Yemen for that, let's hope they don't destroy us before we can make ourselves known."

"No, man. They won't be coming. They were scared enough being here when the lid was on. The best recruits used to come from Najd, the power base of the Al Saud family, and now that they've been kicked out, no one in the army is up for actual fighting."

Hugo nodded, relieved.

"Look, who was that guy that died yesterday?"

"Late to be asking that, no?"

Hugo realized he should be doubly grateful for Devon rescuing the PSD, given that it was their boss who'd set off the conflagration. Still, he wanted to know.

"The way he was dressed, he didn't look like anything special."

"What about his headdress?" asked Devon.

"That's what I mean: it was just plain white, nothing fancy."

Devon gathered his patience before replying.

"A white headdress means you're *sayyid*."

Hugo had no idea what that meant.

"Descended from Mohammad."

"But he wasn't armed. Didn't even have a dagger. The guy looked like he couldn't afford a decent one."

"They don't need to be armed, not even with something symbolic like a *jambiya*, because they're considered above feuds. They're the ones people go to when they want a feud resolved. They've got clout with everyone."

Now Hugo was getting it.

"Jesus."

They drove on in silence for a couple of minutes before Hugo spoke again.

"So it should be, what, a couple of hours to the border?"

"Right. If all goes well."

Hugo's headdress shielded him from the sun and dust better than his usual baseball cap. Having had just a few hours' sleep, he nodded off for a few seconds at a time between potholes.

Before he knew it, they were passing through a small town. He looked at his watch: still morning. Most of the buildings in the town were in ruins, their roofs blown off and walls pitted by bullets. In front of a bombed-out hospital, a man squatted behind a small pile of onions for sale and scowled at the pickup as it passed. Among the intact buildings, none was open.

Devon saw him looking around.

"This is Kitaf. Salafis had an educational center here till the Houthis forced them out and demolished it."

Devon indicated up ahead and to the left. They had passed through the town already, and the remains of cement block buildings were scattered on bare land. One you could imagine as a classroom, another as a dorm, smooth piles of windblown sand on their leeward sides.

"And the hospital was bombed by the Saudis."

Hugo nodded. The people here had had all sides trying to wipe them out.

"This was one of the places I thought we might get challenged," said Devon. "See if you can doze some more. In about an hour I'll wake you up."

Sure enough, next time Hugo looked at his watch, an hour had passed. They were passing through more mountainous country, although ahead the road headed down and there was a broad valley with a few bushes scattered on the hills on either side.

Now it was Hugo's turn to keep alert while Devon and the others slept as best they could. It was nearly midday and the sun was beating straight down on the pickup. Hugo scanned the rocks on both sides of the road: no trace of anyone. Then he peered up into the hazy cloudless sky. He thought he saw something moving, but it was close to the sun, and after a few seconds he had to look away.

Hugo looked up again and this time he could see it properly: a small aircraft, straight wings, lazily drifting over the mountains behind them.

He kicked Devon's leg, snapping him awake.

"Drone," said Hugo, jerking his head towards it in the sky.

Devon squinted into the sky till he saw it. "Shit."

He thought for a few seconds. "Not much we can do for now. Looks like an Iranian one."

Hugo nodded.

"There's no cover here," continued Devon, turning his head towards the bare mountains, "and anyway if they're onto us, then there's more need for us to keep going. If we start switching up our speed, trying to make a harder target, then they'll realize we saw the drone and it'll prompt them to attack. And the guided weapons are lethal to thirty meters, so we don't have good odds. We'll be out of the mountains soon—then the road is straight, clear to the border. We'll be an easier target then."

Devon thought some more before speaking over the radio to Hettrick in the cab.

About twenty minutes later, the pickup had come down out of the mountains, but instead of speeding up on the flat road ahead, it slowed down just enough for Hugo, Devon and the others to jump out. They scrambled behind a rock outcrop, hidden from the road but still baking in the sun.

The vehicle speeded up. Now the drone was flying lower and straighter. Hugo and the others watched as it aligned itself with the road. But before it could release one of its guided bombs, Hettrick reached the town of Albuqa, which was strung thinly along the road. The pickup skidded to a halt alongside a dented metal barrel topped by a hand pump.

Hugo took a deep breath as the drone wheeled away and circled higher.

Tamura got out of the pickup, leaving Hettrick at the wheel, and walked over to the man by the barrel.

"Gasoline," he said in Arabic, reaching slowly inside his jacket for money. But before completing the action, he turned around and glared at someone sitting on a homemade wooden bench twenty yards away, in the shade of dry palm fronds tied over a makeshift frame.

"What'd you say?" he asked aggressively as he strode towards the bench, fingering the M4 carbine by his side.

The man stood up, one hand on his AK, and waited.

Hettrick cursed, got out of the cab of the pickup, and stalked to one side of the road, keeping both Tamura and the man on the wooden bench in view.

The other handful of men who'd been hanging around had now been joined by half a dozen others, spread out around a perimeter to get a better view.

Hettrick stepped slowly away from the road, closing down the angles of the man confronting Tamura.

The silence was broken by the pickup ignition: one of the onlookers was trying to drive it away.

Tamura reached for his M4 but let it go again on seeing all the Yemenis reach for theirs. Instead he headed towards Hettrick, cursing him for leaving the vehicle unguarded.

The tension broken, the onlookers laughed at the discomfort of the outsiders.

Tamura and Kettrick walked back to the road and turned to watch the pickup disappearing down the road, the way they'd come. Admitting defeat, they turned the other way, to the jeers of the group of men by the gasoline drum.

Devon watched the drone break its holding pattern, drift lower, and start to track the pickup again. He stood up and led the group further away from the road, heading north, to the west of Albuqa. The drone leveled out and held a course directly above the pickup, closing on the pickup. Hugo saw a bomb released from under one of the drone's wings and called to the others. They watched the bomb fall parabolically, accelerating towards the ground. The pickup's new driver and passenger were still laughing at the expense of the foolish strangers when the bomb exploded a few meters away and they were torn to pieces by shards of metal from its pre-fragmented casing.

Devon and the others turned and carried on north again while residents of Albuqa, among them the men by the gasoline drum, shouted in dismay and crowded onto the road to watch the flames rising from the pickup truck to the south. Some started to run to help but were called back by others saying that the drone would return to deal with them in the same way.

Twenty minutes later, Hettrick and Tamura were joined by Hugo, Devon and the others, and continued on foot over the last ten kilometers to the Arabian-held border post.

12

Arabia

Four hours later, they were on a minibus heading to the military air base near Khamis Mushait.

Having seen them walk up the straight desert road to the crossing, the Border Guard had been dubious. But they relaxed on seeing Devon and the other US Army soldiers show their uniforms under their Yemeni clothes. Now that they were out of Yemen and in an allied country, Hugo, Devon and the rest had been elated and confident of getting home.

First, though, they'd been taken to the police station in Khbash, a few kilometers to the north. There the chief also looked nervous and unsure what to do with them. He politely required them to wait while he called up the chain of command. He wasn't happy about the foreigners keeping their weapons but didn't try to force the issue because the visitors had more firepower than his men. It suited everyone to have them on their way, and after an hour the foreigners got the OK to use their phones. Hugo called up Parthian's office in Riyadh, which arranged for a vehicle to come from Najran, an hour away.

When the driver pulled his shiny minibus into the station parking lot, he wasn't happy to see that his passengers were half a dozen grubby foreigners dressed in Yemeni handoffs and carrying carbines. But he didn't want to lose the job, and they set off within a few minutes.

By now it was late afternoon, and the desert sand was flecked with more and more green irrigated fields. The soldiers and Parthian contractors took turns dozing, leaving one of each team to keep watch.

When Hugo woke up, it was dark outside, but he could feel the bus climbing and turning on mountainous roads. Devon was speaking on the phone. When he hung up, he turned to Hugo and looked at him in the dim light from the dashboard up front.

"So all American military personnel who were in Yemen and made it out are being airlifted again in the next few hours."

Hugo nodded.

"We should make it in time before the last flight leaves. Anyway, they'll wait for us."

"'Us'?" asked Hugo.

"Right," said Devon without embarrassment. "I don't know what they're thinking about contractors, but I'll do what I can." Devon paused. "By the way, everyone's still calling it King Khalid Air Base except when speaking with a politician in the new government."

Hugo looked back as if to ask "so what?"

"The airlift is a political decision from Washington. No more American presence in Yemen."

Hugo still wanted Devon to get to the point.

"But some of the Arabian opposition groups are trying to capitalize on the unrest caused by that video."

Suddenly Hugo felt lost. "What groups?"

"Like the Al Saud family. The Arabian Army is still full of officers who are Saudi, meaning part of the Saudi former royal family. The new government didn't purge them, it's just tried to stop the royals countermanding orders from their superior officers. They still do, though."

They'd gone through Dharhan, having driven half of the five-hour journey. On a flat stretch among the mountains, the driver pulled off the road so the men could take a leak. As they were getting out of the bus, they heard the rumble of vehicles coming from behind, the same way that they had come.

"Get behind the bus," called out Devon, not wanting those in the other vehicles to see a bunch of armed irregulars. Devon watched the road from behind the rear corner of the bus, his carbine hidden. A few seconds later he was dazzled by the headlights of the first of a convoy of six military trucks. As the last one passed, he could see it was full of armed soldiers.

Devon thought for a few seconds before speaking to Kettrick and Tamura. "Make sure some of your uniform is showing, in case we get pulled over. But keep some of your Yemeni clothes on as well: that way they may not notice that not all of us are Army," he added, nodding at Hugo.

Soon they were back in the minibus and underway again. It was the same mountain roads, but now no one felt like sleeping.

Devon leaned over to Hugo and said, "Those trucks looked like National Guard. They were always close to the Al Saud family, while a lot of the regular Armed Forces welcomed the new government. Let's hope we don't get in the middle of any reckoning between them."

As they came into the last town before Khamis Mushait, a police SUV was parked at the side of the road, and an officer flagged them down. The driver muttered under his breath. Kettrick put one hand on the driver's thigh and, looking him in the eye, pushed down on air with the open palm of his other hand, telling him to keep calm.

As the policeman approached, pistol in a side holster, the driver lowered the electric window with a whirring. The policeman's eyes widened at the heavily armed foreigners filling the minibus, and he peremptorily asked the driver a series of questions in Arabic.

At hearing something about Americans, Devon pointed to the US Army insignia on their chests and said, "From Yemen."

The policeman nodded slightly, told the driver to wait, and walked back, talking on his radio. When he got to the SUV, he leaned back against the hood, scrutinizing the minibus as he talked. After a few minutes he ended the radio call, walked slowly back to the window and spoke briefly to the driver. Relieved, the driver thanked him. As the policeman walked away, he rolled up his window and turned to speak to the foreigners.

"No problem. We go straight to King Khalid base."

Which was what they wanted. But now they were even more incentivized. Half an hour later, they turned off the highway and onto the dual carriageway approach to the air base. They passed under a pair of concrete wings, sprouting from a concrete column in the central reservation.

As they approached, the buildings and runway were to their right, behind a fence topped with razor wire. A convoy of three trucks came speeding towards them but passed them as if they weren't there.

At the first checkpoint, a soldier came out of the booth and the driver opened the side door for him to look inside. Although he glanced over them with disgust, he just waved the driver on. Hugo and the rest of the foreigners were relieved, but not the driver, who gripped the steering wheel and muttered to himself louder than before.

As they came closer to the runway, they made out the tail of a C-17 transport plane, overtopping the central building of the air base and lit by floodlights on towers. The minibus went through a second checkpoint as easily as the first and headed on between two parking lots with scattered civilian vehicles. The twenty-year-old building had two stories, whose generic rectangular blocks had, on the side of the approach road, been dressed up with pale yellow concrete to look like bas-relief. The driver slowed up as they came alongside the terminal, passing under a walkway that linked it to the parking garages. A soldier with a carbine waved them to the side. Again he looked disdainfully inside and jerked his head to indicate that they could proceed.

To get into the terminal building, they were patted down and their weapons inspected. Devon went through first, and the Arabian soldier took out the magazine from his carbine and thought about removing the rounds. Devon and the others tensed, ready for a dispute, but the Arabian soldier slapped the magazine back into the gun and handed it back. They were inside the main terminal without any problem.

A few steps further, they were into an open space running parallel to the facade, with a few aloe vera plants struggling in white gravel.

Devon paused and turned to Hugo. "What do you think of the security here?"

"Seems it's not really us they're worried about."

"Right. But then who?"

Hugo looked again at the men on the terminal's entry doors. They were scanning the personnel inside the building, hardly paying attention to what was outside.

"It's like they want to stop people from getting out, not getting in."

"Right. All the security is National Guard. But how did they take over from the regular Armed Forces? Makes me wonder whether those trucks that were leaving the base just now were regular troops that got tipped off and wanted out of the way."

Looking around, Hugo saw some groups of men in dark green Air Force uniform overalls, close together and glancing occasionally at the National Guard while discussing among themselves.

"Let's hope we're airlifted before it hits the fan."

They entered the next building. A wide glass-walled corridor ran its length and, opposite them, one set of double doors was guarded by American soldiers and opened onto the night air. The officer in charge was Orbach, who they'd last seen at Saada airport.

He looked disdainfully at Devon and his men, still with Yemeni clothes. "So finally you made it. Better get rid of those rags and keep whatever's left of your uniforms."

Devon bit his tongue, and he and his men unwound their headdresses and futas and threw them into a corner.

"Sir, four of the governor's PSD made it out with us."

Orbach looked at Carl, then at Hugo, Raul and Lucio. "No TCNs."

Carl sneered at Hugo, then stepped over to join Kettrick and Tamura.

Orbach's assistant used his tablet computer to wave Devon forward, but Devon didn't move.

Hugo stepped up to Orbach to make his case, but Orbach cut him off.

"Your boss got us into this mess," said Orbach, cutting Hugo off. "He's the one that should be taking care of you. Our plane's overloaded as it is. You need to arrange your own exit."

"And him?" replied Hugo, gesturing at Carl.

"He's our compatriot. You've got no claim on the US Army."

Orbach turned away and looked at Devon, wanting to know why they weren't progressing.

"Sir, you can see what's happening here. Anyone left is going to be caught in the cross fire between Arabian factions," said Devon.

"Want to stay in solidarity?" asked Orbach.

Devon gritted his teeth, but Hugo nodded at him, telling him that he and the others would take care of themselves. Devon nodded back, then gestured at Kettrick to proceed.

Orbach's assistant read Kettrick's name from his chest tape, tapped it into his tablet, and asked Kettrick for his DoD ID.

Devon leaned towards Hugo and spoke briefly in his ear before turning back to Orbach.

A couple of the Arabian Air Force officers approached Hugo, Raul and Lucio. Their uniforms had their names in the Latin alphabet: Alghamdi and Rashid.

"You," Alghamdi said to Hugo, gesturing dismissively at the three of them, "come with us."

Hugo's expression made it clear that he wasn't going to be dictated to by them.

Alghamdi put his face up close to Hugo's. To the National Guard security men, it looked like he was cursing Hugo. But he whispered, "We can help each other get out, or we can all die here."

Hugo nodded and indicated to Raul and Lucio that they should go with the two Arabians. The National Guardsmen looked on disdainfully but didn't intervene.

The Air Force officers led them to an office that looked like it'd just been ransacked, with filing cabinet drawers open and papers strewn over the floor. Alghamdi picked a framed photo of the president of the Arabian Republic off the floor and laid it flat on a shelf. Then he turned to Hugo.

"The National Guard are leading a coup to try to get the Al Saud family back in power. They already control access to the base, and when the American forces have gone, then they'll wipe out any Republicans who stand up to them."

He looked Hugo in the eye. "I see the Americans are leaving you behind, but the National Guard aren't friends of foreign military contractors." He paused. "Can we work together?"

Hugo didn't disagree, so the officer continued. "I'm a pilot. You're better armed than us. Maybe we can make it to one of our helicopters."

"Then what?"

"It's a Bell 412 with full tanks. We can make it across the Red Sea and to the nearest part of Egypt."

"We'll be shot down."

"Maybe, but the National Guard aren't pilots, and none of the Air Force pilots from here will come after us. We're hours from the next fighter base, and with the country heading for chaos, we may not be anyone's top priority."

The engines of the American C-17 roared louder. Through the window they saw it slowly turning towards the main runway.

From behind them in the main hall, they heard the sound of small arms and then of a rifle.

"Let's do it," said Hugo.

"Down the corridor to the left, at the end there's an exit door. Last I saw, it had one National Guard on it."

Hugo nodded and looked at Raul and Lucio to make certain that they were ready.

Alghamdi took a deep breath before stepping briskly back out into the corridor. He gestured to Hugo that it was clear, and the five men carried on to the next corner. Hugo and Raul readied themselves, then, on a nod from Hugo, they both stepped out, turned and fired their carbines at the National Guardsman before he had readied his own rifle. The impacts knocked him back against the door before he slumped down to the ground in a growing pool of his own blood and viscera.

Hugo ran to the body, stepped over it, and pushed the door open. No immediate gunfire. They stepped out into the night air. The sound of small-arms and rifle fire reached them from different directions. Rashid fished car keys out of a pocket and the others followed him, running to a civilian pickup parked on the edge of the apron.

Alghamdi pointed to the rear lights and Hugo smashed them with the butt of his carbine. Then they were off with Rashid and Hugo in the cab and the other three in back in the bed.

They skirted the apron, keeping close to the floodlight posts and staying in darkness as much as possible. Distance blunted the sound of gunfire from the main building as they sped away.

Bending forward to the dash and squinting up through the windshield, Rashid saw flashes of gunfire inside and said, "Once the National Guard takes the control tower, they'll see us."

Now they could see Bell helicopters on the apron, half a kilometer from the truck, spaced about thirty meters apart.

"You've been transported by helo before?" Alghamdi asked Hugo.

"Yes, sir."

Rashid pulled up beside the furthest one, behind the one next in line. "Look out for fire from the cab at the top of the tower," he said before getting out and heading for the helicopter.

Alghamdi followed him. Hugo, Raul and Lucio ran back to the helicopter that was next closest to the control tower.

The flashes of gunfire inside the tower cab stopped.

Hugo and Raul shifted uneasily on their feet while Alghamdi and Rashid rushed through preflight checks.

They saw the glass on their side of the tower cab blow out and a split second later heard the shot that'd done it. Hugo hoped that the helicopter they were sheltering behind hadn't been fueled up like the other.

The helicopter engines started behind them.

Now a bullet thudded off the tarmac a couple of meters from Hugo. He crouched down under the tail, just behind the fuselage, and returned a burst of three rounds from his M4.

As he stepped back behind the fuselage, Raul stepped out and fired another burst, as multiple rounds hit the asphalt and boomed into the fuselage of the helicopter they were sheltering behind. Hugo heard the revs of the escape helicopter increase. He looked around and was relieved to see just darkness, meaning that its lights were still off.

Hugo went forward to the nose of the helicopter they were sheltering behind and took his turn firing from there. His feet splashed. He looked down and saw a floodlight being reflected in a puddle. Aviation fuel.

By now the engine sound from the escape helicopter was deafening. He looked at Raul and Lucio, then pointed to the escape helicopter. They ran, but Lucio was hit in the top of his thigh, below his body armor. He sank to his knees and was hit again. Raul returned fire while Hugo dragged Lucio behind the fuselage of the escape helicopter. Rashid pulled Lucio into the fuselage as Hugo pushed him up. Hugo shouted at Raul to join them as he fired at the tower. Raul ran back and he and Hugo climbed into the helicopter together.

The engine pitch increased even further and they lurched upwards and then forwards. Only the cockpit lights were on, and they could still see gun flashes from the tower, without any idea how close the rounds were passing them. The fuel on the ground by the next helicopter caught fire and the flames spread to the fuselage. As Hugo shouted, "Brace!" a fuel tank exploded and their own helicopter was buffeted up and forward, tilting over to one side and then back as Alghamdi tried to compensate.

The smoke from the explosion blocked their view of the tower, but two Humvees were speeding towards them. They didn't have machine guns, but they were letting off more gun flashes, probably from rifles. But by now the helicopter was accelerating, gradually leaving the Humvees behind and clearing the fence at the north end of the base.

13

Red Sea

Now they were high enough to see the lights of Khamis Mushait. Alghamdi leveled off at about a hundred feet and headed to the east of the town, as if towards Riyadh. Hugo clicked on his flashlight and kneeled down by Lucio, who was in a pool of blood from his femoral artery. Hugo held his hand.

"We made it out, headed for the beach now."

Lucio's eyes were glazed. Raul brought a first aid kit. They bound Raul's thigh, then ripped open his shirt to dress the other wound. Red mush oozed out from under his body armor, which had caught the AK round on its way out and sent it back into his chest cavity, ripping his organs to pieces. Hugo and Raul looked at each other. Hugo took another dressing from the first aid kit, covered Lucio's face with it, then made the sign of the cross over him.

Once the town lights were well behind them, Alghamdi steered the helicopter to the west, asked Rashid to take over the controls, then turned to Hugo and Raul.

He saw in their eyes that Lucio hadn't made it. He looked at them, then down at Lucio, and said the Janazah prayer. When he'd finished, he waited a few seconds before speaking again.

"We're going to keep low and avoid towns. Of course the radio's off, but from what I heard on the ground, the military and National Guard have got bigger problems than us to worry about. The fuel should just about get us to the most southeastern part of Egypt, on the Red Sea coast."

He broke eye contact for a second while he thought about what'd happen if they didn't make it.

"We'll start to head out over the Red Sea to the south of Jeddah, but to the north of Port Sudan on the other side. Then we'll turn west again and landing in Halayib.

"That's in a triangle of land that's disputed with Sudan, but it seems to have been quiet there recently."

He smiled hopefully before turning back to the cockpit controls.

Hugo and the others were exhausted, but with their friend's body between them at their feet and the noise and vibration of the helicopter, there was no hope of sleep.

It was still night, but from their low altitude, they could see they were continuing over the familiar flat, arid landscape, with lights few and far between. After about half an hour, Alghamdi turned further west and crossed the main road towards Jeddah. They could see the edge of the Arabian plateau coming ahead of them. As they approached the void beyond, they were sucked towards it by the chilled night air draining down towards the sea. Hugo's head swam as the land dropped away beneath them and they floated in the blackness beyond the escarpment. Alghamdi struggled with the joystick as he took the helicopter through the turbulence at the edge and then down beside the dark gray cliffs.

They turned north again, flying halfway up the escarpment between the plateau and the coastal plain. Hugo's eyes adjusted and he could make out cliffs, pinnacles and the occasional stand of pine trees. After half an hour more, Alghamdi turned to the west again and sprinted for the coast at top speed, zipping over the main coastal road. The sun was coming up behind them so that the helicopter seemed to be chasing its shadow to the west. Hugo looked to the north and strained his eyes looking for Jeddah on the horizon and any signs of conflict there, but they were too far away. They reached the Red Sea, and as they sailed over its crumpled surface, Alghamdi eased off the speed and sat back for a few seconds before turning to Hugo.

"From here it's a straight run to Halayib."

Hugo nodded.

"But the way we're going, we'll be running on fumes before then."

Hugo had an idea what was coming.

"We need to lighten the load," Alghamdi continued. He didn't need to glance down at Lucio's body. "We're over the sea now."

Hugo looked away. Alghamdi was right. Hugo was grateful that he'd held off asking till now. Hugo wouldn't have wanted to tip Lucio's body onto the desert that he'd fought so hard to escape, but the sea was something different, even though there was nothing to take his body down, so it'd stay floating till it was eaten, or washed ashore on the same desert...

Hugo forced himself to stop his train of thought, looked back at Alghamdi, and nodded.

Alghamdi went back to the pilot's seat. Hugo and the others patted down Lucio's body and found a wallet. Hugo opened it to see a passport photo of his girlfriend. He quickly flipped the wallet closed again before pocketing it. There was nothing else. Raul opened the passenger door and the humid sea air blew in and around them. Hugo tied the dressing tighter around Lucio's head, then made the sign of the cross over his chest. He nodded at Raul to lift the legs while he took the shoulders. They staggered over to the open door, swung the body beyond the helicopter's skid, and watched it tumble gently into the sea.

Hugo and Raul sat down again and set their eyes forward. Alghamdi looked around and nodded acknowledgment before turning back. There were a couple of hundred kilometers to go, and Alghamdi was following a diagonal line, staying equally far from Jeddah to the northeast and Port Sudan to the southwest.

He and Rashid were watching the fuel gauges, but they couldn't do anything but keep a straight course and a steady cruise speed of about two hundred kilometers per hour.

In a bit less than an hour, the east coast of Africa started to materialize through the haze on their left side. As they approached the coast, Alghamdi determined their location thanks to a natural harbor he could see on his old paper map, and he relaxed slightly.

Hugo approached Alghamdi. "How long till we get to Egypt?"

"About half an hour." He paused. "If ever." He pointed to the fuel gauges, which were well into the red.

Hugo nodded before heading back into the passenger compartment.

There was nothing to do but look down at Sudan's Red Sea coastline. Dark blue water directly below them, then aquamarine between the reefs and the sand beaches. The occasional village with a jetty and small boats.

Hugo thought about Valentina. He'd spoken to her once a week or so from Saada, a voice-only call after a long day trying not to get shot. He'd gotten angry when she'd told him she was moving to the US. He thought that she was doing a tit-for-tat and that she should've at least discussed it with him first. Now he cursed himself for scolding her, not wanting to think that those phone calls could be the last they ever knew of each other. He wondered whether she'd seen Yemen in the news and how far the rioting had spread. This job of his hadn't turned out to be about learning English and making lucrative contacts. She'd been right about that.

His thoughts were interrupted by a clattering from above his head. He instinctively looked up, then over to the cockpit, where Alghamdi and Rashid were talking to each other and working switchgear on the dashboard. A few seconds later, when they were done, Alghamdi turned to Hugo and explained.

"One of the engines ran out of fuel. It's going to be close."

Up ahead, now they could see a fence heading perpendicularly inland from the coast across the sand, a straight line into the continent.

"Here we go," Alghamdi called out. "Open the left door."

Hugo slid it back, and the clammy tepid sea air rushed in over them.

On the Sudanese side of the frontier, an unpaved road ran north as far as a ramshackle single-story border post, isolated in the sandy arid landscape. On the Egyptian side, the small town of Halayib, a scattering of tin-roofed buildings, petered out a couple of hundred meters north of the border, but the main road carried on as far as a well-maintained concrete building with a tall communications antenna.

A couple of men came out of the Sudanese border post and alternated between gesticulating at each other and looking up at the helicopter as it sped up the coast towards them, about fifty meters above the water. A third man came out of the building with a rifle. Hugo and Raul knelt in the open doorway with their arms up, hands behind their heads, trying to show they weren't hostile. The Sudanese soldier tracked them with his rifle. They heard a shot as he lowered his weapon. It took them a second to realize that the gunfire had come from the Egyptian side.

They had already crossed the line of the border fence. Alghamdi slowed down but kept heading north into Egypt. Hugo looked for the source of the gunfire and spotted a sandbagged position between the border post and the fence.

Alghamdi shouted, "They're firing ahead of us, to turn us back, but we have to touch down. There's no choice."

Again Hugo and Raul knelt in the open doorway with their arms up, silently pleading forbearance. Alghamdi took them lower. They were almost opposite the gun emplacement and could hear the shots more clearly. Hugo realized they were facing a fifty-caliber machine gun, not a rifle. Seeing the unknown helicopter approach them, the Egyptian gunner switched to targeting it directly. One round went through the acrylic windshield and another into the engine compartment. Whether that finished off the remaining engine or whether the fuel ran out, the helicopter lost power and plummeted down vertically, its rotor blades spinning idly.

Hugo and Raul had a couple of seconds to brace themselves by grabbing seat harnesses. But when the helicopter hit the water, they were thrown upwards, their bowed shoulders denting the ceiling, before they smashed back down onto the floor. They tried to put their concussed thoughts back together as seawater welled up to the bottom of the passenger doorway and spilled inside.

Hugo looked up and saw the shore about fifty meters away. Were they still under fire? They had to get out. He looked around and saw Raul struggling to lift himself off the floor as the water rose around them. Hugo got out his knife, cut through his bootlaces, and shouted at the others to do the same.

Alghamdi and Rashid had released themselves from their harnesses, but couldn't open the front doors against the weight of water, so they clambered back into the passenger compartment. Alghamdi shouted to Rashid to go. The water was halfway up the passenger doorway and Rashid dived into the gap.

Hugo got his own boots off. Raul was up on a seat, tugging at his shoelaces. Hugo cut through them, but by then the water was just a couple of feet off the ceiling. He pushed Raul towards the door. Raul reached the top of the doorway with one hand and pulled himself out. Before the water filled the compartment completely, Hugo took a deep breath and swam through the door against the incoming current.

Hugo reached the surface and gulped air gratefully. Rashid and Raul were already there, and as he looked around, Alghamdi surfaced as well. He shouted at them to swim to the shore. A squad of Egyptian soldiers were watching them from the beach, guns in hand. Hugo gripped Raul, who was struggling to swim with one of his boots still on. As they approached the shore, the waves dashed them against a submerged reef and the jagged coral sliced through their clothes and flesh. Hugo shouted to stand up and they staggered over the reef with their hands in the air, then splashed down in the calm water on the other side and waded towards the shore, at the mercy of the soldiers.

14

Sacramento, Pelton Medical Center, Orthopedic Ward

VALENTINA WAS on the last day of a stint on the orthopedic ward of one of Sacramento's biggest hospitals. She was responsible for five patients, six at a stretch. At the moment, one of them was Estela, a mother in her forties with chronic back problems, not helped by being overweight. Finally she'd come into the hospital for spinal decompression and to get two vertebrae fused. The surgery itself had gone as planned, but then the site had gotten infected, so she'd been in for a couple of weeks.

Valentina was in Estela's room, draining the surgical site on her back. As she reached for the silicone tube that emerged from Estela's side, she asked about Estela's son, Daniel, who came in to visit her every other day. He was studying water resources management and helped pay his mother's medical bills by working as a dog walker.

"Is he busier, now that it's getting colder?"

Valentina popped open a valve on the bulbous end of the tube.

"September's the busiest time. I don't know why," replied Estela. "That's when he revamps all his social media."

Valentina let the bulb suck out the discharge from the infected wound.

"He's got as many clients as he wants for now."

Valentina detached the bulb from the tube, getting a whiff of the rancid sweet pus.

"That's a luxury, being able to turn down work," she replied.

Estela smiled. "I think nursing has the better prospects."

"Thanks," Valentina replied as she dropped the pus-filled bulb into a biohazard container.

"Soon Daniel will have a degree and a job," she continued as she reached for another bulb. "He'll be able to walk his own dog if he wants one."

The second bulb filled past halfway. Valentina swapped it out and showed it to Estela: "Still a way to go with the healing."

Estela nodded in distaste.

"But that's how it's supposed to look. A lot of white blood cells that've died doing their duty."

Estela forced a smile and Valentina laughed. As she stood up, she changed back to her more formal nurse demeanor and picked up her clipboard.

"And how would you rate the pain in the surgical site?"

Estela knew the drill and answered cheerily, "The same, about a three."

"Good, thanks," said Valentina as she noted that on the clipboard.

Valentina headed back to the nurses' station and accessed Estela's electronic medical record. As Valentina was typing in the information, Sherry, the charge nurse, told her that Jessica Sager needed her.

Valentina walked down the corridor and took a deep breath before going into Jessica's room. She was a media officer for a tech company, in her forties. She'd tripped outside the state capitol and smashed her kneecap against the edge of one of the steps. The kneecap had broken into two pieces, which the surgeon had wired back together the day before. Her leg was now in a splint to stop her from flexing it and forcing the pieces apart again.

"Look, there's blood," said Jessica before Valentina was through the door.

Valentina hadn't gotten used to people in America diving into whatever they wanted with no pleasantries. As she walked over, she could see a fringe of red seeping out from part of the dressing. It was common in this kind of surgery, but Valentina didn't want to seem dismissive.

"You're right," said Valentina. "We can change that dressing now."

"Well, if it's time for it to be changed, why haven't you done it already?"

Managing to ignore the question, Valentina said, "I'll fetch a clean dressing."

When she returned, she went to work, releasing the velcro bands on the knee brace, starting with the one up around the thigh. The next one was over the freshly operated knee, and she went as gently as she could, but Jessica gasped angrily.

"Nearly there," Valentina placated as she released the next band, below the knee.

"Where are you from, anyway?" asked.

Valentina pondered her reply as she released the last band from Jessica's calf.

"Colombia. Now we need to take off this figure-eight bandage."

"But you had to pass American tests to work here?"

"Yes, ma'am," replied Valentina as she unwound the bandage, lifting Jessica's knee slightly to get it out from under.

"Ow," complained Jessica. Valentina wondered whether she really was going too fast, just to get away from Jessica's xenophobia.

"And the padding...," said Valentina, slowly peeling back the white material. Close to the knee it was stuck to Jessica's skin with clotted blood.

"I hope you're grateful to those SJWs outside the capitol."

That one was easy for Valentina to ignore, because she didn't know what it meant. Valentina wetted a ball of cotton with saline and started to swab away the dried blood, so she could ease the clotted padding away from the skin.

"The surgical incisions have healed well, and I'm going to give you a new dressing."

"I was trying to get away from someone with batwing arms and a handmade sign when I fell over," added Jessica, gesturing at her knee.

Valentina kept on wrapping her knee with fresh padding.

"Those whiners are turning Capitol Park into skid row."

Valentina concentrated on looping the new figure-eight bandage around Jessica's leg.

"Now I need to lift your leg onto the brace again."

"Illegals should just get in line," continued Jessica.

Gritting her teeth, Valentina closed the velcro bands again, from the calf upwards.

"You know, I spend a lot of time in the capitol. After Nemeth gets elected, more jobs are going to be for Americans rather than foreigners."

Valentina finished up as quickly as she could and, in the corridor, closed Jessica's door behind her and leaned back on it.

Luz, another of the nurses on the ward, seeing that she was upset, approached her and put her arm on her shoulder. Valentina put her own hand gratefully on top of Luz's.

Valentina rubbed her eyes. "Thanks, Luz. Aren't we looking after them well? What's the matter with them?"

Luz stood with Valentina till she moved her hand away, letting her know that she was OK to continue.

15

East Sacramento, California

VALENTINA STOPPED at traffic lights on Stockton Boulevard. She'd gotten off her shift at 7 a.m., half an hour ago. She reached over to the cell phone clipped to the grille in the middle of the dashboard and pressed play on another social media video. She didn't want to think that Hugo had had anything to do with that guy in Yemen getting killed, but she knew he must have.

The sound of the video came over the phone's tinny speaker. The voiceover explained how the footage of a Yemeni cleric being killed had gone viral round the world. The video was a montage of American interests being attacked and trashed: a McDonald's in flames in Jakarta, an Apple store reduced to a pile of glass shards in Turkey, demonstrators lobbing Molotov cocktails at the wall of the embassy compound in Senegal.

The car behind Valentina honked. The lights had changed. Valentina looked up to the road ahead and drove on. She heard the news anchor say that Islamists had taken over the former Saudi Arabia and that America had made the same mistake as with Iran fifty years earlier.

The small imported car followed S Street under the freeway into midtown. The people at the agency had said it would be better to live in Gardenland or Mikon, that there were plenty of Latinos there, but she wanted to live in a building, not a house. An apartment building, like they called it here in America. That was what she was used to in Bogotá.

Valentina circled the blocks around her building, one eye on parking spots, the other on the videos spooling on her phone: a news anchor talking about insurrection in the former Saudi Arabia, then footage of a crowd pouring into government offices in Riyadh and trashing them.

Once into her flat, Valentina sat at the table against the wall of the small kitchen, and pressed stopped on the videos. She found a number for Parthian and eventually got through to a human, but they wouldn't even acknowledge that Hugo was working for them. She browsed more videos between searching for other ways to get through to Parthian.

She woke up with her head on the table, with a few hours to go till her next shift.

16

Sacramento, Pelton Medical Center, Orthopedic Ward

VALENTINA WAS going through Brandon Werner's pre-op checklist for his hip replacement. She told herself to concentrate on Brandon, not the news she'd seen on her way in. Brandon was a cook. Well, he worked at one of the higher-end Sacramento restaurants. But no one understood his job title when he said it in French, so he was a cook as far as the nurses were concerned. He was young, in his thirties, but needed a hip replacement because of avascular necrosis in the ball joint at the top of his femur. The end of the bone was dying, its jagged surface snagging like a cheese grater on the inside of his hip joint. Brandon hadn't wanted a hip replacement: that was for old people. But the pain had gotten so bad that he couldn't pretend to walk properly any more.

Valentina handed him a tube-shaped device with a mouthpiece and a gauge running down its length. "This is a peak flow meter. Put this end in your mouth, make sure that your lips are making a seal around it, and blow as hard as you can."

Brandon took it reluctantly. The burn marks on his arm, an occupational hazard, reminded Valentina of Hugo.

"They're operating on my hip, right?" asked Brandon, looking askance at the flow meter.

It took a second for Valentina to return to the present. ""Right. It's to make sure your lung function can cope with the stress of surgery."

Brandon blew aggressively into the meter and handed it back to Valentina.

"Thank you," she said and noted the result on the form before carrying on.

"Do you have diabetes?"

"No."

"To check for early signs of diabetes, we need to test your urine." She handed him a plastic container.

Instead of reaching out to take the container, he replied angrily. "Diabetes? Isn't my data in the system?"

"You can provide the sample when we've been through the rest of the checks," she said, nodding at Brandon's bathroom.

Brandon looked at the floor. When he spoke again, his tone had changed.

"The sooner they fit the thing, the sooner it'll need to be replaced. I'll be in my forties and already on my second... operation."

He found it humiliating to say "hip replacement."

Valentina thought of the prosthetic joints that teenage soldiers in Colombia got fitted after their limbs had been blown off. She wondered what state Hugo was in now. Although it was against procedure, she rubbed one of her eyes with the back of her hand.

Brandon noticed and looked at her uncertainly.

"You're going to be fitted with the latest-generation prosthesis," said Valentina, trying to convince herself, but hearing her voice break.

Brandon looked away awkwardly.

Valentina tried to stop herself imagining Hugo broken and far from help.

For once, she was relieved to see Sherry at the door, gesturing at Valentina to be elsewhere.

"Maybe you can produce the sample now," she told Brandon, nodding at the plastic container as she rushed out of the room.

For the rest of the shift, Valentina told herself to keep her head together, to be ready for when Hugo made it out of Yemen.

Back in her flat, she went back to trawling social media for clues about him. Not wanting to fall asleep at the table again, she got into bed in her pajamas.

The usual channels were just repeating segments that she'd already seen.

Digging deeper, she came across a different channel called NordStar, which looked just as professional as the others. The blonde anchor was interviewing a sunburned man in his 30s, who had a couple of bruises on his face, but was dressed in well-fitting civilian clothes. The chyron running along the bottom of the screen said that he was Carl Mack, a security expert.

"And you have first-hand knowledge of the war in Yemen?"

"Yes, Ma'am."

"Were you a contractor with Parthian?"

"Anyone with Parthian will have signed a watertight NDA," replied Carl, smiling conspiratorially.

"Why would a White Nationalist join a globalist war?"

Taken aback, Valentina searched the screen for clues about the kind of channel it was. She noticed that its logo, in the corner of the screen, was a stylized tree, its branches looping round to join its roots, forming a circular braid around its thick short trunk. Meanwhile, Carl seemed prepared for the question.

"Remember that this war wasn't started by the United States. Keeping a lid on a war of attrition is better for us White Nationalists than a regional meltdown unleashing another tsunami of migrants on our shores."

Valentina felt her stomach twist, and jabbed at the stop button on her phone.

She got out of bed and paced across the small living room, to the kitchen doorway and back.

What kind of people were in American private security forces?

She told herself that she needed to sleep. She got back into bed and started rehearsing mnemonics that she'd been relearning in English.

The Lazy Cat Sleeps Safely. Temporomandibular, Lambdoid, Coronal, Squamous, Sagittal.

Can The Ladies Stand Comfortably. Cervical, Thoracic, Lumbar, Sacral, Coccygeal.

Cats Run Circles Under Dogs Stomachs. Carpi, Radialis, Carpi, Ulnaris, Digitorum, Superficialis.

The Lazy Cat Sleeps Safely...

Valentina was woken by her phone ringing on the blanket next to her: unknown number.

17

Sacramento International Airport, a couple of days later

VALENTINA WAS driving up and around Sacramento airport's multi-story parking garage, enjoying the g-force on the corners as if she were eight years old again. She told herself to calm down, otherwise she'd rear-end someone and be filling in paperwork when Hugo came out into the arrivals hall. Hugo was safe, his debriefing had finished, and now he was arriving on a flight from Washington.

She spotted a free parking space, swung straight into it, turned off the engine and tried to calm down.

Walking towards the terminal on the elevated walkway she looked for the giant red rabbit. It was a fibreglass art work, suspended from the ceiling, bounding down into the baggage hall. It'd be one of the first things Hugo would see.

In the arrivals area, she paced up and down, looking sideways at the tags on the passengers' bags as they came out. When tags from Hugo's flight started to appear, she jockeyed herself into position opposite the doors. Each time they opened, she could see into the baggage hall for a couple of seconds.

A few minutes later, the doors opened and her stomach twisted as she saw Hugo walking between the luggage carousels towards her. He was wearing new clothes, outdoors style as usual, but a bit less niche. Valentina realized that he must've gotten out of Arabia with nothing, with even his clothes ruined, and replaced them the best he could. As she waved to him, she couldn't help wondering what he'd been through.

Then he reached her and dropped his backpack to the ground. He bent over her to kiss her on the mouth and she put her arms round his neck and pulled herself up to him. He wrapped one arm around her hips and the other around her waist, and while he kissed her, he lifted her off the ground and squeezed her so that she could feel him against her.

They went back to Valentina's flat and stayed in the bedroom till it was time for her to leave for her night shift on the cancer ward.

The next morning she came back and fell asleep next to him and when she woke up they went out.

They walked hand in hand towards State Capitol Park. On the way they bought a net bag of tangerines. They crossed Fifteenth Street into the park and carried on west, towards the capitol. As they passed the Firefighters Memorial, they started to hear chants in English from demonstrators around the capitol, calling for ICE to be abolished and for deportation raids to stop.

Hugo came to a halt.

"What's the matter?" asked Valentina.

"The ICE officers are just doing their jobs. If people want to come here, they should do it legally, like we did."

"Sometimes people are going to die if they stay in their countries. So they leave, whether or not they have the right papers."

Hugo grunted.

Valentina let go of Hugo's hand, turned to face the way they'd come, and took his other hand. They headed back and found an empty park bench near the Rose Garden. They sat down and started to eat the tangerines. Both understood that it was time to talk about the future. Valentina started.

"Thank God you finished that mission in one piece. You said you wanted to learn, but what's left for you to learn now?"

"Well, at least I don't want to work for any more security contractors."

Thank goodness, Valentina thought, and she squeezed his hand. *But...*

"What do you mean, 'At least'?"

"Parthian and the rest of them, they're just there to do their mission, that's it. There's no accountability." Hugo paused. "I wouldn't've made it out of Yemen without the regular Army soldiers. There's some kind of bigger picture for them."

A passerby heard them speaking Spanish and called out to them as he walked past.

"Hey, you're in America now! Speak English or I'll call ICE on you."

Hugo was furious and started to stand up to confront the man, but Valentina put her hand on his thigh.

"He's gone already, don't let him spoil our day."

Hugo relaxed. "What does he know about America?" he asked rhetorically.

"You were talking about the future," Valentina prompted.

Hugo nodded and took a breath. "I want to be a Green Card soldier."

"What?"

"I already went to the recruiting center in Virginia and I'm due at Fort Benning in a few days."

"A Green Card soldier?"

"A lot of the American military aren't American citizens."

"How's that?" she asked incredulously.

"Devon, the lieutenant that led us out of Yemen, is from Jamaica."

"What happened to making contacts, setting up your own business?"

"Signing up with Parthian was a step. I'm trying to learn from that. Now I'm going to take another step."

Valentina decided to look for the positives. "So you get a Green Card at the end?"

"You need an honorable discharge and no criminal record. Anyway, we're not going to stay here, right?"

"No, but it's good to have options."

Hugo squeezed her hand and they sat quietly for a while.

18

South Sacramento, a few weeks later

CARL WAS driving north on Franklin Boulevard, parallel to the South Sacramento freeway. He was driving an ICE truck with his colleague Vic Di Grigoli in the passenger seat.

Carl was thinking back on his interview with NordStar. The anchor had had a point. As a white man, his calling was to be in America with his family. He'd seen how it was going to play out with American security contractors, that they were going to get their wings clipped because of the Yemen shitstorm. Lots of Parthian people were looking for work, but he'd got started on his ICE application as soon as he was off the evacuation plane from Arabia. When he got the interview, he could tell within a couple of minutes that the job was his. White men could still make it there, unlike the police.

He turned west onto Sutterville.

"How many more to make the quota?"

"Half a dozen," replied Vic.

Carl grunted. It was afternoon already. ICE units in half a dozen states were rounding up and detaining thousands of people for deportation. ICE had a target list of people, some with outstanding warrants, most just suspected of being noncitizens. Any collateral pickups would count just as well to the quota.

"Got one coming up on the right," said Vic as he looked at his tablet computer.

Sutterville was a four-lane road with big houses on either side and the odd gas station, chain pharmacy and supermarket.

"Jaime Gutierrez. Sometime security guard, suspect in armed robbery."

As they passed a young Latino man taking his mastiff dog for a walk,

Vic pointed him out to Carl by tapping the window.

"Got him," said Carl.

He drove another couple of blocks, turned right, dropped Vic off, and looped back around to Sutterville.

Carl came up behind Gutierrez again, but instead of passing him, slowed down, then revved the truck onto the sidewalk behind him. Gutierrez turned around to see what was happening, saw it was ICE, and turned back again to run, only to find Vic's gun in his face. The mastiff launched himself at Vic, snarling, but Gutierrez held him back on the leash.

"Control your dog, beaner," Vic shouted at Gutierrez, who stared back, knowing that he was already controlling it as best he could.

Bystanders were caught with Gutierrez, between Carl and Vic. A young Latino man had been walking three more dogs the opposite way on the sidewalk. Excited and bewildered by the mayhem, one of the dogs, a beagle, lunged towards Gutierrez's mastiff, but its walker held it back. Another of the dogs, a collie, howled at Carl, who was aiming his own gun at Gutierrez. The walker struggled to hold the two dogs pulling him in different directions, but Carl shouted at him.

"Stay back, puto."

In a frenzy, the collie bit and held the arm of a ten-year-old girl who was cowering against the wall of a pharmacy with her mother.

Obeying a call from its walker, the collie dropped the girl's torn and bleeding arm.

"Tie up your dog and get in the car," Vic shouted at Gutierrez.

"No way," he replied, pulling the mastiff a couple of inches nearer.

"Leave the dog here, or it gets a bullet."

The mother lifted her hysterical daughter into her arms and tried to comfort her, zoning out the rest.

Gutierrez looked down the barrel of Vic's pistol, nodded slowly, then tipped his head towards a post holding up a set of traffic lights that hung out over the street. Vic nodded, telling him to go ahead, and Gutierrez walked slowly over the post, and tied the dog there, trying to calm it down.

The other dogs eased off their yowling, letting the little girl's screams be heard.

Gutierrez put his hands behind his head and walked towards the ICE truck. He leaned over the hood and put his hands behind his back to be cuffed by Vic.

As Gutierrez was bundled into the truck by Vic, the walker called to the other dogs. He squatted down and tried to calm them.

"You too," said Carl.

The walker looked up and found himself looking down the barrel of Carl's pistol.

"What the hell, man?"

"Into the car. Immigration Enforcement agents. You are under arrest on suspicion of being in the United States illegally."

"Bullshit, man."

"I'm not going to say it again."

"I can't leave the dogs here."

"Tie them up and we'll call animal welfare."

"Jesus! You can see they're not my dogs, right? People paid for them to be out here."

"Since you let one of them bite through a little girl's arm, maybe a spic's not their best guardian. Now go," Carl said, twitching his head towards a traffic sign at the edge of the sidewalk.

Cursing under his breath, the dog walker wound the leashes around the signpost, in slow motion, with Carl's gun on him. When he'd finished, he said, "I'm going to need my fucking phone call."

"We'll see about that. Now do like your greaser friend and bend over," said Carl, stalking around behind the dog walker and steering him towards the truck.

When the walker was cuffed and with Jaime in the back of the truck, Carl and Vic holstered their guns and nodded at each other to acknowledge a job well done.

On their way to the processing center downtown, Jaime kept on cursing out Carl and Vic, who just ignored him. Finally the dog walker nudged Jaime and spoke to him under his breath.

"Think ahead. How you're going to play it when we get there."

Jaime sat back a second and the dog walker called forward.

"Do you realize how much those pedigree dogs cost? Maybe it's time to make that call to animal services."

Without turning around, Carl replied, "They're surely worth a hell of a lot more than you wets."

But, after a couple of seconds, he still took out his phone and made the call.

ICE had turned part of a downtown office building into a processing center. They could no longer use the city jails and prisons because the state attorney general, Gabriel Rangel, had pressured Californian cities into stopping cooperation with ICE.

Carl drove into the basement parking garage, past a couple of protesters camped outside the building, who jeered at them as they went down the ramp.

Carl and Vic took the detainees up in the elevator to the fifth floor. They stepped out into a corporate reception area that had been repurposed as a gateway to the immigration labyrinth.

Carl pushed Jaime up to the counter and spoke to another ICE officer who sat behind it by a computer.

"Need to book this gangbanger."

Jaime clenched his jaw but kept quiet.

"You should be here for about a year before you get to see a judge," Carl said to Jaime.

The dog walker tried to step closer to the counter, but Vic held him back.

The desk officer took a calmer tone.

"Unfortunately my colleague's right about the judicial track. A lot of cases backed up."

Carl slapped Jaime gleefully on the back.

The desk officer looked up for a second at Carl as if annoyed with him, then turned back to Jaime.

"But you have options here."

"Shit," muttered Carl, feigning disappointment.

The desk officer reached down under the counter and brought out a form. He put it in front of Jaime, who started to read it warily.

"That's a stip order, don't sign it!" shouted the dog walker, trying to shrug off Vic and get closer to the counter.

Vic, infuriated, grabbed the walker's wrists behind his back and yanked him away from Jaime. There was a crack as one of the wrists broke. The walker cried out and staggered, cringing with the pain.

"Jesus," said Carl, looking at Vic and jerking his head towards the other side of the counter. They went into an empty cubicle and spoke quietly.

"Now he's going to make a complaint and we'll have that over us," said Carl.

"No, man, we'll just deport him with the rest. Let him see if he prefers whining to the Mex police."

Carl nodded. Doubtfully at first, then convincing himself. They stepped out of the cubicle and back to the booking station.

The dog walker told them that his name was Daniel Martinez, and he gave them his contact details. He wouldn't tell them anything else. Having been denied a phone call again, Daniel was dragged to his cell. It was the office of a midlevel manager, more than a cubicle but with no window to the outside. The walls were partitions that shook when the door closed behind him. Translucent sections below the ceiling let in light from the adjacent cells.

Vic cut the cable tie around Daniel's wrists and he groaned with relief. The fractured wrist had already swollen up and around the plastic cuff. Cradling his broken hand with his other arm, Daniel looked around his cell. There was a plastic foam mattress on the floor, and a chemical toilet in the corner. On one of the walls was a shelf unit and a cluster of thumbtacks that no one had bothered to remove.

He paced from one side of the cell to the other, thinking what he could do.

"Hey, my wrist's broken," he shouted out. "I need medical attention."

Now they couldn't say they hadn't known about it. He called out a few times before letting up. Any more and he'd just be giving them satisfaction. He lay down on the foam mattress and breathed in its bleach vapors. He tried to relax, telling himself that at least his dogs should be OK, that his mother was still in the hospital but getting better. For hours, the pain of his broken wrist kept him awake. Finally tiredness overcame pain and he dozed fitfully for a few hours.

He was woken up by an ICE officer banging on the door and telling him to get ready to leave. He looked at his watch: 6 a.m. He started to get up off the mattress but flinched at the pain from his wrist. He paused a second and, with deliberate movements, stood up at the second attempt. Still in his clothes and shoes from yesterday, he went over to the door.

"We're going to come in and cuff you."

"You broke my fucking wrist and now you're going to cuff me again? I need medical attention."

But the ICE officers were already through the door with a pair of metal handcuffs.

Daniel turned around slowly, putting his hands together behind his back. He heard one of the officers swear under his breath, then the sound of the handcuffs being put away. He groaned with pain as a zip tie closed on his broken wrist.

"Your fucking cuffs can't even fit around my wrist now, it's so swollen."

"Come on," one of them said defensively as he pressed his palm on Daniel's shoulder to turn him back around towards the door.

At least one of them's got some kind of shame, Daniel thought, as the officer guided him towards an office on the opposite side of the former office space.

Inside the cubicle was another ICE officer at a desk, with a computer to one side. He nodded at the escorts, who took their hands off Daniel and stepped back, pressing themselves against the frosted acrylic of the temporary wall. The seated officer turned back to his computer and read from a script.

"Daniel Martinez, you are hereby notified that, having been found within one hundred miles of the border without proper entry documents—"

"One hundred miles of the border? We must be five hundred miles from Mexico," Daniel tried to interrupt.

The seated officer just carried on.

"And having broken public order by affray, pursuant to the Immigration and Nationality Act, Title 8 of the United States Code—"

One of the officers behind him replied to Daniel. "The sea border, moron."

"You are hereby ordered to be removed from the United States."

Daniel cried out in pain as the two officers behind him grabbed his arms again and pushed him towards the door.

As he was being taken back down to the basement and out of the building, the officer upstairs started to fill in the computer form to show that he'd arrived.

19

Sacramento, Pelton Medical Center, Cancer Ward

VALENTINA WAS in the locker room of the cancer ward, changing out of her scrubs. Cancer nursing wasn't her specialty, and she hoped that her agency would find her orthopedic work again after the stint here. In fact, she was already counting the days left. Yes, she could do her job on a cancer ward. But she could make more of a difference with orthopedic patients.

Valentina put her scrubs in the laundry basket and headed for the elevator.

Orthopedics was more of a craft. It needed good hands. The cancer ward was more about drugs, overpowering drugs that killed a part of each patient, because that's what the cancer was. So a lot of her work was not with the patients but with the computer, checking the prescription dose, then getting another nurse to check the calculation. At least on the ward, they had all the drugs they needed. And right there, in the automated dispensing machine.

Valentina came out of the elevator into the lobby and walked out into the parking lot.

And the cancer patients were really sick. Systemically sick. More than the orthopedic patients. The cancer patients were usually older, with conditions that were only just under control, even before the cancer. So any progress with the cancer seemed to make something else worse.

Valentina got into her car and headed for the exit.

Like Mr. Pfeiffer today, with his acute episode of swelling and rash. His face and neck had blown up like anaphylaxis. She'd paged his attending physician, who said it was hereditary angioedema. So she'd gotten him hydrochlorothiazide from the ADM. The charge nurse had told her to use the override to get it out of the machine. You couldn't even get saline out of that machine without an override, she said. Valentina had put all the episode and treatment into Mr. Pfeiffer's record as a verbal before going off shift.

"Shit!" she said out loud.

She looked back towards her parking space, but there was already a line behind her, and no way to turn around. She pulled to the side of the exit lane, blocking a couple of cars in. Those behind her would have to squeeze past as best they could. She turned off the engine, got out of the car, and ran back towards her building, ignoring the shouts of the drivers in the line behind her.

Valentina had realized that Mr. Pfeiffer's HAE episode had happened after she'd left him to help another patient recover from a fall. And that had happened as she was about to give Mr. Pfeiffer his cancer medication.

She got back to the nurses' station out of breath. The charge nurse for the new shift looked at her disdainfully.

"Mr. Pfeiffer," Valentina gasped. "Before he could get his cyclophosphamide, he had hydrochlorothiazide for an acute edema episode."

The charge nurse raised her eyebrows, wanting more.

"I got the hydrochlorothiazide from the ADM by the override, so there was no check for drug interactions."

Now the charge nurse understood. Mr. Pfeiffer shouldn't've gotten the two medications so close together. She scowled at Valentina while lifting the handset of her desk phone and paging the attending physician.

She replaced the handset.

"Is it all charted?" she asked Valentina, who nodded.

The phone rang with the callback, and the charge nurse explained the situation to the attending physician.

"There's a risk of prolonged neutropenia," she informed Valentina. "You did the right thing to raise the concern." The charge nurse paused and Valentina knew what was coming. "But you've had a fall and a drug-drug interaction on the same shift. That's not meeting expectations."

Valentina nodded and turned to leave the ward again. Like most medical errors, it was a chain of things that shouldn't have happened, but she would be the easiest one to blame.

20

Gardena, Los Angeles, California

Raul was waiting to meet Devon in Los Muchachos bar in Gardena. After his debriefing back in the States, Raul had decided to leave the Parthian. His citizenship had come through while he was in Yemen, and he'd promised his wife, Marina, not to take on any more security contractor work. He was staying in her apartment while he found work.

He sipped his beer, watching a couple of guys play *billar* in the partly covered space out the back of the bar.

Tracking down Devon hadn't been difficult. The first internet search hit had been for something called the American Foreign Legion. Raul was remembering Devon's photo on social media when he saw Devon himself in front of him.

Raul stood up, and they embraced. He got Devon a beer and sat back down opposite him. They both drank.

Raul explained about leaving Parthian.

"That was easy. Getting a new job, not so much."

Devon looked at Raul and shrugged as if to say that he should have plenty of options.

"I applied to the CBP, that could be my best shot," continued Raul.

Devon raised his eyebrows.

"You were just made a citizen, and you're going to go right back to the border and start hunting down immigrants, locking them up, and sending them back to Mexico?"

Devon's tone took Raul by surprise and he replied defensively.

"Did you question your missions when you were in the US Army?"

"No, because, before signing up, I thought about what they might be. I never had any beef with the Army, just with the DHS."

Devon changed his tone. "I know, it's a steady gig and you've got the tools to do it well."

Raul nodded. This was more like what he'd expected.

"You'll need to get on board with the way the other CBP officers think and talk about people, and the way they treat them," Devon continued.

"You know, I'm kind of a by-the-book guy. I don't think I'll go far too wrong if I treat people how they're supposed to be treated."

"Well, you can try the inside-the-tent-pissing-out, now that you're a citizen."

Raul paused before changing the subject. "So you got discharged."

"Sure did."

They drank to that.

"Unlike you, though, my citizenship got denied," said Devon.

"Jesus, man. You saved us all in Yemen. What more d'you have to do?"

"So that's your beef Homeland Security," Raul continued, shaking his head.

"They said my Jamaican identity papers were off, which is bullshit."

"Maybe they just don't like that American Foreign Legion that you're heading up."

"Good that you've seen it. Since the security contractor gigs dried up, a lot of people are looking for work, and ICE is looking for them, to deport them."

"So, you're like a campaigner now?"

Devon laughed. "One step at a time," he replied.

"So what step is next?"

"Right now we're reactive. ICE fucks someone over, we let everyone see it. They try to duck out of sight, cut more corners. We show everyone that as well. We get more support, ICE gets more pissed and lashes out even more."

Devon saw that Raul wasn't comfortable with this, with him potentially being a new Border Patrol officer.

"Hey man, maybe you'll prove me wrong and show me that *la migra* can do the right thing."

They drank to that.

21

Sacramento, Valentina's apartment

THERE WERE no frozen chicken legs left, so Valentina made a one-egg omelet and flopped it on top of the rice on her plate.

Hugo had gone to Fort Benning to start his basic training. The cancer ward stint had finished a week ago and the agency had done nothing for her since, despite her calling them every day. The little money she'd had had gone on deposits for the apartment, the car, the phone, cable. The money from the first job had covered the monthly payments, but she had next to nothing left.

People always needed nurses, so if the agency couldn't find her anything, she would find something herself. She hacked at the egg with the edge of her fork while browsing the phone with the other hand.

She saw something, then pushed back the plate with its half-finished food. She plugged a flimsy hands-free set into the phone and tapped a number from the website.

"Bellevue Clinical Recruitment, how may I help you?"

"Yes, hello, it's about the ortho nurse position in Aurora Hospital in Sacramento."

"Yes, ma'am. You've seen the ad? You've got your NCLEX and BLS?"

"Sure do."

"And are you an independent contractor, or with an agency?"

"Well, I'm with an agency, but I want to apply directly myself."

There was a pause.

"Agency contracts are typically exclusive."

"Sorry, what does that mean?"

The call center staffer took pity on Valentina.

"Most likely you can only work through them, dear. How long's your contract for?"

"Three years," said Valentina, downbeat.

"Why don't you check the wording and call back if you're clear to apply?"

"Right, thanks."

"Have a good day."

"Oh, yes, same, thanks," said Valentina, whose mind was already elsewhere. She hung up but didn't look for her contract to check it. The idea of trying to read that small print in English made her brain freeze. What business was it of the agency's if she looked for a job for herself?

She messaged Leidy in Bogotá.

> Hi, how's it going?
>
> Look, the agency hasn't got me anything so I found something myself, but they told me I have to do it through the agency.
>
> Is that right??

Keeping one eye on the phone, she reached for the plate and started picking at the rice again. The phone pinged with Leidy's reply.

> Yeah, all good.
>
> That's right.
>
> With most contracts you can only work for that agency. But let them know what jobs you've seen with clinics where they place people.

Valentina swore under her breath.

> What if I just start a different job and ignore them??

> The agency?
>
> They'll take you to court for the damages in the contract.

> If I don't get a job then the car leasing people
> will take me to court instead...

People have tried saying that agency contracts are unfair but that's even more time in court...

> God!

Haha. Look I need to go now.

Don't worry, there's plenty of nursing work out there.

Valentina tossed the phone onto the table. Maybe the agency would come through with something, but she didn't want to be just waiting in the meantime. She ate what was left of her meal while she thought.

She found Luz in her contacts and almost pushed the green button to call but caught herself and messaged instead, asking Luz to call her back sometime.

She was watching a soap opera—to improve her English, she told herself—when Luz called.

"Hi, thanks for calling."

"No problem, what's going on?"

"Not much, that's the problem."

Luz waited for Valentina to explain.

"My agency, Mediquet, isn't getting me any work, so I found something myself, but they told me I can't do it, because of the contract or something."

"Right. If you try that, they threaten to sue you."

"They'd sue their own people?"

"It suits them to have plenty of nurses on tap, really needing work. It doesn't matter to them if some of them can't pay the bills."

Valentina was speechless.

"But they're bullies," continued Luz. "If they think one of their nurses will fight back, then they're liable to back down."

"So, what can I do?"

"You said you've got no work, nothing, just now?"

"Right."

"Be ready to head down to the Mediquet office when I call you, OK?"
"Sure. Thanks."
"Remember to bring your contract. I hope I can help you."

22

Rosemont, Sacramento

Valentina was watching a daytime soap when her phone rang: Luz.
"Hi, be at the agency office at twelve thirty, OK?"
"Got it, thanks."

The Mediquet office was in a strip mall on the north side of Rosemont, about twenty minutes east of Valentina's apartment. She got out of her car and looked around: lights flashed on a minivan a couple of spaces down. As she walked over, the driver's window slid down and Luz indicated for her to get in the back. Luz introduced her to the young man in a dark suit in the passenger seat.

"Valentina, this is Ernesto Sandoval. He's a labor lawyer. He's helping us out with a bit of time he found from his schedule."

"Thanks a lot, Ernesto," she replied.

"Did you bring the contract?" asked Luz.

"Oh, yeah." Luz fished it out from her handbag and passed it to Ernesto.

"The plan is for you to go in and state your grievance clearly and confidently. We'll be there behind you to back you up and show that you have a serious team onside."

Valentina nodded.

"Let's go. Ernesto needs to be back at his office in midtown in half an hour."

Valentina hadn't expected Luz to call in a favor for her. She walked across the sidewalk to the door of the agency office.

As the other two walked in behind her, she felt strength in numbers. The agency hadn't invested a lot in decor. There was a big framed poster with the Mediquet Agency name and a logo with a couple of stylized humans coming together to make a heart shape. A middle-aged woman sat behind one desk and a younger one at the other. From the desk nameplates, they could see that they were Myrna Fahey and Uma Kallio. There was a dispenser to take a number, but there was no one else there. The younger woman, Uma, smiled a readymade smile at Valentina, indicating that she should speak with her. Valentina sat down, and Luz and Ernesto stood behind either side of her chair, but Uma tried to ignore them.

"How may I help you?" she asked Valentina.

Valentina took a breath. She was used to being polite, but by being formal, not in the American way of pretending you were having a great time.

"Well, the first job you found for me was good, but I'm definitely ready to start another one soon."

Uma nodded, trying to emote sympathy.

Valentina could hear Ernesto leaf through the pages of her contract behind her.

"It seems there are quite a few jobs out there," Valentina continued.

"We're sure you'll be best served by the opportunities Mediquet finds for you."

"Well, that's what my contract says."

"Mm-hmm," Uma replied thinly, trying to avoid glancing up at Luz and Ernesto.

"You know, the bills keep coming in."

Uma didn't reply.

"At some point, if I find something suitable anywhere, then I'll need to take it."

"If you break your contract, we'd have to defend ourselves."

Ernesto interrupted. "Don't you think that a penalty of thirty thousand dollars constitutes undue harm?"

Uma looked up at him without replying.

"Oh, excuse me." Ernesto took a card from his inside suit pocket and gave it to Uma, who glanced at it with distaste before putting it on her desk. She still didn't reply, so Ernesto repeated.

"So, undue harm?"

Uma had had enough and looked over to her boss, Myrna, who stood up and walked over to stand behind Uma's desk.

Valentina stood up as well. Uma seemed relieved, even though the others were now talking over her head.

"I suppose you know that things haven't gone smoothly for Valentina,"

Myrna told Luz.

"It's her responsibility to notify clients of any risks to patients," Luz replied.

"Involvement in incidents can affect employers' perceptions."

"If you don't have work for me, then let me find it myself," said Valentina.

Myrna looked between Valentina and the two people backing her up and made a judgment as to whether it'd be more inconvenient to risk publicity fighting them or to start listing Valentina's resume again.

"How can we better meet your needs?" Myrna asked Valentina, softening her tone.

Valentina looked at Luz, who nodded.

"Why don't you show me some of your current vacancies?"

23

Nogales, Arizona

Raul was on a CBP night patrol. They'd left their truck on the dirt road and headed on foot towards the border. Most coyotes chose nighttime to move their human traffic on this side of the border, trying to get them to a safe house. He was with three other CBP officers. Alongside him was Carmen, while Tyler and Jayden were on a parallel course, on the hillside a couple of hundred feet higher. There was no path, but in the light of the half moon they could pick their way between the boulders and over the sand.

The coyotes could have eyes on them already, but Raul and Carmen trod carefully, spoke in whispers, and kept radio contact with the other two to a minimum.

They lengthened their strides as they came out of the moonshadow of a twenty-foot boulder. Raul let his mind wander to the social media group that he'd joined on Carmen's invitation. All the members seemed to be CBP officers, and most of the posts were mocking the would-be immigrants. Every other day there was a picture of a Rio Grande floater, or a dead bleacher in New Mexico. Raul hung back from commenting on the posts. When he was at Parthian, he hadn't beaten himself up about the people he'd shot, but he hadn't spent time denigrating them either.

Sometimes Raul would be in the back of the truck and the others would be chatting out loud as they were replying online about the latest affronts by guats or tonks. He'd keep quiet unless the others asked him what he thought, in which case he'd make a noncommittal answer and get sidelong looks in return. Then they'd start testing his support for Nemeth in the upcoming Senate special election.

Nemeth was a former sheriff of a border county who'd been found guilty of negligence over the death of a Haitian immigrant who'd died of dehydration and heat stroke. The Haitian had been handcuffed in the back of a car belonging to the sheriff's office, which had been left in the sun for hours in the middle of the day with the windows up. Whenever they picked up a black immigrant, Jayden would make jokes about it being time for another roast.

When they asked him about Nemeth, Raul would talk about how he'd performed as a sheriff: not about abuse of migrants, but how Nemeth had left the people under him to carry the can for his decisions. But the others wouldn't engage at that level. They'd just take his answer for what it was: a way of avoiding the main point, which was freedom to abuse immigrants.

Despite his argument with Devon, he did follow the American Foreign Legion on social media. The others in the CBP team talked about the AFL more and more frequently, and not because they'd seen it on Raul's phone. The AFL was advocating the exact opposite of their everyday mission, and they were enraged even more because most of the AFL leadership had combat experience that put their petty bullying in the shade. For example, they made jokes about Devon being a stoner just on the grounds of him being Jamaican. They played out the same dynamic with Raul, belittling his experience with Parthian because they found it intimidating.

Radio crackle brought Raul back to the present. Carmen answered, and Tyler told them to move about twenty yards to their right before carrying on south. A couple of minutes later they found some blankets on the ground where migrants had been resting. Carmen took out her knife and started to slash the plastic gallon containers of water. Raul followed suit. The migrants couldn't survive for long without water. As he tipped out the containers, Raul thought of the people he knew who'd made it into the country this way. Maybe they wouldn't have made it if the CBP had been ditching people's water back then. But Raul kept at it. This was what he'd signed up for: stopping people from making it. There were some packets of crackers and dried fruit, which Carmen and Raul opened and scattered. Then they looked at each other, ready for the next stage.

Carmen spoke to Tyler over the radio. "We've trashed their food and water."

"Roger. See that boulder on top of the next ridge, to the east?"
"Affirmative."
"When the wets spotted us coming, likely one or more would've gone over the ridge behind that, to avoid showing on the horizon."

"Roger. We'll head over there. Out."

Raul followed Carmen up to the crest of the ridge. They took a few seconds to orient themselves in the dark gray moonlit landscape. There was one obvious way down the other side of the ridge and away from the border. A hundred yards further on, they found a couple collapsed on the ground.

Raul and Carmen took their flashlights from their belts and scoped the couple. They were at least middle-aged. The man was lying splayed on his back on the rocky ground, unconscious. The woman was holding his head up in both her hands, telling him that they needed to carry on. When Raul and Carmen turned on their flashlights, she stopped speaking to the man but still looked at him for a few seconds, as if a change in his condition had made the light come. Then she laid his head down gently on the rocky ground.

The woman stood up between the unconscious man and the two CBP officers.

"Speak English?" Carmen asked her.

The woman shook her head and replied in Spanish, gesturing at her companion on the ground.

"We need help."

The CBP officers spoke to her in Spanish.

"Step towards us please," said Carmen.

"Your husband?" asked Raul.

The woman nodded.

"What's he called?"

"Tolo."

"And you?"

"Kemena."

Raul crouched down beside Tolo. With one hand he reached for his neck pulse, while the other shone the flashlight on his face.

His wife sobbed at seeing him oblivious to Raul's probing.

Raul stood up again and spoke to Carmen in English.

"Rapid heartbeat, sunken eyes, looks like he lost consciousness due to dehydration."

Carmen turned to Kemena and spoke to her in Spanish.

"You have to come with us. Try to wake your husband up."

Kemena dried her eyes with her hand and looked at Carmen incredulously for a couple of seconds before replying.

"What do you think I was doing when you got here? Look at him! Do you think he's going anywhere?"

Raul saw Carmen tense and her hand move on the taser on her belt. She took a deep breath before replying.

"You've put yourselves in harm's way by acting illegally. We're taking you into custody. If you can do anything for your husband, then do it now."

Kemena wasn't backing down, but Raul spoke before she could.

"I've got him," he said to Carmen in English.

"What do you mean?" she replied skeptically. "We report this one and maybe they'll send a chopper in the morning."

"That's a long time for someone in his state. He weighs less than a hundred pounds. I can get him back to the vehicle."

Although Kemena couldn't understand the English, she could tell that Raul was trying to help her husband over Carmen's objections. She knew better than to intervene but just looked at Raul through the shadows, trusting her body language to encourage him.

Carmen didn't want to push the argument any further in front of a detainee.

"You got it," she said derisively in English before turning back to Kemena.

"Put your hands together behind your back," she said to her in Spanish. Carmen cuffed her, then updated Tyler over the radio.

Raul lifted Tolo over his shoulder, to a disdainful sigh from Carmen, who led them back to the vehicle. They rested a couple of times on the way, with Raul changing the shoulder on which he was carrying Tolo, who was inert and oblivious. While Raul got his breath back, Carmen fidgeted with impatience and exasperation.

Tyler and Jayden had gotten back to the vehicle before them, and there were two young men in the cage on the back. Carmen shone her flashlight in at them. They were dejected, and bleary-eyed from exhaustion, but nothing worse. Carmen opened the back of the cage and Raul laid Tolo down inside. Before getting inside herself, Kemena put her hand on Raul's shoulder and thanked him.

Before setting off, Carmen asked the three conscious migrants some questions, but of course none of them would say anything about how they got across the border. The coyotes, in better shape than their captives, had been the first to see the CBP coming and had made it clean away.

The four officers got into the double-cab vehicle in the usual seats: Tyler driving, Jayden next to him, with Raul and Carmen in the rear cab. They set off on the dirt road.

From the way Tyler smiled at him in the rearview mirror, Raul knew that he was going to give him a hard time.

"What's with carrying a wet for miles through the hills, man? That way, pretty soon, whenever we catch them, they'll have a lie-down and expect to ride on our backs."

Raul was too tired from carrying Tolo, and too disillusioned with his colleagues, to take issue.

"You know how long we'll be tied up in paperwork for this guy?" asked Carmen. "Trying to find someone to sign him off to?"

"Better have a long shower before getting into bed—that wet smells like death," said Tyler.

Carmen and Jayden laughed.

When Raul started his shift the following afternoon, he found Tolo lying in a cell, looking up at the ceiling. Raul called his name but he didn't respond.

The other three from last night still hadn't been shipped out. They would be sent west to Texas to be put back over the border there. Raul and Jayden took the two men out of their cell, and Carmen did the same for Kemena. When they went past Tolo's cell, Kemena grabbed the bars and called out to him. He heard her but just sent a glazed look in her general direction, without trying to move.

Carmen pushed Kemena on, but she kept holding on to the bars. She realized that Tolo wasn't in a state to go anywhere and started shouting at Carmen in Spanish.

"I'm not going to leave my husband by himself! Look at him, he can't even stand up!"

Carmen tried to heave Kemena away from the cell but couldn't pry her hands off the bars.

"You bastards want him dead! And that's how he'll end up if you get him alone!"

Carmen got one of Kemena's arms free from the cell bars, but Kemena twisted free and elbowed Carmen in the face. Carmen lost her patience, took her billy club from her belt, and drove the end into Kemena's back, aiming for the kidney. Kemena bawled and collapsed into a squatting position. Her blood up, Carmen pushed Kemena over and started smashing her head with the club.

Raul looked to Jayden to help him to get Carmen to back off, but he was smiling, enjoying the spectacle. So Raul stepped forward himself, lifting Kemena up off the floor, taking some of Carmen's blows in the process. Kemena was bleeding from a gash above the eye and had other cuts on her lips and above the cheekbones. Dizzy, she clung to Raul for fear of hitting the floor again, wailing and cursing Carmen.

From the way Carmen and Jayden were looking at him, Raul saw that they would have kept beating Kemena if he hadn't been in their way. Raul pulled Kemena out of the building and towards a battered bus that the CBP had contracted to take the detainees to Texas. She was bewildered, realizing that Raul was both protecting her from the other two officers and taking her away from her husband.

"Don't do this to me," she begged as Raul dragged her closer to the bus.

"There's no other way."

Two more CBP officers were waiting on each side of the main door of the bus. Raul let Kemena go. She stood and looked in turn at the three officers, then, seeing no way past them, walked disconsolately up the steps of the bus.

Raul hardly spoke with the other three before they went out on patrol again that evening. Tyler didn't have much time for Raul, but nor did he want infighting among his team. As he drove them out of town, and the roads got smaller and rougher, he kept up the small talk while trying to make an opening for Raul to join in. But Raul was running out of ways to convince himself that joining the CBP had been the right decision. He thought about Devon's advice and started scrolling through the AFL's social media feed.

"What're you looking at that traitorous shit for?" Carmen challenged him.

Raul looked at her, unsure what she meant, because he'd been holding the screen away from the others. Then he realized that, in the darkness, she must've caught the AFL logo in the reflection from his screen in the passenger window. That just annoyed him more.

"If they're not citizens, how can they be traitors?" he challenged Carmen.

"They call themselves American, right? How can the American Foreign Legion be against our law enforcement?"

"When the law enforcement doesn't follow the law."

Jayden turned round to have a go at him.

"We're a team and we've got to have each other's back. Not leaking shit to a bunch of illegals who are out to get us."

Raul was still thinking about Kemena and wasn't going to back down.

"I'm not leaking anything. You saying I did?"

"So you're just a lurker on those fucking brazer channels?"

Raul was going to reply, but Tyler spoke first as he braked the truck, pulled it over into a bare patch of ground beside the unpaved road, and turned on the light inside the cab.

"This is where we start tonight's operation. We need to stow those beefs and pull together like we have been."

He scanned the faces of the other three for any signs of dissent. Satisfied, he turned away and opened the door of the truck.

"Let's get to work."

When Raul was driving to work the following afternoon, he got an IM from Tyler to go straight to his office to meet him.

Once there, Tyler looked up at Raul, turning away from the promotion application he was working on the computer. He gestured at a seat on the other side of the desk.

"I'm going to cut to the chase, Raul."

Raul kept his poker face.

"There's been a complaint that you assaulted one of our detainees."

Raul was furious. Not initially at Carmen and Jayden for lying about him to get him out of the team, but at himself for having ignored what Devon and the others had told him.

Tyler was still talking.

"The allegation is that yesterday you assaulted Kemena Fuentes, when she resisted removal from this facility. As you know, this goes against our values and Standards of Conduct."

Raul raised his eyebrows sarcastically. Tyler paused for a split second but decided to ignore the challenge.

"On that basis you will be investigated by the Office of Professional Responsibility and will be assigned to duties which do not involve immediate contact with suspected illegal immigrants or detainees."

"Yes, sir."

"Do you wish to respond or ask any questions?"

"No, sir."

Raul was already standing up. Tyler let him go and turned back to his computer.

24

Nogales, Arizona

RAUL GOT reassigned to the intelligence group while the complaint was investigated. There were three others, and a couple of them treated Raul like he'd expected. They weren't worried about him having supposedly beaten down an illegal migrant woman. But if Raul's former teammates had a problem with him, bad enough to make them screw him over, then they had a problem with him as well. The third member of the intelligence group seemed like he was trying to get friendly, but Raul recoiled from what seemed like pity.

Whenever Raul saw Carmen and the others in the building, they wouldn't say anything, they just looked smug as they went past. They knew that the OPR was only interested in CBP people as witnesses. They weren't going to spend time and money chasing after statements from Kemena or Tolo or any of the other illegals, who had quickly been scattered to the four winds.

Raul hadn't had any previous experience with the intelligence group, and one way or another, he probably wasn't going to be with them for long. Plus, most of them wanted to spend as little time around him as possible. So they just handed him down the most tedious tasks: sifting through emails and transcripts from surveillance or existing cases, browsing news websites in the US and Mexico, downloading extracts from CBP databases and making spreadsheet graphs.

He could do the work OK, and was even learning, but being inside windowless rooms all day got to him. On break he would go to the parking lot and look at the mountains on the horizon. Then he'd look over to the group of smokers under the awning that'd been put up on one side of the building and wonder what it'd be like to smoke and chew the fat with them.

He was on his way out of the Border Patrol, that was clear. Even if the OPR acquitted him, he'd be stuck working menial tasks indefinitely. His colleagues would look at him with contempt. Even the transient few who still imagined that the CBP helped people would avoid him once they heard what he'd supposedly done.

Across the parking lot, under the awning, one of his colleagues stubbed out a cigarette and the group made to go back inside.

Raul realized that he'd already checked out mentally from the CBP.

His wife, Marina, was telling him that the sooner he quit, the better. She was a catering manager for off-site events and was still trying to build up contacts in Nogales. They'd been away from Los Angeles for six months. If they went back soon, then some people would hardly have noticed her absence, and with a bit of luck she'd soon have the amount of work she had before. In fact, she was probably getting a quote from U-Haul right now. Raul smiled to himself as he walked back to the building.

25

Pico Union, Los Angeles

A MONTH LATER they were living with Marina's parents' house in Pico Union. That was a positive for her, but it would start to grate on Raul after a few weeks. The short stint with CBP, and the lack of a reference, was making it harder to get a job with any responsibility.

He started looking for work, but there was only a lot of low-paying mall security and night watchman work. Devon had been right about the CBP, which made Raul hesitate to call him, but after a week he realized that a different take on things wouldn't hurt.

They met up again in the early evening at an old-fashioned bar in Atwater, near to Devon's ambulance headquarters in Glendale. Before going in, Raul took a breath and cast his mind back to his security contractor days, trying to assume that military demeanor. As he walked in, some of the regulars sized him up before turning back to their beers, untroubled.

Devon was waiting for him at one of the built-in tables near the wall, sitting on the wrap-around curved leather banquette.

Raul sat down opposite him and relaxed.

"How're you settling back into LA?" asked Devon, getting back with a couple more beers.

"Well, under the circumstances..."

Devon smirked, then they both laughed, then drew on their beers.

After a few seconds' pause, Raul got on to the reasons for wanting to meet Devon.

"So, you were right about the CBP."

"Gives me no joy."

"Bullshit."

They both laughed again.

"You know, seeing the AFL on my phone was one of the red flags for them."

"We're not being ignored anymore. Some people love to hate us, they use us to drum up support for their nativist policies, but our message is getting through. Every day we show ICE fucking people over, and what we're doing to stop them."

Raul nodded.

"How do I get to do more than 'liking' your posts and flaming redneck trolls?"

"Remember what I said last time? About escalation?" Raul nodded.

"We're planning a couple of steps ahead. We do have armed men and women to count on, for when the time comes."

Raul raised his eyebrows, asking Devon to get to the point.

"I can find you work. With you being a citizen, that'll be easier than it is for some. But you need to keep your nose clean till I have something more interesting for you. OK?"

"Sure thing."

A couple of days later Raul started as an assistant in a nursing home in East Hollywood. To be honest it wasn't the kind of job he'd considered before meeting Devon. And he probably wouldn't have needed any help to get it. But he'd stick with it, in the meantime.

26

Fort Benning, Georgia

THE BUS pulled up in darkness outside the headquarters of the 30th Adjutant General Battalion at Fort Benning. Some of the other recruits were teenagers, ten years younger than Hugo. A Drill Sergeant Schulz, in his big campaign hat, got on and walked up to the back of the bus and down to the front again, shouting at the recruits at the top of his voice.

"The only things I want to hear from you dog-breaths are 'Yes, Drill Sergeant' or 'No, Drill Sergeant' Do you understand?"

"Yes, Drill Sergeant," the recruits all replied.

"Bullshit! Say it like you've got a pair!"

"Yes, Drill Sergeant!" they shouted.

Schulz shouted at them that they had to be off the bus, with their bags out of the luggage compartment, and lined up outside the building, within thirty seconds. Hugo knew this wasn't going to happen, but he jumped up with everyone else and jostled down the aisle to get off the bus. Anyone acting like a smart-ass would be a marked man. He stepped over a kid who'd fallen down the steps of the bus, then went for his bag. Since they weren't ready within the impossible thirty seconds, the punishment was for them all to hold their bags over their heads till Schulz told them otherwise.

"Do I have the attention of you dolts?"

"Yes, Drill Sergeant!"

"Get this into those moldy brains of yours. The Army code is to treat everybody with dignity and respect, regardless of race, religion, color, national origin, gender, sexual orientation, and all other protected categories. Do you clowns understand?"

"Yes, Drill Sergeant!" they all shouted. The bags held over their heads wobbled more precariously.

Schulz faced up to a teenager with a stylish haircut whose fingers were scrabbling to hold up the shiny rounded corners of a big new suitcase.

"Is that bag heavy?"

"No, Drill Sergeant!"

"Did your mom pack you your wetback maid inside?"

"No, Drill Sergeant!"

"Hold that thing up straight, you runt."

"Yes, Drill Sergeant!"

Schulz turned away and confronted another recruit, who was resting his bag on his head.

"Grown a third arm, have you, butt muncher?"

"No, Drill Sergeant!"

"When one of you dipshits gets himself wounded in action, are you going to carry him on your head?"

"No, Drill Sergeant!" he replied, trying to lift his bag clear of his head and almost falling over backwards.

Before Schulz could answer, there was a crashing sound as the first recruit finally lost his grip on his suitcase and he fell with it onto the concrete floor. Schulz went back to the front of the group and harangued them as the recruit picked himself up.

"Do you vermin think you can be soldiers when you can't even carry your own bags?" He waited a split second before demanding, "Answer me, scumbags: are you going to be soldiers?"

"Yes, Drill Sergeant!"

"You bullshitters take your bags and report inside!"

"Yes, Drill Sergeant!"

That was the start of processing. Over the next few days they had to watch any number of PowerPoint presentations and motivating speeches, fill in questionnaires, sign disclaimers, hand over their cell phones, and get prodded, probed and vaccinated. At the end, they had their last chance to back out before being bused to their barracks for the start of their actual training.

The barracks was a new building and their bunk room was big and windowless, lit by rectangular neon units. The bunks and lockers were made out of gray-painted metal. Hugo was assigned Logan Miller as a battle buddy. That meant each was supposed to have the other's back at all times, and in particular during training exercises. Logan was a twenty-year-old from rural Wisconsin. He didn't need to be told to keep his head down. In fact, he hardly spoke. And he had no problems with the exercises, not even with the food.

What Logan couldn't do was get into the mindset of the drill sergeants. When he was on the weapons range, a sergeant asked him to pass a can of cola that was on top of a wall. When Logan picked it up, the sergeant said, "You're dead, shit-for-brains, and I'm wearing your guts as a scarf." On the bottom of the can, "IED" was written in black marker.

When Logan was on guard duty for the dorm the first time, Hugo made sure that he knew not to let *anyone* through without ID and password. So that's what Logan asked for when a drill sergeant turned up about 2 a.m. wanting to get in. The sergeant showed him a pizza coupon as ID, and Logan kept a straight face, telling him he was denied entry. But then the sergeant said, "Okay, good job, now let me in, I've got work to do." Logan just stood aside to let him through and got himself an earful from the sergeant, and was assigned to cleaning the bunk room floor for a week. The next time Logan was on guard duty, Hugo went through with him how he wasn't going to let any drill sergeant through, no matter how much he threatened him, and Logan held up.

On Sunday night they had cell phone privileges for an hour. Hugo had called Valentina the week before and his call had gone to voice mail. He received his phone from one of the drill sergeants and saw messages from Valentina. Like he'd hoped, the only reason she hadn't picked up was that she'd been on shift, with her phone in her locker. After Luz had helped her stand up to the agency, Valentina was back working on an orthopedic ward. From the way she'd written the long messages, Hugo could tell she was well past the downer of being out of work.

Although she'd told him she'd be on shift again, Hugo tried calling anyway. When it went to voice mail, he wrote her back, telling her that he was getting through basic training without any real problem and how he was trying to help Logan.

There was also a missed call from an unknown LA number. He called back and a man answered.

"Hey, man. Hugo. Devon Reid."

"Devon, what the hell?"

"Yeah, man, I finished my tour in the Army. Now I'm an ambulance dispatcher. You did a good job over there, not least getting yourselves out alive."

"Not all of us."

"Basic training sucks, but you should handle it better than most. Anyway, I just wanted you to have my number."

"Thanks, man."

"If that nativist shit comes your way, maybe I can help, OK?"

"Nativist?"

"You know, anti-immigrant."

Hugo didn't think that was anything to worry about, so he changed the subject. "You know I was in California a few weeks ago. My girlfriend is a nurse in Sacramento."

"So look me up, man."

"Sure thing."

"See ya."

Devon hung up and saw a notification had just arrived on his phone: a direct message from Devon, with a link. He followed it to a social media account for the American Foreign Legion. The avatar was a military-style badge in the shape of a shield. On the shield was a dagger on top of a drab green American flag, but with an elliptical globe symbol where the stars would have been.

Hugo scrolled through some of the American Foreign Legion posts. They seemed to be mostly about immigrants standing up for their rights. Hugo wasn't against that, but he had no need for it himself.

The platoon had gotten through a live fire exercise, fighting their way through a Potemkin village in the Georgia woodlands, when Schulz told Hugo to report to the company commander, Lieutenant Monro. In the office, a civilian in a cheap suit stood to the side of Monro's desk, his hands behind his back. Hugo saluted Monro, identified himself, and waited while Monro looked him up and down.

"You were in the news on account of that Parthian lynching. And of how you managed to get out of Yemen."

"Yes, sir."

"Seems like someone in Washington remembered you." Then he nodded to the civilian, who stepped forward and handed him an envelope.

"Subpoena to appear before the House Foreign Affairs Committee. Enjoy your day."

Monro looked at Hugo dryly while the civilian left.

"The committee is investigating human rights violations in Colombia."

Hugo tensed. "Yes, sir."

"Before they question you, you need to provide a written witness statement. Inside a week. Bring it here within five days and we'll send it to Legislative Liaison in Washington."

"Yes, sir."

"It'll probably be on C-SPAN."

Hugo's expression didn't change, so Monro added "Television" by way of explanation.

"Yes, sir."

"Just keep to the facts. No politicking."

"Yes, sir, I can do that, sir."

Monro picked up the file, flipped back through it a few pages. "I guess you can." He took a breath before wrapping up. "Go to the Defense Travel Administrator's office, Building 35, for your authorization and papers."

Hugo saluted, left the office and walked down the corridor and out of the building. Someone in Washington must've done their homework on him. They thought he could tell them about human rights abuses. In his mind, he reached back towards those times in the Colombian military.

27

Washington, DC

A WEEK later, Hugo left Fort Benning for Atlanta airport on one of the same buses he'd arrived on. This time it was empty except for him, the driver, and a specialist charged with rounding up a new batch of recruits at the airport later. It was daytime and Hugo could see that the entrance to Fort Benning was marked by four sets of columns, fifty feet high, on each corner of the double overpass of I-185. On the two sets of columns facing the Fort, an eight-foot-high bronze bald eagle saluted those leaving. As they went under I-185, Hugo looked round and saw an infantryman and a cavalryman on top of the other two sets of columns, encouraging new arrivals.

On the way north, Hugo looked out the window as patches of forest came and went. At the airport, he went through security and headed to the gate for his afternoon flight to Washington, DC. This was his first time off the base in a US Army uniform, and he was surprised and thrilled by how people treated him with respect, even exaltation. In Colombia, the more likely reactions ranged from distrust, to fear at being next to someone with a target on his back, to barely hidden contempt. Well, in Washington, he was going to do what he could for a better Colombian military.

On the flight, he looked over the seats in front of him, at the other passengers sipping coffee, tapping on electronic devices, or just trying to find a position comfortable enough to relax for half an hour. Hugo reached into a shirt pocket, fished out a small notebook, and thought through answers to some of the questions he'd imagined the committee could ask him.

He'd been booked into a chain hotel in Rosslyn: across the Potomac River from Washington and Georgetown, and to the north of Arlington. Although the view from his room was just a gray wall on the other side of a light well.

The next morning he was met in the lobby by a specialist from Legislative Liaison and they were driven to Congress. As they lined up outside to get their passes, Hugo looked up at the dome and smiled, proud that he was going to be part of this building's work for a few hours.

Hugo sat with the specialist in the back rows of the floor of the committee room. The committee members, from the House of Representatives, sat on tiered rows of seats banked against one of the walls. Each new witness had to make their way to an old wooden desk under the eye of the committee chair, Elijah Cantrell.

The room was well lit, not by windows but high-intensity LED panels for better photography. The only windows were hidden behind blue velvet curtains that hung from floor to ceiling behind the committee benches. The liaison specialist had told him in the car that each committee member had up to five minutes to question each witness.

For this hearing on Colombia, most of the witnesses were State Department officials, including some who'd staffed the US embassy in Bogotá, or workers from NGOs relaying accounts of abuses by guerrilla groups, drug gangs, and the Colombian military. Finally Hugo was called and he made his way to the big central desk, its sides piled high with paper files, and sat on the leather upholstered chair.

"Mr. Ayala, would you like to make an initial statement?"

"No, sir. Thank you."

"Mr. Ayala, you are currently undergoing basic training as a US Army recruit at Fort Benning."

"Yes, sir."

"You are a Colombian citizen and were previously a corporal in your country's Naval Infantry."

"Yes, sir."

"Your written testimony states that you had knowledge of extrajudicial killings."

"Excuse me, sir?"

Cantrell flipped through some of the papers in front of him before clarifying, "The so-called false positives."

"Yes, sir."

"Could you summarize for us how you tried to testify about these extrajudicial killings, how your superiors stopped you from doing so, and how you were treated from then on?"

"Yes, sir." Hugo took a breath. "After they set up the JEP—I mean the Special Jurisdiction for Peace—my lieutenant said that he was collecting testimonies from anyone who knew anything about the false positives—"

The chair interrupted. "For the record, which lieutenant was that, please, sir?"

"Lieutenant Lleras, sir." Hugo continued, "I believed him, so I wrote down what I knew."

Hugo paused but continued again when he got the nod from the chair.

"When we were stationed on the Caribbean coast, we went to a village on the Atrato River because of reports of guerrilla activity there. We arrived after an army unit, and they said they'd carried out an operation against the guerrilla the night before and killed some of them. I saw some of the bodies because they didn't have body bags."

"So the army was doing their job?"

"They'd been shot in the face so you couldn't recognize them that way. But I'd seen one of them before."

The chair gave the nod for him to continue.

"I'd seen him getting into an army vehicle, in a town downstream, nearer the coast. He was a young guy, his clothes were ragged, his hair was a mess, but he seemed excited to be with the army." Hugo paused and looked down at the floor.

"I noticed the tattoo on his wrist. It was a band in a geometric design, a square divided into triangles, and then zigzags. Like it was supposed to be indigenous. And then I saw it again on the wrist of the dead man in the village. It was a homemade tattoo. It was the same guy."

"What would be the motive for the army to kill him?"

"There were incentives so you were paid according to how many guerrillas you killed."

Hugo heard some murmuring from those around him.

"And what happened when you wrote that down and gave it to the lieutenant?"

"He looked it over, then laughed. He took out a lighter and set fire to one corner of the paper. While it was burning, he said to me: 'We need to know who's a soldier and who's a *sapo*.' A snitch."

There was silence for a couple of seconds before the chair continued.

"So the officer in charge, Lieutenant Lleras, now Colonel Lleras, destroyed your evidence of an extrajudicial killing, and criticized you for submitting it."

Hugo paused for a couple of seconds before replying, "Yes, sir."

"And what happened to you after you'd tried to denounce this apparent crime?"

"Sir, I was put in harm's way whenever possible. By my own unit. I know we were fighting a guerrilla conflict, but I was ordered into situations contrary to our training."

"And what was the result?"

"We had intelligence that a riverboat was being used to transport drugs. I was ordered to go inside and clear the cabins while the rest of the unit stayed outside. I was shot in the arm before the rest came for me."

Hugo looked at the grain of the wood in the desk in front of him till he could speak again without crying. The chair paused.

"So they needlessly put you at risk of death, but only after you'd denounced evidence of extrajudicial killing."

"Yes, sir."

"Thank you, Mr. Ayala." Then the chair looked down to the papers on his desk, frowned, turned to look at a colleague to his left, and said, "Representative Roebert."

"So, Mr. Ayala, you ratted out your former comrades in arms, but only once you've reached the safety of the United States?"

Hugo was taken aback by the hostile tone and took a second to reply.

"Ma'am, I was invited here to testify and I've answered the questions truthfully."

Roebert was looking for soundbites rather than engaging in dialogue with Hugo.

"Why should the United States pay to train you in deadly force when you couldn't go the distance for your own country?"

"I was wounded in the line of duty. If I hadn't gone the distance, I wouldn't have been honorably discharged."

"Are there foreigners in the Colombian military?"

"Not to my knowledge, ma'am."

"Because only Colombians will risk their lives to defend Colombia, isn't that right?"

"Ma'am, whoever lives in Colombia will benefit from defending it."

Roebert was winding herself up and ignored the answer. "Just like America can only be defended by Americans." She turned to look at the chair. "Mr. Chairman, I want to put on the record my demand that all

American military personnel be American nationals. None but Americans shall rule America!"

She sat back, relaxed, and nodded at the chair to indicate that she'd finished.

The chair took a deep breath. "I remind the committee that our charge today is to investigate human rights abuses in Latin America, not to discuss the immigration policy of the United States. Any more questions?"

There weren't any, so he looked back at Hugo. "Sir, I hope you will serve this country as well as you did Colombia."

Hugo stood up and made his way back to his seat.

28

Fort Benning, Georgia

From the time Hugo got back to Fort Benning, Drill Sergeant Schulz was on his back. He'd call Hugo out for something like a loose thread in the inside of a uniform sleeve. Then, when he did the punishment push-ups, they weren't flat enough, so he had to do them again with his hands off the ground on bricks. For Hugo, this went with the territory, but Schulz could see that, so he just kept pushing him harder and harder. Schulz tried to provoke Hugo verbally, but he kept himself to the three-word answers they'd been taught.

On one of the field exercises, Miller got himself killed by stepping on a mine, and Hugo had to carry his body over his shoulder up the hill to a medic post. When he got there, Schulz told him that he hadn't carried Miller fast enough and that he had to carry him down to the bottom of the hill and up again. When he did that, Schulz told him he hadn't kept low enough and he would've been picked off by the enemy. By the time he got to the top of the hill the third time, with Miller over his shoulder, he was starting to see white spots before his eyes.

Schulz saw he was struggling, and he laughed. "Come on, beaner. Just imagine that you're trying to carry your kid over the Rio Grande into the USA."

Hugo knew that Schulz wouldn't let up as long as he was standing. When he got to the bottom of the hill again, Miller whispered to Hugo to just keel over halfway up the next time. But Hugo's challenge wasn't to get past Schulz: it was to leave nothing out on the training ground.

As he went up the hill again, the white spots cleared away and he was back in Colombia, in the Naval Infantry, on the River Atrato. Their boat had been blown out of the water by an explosion and flipped over on top of Hugo and another corporal. They had their heads above water in an air pocket under the boat, and Hugo knew they had to use what oxygen was left to dive under the boat and up again, but the other soldier was scared and held him back. Hugo dived down into the water, but the other soldier kept hold of his feet. Hugo tried to kick free but just used up his air faster till there was none left. But it didn't matter because he was a manatee now. He sensed that the other soldier was going to be OK, and then Hugo was by himself. He let the river current take him downstream till finally he got to the Caribbean. He got washed up on a beach but, being a manatee, he couldn't breathe air anymore, and he was trying to flap himself back into the sea with his stubby flippers when he woke up.

He was in a hospital bed, which had been tilted to put his legs in the air and his head down. A medic turned around to face Hugo and looked at him quizzically. Hugo realized that he'd passed out, due to lack of oxygen, and had been speaking while hallucinating.

Schulz also started to use the kind of lines that Representative Roebert had come out with at the congressional hearing. Most of the rest of the platoon started to avoid Hugo for fear of being collateral damage to Schulz's spite. Now, when Miller looked at him, it was with apprehension.

On the parade ground, Schulz took issue with Hugo's execution of the about-face.

"Can't you beaners ever stand up straight?"

Hugo chose this moment when all his platoon would hear.

"Nationality is a protected category, Drill Sergeant!"

Schulz stepped back, then threw himself forward again, straight-arming the heel of his hand into Hugo's cheek. Hugo staggered back, tried to recover, but Schulz's face against his prevented him from stepping forward into line.

"Beaner is not a nationality, assface!"

Hugo had made his point already, so he looked back into Schulz's eyes without speaking.

"When you're under fire, do you think any *category* is going to protect you?"

"No, Drill Sergeant!"

Then he stepped forward into Hugo's face and hissed at him, "What I hear, soon we'll be done with your kind around here."

Then he shouted to the platoon, "Thanks to Ayala here, you worms have no phone privileges this Sunday." Hugo kept staring straight ahead, but he could feel the contempt of the other recruits.

Mail call was every evening, Monday to Saturday. One of the drill sergeants came through the barracks calling out the names of those who'd got a letter. Nowadays not many people had family or girlfriends who wrote letters, and that included Hugo. But one evening, when he'd got back from doing his laundry, and was folding his uniform ahead of inspection the following day, he heard his name called out. The sergeant handed him a small manila envelope with something inside that felt like a small booklet. Hugo opened the envelope and tipped it out onto his bed. He picked it up and looked into the placid eyes of the Virgin María, who was carrying the baby Jesus in her arms. They were in a small reproduction of an altarpiece, set into a rectangle of black satin. A *sufragio*. A kind of elaborate condolence card, received after a death in your family. He steeled himself before opening the *sufragio* and reading the message.

> You looked great on TV, you snitch. Do you think your gringo ass is too fancy for the Colombian Navy? If you ever come back to Colombia your TV face won't last for long. And we'll make sure you can't satisfy that uptight girlfriend of yours.

The note was handwritten. They weren't even worried about being identified. He looked at the return address: Massachusetts Avenue in Washington. The Colombian Embassy. Hugo swore under his breath.

Finally it was time for the bivouac, the last serious exercise before graduation: two days out in the elements, digging foxholes, fighting their way through enemy territory, then overrunning one of their outposts. The instructors still chewed out the recruits, but seemed invested in their success, like it would reflect badly on them if any failed to become soldiers.

At the end of the exercise, the recruits stepped out of the forest and onto the grass surrounding the Afghan Village. Lieutenant Monro, the company commander, was there to congratulate them one by one. Hugo let Miller go first and smiled to see how exhilarated he was to have made it.

But then he saw Monro's expression change when it was his own turn.

"Ayala, step aside," he ordered.

"Yes, sir," he replied. It seemed serious, but he didn't think he'd made a major screwup, so he wondered whether something had happened to his parents or to Valentina.

Monro led Hugo away from the group of recruits. Exhausted, they had sat down on the ground, but they wanted to hang on to the experience of the bivouac and were bullshitting each other about how they'd excelled or messed up over the previous two days.

Once they were a few yards away, Monro turned to Hugo and frowned.

"Ayala, as of today, by executive order, no foreign nationals can be soldiers in the US military, nor can they be recruited for that purpose."

Hugo was stunned. "What does that mean for me? Sir?"

"We have no choice but to escort you from Fort Benning and release you from the Army."

"But, sir, a soldier in the US Army is what I'm meant to be. This is what I want to do with my life."

"I know Ayala. I've had my eye on you. I thought you were going to go far. If it were up to me, then you would."

"Thank you, sir," said Hugo before turning away, tears in his eyes.

Miller ran after him, wanting to celebrate, but Hugo couldn't face him and just carried on walking straight ahead. After a few seconds, Miller stopped and looked after Hugo, not understanding.

As he walked, Hugo tried to make sense of what America was doing to him. He'd signed up for the Army to make sure that people were treated fairly, and then they kicked him out and left him to die. He couldn't accept it. He didn't want to think that he'd been wrong about his adopted country. Instead he thought about what he was going to do. He didn't even think about going back to Colombia. The only thing there for him now was a slow and painful death. He'd known that when he'd decided to testify in Congress. He'd assumed he'd get citizenship after finishing his tour of duty in the US Army after graduating. He wasn't going to be one of those stupid kids that blew their chance for some petty crime. He was going to do things by the book. That's what he'd thought.

29

Sacramento, Pelton Medical Center, Orthopedic Ward

A COUPLE of days after the showdown at the Mediquet office, the agency called Valentina, and the following Monday she was back on the same orthopedic ward as a few weeks before. She'd messaged Luz to thank her and was expecting to see her on the ward. But when she got there, Luz wasn't there. In fact, Valentina had been contracted as cover for her.

Estela wasn't one of Valentina's patients on her first shift, but when she finished everything up, before changing out of her uniform, Valentina went to see her. Estela's medical record showed that she was due to be discharged soon, but she didn't seem too excited about it. Trying to cheer her up, Valentina asked about her son, Daniel.

Estela burst into tears.

"The fucking *migra* got him and they're going to deport him."

Valentina was taken aback.

"We don't even know where they've got him now, and no one can make them listen," continued Estela.

"They can't do that," said Valentina, taking Estela's hand.

"Daniel's a citizen, but they don't care. They do what the fuck they want."

Estela put her hand on top of Valentina's to thank her.

"Luz is using some of her leave time to try to track him down and *ojalá* get him released. May God bless her."

Estela took a breath.

"I want to get out of here and help him, but I've still got these tubes coming out of me, leaking pus like a squashed cockroach."

Valentina kept her hand on her arm till she stopped crying.

When she got home, Valentina called Luz.

"Why didn't you tell me about Daniel?" asked Valentina. "I started talking to Estela about him and just upset her."

"Well, some people don't want to know about patients outside work. They want to forget them once they're through the swing doors."

"You're right," said Valentina, thinking of Leidy. "But I can't just switch them out of my mind. For better or worse. My boyfriend was a patient, you know."

They both laughed.

"So what happened to Daniel?" asked Valentina.

Luz sighed. "We don't know for sure yet, but it sounds like he was out working, and his dogs got into a fight with some other guy's dog. A kid passing by got too close and had her arm bitten."

"Ow."

Luz switched to nursing mode. "Yeah, I managed to track down where the little girl was taken. Puncture wounds between the radius and ulna. Clean, no complications, she's fine."

Luz took a breath.

"Anyway, somehow ICE got involved and they took Daniel, and the owner of the other dog."

"My God, when did that happen?"

"A few days ago. We're not even sure where Daniel is right now. When we call ICE, they won't tell us anything. It doesn't help his mom being in the hospital and not in a good way. They give us bullshit about protection of privacy."

"Who's we?"

"I'm working with a nonprofit to try to track him down and help him. Remember Ernesto? He's helping as well. We don't want Daniel to be deported."

"But he's a citizen? And they have to go to court for that, with a lawyer and everything?"

"They shouldn't deport citizens, but they do. And he doesn't have the right to a lawyer because he's accused of a civil offense, not a criminal one. He's supposed to have due process, but the whole system is done on the cheap, so by the time someone's wrongly deported, then it's too late to be fixed."

"*Hijueputa.* That's not right."

"No, but that's how it is. When you're back on the ward, I think it's better if you see Estela, even if she's not your patient. Maybe you think you're upsetting her, but being alone's not good for her either."

"You're right, thanks." Valentina thought for a second. "Why don't you forward me a link to that nonprofit you're working with?"

"Will do, thanks. Bye"

30

Fort Benning, Georgia

On Sunday, Hugo's platoon had cell phone privileges again. He couldn't face calling Valentina first. He didn't want to speak to her when he didn't know what he was going to do.

Instead he messaged Devon and called him as soon as he messaged back.

"Hey."

"Hi, glad to speak with you, man," said Devon.

"What's up?"

"I guess you saw the news about Green Card soldiers. So I'm out of the Army, and if I go back to Colombia then I'm dead."

"If you're lucky."

"Yeah." They laughed and Hugo eased off slightly. "So I've got to stay here," he continued in a lower voice. "In America."

"Some of us don't have a choice."

Hugo hesitated before referring to Devon's own situation.

"It sucks that your citizenship was blocked."

"If you speak up too loud about certain things, they'll try to smear you. Being undocumented does require a certain mindset," Devon continued. "But do you think it's more stressful than being on active duty in some of the places you've served?"

"No."

"Let me suggest something."

"Yep."

"Not all states treat undocumented people the same. California is one of the better ones."

"Well, Valentina's there, but I don't want to get her into trouble."

"I get it. But California's bigger than Sacramento. And you can get a driver's license, for example."

"Really?"

"Yeah, and Hispanics are the biggest ethnic group. The state government's got no reason to buy into this nativist shit. Why don't you come out to LA? I'll see if I can help you set yourself up."

"That'd be great, thanks."

"OK. It's not all irie, though. If ICE has a reason to get on your ass, at any time, anywhere, then you're liable to be detained. Some local police love to kiss ICE's ass as well. So you keep your head down."

"I don't tend to make trouble."

"Good. But better travel by land."

"Right."

"Remember, one in thirty Americans is undocumented. More than ten million."

"Thanks, man."

"No problem."

Hugo hung up. Now he felt ready to call Valentina. She cried when she heard what'd happened to him, but he could handle it now that he had a plan. When they'd both calmed down he said, "I think I'll go to LA. I know someone there who can help me."

"What? You should come here to Sacramento."

"It's Devon, I told you about him. He can help me find a job."

"So can the people I know here."

"You've had your own problems getting work even though you've got the right visa and all that."

"Well, it's because I've got the right visa that I'm in a position to help you. Is Devon undocumented as well?"

"Yes."

"And that's a good thing?"

"He knows what I'm going to need."

"Why won't you accept help from me?"

"That's not true." It was. "Do you know anyone in LA?"

Valentina decided that this wasn't the time to argue. "One of my colleagues from the military hospital went to work there. I can get in touch with her and see if she knows anyone that can rent you a room. I guess that's what you need?"

"Right. That's great, thanks."

There was a pause.

"I have to be out of here in a few days."
"I'm sorry, Hugo."
"I've got some kind of a plan now."
"I'll send you the phone number when I know something."
"Thanks. Bye, my love."

A few days later, before the graduation ceremony for all the others, Hugo cleared out his bank account via an ATM on the base and got on an Army bus to the Atlanta airport again, for the last time. It was afternoon by the time they arrived. The driver seemed to know the deal about him, and they fist-bumped when Hugo got off.

And that was the Army behind him. From now on he was illegal. *Undocumented*, Devon's voice told him.

From the airport, Hugo got the MARTA subway to Garnett, then down the stairs of the elevated station. Hugo looked around him as he crossed over the street: the only visible businesses were a couple of bail bond agents. He walked into the bus station, a nondescript two-story building of grimy concrete and brick.

As he lined up to buy his ticket, Hugo felt the eyes of the security guard on him. But he told himself that he was a typical customer and the guard had no reason to do anything. When he got to the counter, he spoke through a microphone to a middle-aged woman on the other side of the solid glass and asked for a one-way ticket to Los Angeles.

"Leaving twelve forty a.m., transfer Houston," said the agent, her finger poised on the mouse, confident of closing the deal.

Texas, Hugo thought. Who knew what bullshit they had for undocumented people? Then he caught himself: already thinking scared. But he was right. This was how it was going to be from now on.

The clerk tried to keep looking positive, but her lips were pursing.

"I've got time. Any other routes?" asked Hugo.

The clerk shrugged and went back to navigating her screen.

"Well, you could transfer at Memphis and Oklahoma City."

"Yeah, I'll take that, please."

31

Los Angeles

A COUPLE of days later, Hugo walked out of the bus station in LA, with his olive-green backpack on his back, feeling oil ooze from his pores from the cheap food he'd had on the way. He walked south, parallel to a train pulling slowly in towards Union Station. He found the stop for bus number 40 and got on the next one south to Hawthorne. He took out his phone and looked again at the messages that Valentina had sent him while he was on the bus. Her ex-colleague knew someone with a room to rent. She was a retired nurse, originally from Colombia, called Esme Torres, who could do with the income and feeling of security from having someone in the room. Hugo messaged Mrs Torres to say he was on the bus and expected to be at the house in a couple of hours.

Hugo got off opposite Hawthorne Plaza. Hugo hadn't realized from the map on his phone that it was a dead mall, with its windows boarded up and external walkways blocked off by metal railings. Hugo walked past it heading east, and a few blocks later turned north onto Dumbarton Street. The houses were small 1940s tract homes with a frill of Mission-style brickwork on top of each front wall. He rang the bell of Mrs. Torres's house and she came to the door. She looked younger than Hugo had expected, her hair still black and her face smooth. For a second he wondered whether Valentina wouldn't also want to retire early from the physical and mental challenges of caring for broken people every day.

"Hi there, you must be Hugo," she said in English.

Hugo snapped back to the present. "Yes, good afternoon, Mrs. Torres. Hugo Ayala. Pleased to meet you."

She invited Hugo in and showed him around. The furniture and decoration seemed to need more space than they had available: heavy wood carved in a rustic style, a reproduction of a fat Botero queen in an ornamental gilt frame.

In the kitchen, Mrs. Torres started to ask. "Do you think..."

Hugo flinched as a large aircraft screamed over the house. Involuntarily, he looked up and around at the ceilings and walls. Then he realized it must be a cargo plane taking off from Hawthorne Municipal Airport, a few blocks to the east. He fidgeted while the noise abated enough to talk again.

The noise was second nature to Mrs. Torres, who just carried on again in midsentence.

"...you'll want to use the kitchen a lot?"

Hugo smiled. "Not really, Mrs. Torres. If I was on *MasterChef*, I'd make rice and tomato ketchup."

She laughed, relieved at not having to share her kitchen with a stranger. They went on to the spare room, which was going to be Hugo's. It had a single wooden bed with a multicolored cotton bedspread. Next to the light on the bedside table was a photo of the cathedral in Zipaquirá. Hugo thought this would've been one of her kids' bedrooms. He looked out of the window and saw an identical house next door. The curtains looked thick enough to keep the room dark.

"This is just what I need," he told Mrs. Torres.

They went to the living room and sat down at the table, and Hugo paid her a deposit and a month in advance in cash. Nothing in writing. Hugo went back to the bedroom and started to take out his neatly folded clothes and put them away in the wooden closet, and it reminded him of being at home. Suddenly he felt exhausted, not just from sleeping on a bus for the past two nights, but from having been on call for almost all of the past six months. Now there was no wake-up call, no guard duty, nothing.

He put his phone on silent, took off his clothes, got into bed under the colored bedspread, and fell asleep. He woke up the next morning, walked around the house in his socks till he found the bathroom, and had a shower. In the kitchen he found a breakfast that Mrs. Torres had made for him, of arepa and eggs with scallions and tomato. He ate it, went back to bed, and slept again till late afternoon. When he woke up, he messaged Valentina that everything was good. Then he messaged Devon asking him to meet, and they agreed on the following afternoon in Glendale.

32

El Paso Centro Legal, Sacramento

VALENTINA PARKED her car and walked to the storefront office of El Paso Centro Legal in Northgate. She walked uncertainly through the door. A middle-aged woman was speaking from behind the counter to a young man who had his back to Valentina. In the meantime, Valentina looked around. A pinboard was covered in multiple layers of flyers, posters, and laser-printed sheets with hand-cut tear-off tabs. The outer layer of paper included a poster calling for people to march on the state capitol in support of Cheddi Maharaj. From something on her phone, Valentina knew that he was an undocumented immigrant who said he was being targeted by ICE because of his activism.

Her thoughts were interrupted by the woman behind the counter.

"May I help you?"

"Yes, thanks. Maybe you know Luz Rivera. She told me about the center and I want to help."

The woman stood up to shake hands with Valentina. "That's great, thanks a lot. I'm Eugenia."

"Valentina Díaz."

Eugenia picked a leaflet out of a stand on the counter. "This describes our work supporting the legal rights of the disadvantaged, including immigration and tenancy rights."

Valentina took the leaflet, put it down on the counter and left her hand on top of it, to show that she'd read it later.

"For volunteering, one role that we always need is interpreter."

Valentina nodded to say that that was something she could do.

"Good. Have you had any experience in doing that?"

Valentina shook her head.

"No problem. It's probably best to start with a less formal situation, like an initial interview with a potential client. Not all our attorneys are fluent in Spanish."

"Sounds good."

"How's your time availability?"

"Well, I'm an agency nurse. I work shifts according to what work comes in. So there isn't really a fixed time. I know a week or two in advance when I could be available."

"That works."

A bell rang as the door opened behind her. Eugenia nodded past the side of her head at the person coming in.

"Hi there, Mr. Litman. Would you mind waiting a minute?"

"Sure." A young man, looking slightly ill at ease in his suit, stepped forward to the counter and waited for Eugenia to finish with Valentina.

"Look, Valentina, the way it's turned out today, if you wanted, you could try being an interpreter right away, to get an idea whether it'd suit you."

"That'd be great."

"Wonderful. Mr. Litman here is one of the lawyers that works with us," she said, indicating the young man.

He held his hand out to Valentina: "Please call me Mark. And you too, please, Eugenia."

"Thanks, Mark. There are a couple of people waiting for an initial consultation," said Eugenia, motioning to the wall opposite her, "and the meeting room is free."

Valentina turned to look at a handful of people sitting on stackable chairs, waiting with their backs to the storefront window. She felt guilty that she hadn't paid them attention before.

"Ms. Morales?" asked Eugenia, and a woman in her forties stood up. She was much taller than Valentina, even without the curls, which added a few inches before cascading down past her shoulders. Valentina found herself looking at a gold chain around her neck that carried the image of a saint.

Eugenia continued in Spanish. "Mr. Litman is a lawyer and will ask you to describe your situation and why you've come here to the legal center. Ms. Díaz will interpret if necessary." Valentina nodded at Ms. Morales, who glumly identified herself as Aura.

"Please come through," said Eugenia, opening the swing gate from the reception area into the office.

The three of them sat down around a laminate table in a small windowless meeting room towards the back of the building. Mark explained that it was an initial meeting to see whether and how the center might be able to help. Then he made sure that it was OK for him to record the meeting and did so using an app on his phone, which he put in the middle of the table. He got ready to write notes on a yellow legal pad.

Aura started to tell them why she was there, pausing every few sentences to let Valentina translate.

"So I'm from Venezuela. I've been here about three years. I don't have papers. I'm a maid."

She paused.

"I *was* a maid, I should say. For a family with a big house in Land Park. Just a block from the park. I worked for them for more than a year. I went there every day and they got to trust me with everything. Why not? I did a good job. When they were away on vacation, for work, I would still go and clean, let the gardener in, all that.

"A couple of weeks ago, ICE was waiting for me when I showed up to work in the morning. The family saw them take me away.

"It was the day after I'd been on the demonstration at the state capitol. I'm sure they picked on me for that. That's got to be against the law.

"We heard they were surveilling the demonstration. But it's in a public place, they're allowed to do that," said Mark.

"*Desgraciados.*"

"They're not allowed to be discriminatory, but that's hard to prove."

Aura caught her breath and continued.

"They took me to their detention center and asked me a bunch of stuff, but I wouldn't tell them anything."

"That was the right thing to do."

"But somehow they knew my name and other things. They gave me this paper," she said, fishing out a form from her handbag, "and said I could either be detained or wear a tag."

Aura lifted her cotton skirt above her ankle to show the GPS tag: a military-looking piece of equipment, with black webbing and a rounded black battery pack wrapped around her leg. She sighed.

"Can you imagine what it's like when people see this *grillete*?"

Mark shook his head. "Can I see the NTA?" he said, indicating the form that Aura had in her hand.

Valentina could see that in the top corner, it said "Notice to Appear."

"They didn't bother to complete it," he said, indicating the blank lower sections of the form. He paused while Valentina translated for Aura.

"By law they are supposed to complete it properly. They should say the grounds on which you're supposedly liable to deportation," he said, pointing to a block of white space on the form.

"So they screwed up?"

Mark took a scan of the NTA on his phone.

"Right. But still you need to appear at the Merits Hearing. How about the family you were working for? Will they put in a word for you?"

Aura sighed. "Since it happened, they don't want anything to do with me. They don't want people to know they had an undocumented maid. They seemed friendly with me before, and now nothing. They wouldn't even let me speak with the kids. I used to make *tequeños* for them."

Her voice trailed off as she frowned at the ground.

"Have you got photos or anything that can show you spent time there, or with the family?"

"Yeah, I've got some of me and the kids."

"Good. That's evidence that you were gainfully employed. What about family of your own?"

"I'm with my husband here. He's undocumented as well. Our kids are with my parents in Venezuela." She sighed again. "We didn't want them to risk what we had to go through to get here."

Mark looked at his watch, then flipped through the sheets he'd written on the legal pad.

"Well, Aura, I've got what I need to get started on an argument to the judge at the Merits Hearing for why you shouldn't be deported."

He took out a business card from his pocket and gave it to Aura.

"ICE could pick you up and detain you at any time. If you end up in a detention facility, they should let you make a call. Think now who you want to call, should that happen. And memorize their number. If you want to call me, I'll pick up at any time, but whoever it is, memorize their number."

"Thanks," said Aura, looking at the card.

Mark stood up. Aura and Valentina followed his cue, and they all went back to reception. Aura thanked Mark again, shook his hand and left.

"How did you find that?" Eugenia asked Valentina.

"Well, it was tough. Listening to her story, I mean," she replied. "I felt

OK doing the translation," she added, looking at Mark.

"Yes, you did a good job. Aura was confident in talking to you," he replied.

There was a pause. "Who's next?" asked Valentina.

The other two laughed. "Way to go," said Eugenia.

"Well, Mr. Ortega doesn't need an interpreter," she said, nodding to a young man sitting against the window, "and he's got the last appointment today."

Mark held out his hand to Valentina and thanked her. Mr. Ortega stood up and went with Mark towards the meeting room in the back.

"This kind of time is good for me at the moment," Valentina told Eugenia.

"No problem. As long as you want to help, then you'll be able to," Eugenia replied. She saw the enthusiasm in Valentina's eyes. "Maybe you'd like to take some of these flyers and put them in places where they might help."

"Sure," said Valentina, putting a handful into her bag. They hugged, then Valentina left and walked to her car.

Back at her apartment, Valentina called Luz.

"So I volunteered to be an interpreter at the legal center. They needed someone on the spot and I was able to help."

"Great. How was it?"

"Kind of depressing and exciting at the same time."

"The *migra* are just gonorrhea."

Luz's vehemence shook Valentina for a second. "Seems like the center can help some of them, though. What's the latest you heard about Daniel?"

"We think he's being held in the ICE cells downtown. But no one's heard from him. Sometimes they don't let people make calls even though it's their right."

"My God, that kind of thing really happens here."

"Damn right." Luz paused. "It's great that you're helping with the law center. For now there are still some legal moves that can stop some people from being deported."

"For now?"

"Don't you see the news? If Nemeth wins the election to the vacant seat, then he'll flip the majority in the Senate: all of Congress will be with the president and she'll be able to do what the hell she wants."

"You know, my boyfriend, Hugo, is always going on about how great

America is. It's too much at times. But now you've got me worried because I thought things were done by the law here."

Luz scoffed. "In the thirties, when there was a lot of unemployment, they rounded up hundreds of thousands of people in California and sent them over the border to Mexico. They didn't care whether they were citizens or not, or if it was within the law or not. If we just sit quiet, then they can come for us when they want."

33

Glendale, Los Angeles

THE NEXT afternoon, Hugo got the C line tram from Hawthorne station, then a couple of buses to Glendale. He walked to the ambulance dispatch center where Devon worked, a two-story building in white fiber cement cladding, set back from the street behind its employees' parking lot.

Hugo waited in reception. He wondered whether he should message Devon to let him know he'd arrived, but he came out and met him just after the agreed time.

They walked west on East Colorado Street, looking to get a coffee. Suddenly Devon stopped and turned to face a modern single-family house with some tall green shrubs shielding a small front yard.

"This is where the American Nazi Party had its headquarters."

Hugo wasn't sure whether to take Devon seriously.

"What, like before World War II?"

"No, man, it's still doing its thing. Just that their base is in Virginia now."

Devon turned back to the street and they both carried on walking.

"I couldn't've had this job here in the sixties. Glendale was a sundown town."

Hugo looked at Devon for an explanation.

"All Blacks had to be out by sundown. Or else get arrested or worse."

"America has progressed since then," said Hugo cautiously.

"What I'm saying is, there are still white supremacists, militias, just like there always have been in America."

By now they'd got to the café and sat down.

"Anyway, how are you doing?" asked Devon.

"I'm renting a room in Hawthorne from a Colombian lady, friend of a friend of my girlfriend."

"Good."

"How do you hold down your dispatcher job?"

"I got the job offer when I was still in the Army. If anyone suspects anything, they don't mind as long as I'm good at the work. And it helps when I recruit good people."

Devon paused for a second.

Hugo realized that he was expecting a tacit commitment in return.

"Look, things are not going to get easier, with the new Congress," Devon continued. "ICE is bad enough already. The American Foreign Legion is a network that can push back. A lot of people like us put our lives on the line for America, and now they want to throw us out. If we stick together, we can stop that from happening."

"I don't know, man."

"We're not the ones picking a fight here. But are you going back to Colombia?"

"No."

"Do you want to be on the run?"

"No."

Devon raised his eyebrows, inviting an alternative, but Hugo had none.

"OK, man. So, you can drive, right? Even in basic just now, you had to off-road?"

Hugo nodded.

"We're always needing ambulance drivers: EMT drivers, we call them. We get a lot of applicants too, but most of them haven't got it, haven't thought it through. They've tailgated ambulances and like the idea of being up front. It's liable to go to their heads, so they hit a curb and flip the vehicle."

"What's the catch?"

"Well, you'll always be liable to come up against ICE and get deported. It's a highly visible job, so you'll come across people who could want to call ICE on you."

"But ICE could get me anyway, and I can't just hide away, even if I could stand it, because I need to eat."

"Exactly. You need to go through EVOC. Emergency Vehicle Operator Course."

Hugo nodded.

"Some of it is theory, like a class, and some of it's actual driving. There's one I know where the instructor won't ask too much about your papers."

Hugo nodded.

"It's five hundred bucks, and I need to help the instructor with a couple of hundred."

Devon could see that Hugo was doing calculations in his head.

"Pay me back when you can, OK?"

Hugo realized that he was owing Devon more and more favors, but it wasn't like he had many options.

"Thanks, man."

A few minutes later, Devon acknowledged a man who'd come in through the front door of the café and was looking around. When the man left again, Devon got up and took his leave.

Hugo wanted to sit a while longer before the trip back to Hawthorne. Through the window, he saw Hugo and the other man get into a white station wagon with a couple of round white decals on the driver's side door. One of them had a design that looked like a fire helmet.

34

Downtown Sacramento

VALENTINA CHANGED out of her uniform in the locker room, then logged on to the ICE locator on her phone. She checked for Daniel and the others who were missing, presumed detained, from a list from the legal center. She did that four times a day now. She could search for some of the people by their A-Number, but Daniel was a citizen, so he didn't have one. She entered his first name and surname and felt a surge of excitement when she recognized him at the top of the list.

She hurried to her car and headed for the ICE offices downtown. She got the elevator from the basement parking garage and stepped out into the fifth-floor lobby. She saw the desk officer's eyes glaze over when he saw she was a Latina.

Valentina told him that, according to the ICE locator, Daniel was right there with them in the building. The officer typed Daniel's details back into the computer.

"Sorry, ma'am, he's no longer here," he said, pleased with himself.

35

Sacramento to Oakland Airport

THE ICE officers took Daniel down in the elevator and out of the back of the building to the delivery area, where an unmarked old bus was waiting. Through the windows of the bus, Daniel could see half a dozen people sitting on bench seats with their backs to him.

"What the fuck, man?"

"Enjoy the mystery tour, brazer," replied one of the officers as he pushed Daniel towards the bus.

As Daniel stepped up into the bus he was met by the hostile glares of the others, mostly young men like himself. The officer shoved Daniel down onto the seat and tied his cuffs to a bar that rang the length of the bus, behind the bench seat of ripped black vinyl. Daniel cried out again from the pain of his broken wrist. The disdainful looks of the other detainees told him to toughen up.

As the bus pulled out onto the street, a couple of demonstrators held up their phones to record the bus, while yelling anti-*migra* slogans.

The bus crawled through downtown, crossed the Sacramento River and kept on west on I-80. Daniel looked out of the window, trying to figure out where they might be being taken. Others just stared at the floor.

An hour later they came out onto the shore of San Francisco Bay, then turned south, past Berkeley, over the causeway through the Aquatic Park, through Oakland, then past big box stores and warehouses.

"Shit," said Daniel under his breath when he saw the bus following signs for the cargo area of Oakland Airport. They stopped at chain-link fences to go through one security check, then another, then they were out on the aircraft taxiway.

Ignoring the faded lane markings on the asphalt, the bus headed towards an aging 737 airliner, which was parked a couple of hundred yards from the cargo terminal building. It was unmarked except for a fading "Atlas Air Charter" decal on the tail.

They stopped twenty yards from a wheeled aluminum stairway that led up to the plane door. Another ICE agent stood on each side of the bottom of the steps. The bus driver cut the engine, but none of the detainees moved. A couple of ICE officers got out of the cab. One waited on the ground, eyeing the length of the bus, while the other agent walked up the passenger steps.

"This is the next stage in your removal from the United States. You can get on the plane peacefully yourselves, or we can put you on it."

He took a couple of steps further down the aisle of the bus and stood in front of the first detainee, a woman in her forties, who squinted back at him as if she needed her glasses. She flinched as the ICE officer reached behind her back. He unlocked her cuffs from the rail, stood back, and made a shooing gesture towards the plane. The woman looked around her but, with no reaction from the other detainees, stood up and disconsolately made her way off the bus.

The officer turned to face the first detainee on the opposite bench seat, a man of about fifty with a weather-beaten face and beer gut. He looked the officer in the eye, as if to say that he'd seen worse than him. The officer released the cuffs from the rail behind the detainee, but still he didn't move.

The officer signaled to his colleague on the asphalt, who bounded up the steps to the detainee and grabbed him under one armpit while the first officer took the other. The next detainee on the bench seat struggled to free himself to help but just drew his own blood as the cuffs cut into him. Meanwhile the officers had hauled their target to his feet. With his hands still cuffed behind him, he tried to lash out with his feet, but the officers were too close to get any force to his kicks. The officers dragged him to the top of the steps of the bus and threw him down. He bounced off the sidewall, tumbled headfirst onto the taxiway, and lay still.

The two officers manning the steps walked over, picked up the detainee from the asphalt, and dragged him towards the plane.

No one struggled after that. Daniel zoned out and tried to think ahead, how he could get word to his family, how he should hold his arms to reduce the long-term damage from the fracture. When it was his turn, he walked as steadily as he could out of the bus and up the shaky aluminum steps towards the plane, under the eyes of the ICE officers on the ground and in the doorway of the plane.

He stepped inside the fuselage but recoiled from the reek of urine.

Seeing his reaction, the ICE officer sneered at him, "Fucking chuco pigs." He jerked his head towards the back of the plane, telling Daniel to move on.

Daniel turned right and saw three more ICE officers halfway down the plane. Behind them, the plane was packed with other detainees. Some of their heads lolled to the sides, some flopped forward, and some were still upright but with their eyes blank. A movement behind him prompted Daniel to walk up towards the nearest officer, who waved him to the right. The seats and backrests were sheets of thick vinyl. Under the urine, Daniel now also caught the smell of bleach. He squeezed himself towards the next detainee, a tall man with a bull neck. He caught Daniel's gaze and held it, letting Daniel know that he'd take this shit out on him if he got a chance. With nowhere else to go, the tall man's legs spilled over into where Daniel had to sit. Nursing his broken wrist behind him, Daniel levered himself onto the sling seat, wedging his legs under his neighbor's.

An officer reached over Daniel, grabbed a seat belt, snapped it into the buckle and pulled it taut. Daniel cried out as his torso was forced back onto his inflamed wrist. Already the next detainee, a heavyset middle-aged woman, was filling the space on his other side, her legs and torso pinning back his. She bowed her head and sobbed quietly.

Daniel willed sleep to take him over, but he was snapped back to reality by the shouts of another man standing in front of him in the aisle.

"So kill me, motherfuckers. I told you I'm not going back."

Another officer approached the man from behind.

"You fucking pussies have no idea. Do you think you've seen half of what I've been through?"

Daniel reflexively cried out a warning as the officer unholstered a weapon. The detainee's shouts turned into strangled groaning as he was tasered in the neck. The officers shoved the twitching body into the available space, cinched a seat belt tight around him, and looked around for the next one.

Daniel closed his eyes till the engines turned shrill and the plane pushed him forward.

36

Sacramento

Valentina was on her way home after her shift. As soon as she stopped her car at a red light, she called Luz again on speed dial. Valentina had called her earlier, on her way out of the ICE building, to tell her that they'd denied having Daniel there. Luz had told her that he was probably with a batch of other detainees that protesters had seen leaving the building around the time that Valentina had gotten there. Now Valentina was checking in again.

"Well, we've got an idea where they could've taken Daniel and the others," Luz said.

"Great."

"Let's see," cautioned Luz. "but ICE has chartered a lot of flights out of Oakland Airport."

"What?"

"One of the people we called this morning is on the airside staff. A few hours after the bus left Sacramento with the ICE detainees, one like it drove out onto the airport taxiways. The people inside were cuffed and they were forced onto an old charter airliner."

"Shit. What about the destination?"

"Yep, that's public information. It went to San Diego."

Valentina didn't get it.

"They take a lot of people there and then to the Otay Mesa Detention Center before busing to the border and deporting them."

"My God. Is there anything we can do?"

"The same as always—put together what we know, make a case, try to get a judge to issue a ruling to stop what ICE is doing."

"But we can't even find out where he is."

"At least we know that ICE had him in Sacramento and moved him.

They should know where he is, even if they stop their own systems from making that public. So we have a chance to get an injunction from a judge to stop ICE from deporting him."

37

William Ridgeway Family Courthouse, Sacramento

CARL AND Vic were on courthouse duty. Easy pickings compared to wrestling cholos on the street. All they had to do was sit quietly at the back of the court till it was time. The best part was that the wets had to identify themselves.

They had a source in the courthouse who, every week, ran them down the witnesses that were most likely illegal. The informant knew that if she didn't come through with good tips, then her big brother would be on his way out of the country.

Carl sat back to enjoy today's novela bullshit. They were in William Ridgeway Family Courthouse in Belvedere, five miles east of downtown. It'd been built a few decades ago. There were arched windows on the outside, but Carl had never seen the inside of them. The interior felt like a midrange hotel, and today's courtroom was like an oversize meeting room which the furniture wasn't managing to fill. Some gorda was trying to get child support out of her loser ex for her anchor baby instead of pissing it away on beer.

Carl and Vic were in civies so the target didn't get nervous about them being in court. When the hearing was wrapping up, they left and waited for her in the corridor of the courthouse.

The gorda was so wound up after her testimony that she started screaming when she realized she was going to be arrested. As Vic was cuffing her, a couple of Sheriff's peace officers ran up and challenged them, hands on their sidearms. Carl pulled out his ICE badge, taking a deep breath. These guys knew who they were, their pride just wouldn't let them see ICE taking illegals from under their noses without putting on a charade.

By their body language, Carl and Vic let the peace officers know that they weren't letting go their detainee, but they weren't looking for trouble either. Shadowed by the peace officers, they pressed through a knot of rubberneckers calling them fascists and goons, which just told Carl that he was doing his job right.

38

Inglewood, Los Angeles

A WEEK after meeting Devon, Hugo rolled his recently purchased secondhand Subaru into an ambulance station in Inglewood, across Interstate 405 from LAX, just fifteen minutes from Mrs. Torres's house. He introduced himself in the small office, then waited for the emergency medical technician to arrive and complete the team. He arrived just about on time, introduced himself as Joseph Omondi, and suggested they talk more on the road.

Heading out to Huntington Park, Joseph sat up in the cab next to Hugo and went through the day's roster. After half an hour, they got to their first patient, who lived in a single-story 1960s house a few blocks to the east of Pacific Boulevard. Hugo watched from the cab as Joseph spoke with an elderly woman at the door. She stepped back, and an overweight middle-aged man appeared, stepping uncertainly, with his eyes alert and twitching. Hugo stepped out and walked around to the back of the ambulance as Joseph guided the patient to the door with the serenity of a maître d'. As the patient swayed up the steps, Joseph glanced at Hugo, tipping his head towards the front of the vehicle, telling him that he could best help by staying put in the cab.

Hugo set off when he got the call over the intercom from Joseph in the back of the vehicle. Forty-five minutes later, in Baldwin Park, he drove right on past the address shown on the GPS screen, and Joseph called out.

"Mr. Hugo, we passed the clinic."

"Roger," replied Hugo. He went straight into a three-point turn because they were on a broad suburban residential street with no other traffic. Having turned around, he pulled up on the street outside the clinic, which looked like any other house on the street except for two porta-potties off the side of the driveway.

"Mr. Hugo, you can use the driveway."

Of course, Hugo said to himself. He still hadn't gotten it into his head that this was their destination. He drove up the driveway and waited while Joseph helped the patient out of the ambulance and onto the porch, which ran along the front of the house/clinic. They were met by an attendant in a blue-and-white nursing-style uniform, who guided the patient to a rocking chair on the porch and helped him sit down. Then she brought him a soda in a big plastic gulp cup. When he set down the cup on a small table beside him, the attendant brought him a tablet computer and left him playing some kind of game.

Hugo was still watching the porch when he heard Joseph close the door behind him on the passenger side of the cab.

Ignoring Hugo's bemusement, Joseph asked politely, "I think our next patient is Mr. Lewis in Bellflower, is that right?"

"Yes, sir," replied Hugo automatically.

When they were cruising on the I-605 he said, "Joseph—Mr. Joseph—we came north from Huntington Park, now we're going back south again. The patients have scheduled appointments. Do you think the dispatch office has chosen the most efficient route?"

Joseph nodded indulgently. "Our priority is patient satisfaction," he reassured Hugo. "We fit in around their other appointments."

Hugo raised his eyebrows, wondering how many other appointments their last patient could have in a day.

"And their carers' schedules," added Joseph.

It was Hugo's turn to nod, trying to convince himself.

He got back home to Mrs. Torres's house at about 8 p.m. In his room, he was going to call Valentina, but he knew she'd tell him that there was something not right about the work. He didn't want her to hear that yet. He wanted to tell her after he'd worked out what to do about it. So he just exchanged a few superficial text messages with her, about how well everything was going.

Then he ordered in Italian food and sat chatting with Mrs. Torres while he ate lukewarm pasta. She had the television news on and an item came on about the AFL. There was some footage of the Sacramento demonstrators, then a still of Devon, which looked like it was taken as he came out of the ambulance dispatch building.

"What a troublemaker that guy is," said Mrs. Torres.

It wasn't polite for Hugo to disagree with his landlady, but he had to say something.

"Well, I knew him when he was in the US Army. He got me out of a tough spot."

"So let him be a soldier, not a politician."

"He's done his time in the Army. If he wants to stay, he should be here legally."

Mrs. Torres had never asked whether Hugo was legal.

"How can anyone trust him when he goes on a fake passport?" continued Mrs. Torres.

"All I know is, Mrs. Torres, is that he did a good job in the Army and got an honorable discharge, so he can't be all bad."

Mrs. Torres huffed.

The next day, he was in the ambulance crawling up La Brea Avenue on the way to their first patient in Crenshaw. Joseph was in the cab with him, telling him about his favorite places to eat in LA, when a call came in for units to respond to a multivehicle accident on Centinela and Field. That was half a dozen blocks away. Hugo reached for the mic. He was going over in his head how he was going to respond when he realized his hand was on top of Joseph's, rather than the mic.

Gripping the mic as if he were squeezing a lemon, Joseph said, "No emergency response. Did they not tell you that at the station?"

"In training they told us that emergencies are our first priority."

"Do you think a real emergency service would take you on?"

Was Joseph threatening him? But Hugo didn't care about that. The point was that they should answer the emergency call. Joseph was in the wrong. But as long as they were illegals, Joseph was right: Hugo had no other place to go. He gritted his teeth and put his hand back on the steering wheel. Joseph let go of the mic.

"We don't want to bring in an emergency casualty and have some hospital going over our paperwork," continued Joseph in a more conciliatory tone.

Hugo grunted noncommittally, keeping his eyes on the road.

At the house in Crenshaw, Joseph fetched an elderly woman who shuffled slowly to the ambulance with the help of a folding walker. Fifty minutes later they arrived at the so-called clinic in Baldwin Park and parked behind another ambulance from the same station on the driveway. Joseph helped the woman to a seat on the porch, then stopped to talk to the crew of the other ambulance, who were both waiting outside their vehicle.

Hugo watched them chat for a few minutes. He didn't want to sulk, so he got out of the cab and joined them. Joseph was debating with the other ambulance's EMT about food, and where to buy fresh meat. Hugo just stood by till there was movement on the porch. The uniformed woman took the tablet from one of the patients and started to get her ready to leave, so each crew went back to their own vehicle.

On the way to their next patient in South Gate, Hugo got to wondering.

"So how do you make that goat meat?"

"Nyama choma?"

"Yeah. Do you—what's it called—use herbs on the meat before?"

"Oh yes, with garlic, onion, rosemary, lime juice..."

"Lime juice?" Hugo interrupted. "No, no. We never do it like that. You have to marinate it, but not with lime juice. Garlic, onion, OK, beer maybe..."

In the end, they agreed to disagree, but also to try out the Kenyan way at a restaurant.

39

William Ridgeway Family Courthouse, Sacramento

CARL AND Vic waited in an unmarked car in the parking lot to the east of the family courthouse. For now they couldn't work inside, because the state AG had gotten a judge to rule that arresting people in a courthouse was against common law. What a joke. So, while their lawyers appealed that, they had to catch wetbacks in the parking lot instead. Carl sipped coffee while scrutinizing people walking back to the parking lot from the court. Finally he saw who he'd been looking for. Isabela Campos was a fifty-year-old Argentinian who volunteered at one of the so-called legal defense centers in town.

"Let's go."

Campos had been a Green Card holder for twenty years, but they were going to deport her.

They'd parked their car near the entrance, and they got out of the car as Campos walked past them. They had their POLICE—ICE jackets on, and they followed Campos as she walked towards her car in the far corner.

When Vic was in place, Carl quickly looped around in front of Campos and held up his badge at her.

"Isabela Campos, you are being detained for defrauding the United States."

"Fuck that, I've never defrauded anyone."

Carl couldn't resist contradicting her, at the cost of tipping their hand.

"Oh no? Green Card holders can't vote."

"Jesus," she replied, but not as confidently. She looked at Carl contemptuously but said no more.

Carl was busy cuffing her when he heard Vic shout out.

"Keep back!"

Carl looked up and saw that a man in his thirties, wearing a suit, had walked up to them and stopped a couple of yards away. Carl recognized him as Ernesto Sandoval. He was another one that Carl and the others joked about deporting. Maybe that'd fly now that Nemeth had been elected. But for now Sandoval was challenging them.

"You know that Judge Grovan ruled that ICE can't make arrests on the grounds of the court?"

"We're not *on* the grounds," Carl replied.

Carl noticed another young guy standing behind a car about twenty yards away, recording the events on his phone. It looked like the brazers had been expecting this move from ICE. Still, they weren't going to back off now.

"I guess we'll see about that," said Ernesto before turning to Isabel and adding, "We won't let them get away with this."

But Carl and Vic were already taking her away in cuffs towards their car.

40

Office Building, P Street, Sacramento

Finished for the day, Carl got the elevator down to his parking level. As he approached his car, he pressed the unlock button on his key fob. Two men got out of the car next to his and walked towards him. Carl was considering going for his weapon when one of the men had pulled out an ID and held it open towards him.

"Sacramento Police. Carl Mack, you are under arrest for contempt of court."

"What the fuck?"

Carl couldn't believe that the city police were arresting a federal officer.

"There's a bench warrant for your arrest."

The cop moved to take one of Carl's wrists.

"OK, I get it."

Carl turned round slowly and put his wrists together behind his back. As the officer cuffed him, he saw another plainclothes officer, her ID around her neck and hand by her pistol holster.

The first officer cuffed him, took him by the shoulder and guided him back to the elevator. Then up to the ground floor and to a badged truck parked outside. He was put in the back. One of the officers got in beside him, the other two in front.

They headed north. Up ahead, Carl caught sight of the Hall of Justice, which held the main jail for Sacramento County's superior court. The building had sixteen stories and the jail held more than two thousand inmates. Carl took a deep breath. He'd like to give the cops grief, but in the current situation, he'd get more mileage by trying to treat them as peers.

"Look, is this about picking up illegals outside the courthouse?"

None of the three paid any attention.

Carl turned to the one next to him.

"We were advised that we were outside the reach of the order."

"You guys like to cut it fine. You'd better hope that whoever came up with that advice will come through for you."

At least they'd confirmed what it was about. And his ICE colleagues should've realized what'd happened. The cops had likely left their truck outside because they thought that ICE would've been tipped off by building security if they'd parked it inside. And they would've been right. At least, that's what the head of security had told them. And the people in the lobby should've gotten straight on the phone to the fifth floor when they'd seen Carl taken out in cuffs.

By now they were close to the Hall of Justice. It was made of half a dozen yellow concrete blocks, with the same height and facades, put together with no apparent consideration for symmetry or harmony. It didn't have visible windows, just a black slit across each floor, as if to snipe at passersby.

They approached the entrance to the main jail on I Street.

"Shit," muttered Carl as he saw a small crowd of about thirty people on the sidewalk outside the moving doors. Carl doubted that the leak had come from the police. Despite everything, they hadn't seemed keen on taking him in. So the news must've come from their own building, or else from someone seeing him come out in custody. Didn't they have better things to do?

The truck pulled up. Two of the cops hustled Carl out of the truck, then guided him through the crowd as the driver pulled out. Carl couldn't believe he was doing the perp walk through a crowd of wetbacks. He heard them shout slogans about abolishing ICE, and a bunch of things in Spanish that he couldn't understand.

It seemed a long way to the door. Then they led him to the booking desk where they took his details.

"Who do you want notified?" the desk sergeant asked him.

"Vic Di Grigoli, ICE office on P Street."

The desk sergeant dialled a number, then nodded towards a wall phone. Carl picked up the handset and waited for Vic to answer.

"Hey, it's Carl. You know what happened, right? I'm in the main jail, about to be booked."

"Bullshit, right? The lawyer says he's working on an appeal, but you'll be in a cell for a few hours at least."

"Jesus." He paused. "OK, call the wife, will you?"

"Sure."

"And make an effort, alright? Don't leave her thinking I'm going to be dead meat in here."

They laughed and Carl hung up.

Carl turned back to the police and looked the ranking officer in the eye, raising his eyebrows to ask whether they really needed to cuff him again. He acquiesced and just waved Carl towards the booking desk.

Carl stepped over to the desk sergeant.

"I work the street. I know you're not allowed to keep our detainees anymore, but still, I'm known to a lot of the scum you've got locked up here. To avoid trouble for all of us, the best would be for me to be in protective custody."

The sergeant nodded like he'd already thought through all of that. He picked up the phone and a few minutes later a couple of sheriff's officers came out into the booking area and took Carl up to a cell.

41

Lorenzo Patiño Hall of Justice, Sacramento

CARL WAS woken up by a guard banging on the door. It took him a few seconds to figure out why he was in a concrete cell. He was on the upper bunk, and he remembered they'd put him in a cell by himself.

Carl jumped down and stood in the middle of the floor, where the guard could see him.

"You're free to go."

So the ICE lawyers had done their job and kicked the charge down the road. Carl hadn't doubted the outcome. In any case, he'd need to make someone pay for taking him on.

42

Van Nuys, Los Angeles

Hugo was driving Joseph and Baptiste, a Haitian EMT, to Joseph's favorite Kenyan restaurant in Van Nuys. Although it took nearly an hour from Inglewood, Hugo didn't mind, driving past the Getty Museum, up into the hills, past Bel Air and the MountainGate Country Club before coming back down and into Sherman Oaks.

From the street, the restaurant looked like a normal house, but there were parked cars clustered around it, including on the lawn in front. Joseph had told them that this was the day of the week when they had nyama choma.

Hugo found a gap fifty yards up the street and they walked back. The oldest part of the restaurant was a simple prewar bungalow with a tile roof. About twenty years later, an extension had been built to one side, and further back from the street, with a porch along the front, but with the same red tiles.

Joseph led them around the back of the building. While the front yard had a plain tidy lawn, the backyard was randomly scattered with the components of an ad hoc restaurant. To one side was an off-white tarp over a metal frame, giving shade to an old sofa and a couple of plastic tables with a miscellany of chairs. In the open air were a couple of hefty wooden picnic tables that looked like they could've been lifted from a public park. Taarab music filtered through a small window in the back wall of the house.

All the backyard tables were full of people talking, laughing, and digging plastic forks into polystyrene containers of different kinds of meat stew, cornmeal cake and greens.

A man wearing an apron over a T-shirt and polyester shorts lifted the lid of one of the coolers sitting on the worn grass. He pulled out a couple of large bottles of Tusker beer and took them over to one of the wooden tables. He caught the bottle opener dangling by a string from his apron, lifted the caps, and gave the bottles to two of the clients.

Joseph looked around, disappeared under the shade of a tree, and came back carrying a square plastic table, which he set up opposite the tarp. The three of them trawled the backyard and found a couple of plastic stools and an old wooden chair missing its back. Joseph, in his element, whistled at the aproned waiter and held up two fingers to get them beers. When they came, Joseph asked for a glass as well. He poured some of his bottle into the glass for Hugo and they toasted. Hugo drank down the freezing liquid with relish, realizing it'd been months since he'd had a drink. They lingered a few seconds on the bitter aftertaste. Then their senses were drawn to the driveway along the side of the house, where fragrant smoke was coming from a charcoal-burning barbecue. Hugo and Baptiste looked at Joseph and nodded their appreciation.

When the food came they ate in silence for a few minutes.

"It's good. You could serve this goat in Santander, no problem," said Hugo.

Joseph nodded to acknowledge the compliment.

"This," said Hugo, pointing carefully at the ugali, "for us it's a bit plain. But it's like what we have in tamales. I imagined I was eating a tamal that'd been left in pieces."

The other two laughed.

"Maybe next time we can go to this place in Canoga Park that serves taso kabrit," suggested Baptiste.

"Deal," said Joseph.

Those two kept drinking and their conversation left Hugo's sobriety behind. They touched on why each of them had left their own countries. Joseph had gone strong for a Kenyan politician who hadn't made it. Baptiste's home in Haiti had been wiped out by an earthquake, and he'd gotten a construction job in Brazil. But that work had dried up, so he'd had to leave, and he still had family to support in Haiti.

But this wasn't the evening for going over painful histories. The two of them talked about music, nightspots in LA, side hustles.

"Who knows how long the ambulance scam is going to last?" said Joseph.

"What do you mean, scam?" interjected Hugo.

Joseph looked at Hugo patiently. "How do you think our users get such a tailored service?"

Hugo shrugged.

"You know the attorney general that's always on social media talking tough about ICE?"

"Yeah?"

"Till a few months ago, he was on the County Board of Supervisors."

Hugo didn't get it.

"They run the fire department, and it's the fire department that contracts ambulances."

Hugo nodded slowly and leaned back in his seat. He thought back to the logo on the car that Devon had gotten into, when they'd met in Glendale.

Gradually the other diners left till the only people left at the main tables were a couple who were splayed out on the battered sofa like they had no plans to leave. The three ambulance men were still off to one side in the darkness.

Joseph was explaining to Baptiste how he'd gotten an informal loan to buy a secondhand car and that it was being driven as a rideshare by the cousin of one of the other ambulance drivers. Hugo heard raised voices coming from the side of the house. Joseph and Baptiste were too immersed in conversation, or had had too many beers, to pay attention.

Four men pushed past the waiter and into the backyard. They were silhouetted against the floodlight on the low eaves of the house, but Hugo saw at least one baseball bat.

"This is a fucking residential area. We're fed up with this jungle music," shouted one of the intruders at the darkness at the far end of the backyard.

The waiter caught up with them and put his hand on the shoulder of one of them.

"Don't fucking touch me, jiggy."

Now all three of the ambulance men had realized what was going on.

Two of the other thugs grabbed the waiter's arms from behind and the first one stepped up close and put an uppercut into his midriff.

Hugo, infuriated, stood up to intervene, but Joseph took hold of his lower arm.

The two intruders let the waiter go and he slumped to the ground.

"Do you want to get us all arrested?" whispered Joseph. Hugo tensed but kept still.

The intruders' leader stepped over to the barbecue.

"We don't want your stinking bush meat here."

He tipped the barbecue over onto the ground, scattering chunks of red-hot charcoal.

"Get yourself a roach coach and sell it to your own people in South LA."

The couple on the sofa woke up and clung to each other, looking around for a way out and not sure whether to run for it.

The charcoal set fire to small clumps of grass and melted a polystyrene container, sending up a thin plume of chemical fumes.

A couple of the intruders walked over to the couple, eyeing up the girl.

Hugo cursed them under his breath but didn't try to take Joseph's hand off his arm.

The two intruders stood over the couple on the sofa.

"Stand up."

The man did as he was told. As he reached full height, he was briefly eye to eye with the man standing in front of him, who then pushed him back down.

With his free hand, Joseph indicated to Baptiste to stand up. He did so and went around to stand on the other side of Hugo.

"Stand up, both of you, or we'll pick you up," insisted the intruder to the couple.

They both stood up, with the woman leaning back as far as she could to avoid pressing against the intruder in front of her, who grinned lasciviously.

Baptiste could see that Hugo wanted to take the intruders on, so he whispered to him.

"If I get deported, there'll be three generations of us on the street in Port-au-Prince."

Hugo gave in. He dropped his head and turned towards the front of the house. Joseph and Baptiste followed him. They stepped onto the floodlit part of the lawn and were noticed by the intruders.

"Yeah, get out of here, coons," one of the intruders shouted after them.

The woman was forced to drop back onto the sofa as the intruder leaned into her.

The intruders all laughed, then called for her to stand up again.

His jaw locked, Hugo strode over the front lawn and up the empty street to his car, with the other two trailing behind. Hugo got in, started the engine, and sped off in silence while Baptiste was still closing the rear passenger door.

Hugo absently followed the road south, out of the San Fernando valley, back the way they'd come. The other two kept quiet while Hugo thought about how the intruders had humiliated the girl in the restaurant. Joseph and Baptiste had been right: if he'd gotten involved, then all three of them could've been deported. And maybe it would've ended up worse for the girl as well. But how could it have been right to hide in the darkness, just looking on?

By now they were on the 405, and Hugo had his foot down. After passing the country club, they crested a hill and the car floated.

"Hugo, isn't the speed limit sixty-five here?" asked Joseph nervously.

Irritated at the intrusion, for a split second Hugo felt like flooring his foot even more, but he eased off. He didn't reply to Joseph and went back to his musings.

As an undocumented person, it was wrong to do the right thing. At least he was helping people with his ambulance job. He looked down on the lights of Los Angeles as he passed the Getty Museum. He'd better avoid situations where he might get himself involved. That was something like a plan, at least for now. He eased more off the gas and started to visualize the route home.

43

Downtown Los Angeles

DEVON HEADED north on Maple Avenue for an ambulance operators' meeting downtown.

Parked under the Santa Monica Freeway, a couple of ICE officers were expecting him. When Carl had been released from jail on the contempt charge, ICE had doubled down by sending him to Los Angeles for this high-profile mission. With him was another ICE officer, Josh Minassian.

As Devon emerged from the shadow of the freeway, Josh pulled out and accelerated to get behind his Ford. Then they turned on their lights and siren, and Devon pulled over.

When Carl stepped out of the car, he heard Devon's engine still running.

"Turn off your engine and drop the keys out the window!"

Devon complied. By now Carl had drawn his pistol and was walking slowly up the side of the Crown Vic.

Devon restarted the engine with spare keys, floored the gas, and sped off.

Carl raised his pistol and fired at the Ford as it left him in its trail of exhaust fumes. One round hit the rear window, but it didn't shatter. Another hit a tire but left it intact.

Josh pulled up alongside in the ICE truck, and Carl jumped in.

"He's got himself run-flat tires."

"Whatever. He's not getting far," replied Josh as he tried to narrow the gap to the Ford.

A few blocks further on, they made a hard left, then a right, passing empty lots and homeless tents. As they kept north, more of the units were occupied, mostly selling fabric and clothing accessories. Halfway down a block, Devon suddenly pulled over in front of a nondescript single-story storefront. Josh braked to a halt twenty meters back on the other side of the street, then reversed back at an angle, back wheels on the sidewalk, scattering pedestrians, to point their truck at Devon's car.

Both ICE officers opened their doors and crouched behind them, training their pistols on the Ford's driver-side door. The door opened and Devon's head showed for a split second. Carl squeezed off a round, but as he did so, the windshield was punctured by an incoming shot.

"Shit!"

Carl and Josh tried to locate the source of the fire.

A woman pedestrian screamed as the street emptied and shopkeepers scurried to close their shutters. Only a homeless man, curled up on a cardboard box in a doorway, stayed put, apparently oblivious to the firefight picking up around him.

Devon ran, crouching, around the car and into the storefront door before the ICE officers focused back on him.

"Someone's on the roof with a rifle," said Josh. He let off a couple of shots, blowing geometric chunks of 1930s stucco off the cornice.

One of the storefront windows blew out as a fire extinguisher crashed out through it. A pistol shot from one of the ground-floor windows smacked into the driver's-side door. The officers flinched, looked at each other to make sure they were OK, then back to the storefront. Venetian blinds flopped back over the window and stopped them from seeing inside.

"We're going to need the backup team."

"Right."

Josh got on the radio while Carl tried to cover both the roof and the window.

"They're a block away."

Meanwhile, the AFL social media channel had started livestreaming the shoot-out. Hugo got an audible alert on his phone when he was driving the ambulance east on Whittier Boulevard towards Pico Rivera.

Carl saw something move behind the window and fired. The bullet thudded into something behind the blinds.

"Some kind of shield."

At the next red light, Hugo picked up his phone and opened the AFL video. It was a street-level view of the gunfight outside the storefront. Along the bottom ran a chyron: "Armed ICE officers try to capture Devon Reid, leader of the American Foreign Legion."

"*Hijueputa*," muttered Hugo.

Above the video, in the social media feed, he saw that a couple of thousand people were tuned in. In the passenger seat, Joseph coughed intentionally, and Hugo realized the light had changed. He drove on, but without blanking the phone screen.

Another ICE truck sped towards Carl and Josh from the far end of the street. Just as it seemed bound to crash into Devon's Ford, it braked sharply and the bumper kissed the side panel. Another ICE officer jumped out of the passenger side with body armor and carrying a carbine. He crouched down beside Devon's Ford and edged his way forward as bullets from the storefront shattered the car windows. A fourth ICE agent, also in body armor and carrying a carbine, stepped out and down behind the open driver's-side door, aimed at the roof, and blasted away more of the concrete cornice.

His partner lifted his head and shoulders above the hood of the Ford and fired a burst through the window. Sounds of metallic blowout echoed out onto the street.

There was a second's silence, enough for the ICE agents to think that maybe the job was done. But then Devon and the other AFL fighter returned fire simultaneously from the window and the roof, shredding the panels of the Ford and leaving dents in the reinforced panels of the ICE trucks.

The two ICE agents behind Devon's Ford looked at each other, counted down from three, then unleashed more automatic fire at the building.

Carl and Josh put on their body armor. The four ICE agents were wired for radio.

"We can tie them down, but we're not going to breach this way."

"Roger."

"Another unit's getting in place round back."

"Copy."

From his computer in Sacramento, Loy was part of the radio conversation with the attacking officers. He got an alert on his screen, clicked through, and opened up the AFL livestream.

"Shit, this is going out live."

"Jesus, tell the wife not to miss it," shouted back one of the officers over the sound of gunfire.

Loy had been talking to himself as much as officers in the field. They had Devon pinned down, but the video stream stopped them defining the narrative.

LAPD had closed off the street at both ends of the block, and small crowds were gathering. Some just wanted to see the action, others chanted slogans: "Abolish ICE," "Deport ICE from California," "*Chinga la migra.*" Some of them kept one eye on the livestream on their phones.

There was a service alley behind the unit where Devon was holed up. A third ICE truck slalomed between the dumpsters, skidding through the garbage, and came to a halt by the rear entrance. The alley was too narrow to turn the truck to face the back door, so both officers scrambled out of the passenger-side door and took cover behind the vehicle, one behind the hood and the other behind the rear wheel.

"Stay back," shouted an AFL voice from inside the building.

Reflexively, each ICE officer strafed the back door with a burst of automatic fire. Some of the rounds hit the checker plate of the door but only left dents. The AFL returned fire from a couple of holes in the wall. One was a round air vent, another where a brick in the wall was missing.

In Sacramento, Loy saw the camera switch from the street to the back alley. He realized that ICE had fired the first shots again. This footage was going to get a lot of views. But as long as they got Devon, the rest would be details.

At the front of the building, one of the ICE officers continued firing towards the AFL gunman on the roof behind the cornice.

"Changing clip."

"Roger."

No one on the roof took the chance to return fire.

Out the back, in the alley, the two AFL shooters concentrated their automatic fire on the cab of the ICE truck, which buckled, then shattered in a shower of glass and shrapnel. Now there were knots of people at each end of the alley as well, and they cheered.

In front, the four ICE officers switched from targeting the roof to the window, shredding what was left of the blinds. Now some of the bullets were getting through the shield behind the window and ricocheting inside the unit.

They paused for ten seconds.

"Seems like they're done."

"Roger. We're going to breach."

Josh went back into the truck and came out again with a door-breaching ram. He hefted it slowly over to the door as Carl walked alongside him with his pistol aimed at the window. The other two agents covered the building with their carbines.

In the back alley, the other ICE agents were no longer under fire either, but they kept their weapons trained on the exit.

When Josh got to the front door, he looked around at the others and they nodded at each other. He swung the ram and the front door gave way.

Carl went through the front door as Josh dropped the ram, drew his pistol, and followed him.

Their eyes adjusted to a dark office space. The only window was beside the door, and had been blocked off by three full filing cabinets, one laid horizontally on top of the other two. These had been Devon's shield. The metal of the cabinets had been ripped apart by ICE gunfire. The paper contents had been blown out and now lay like a layer of confetti on the grubby linoleum. Around the window was a scattering of automatic pistol cartridges.

Further back from the window there was a man-sized hole in the floor. Carl jerked his head towards it, and both ICE agents approached, guns drawn. A plank of wood lay across the hole with a rope tied around it and going down into blackness.

Carl stayed by the hole while Josh cleared the space. There were some bits and pieces discarded on the floor and shelves, as if the movers had been in recently, but the side rooms were otherwise empty. By the back wall, on either side of the door, the floor was strewn with automatic rifle cartridges.

Josh walked back towards Carl, shrugging his shoulders to indicate that the place was clear.

Carl sighed, realizing that the AFL shooters had gone. He indicated to Josh to watch the hole while he stepped away and called Loy on the radio.

"Sir, we've breached the building."

"I can see that. You're going out live, remember? Why aren't you taking that jump-up Reid into custody?"

"Sir, they escaped through some kind of tunnel."

Carl heard Loy swear under his breath.

"Wrap it up, but make sure you find the cameras they were recording you with. One out back opposite the door, one out front and to the north."

"Yes, sir."

On his computer screen, Loy was looking at a selfie taken by Devon and posted on the AFL's live feed.

The crowds at the street corners had seen it as well and turned up the volume, mocking ICE by singing the hook of "Illegal en Estyle" by María del Pilar.

Devon had taken the selfie in one of the abandoned tunnels that had been dug under downtown LA in Prohibition days. He was leaning back against a mural that showed customers of a speakeasy like the one that, in the 1920s, had operated in that same tunnel. Devon grinned at the ICE agents who'd been trying to kill him as he chilled, flouting the law with his century-old companions.

Joseph finally voiced his disapproval.

"I hope we don't get pulled over," he said, eyeing Hugo's phone.

"You're right," Hugo replied, and he tossed the phone out into the next lane.

"Hey, that's not what I meant!"

In the side mirror, Hugo watched the phone shatter under the wheel of an oncoming car.

"ICE agents are shooting up someplace downtown where Devon's holed up and he's shooting back. His phone contacts are going to be on their shit list."

"I see." Joseph, taken aback, absently traced the outline of his own phone through the cloth of his trouser pocket while looking at Hugo's face for suggestions on what to do.

"I knew Devon when he was in the Army. I guess I'd be the one ICE would be most interested in."

"Indeed. Thank you," said Joseph, relieved.

The ICE officers found all but one of the phones that'd been used to livestream the event. From the camera angles, the remaining one had been used by the homeless guy, who'd left his spot sometime towards the end of the shoot-out. In frustration, Carl kicked his cardboard sleeping mat out into the street.

He took a deep breath before speaking over the radio to Loy in Sacramento.

"Sir, have you got the phone GPS on Reid's contacts?"

"They all went dead during the shoot-out. I've just set an analyst to make a report on the contacts of the contacts."

44

Plaza de Cultura y Artes, Los Angeles

Hugo walked across the paved square, looping around the bandstand and back again to stand under a row of trees on one side. He watched the miscellany of families, tourists, and homeless people. This was the place and time he'd arranged with Devon, for when they couldn't use their phones. To the east, across more open space and a couple of streets, he could see Union Station, where he'd arrived just a few weeks ago.

Hugo set off strolling again and paused in front of a plaque commemorating the mass deportations of Latinos in the 1930s. He'd read part of it when he heard a voice at his shoulder.

"Hugo."

He turned around and saw a young man in a plaid shirt and chinos. He looked so bland that, for a second, Hugo couldn't believe that this was the go-between. Seeing his confusion, the man smiled and extended his hand.

"I'm Luke. Devon sent me."

He paused and the two set off walking around the plaza together.

"His face is famous now," Luke continued. "The downtown shootout made ICE look ridiculous. They know they're losing the fear factor, and they'll try to get it back by tactics that are even more hostile than before. But as long as we're one step ahead, then we can keep turning people against them."

"So, we want them to escalate?"

"We want things to change, and if they're reacting to us, we have more control."

"Tell me more."

45

McClure, California

McClure was a farm town in the San Joaquin Valley. Most employment was in the fields and warehouses: sowing, growing, harvesting and packing grapes, cotton, oranges and other crops. More than ten percent of the population were undocumented.

McClure also had a private prison that was contracted by ICE to hold its detainees. The prison buildings were two single-story off-white concrete blocks, of different sizes but with a shared wall. Two concentric razor wire fences, ten feet apart, surrounded the prison. On the north and south it was bordered by new single-story terracotta-colored houses. To the west there was an elementary school, and State Route 99 was to the east, running north–south through California's Central Valley.

An ICE bus entered McClure from the south on SR 99, bringing detainees to the prison from Los Angeles and further afield. From the northbound lane, the driver looked across at the prison gate as he drove past. A few hundred yards further on, he left the highway, crossed over the bridge, and came down the access road to join the southbound lane. He could see the tall floodlight poles a couple of hundred yards from the entrance. But his way was blocked by workers in overalls and sun hats who'd blocked off the road and were getting their jackhammers ready to dig it up.

A diversion sign told the driver to turn right, to the north of the prison. Before doing so, he shouted out to the laborers, asking them how long they'd be digging up the road for. They shrugged their shoulders expansively. The driver cursed immigrants' language skills, then set off to loop around and get to the entrance from the south. At the next corner he turned south and groaned as he saw the road was jammed with cars.

The word in the parents' social media group was that they should pick up their kids early because the school's water supply had been cut. As more cars rolled up, a couple of parents turned away from the intercom on the front gate. One of them started texting on their phone while the other started shouting out to the rest of them, some still in their cars.

"The school secretary says there's nothing wrong. The kids are going to come out like usual. They're going to post in our group."

The waiting parents started grumbling. Some scrolled back through the chat to see who'd started the rumor.

The ICE bus had to stop because some parents' cars were U-turning, some were behind the bus, still trying to get to the school, and others were coming towards the gates from the far side.

The bus driver was wondering whether he'd get the bus back to the depot in LA before rush hour, when he heard a flurry of shots.

"What the fuck?" said one of the officers alongside him in the front of the bus. They all unholstered their pistols.

The bus swayed and settled as its tires were blown out.

The parents scrambled for cover. Most ducked down inside their cars, but some tried to escape by driving through the mess of traffic, only making it worse.

The three ICE officers looked around but couldn't make out any shooters. The pickup truck behind them pulled up alongside the driver's side of the bus. Raul was sitting in the bed of the pickup. A couple of days before, the unknown caller had told him to drive to Bakersfield and check in to a chain motel. There he'd met the rest of the AFL team and they'd gone through the operation.

Raul stood, lifted an MP5 submachine gun, and put a single shot through the driver's-side window of the bus. The round went in front of the officers and punched a bigger hole as it left through the passenger-side window. By the time the officers had aimed their pistols at the pickup, another man had joined Raul and was pointing another MP5 at the officers.

A couple of the parents were capturing video on their phones, squatting between cars and trying to get closer to the bus.

Two more AFL members, a man and a woman, climbed onto the hood of the bus. The woman took a pickax to the corner of the windshield and pulled out the laminated glass. The man aimed his MP5 at the ICE officers and shouted, "Lower your weapons!"

"Do it, guys," the ranking officer told the others.

"Hold your weapons by the finger and thumb and toss them out onto the hood," the AFL man continued.

One of the officers looked around, but with four MP5s pointing at him, he did what he was told. The others followed.

Someone in the crowd shouted "*¡Chinga la migra!*"

The pickax woman tossed a pair of handcuffs to the driver.

"Open the passenger door, then cuff yourself to the wheel."

As the door of the bus opened, Raul and another AFL member ran up the steps of the bus.

"You want out of here?" Raul asked the nearest detainee.

He nodded, and the other AFL man cut him loose from his plastic cuffs. The detainee ran out onto the street, to cheers from the parents who'd remained.

Raul and the other AFL man went down the aisle of the bus asking each detainee whether they wanted to run or to go to prison. A few, in their sixties or older, wanted to stay, and they left them cuffed. They told the rest of the detainees, including Jaime Gutierrez from Sacramento, to go south past the school, then turn right into the residential streets of the town.

The ICE officers in the cab had cuffed themselves to the wheel and did their best to pretend they were sitting comfortably. The crowd of parents gradually gained confidence. They edged closer and started verbally abusing the ICE officers, recording the scene on their cell phones.

The sound of gunshots reached the crowd from the direction that the bus had come from. A few hundred yards back up the road, a couple of vehicles had blocked a truck with correctional officers from the prison, who were trying to come to the aid of the ICE officers.

Inside the bus, the last of the detainees was freed. The AFL men followed him out onto the street. A couple of men in the pickup next to the bus fired towards the roadblock, covering AFL men there as they pulled back. Once they'd made it safely to the main group, all the AFL men piled into the truck. It drove off onto the dirt off the side of the road to get around the parents' vehicles, carried on past the end of the school compound, and disappeared into the residential streets.

Some of the parents took the chance to spit on the immobilized ICE officers before their colleagues from the prison arrived.

46

Maywood, Los Angeles

Two teams, each of two ICE officers, sat in their cars in the parking lot opposite the Methodist church in Maywood. From there they could see through the open front door of the church and as far as the round stained glass window with the simple abstract pattern that decorated the far wall. Around the corner, another couple of officers were monitoring the side entrance. For months they'd wanted to go into the church and detain Cheddi Maharaj, but they kept getting told that it'd cause more trouble than it'd be worth. So Maharaj was free to run his organization from inside the church and laugh at them through the door. Maybe now, with Nemeth getting elected, churches wouldn't be off-limits anymore.

In the meantime, they reckoned that Maharaj was going to try to sneak out to his wife's bedside, now that she was critically ill with kidney disease. Coming out with the crowd after a service was one of his better options. But they were ready for him.

Just then the minister blessed the congregation and they sat down. Then upbeat organ music started to belt out. The congregation stood up again and started to file towards the main door. The ICE officers in the parking lot could see the congregation head towards them and spill out onto the street.

They used to have officers undercover in the church, but they got made by the real worshippers, who made a big deal out of it. Tonight, a plainclothes officer went and stood by the door and gave them a rundown over the radio on what was going on.

"Maharaj is getting together with his usual gang."

That meant people from his own organization, Methodist deacons and elders, and clergy from other churches, even a rabbi.

"They're heading towards the door."

"Ready all units," said Josh over the radio.

A minivan veered suddenly out of its lane and pulled up smartly outside the church door.

"He's going to make a break for it. Close up."

Maharaj, in his early forties with a goatee and graying ponytail, got to the church door with two clergymen on each side, each linking arms with his neighbor.

The congregation bunched up around Maharaj's group, ahead of them and behind them.

A sliding door opened on the passenger side of the minivan. The congregation surged forward, sweeping along Maharaj and the clergymen. But Josh and another ICE officer stepped around from the street side of the vehicle and blocked Maharaj's entry.

The congregation started to sing "We Will Overcome." The first members reached the curb and struggled with the ICE agents, trying to shove them out of the way.

Twenty yards away an agent called over his bullhorn.

"We are federal agents arresting Cheddi Maharaj. Disperse now or face the consequences."

Some of the congregation booed while others continued singing the protest anthem.

The agents on the curb stopped grappling with the congregation. By now another couple of agents had stood in front of the minivan. The four of them unhooked gas masks from their belts and started putting them on.

"They're going to gas us," one of the congregation cried out.

The singing wavered and the group around Maharaj loosened around the edges. The four clergymen flanking Maharaj held firm but flinched as a tear gas canister was lobbed into the congregation, hitting one of them on the head.

Now the congregation scattered in panic, some trying to head back into the church, others into the street, but in random directions, unable to see out of their burning, streaming eyes. ICE officers in gas masks shouldered their way between the writhing worshippers, heading for Maharaj. They ripped him from the arms of his middle-aged defenders.

The canister was kicked away into the street, and from there into the parking lot opposite. The minister vomited onto the sidewalk and, as the tear gas cleared, stumbled his way into the church, fishing for his mobile phone in his pocket.

By then, Maharaj was already a couple of streets away in the back seat of an ICE truck, hands cuffed behind his back, Josh on one side of him, another officer on the other.

Elated by the successful struggle, Josh softly slapped Maharaj on the cheek a couple of times.

They were too full of themselves to notice that they were being boxed in. A delivery van ahead of them stopped suddenly and they were all jolted forward as their driver piled on his brakes. In the back, without seat belts, the two officers thudded into the seats in front. Maharaj, helpless with his hands cuffed behind him, flew forward and cried out in pain and surprise as he got wedged between the driver and front passenger seats.

Instinctively the officers realized that this wasn't an accident. As they reached for their pistols, they were rammed from behind, hurling them forward again. Their eyes refocused on a man jumping up onto the hood of a truck. He lifted an MP5, aimed it at the front passenger and shouted.

"Drop your weapons!"

The three officers who weren't driving held on to their pistols but didn't raise them, taking a couple of seconds to think.

A pistol round exploded through the street-side rear passenger window, ricocheted off the column behind the driver and thudded into his seat. The officers tried to blink the glass dust out of their eyes as another AFL gunman shouted at them to drop their weapons.

Maharaj was pulling himself out from between the front seats of the truck and blocking the view of the AFL man. Josh and the other officer looked at each other, deciding whether to open fire, when another shot burst down through the roof and slammed into the floor between Josh's feet.

As the officers reflexively cursed and looked up, they heard the pull-start of a power saw. A second later, the diamond-tipped edge of the circular blade cut down through the roof of the truck, over their heads.

One of the officers fired his pistol up through the roof but was shot in the chest by an AFL man standing by the side of the truck. The officer was knocked back into his seat as his body armor blocked the bullet.

"We said drop your fucking weapons!" shouted the AFL man outside the car.

The officer who'd taken the bullet was still dazed. Josh looked the AFL man in the eye and gradually lowered his pistol before letting it drop onto the car floor and raising his hands behind his back.

The saw blade surged forwards, cutting the roof open parallel to the windows.

The ICE officer in the front passenger seat dropped his weapon as well, looking down the barrel of the MP5 of the AFL man on the hood.

The circular saw blade reached the front of the roof and disappeared. A second later it cut back down at a right angle and sliced through the roof parallel to the top of the windshield.

Another AFL gunman had appeared by the other side of the truck and shouted at the driver to keep his hands on the wheel.

The driver did as he was told but flinched as metal shavings sprayed his face as the saw passed above his head.

The circular saw lifted out of the truck again, and the AFL men outside looked at each other and nodded.

The AFL man outside the passenger window dropped to the ground and a pickup pulled up alongside. A gunman in the truck bed aimed his weapon at the ICE officer nearest to him in the rear passenger seat while the man with the saw jumped down into the bed from the roof of the ICE truck. He carried on cutting along the third side of the passenger compartment. Inside, the ICE agents looked around but couldn't see a way past the AFL men with their guns trained on them.

The circular saw reached the back of the passenger compartment. Another pickup drove up onto the sidewalk on the passenger side of the ICE truck, with two men in the bed. On the driver's side, the man dropped his saw and was handed a crowbar by someone inside the car. On the opposite side, one of the two men also had a crowbar, and the two of them started peeling back the roof of the ICE truck as if it were a can of sardines. The man in the pickup bed was Hugo, with an MP5. As the man off the roof worked his way back, prying up the roof of the ICE truck as he went, he passed Hugo, who kept his gun trained on Josh, who was the nearest to him in the rear passenger seat.

On the driver's side, the AFL man dropped his crowbar, tossed a blanket over the jagged edge of the roof, and beckoned Maharaj out. Maharaj looked doubtfully at the ICE agent to his right. The agent glanced down at his pistol on the floor of the truck, then raised his eyebrows at Maharaj, challenging him to make a break for it. The AFL man offering his hand to Maharaj encouraged him.

"Leave these racist fuckers behind."

Maharaj still didn't move. The ICE officer realized that the AFL men were feeling the pressure of the standoff. He looked across at Josh on the other side of Maharaj. They saw agreement in each other's eyes.

Maharaj stood up and raised a hand through where the roof of the truck had been towards the AFL man. On the other side, Hugo saw Josh slowly reaching down for his pistol.

"Don't move!"

Josh heard apprehension in Hugo's voice and kept his hand edging down towards his pistol on the floor.

"Cheddi, look out!" said Josh, feigning concern for Maharaj. His hand kept inching down.

The AFL man took Maharaj's weight as he lifted him towards the pickup. The two vehicles swayed under their shifting loads. Both ICE officers on the rear passenger seats reached for their pistols and aimed for the AFL gunmen on their respective sides. On the driver's side, the AFL man put a burst from his MP5 through the window and into the officer's chest before he could get a shot off. The officer dropped his pistol and writhed with pain from his broken ribs.

Hugo saw Josh on his side, reaching for his pistol. Hugo knew what was coming and what he should do. He aimed his MP5 at Josh's chest, where he saw his gold badge with the crest and eagle of the United States. Hugo's mind flashed back to the American flag at Fort Benning, the US Army uniform badges in Yemen, the seal of the House of Representatives when he testified...

Josh's neck exploded into a spray of blood and gristle, shredded by a pistol round from the AFL man next to Hugo in the pickup bed.

Hugo had let the situation get away from him till it needed critical corrective action.

They hauled Maharaj up and over and down into the bed of the opposite pickup. All the other AFL men jumped into one or other of the pickups, which sped off, leaving their other two vehicles blocking in the ICE truck. The other two men with MP5s were in the back of the second vehicle, their guns trained on the ICE officer in the front passenger seat. But, having seen what'd happened to his colleagues, and armed only with a pistol, he didn't much like his chances taking on the AFL men and their submachine guns.

By now they could hear sirens of LAPD cars.

A couple of blocks to the north, the first AFL pickup braked suddenly and stopped alongside an anonymous sedan parked on the side of the street. The second pickup sped past Maharaj as he got out and stepped shakily over to the back door of the sedan, which took off as soon as he got in.

The second pickup made a sharp turn and dived into the underground parking garage, whose entrance barrier had been conveniently left up. The AFL men took everything into the back of a panel van, whose driver was waiting in a cab and which headed back out onto the street.

After handing over Maharaj, the first pickup kept going north till it got to a light industrial area just south of the LA River. A garage door opened and the driver drove straight in. Hugo and the other AFL men were thrown forward as the truck jolted to a halt just short of the far wall. They quickly checked the vehicle for gear and shell casings, then scattered out of the garage and into a couple of saloons waiting on the apron outside.

Hugo was in the back of one of the sedans next to Bruno. As they drove past the commercial units, the AFL men were on the lookout for police, but after a few minutes headed northwest towards downtown, with no sign of trouble, they relaxed a bit, except for Hugo. Bruno realized that Hugo was beating himself up over what'd happened with the ICE officers. Well, so he should. Hugo had pussied out and David had had to cover for him, killing a federal agent. That was something he had over his head and it wasn't going to go away. That officer had seen that Hugo was bluffing. If he wasn't ready to do what was necessary, then he shouldn't have joined the mission.

"I'm sorry, man," said Hugo, interrupting Bruno's chain of thought.

Hugo must've realized what was going through his mind. Hell, it was done now and Hugo realized he'd messed up. Bruno replied with the kind of shit talk that was meant to tell Hugo that he was still part of the team.

"Hey, what happened to you, man? You froze like that ICE fucker was your own reflection."

Hugo didn't react, so Bruno tried a different tack.

"One time in Baghdad, on Route Irish, I lit up the car behind, and it crashed and burned. Turned out it was some stupid airport guy trying to get close enough to show us his badge. We got rotated out for that. But here I am, still standing. Better safe than sorry."

Still Hugo didn't reply, just looked blankly out of the window.

Hell, what more was he supposed to do? thought Bruno.

They kept driving in silence till they got to the first drop-off point, outside a mall. Hugo got out and gave the OK sign to the driver, who pulled away. Hugo just needed to call a ride from his burner phone and head on from the other side of the mall. But instead he headed for the movie theater and, without thinking about it, ten minutes later he was watching trailers and eating popcorn.

It was a rerelease of a classic action movie, with space soldiers fighting giant insect aliens who'd carried out a Pearl Harbor–style attack against Earth. Hugo soaked it all up, forgetting about his real world in which he had to fight against the country he'd loved for as long as he could remember. When the lights came up and the staff came in to clean out the theater for the next screening, Hugo pulled out his phone and ordered his ride.

He got dropped off at the mall to the east of Hawthorne Municipal Airport, picked up a burger, and walked for half an hour around its south perimeter to get home. Mrs. Torres had gone to bed and he ate the burger absently at the kitchen table. Then he brushed his teeth, took a zolpidem, and went to sleep.

The next morning it took him a few seconds to remember how royally he'd screwed up. The ICE guy had gotten killed because he'd let him see the doubt in his eyes. Now the AFL had killed a federal agent and that would surely bring all new kinds of trouble for them.

Devon and the others wouldn't be able to trust him in an operation now. He went over where he'd stashed money in the house: some in the pantry in a box of cheesy crackers that Mrs. Torres would never eat, some in a baggie at the back of the freezer, in the frost under a twenty-year-old ice cube tray. That one had his Colombian ID card as well. His passport was inside a VHS tape of a relative's wedding that he hadn't minded damaging because Mrs. Torres had no VHS player.

He went outside and trailed the garden hose from the side of the house out to his car on the street, then went back and got a couple of buckets, one of which had a sponge and other car-washing supplies. He took his time cleaning the car and swapped out the license plates using alternate ones he had in the other bucket.

Back in the house, he showered and put on clean clothes. He put the dirty clothes and all his other things into his backpack and headed back out to the car. He drove around the north side of Hawthorne airport, to the big box stores on its east side. From the parking lot he called Mike, who was a fellow zolpidem user. Hugo hadn't wanted to get into any medical databases via a prescription. He'd met Mike with his girlfriend, Irma, who was one of Valentina's contacts in LA. He'd dropped a hint about sleeping pills and Mike had gotten back to him later about it.

Mike picked up but kept silent, so Hugo spoke first.

"Hi, Mike, Hugo."

"Hey. I didn't recognize the number."

"No. Can we meet? I guess you realize why I'm not on my old phone."

"Gotcha. Yeah. Meet me at Pershing Square at one p.m.?"

"Got it."

Hugo hung up. He got out of the car and put the burner phone under one of the car wheels so it was crushed when he drove off.

That lunchtime, Hugo got a couple of coffees from a stall on Pershing Square and sat with Mike on the steps leading up to the bell tower. Mike now had his hair pulled back in a ponytail, was unshaven, and had dirt on his trousers. Hugo tried to act like he hadn't noticed but Mike wasn't one to beat around the bush.

"Irma got picked up by ICE and they put an ankle bracelet on her. She couldn't keep up with the fees for her own tag. So she got detained. Then I couldn't keep up with the rent by myself, so I'm living out of my car."

"Jesus, man."

"Yeah."

Mike waited for Hugo to spill.

"I need to go off-grid. After what happened last night I'm on the hook for—"

Mike lifted his hand, telling Hugo that it'd be better to avoid unnecessary details.

"Just learn from it, that's all you can do."

"Thanks, man. You're right." Hugo paused. "I've got some money, but I'd just go downhill if I tried to hide out someplace doing nothing."

"Have you spoken with Devon?"

"Even if he wanted to help, I need to sort my head out."

"Why don't you stay with Valentina, or let her help you in Sacramento?"

"That could put her on the spot as well. I just need to get away for a while."

Mike nodded.

"But I can't do anything public. You mentioned that Irma's brother was working in the Central Valley."

"Yeah, but it's grinding him down. He's always on the lookout for something better."

"I've been a soldier for years, I can work the land for a while."

"OK. I've got his number. We've been getting our heads together on how to help Irma. I'll have to level with him, though, this is a different level of shit you're in now."

"Thanks, man."

Mike looked up at the sky.

"He'll be out in the fields now. I'll message him to call me back."

47

McClure, California

A FEW hours later, Hugo had left Los Angeles behind and was crossing the Santa Clara River, going north on Interstate 5 in his Subaru. The road swerved around the edges of the Transverse Ranges before climbing again through the tail end of the Sierra Nevada. Descending into the Central Valley reminded him of the final straight of their escape from Yemen, and he resisted the urge to lower his head to the dashboard and squint up into the sky, looking for a drone. But this landscape had been thoroughly transformed by people, with green fields over most of his field of view, changing abruptly to dust when the irrigation stopped at the boundary fence.

He drove on through fields of almond and orange trees, grape vines and sugar beet, then through the middle of Bakersfield before the final stretch to McClure. He parked outside the packing shed of Irma's brother's company. He walked in through the open end of the building, where the trucks backed up to be loaded. The workers tending to the conveyor belts had no time to look up. Hugo walked up the metal steps to the small office that looked down on the working area. A middle-aged woman looked up from a computer spreadsheet and gave him directions.

Hugo parked outside the workers' dorm, a single-story building with jalousie windows and walls of fiber cement board. Now there was nothing to do but wait. He relaxed and fell asleep in the driver's seat.

He was woken up by wheels churning the gravel behind him. The sun had set. A tractor was towing a trailer with a bench seat down its center line. Both sides of the seat were packed with grape pickers coming back to their accommodation.

Hugo got out of the car, stooping as he walked the feeling back into his numb legs.

The pickers were getting out of the trailer, the younger ones vaulting over the side, the older ones waiting to step down the metal footholds set into the rear flap. Hugo stood to the side of the door into the dorm, lit from above by a single bulb. He hadn't seen a photo of Irma's brother, but he looked over the younger men as they trooped into the dorm, until one of them came up to him and addressed him in Spanish.

"You're the new guy?"

"You're Irma's brother?"

"What's your name?"

"Johnny Rico."

That's what Hugo had told Mike to say.

"Mateo," said Irma's brother.

They shook hands.

"They told me it's OK for you to spend the night here," said Mateo. "Tomorrow you can meet the foreman and go to work with us."

"Alright, good."

"No paperwork," Mateo cautioned.

"That's good for me right now."

Mateo shrugged, as if to say that it's an ill wind. He gestured to the door and Hugo followed him through.

The inside of the dorm was lit by bare fluorescent lights and was one open space except for a bathroom at the far end. Below a jalousie window by the door was a sink with pots and pans stacked neatly upside down on the draining board.

"Together we pay a girl to clean up each day," said Mateo, by way of explanation.

Another worker was already boiling water on a gas stove against the facing wall, which was fed by a butane cylinder on the floor next to it.

"And she makes rice," Mateo continued, pointing at a huge battered aluminum pot that'd been left on the stove.

"By the time we leave tomorrow, it'll be a pigsty," Mateo continued as he led Hugo further away from the door. Against each wall was a row of double bunks, with threadbare towels hanging from their rails. Men were pulling out battered zip-up bags out from below the bunks and getting clean clothes to change into after lining up for the showers. The place smelled of sweat and weedkiller. Hugo was taken back to his time in the Fort Benning barracks and had to force himself not to shout out, warning the workers that the drill sergeant would be along in a minute.

He was brought back into the moment by Mateo's voice.

"Look, the place is overfull, so since you're the new one, you'll have to sleep on the floor till a bunk frees up."

Mateo carried on to the far end of the bunkroom, then turned around and groped at something between the bunks and the wall. Hugo followed Mateo and saw him drag out a thin mattress with foam squeezing out from holes in its synthetic fabric cover. Mateo went down on his knees and pulled out a bedsheet with faded orange and pink stripes, dusty from having been pushed up to the corner of the wall and floor. He patted at it apologetically, knocking grit off onto the floor, and handed it to Hugo.

"You'll have to put the mattress down here," said Mateo, waving his hand along the corridor between the lines of bunks.

"No problem, man, thanks for putting in a word for me."

Hugo felt relaxed, thinking that no one here had a reason to turn him over to ICE.

He put the sheet back under the bunk and asked Mateo where he could buy food.

"Look, I saw you were asleep in your car. I'll give you some canned meat to eat with that rice," he said, gesturing back towards the stove. "Tomorrow I'll show you where to buy what you need."

Then Mateo went with Hugo, looking out at the men in the bunks on either side of Hugo's floor space and introducing them. They shook hands with Hugo without any resentment but not much welcome either: they'd seen plenty of workers come and go.

Hugo ate with Mateo. He was going to wait before going to bed but then thought he didn't mind, and nor would anyone else, if he was lying in the middle of the floor while everyone else carried on around him.

48

San Joaquin Valley, California

THE NEXT morning Hugo was woken up by a mobile phone alarm when it was still dark.

He got on the tractor-trailer with the rest, and it took them twenty minutes to get to the grape fields, picking up where they'd finished the day before.

The foreman was already there, standing beside his pickup on the unpaved track with rows of grapes on either side. The workers got out of the truck and each headed to the end of one of the rows, picked up a flat piece of cardboard from a stack, and walked down between the grape vines, out of sight, folding the cardboard up into a crate. Mateo waited behind with Hugo and walked over to the pickup to speak with the foreman.

"So you're the new guy?"

"Yes, sir," replied Hugo.

"Ever picked grapes before?"

"No, sir."

"Alright, it's not rocket science. First do a row or two with your friend here," he said, nodding towards Mateo. "The main thing is not to pick the unripe ones because you won't get paid for them and you'll just get the weigher pissed at you. You leave them, then you or someone else will get paid for them later, when they're ready. He'll show you what's ripe or not," he said, nodding at Mateo again. "When you have your own rows, you bring your full crates to the track and they'll be weighed when the tractor comes round. The first time, just make sure and tell them you're a new guy, and they get your name right in the book where they note down the weights. All right?"

"Yes, sir."

"Oh, have you got a pruner?"

Hugo shook his head. The foreman went to the cab, fished around in the glove box, and tossed one to Hugo.

"No gloves?"

"No, sir."

"Alright, good luck," said the foreman as he walked off towards the tractor driver.

After half an hour with Mateo, Hugo was working on his own account. He had to stoop down to reach the bunches of grapes, so he decided to shuffle along on his knees rather than risk slipping a disc. When he crossed Mateo in the next row, he laughed at Hugo for working like an old woman, but Hugo just shrugged. He was giving the work a good shot, not just because that was what he always did but also because being a slacker would be suspicious.

As he lumbered up and down the rows, dragging his grapes behind him, he could zone out and think about what he'd done and not done in the AFL operation to free Maharaj. He replayed the scene in his head, and each time he still recoiled from pulling the trigger on the ICE officer. So what the hell was he going to do? A soldier who wouldn't use his weapon was worse than useless. But he couldn't live in constant fear of getting picked up by ICE, always scared to act like he had been at the restaurant with Joseph.

After a few hours, he heard the tractor getting close. He stood up gingerly and staggered to the end of the row to get his grapes weighed. The woman on the trailer looked him up and down in despair.

"Son, look at yourself. You've been working for less than a morning and your knees and hands are cut to pieces. Didn't they tell you to bring gloves?"

"No, ma'am."

"Do you think gringos want to eat grapes with your blood on them?"

They both laughed, but then the weigher turned serious.

"Any more like that, and you can sit out the rest of the day."

"Yes, ma'am."

After a few hours more, Mateo called to Hugo to have lunch.

"Shit, I thought you'd've turned up better prepared than that," he said, seeing Hugo's shredded knees and hands.

Hugo grinned.

"What's the matter with you, man? If you carry on like that you won't be able to walk, and your hands will be so bandaged up that you won't be able to wipe your ass."

Hugo shrugged dismissively.

Mateo shook his head and kept talking to Hugo while he took out his phone. "Mike said you've been around the world and everything, but respect your work, man."

Hugo shrugged again, but this time in acknowledgment.

Mateo dialed one person, then another, while Hugo started on his lunch of sandwiches of white bread and sliced meat.

"OK. Someone's going to go to the store and get you some gloves and knee protectors, if you're going to work like that," said Mateo, looking skeptically at Hugo's knees.

"Thanks, man."

"You can pay her back tonight, right?"

"No problem."

The two of them ate while sat looking at the mountains. Mateo laughed when he saw Hugo had some grapes as well: he'd had his fill of grapes a long time ago.

An hour after lunch Hugo got a cramp in one of his thighs. He struggled to his feet and managed to stretch it out. Then the lack of sleep caught up with him. He lay down and by the time he woke up again, the sun was almost down over the coastal ranges.

49

McClure, California

OVER THE next couple of weeks, Hugo gradually caught up with the speed of the other workers. The cuts on his hands and knees healed slowly. One of the men left for another job and Hugo got bumped up from sleeping on the floor to a lower bunk. He got used to the routine of working, eating and sleeping. In a place where no one had a reason to pick him and deport him to his death, he appreciated being under the open sky and harvesting food, work that'd always need to be done. He wondered how many years his body could handle the work. He looked at the men working and sleeping alongside him, in their fifties, who looked like campesinos in Colombia, the same age as his officers in the military but whose etched faces and fixed eyes made them look decades older. He wasn't going to do this job six days a week for the next twenty years. But he didn't know how to get out and do anything else.

They picked the last of the grape crop one morning and were taken back early to the bunkhouse. The next day they'd start harvesting olives a few miles up the road, but for now they had the afternoon off.

Hugo ate his sandwiches outside the bunkhouse, sitting on an old car seat that someone had left leaning against the wall.

He'd only seen the town on Sundays, so he decided to drive around and see what it was like on a weekday afternoon. McClure Park was almost deserted. As he headed into the empty parking lot, he heard shots coming from the south. He turned the car sharply into a parking space and looked around. A man vaulted over the fence of a garden bordering the parking lot and hit the ground running, but raggedly, like he was exhausted. Hugo recognized Mateo. A couple of uniformed prison officers came over the fence, chasing and closing in on him.

Hugo reached under his seat and tore out the pistol that he'd taped underneath.

One of the officers tackled Mateo and fell to the ground on top of him.

Hugo stepped out of the car, put the pistol in his waistband in the small of his back, and ran towards the men with his head up, looking around for anyone else who was in on the chase.

The first officer got up. As Mateo tried to do the same he was knocked back down by a blow to the head from the second officer's baton.

Hugo swore and started to run faster towards the three men.

"Hugo, stop!"

Hugo ignored the voice in his head. He was Johnny now, anyway.

The first officer was kicking Mateo in the midriff.

"Hugo!"

It sounded like Valentina. He heard a car behind him and looked around. The car pulled alongside. Valentina was in the driver's seat.

"Hugo, get in, for the love of God!"

Hugo was dazed for a second. Valentina didn't belong here in the middle of violence.

"Hugo, are you coming with me or going to jail?"

One of the officers was cuffing Mateo's still body, and the other looked up and around.

Hugo got in Valentina's car as calmly as he could.

"That's it, take your time," she said.

Valentina hung a U-turn and drove out of the parking lot at normal speed. The officer would probably make them for a random couple that had gotten nervous at seeing a little police brutality.

"What the hell, Hugo?"

Valentina was venting.

Hugo gaped back at her, still trying to process what had just happened.

Valentina was weaving the car east through residential streets, getting closer to SR 99.

"You disappear without telling me anything and end up hundreds of miles away?"

"I didn't want to get you in trouble."

"So you were playing things safe by going after a couple of prison officers with a pistol in your belt?"

Hugo grunted.

"How did you find me?"

"You got this job through contacts I gave you, remember?"

"Right," Hugo conceded.

By now they were on SR 99, southbound. Valentina glanced over to the prison on their right.

"What's going on there?" she asked.

Vehicles in different kinds of livery were backed up on both sides of the security gate, some with their emergency lights flashing.

"That's the *migra* prison," said Hugo.

Valentina swore and he laughed.

"I don't know what's going on," he continued. "Those COs back there were beating on someone from our team. Maybe some people escaped and they were trying to catch anyone that the shoe fit."

"Idiots. They just make it all worse."

The last of the town was behind them. There were green irrigated fields on each side of the road, and in the distance the Transverse Ranges with Los Angeles on the other side.

"Hugo, when were you going to contact me?"

He didn't answer.

"You'd have found a way if you wanted."

Still nothing.

"I'm not worried about what you did, whatever it was. I trust you to do the right thing."

She looked over at him and he nodded.

"Maybe I was doing the right thing, but I didn't do it well. I didn't shoot that ICE guy, but if I'd done my job better, then he wouldn't've got shot. The murder conspiracy charge makes sense that way."

Hugo paused. "I froze. Someone like that is a liability." He paused again and looked dejectedly out of the window. "So I went off the grid. Yeah, to avoid being arrested, but really because I didn't think I could help the AFL anymore."

"Hugo, why didn't you tell me?" said Valentina, "I want to help you. Aren't we supposed to help each other?"

"You're right, I know, but help me do what? I didn't want to call up and just say 'I'm in deep shit.' I wanted to have some idea what to do next, some kind of plan."

"And?" asked Valentina.

Hugo looked at her.

"What plan have you come up with? In the month you've had to think it over by yourself?"

Hugo shook his head.

The car fishtailed slightly as Valentina took her hand off the steering wheel and rested it on Hugo's thigh. She waited to feel his hand squeezing hers, then moved it back to the steering wheel.

By now they were leaving Bakersfield behind. Then green irrigated fields, then the thinner air of the Transverse Ranges, between slopes of dry yellow grass and chaparral. As the road crossed over a branch of Pyramid Lake, Valentina looked over at Hugo and smiled when she saw that he'd fallen asleep.

50

Bell, Los Angeles

Hugo woke up in a parking lot in the late afternoon. In front of the car was a sparse row of cypress trees and, beyond them, a block of two-story row houses. He looked behind the car and saw some big metal wheeled dumpsters, and then a three-story residential building. A hotel, he reckoned. He reached back in his memory to work out what he might be doing there. Then, from outside the car, Valentina opened the passenger door for him, and he smiled in happiness and relief. He looked around for anything that he should take out of the car with him and remembered that he only had what was in his pockets, and his pistol. He moved to take the gun out of the glove box and winced from the pain of having slept twisted in the car seat. He levered himself up and out of the car, and embraced Valentina.

"When was the last time we stayed in a hotel?" she asked.

Hugo smiled and shrugged. "Villa de Leyva? How many years ago was that?"

"Plenty."

Valentina locked the car doors with the key fob, then walked to the hotel reception, holding Hugo's hand and dragging her wheelie bag with her other hand.

They got a room on the second floor, which looked out onto the parking lot. Once inside, Hugo made sure he could see Valentina's car from the window, then drew the curtains.

Valentina lay down on the bed, put both hands behind her head, and smiled up at Hugo. He looked at her as he stepped over to the bathroom door.

"It's been a while since I had a hot shower."

"Take your time. I'm not going anywhere."

Hugo went into the bathroom and closed the door behind him. He started to take his clothes off, taking his time, imagining how he'd soon be taking Valentina's clothes off for her.

Through the bathroom door, he heard Valentina calling out to ask who was at the door.

Hugo snapped out of his reverie.

"Don't let them in!" he shouted as he pulled his clothes back on and grabbed his gun. But he heard the main door being smashed in from the corridor side. Valentina screamed as the intruders shouted.

"Federal agents! Hands in the air!"

Footsteps, then, "Where's your boyfriend?"

While they waited a second for a reply that didn't come, Hugo turned off the light in the bathroom and stood to one side of the door.

"Get her out of here."

Hugo thought he heard the sounds of scuffling. He imagined the agents dragging Valentina off the bed and away. He told himself to keep calm.

The strip of light under the bathroom door was silently interrupted by the shadows of an officer positioning himself on the other side.

From the other side of the door he heard Valentina start to shout.

"¡*Migra*! The fucking *migra* are taking me away! Help me!"

She sounded far away. Hugo thought she'd waited to get into the corridor before shouting, so more people would hear her before they shut her up again.

Hugo stepped out into the middle of the bathroom room, judged where the officer would be, and aimed a shot at his chest.

The officer cried out, and Hugo leapt towards the frosted glass bathroom window as the door and the wall where he'd been standing were shredded by gunfire. A shotgun and at least a couple of pistols. Hugo had no chance going toe to toe with them. He used the butt of the pistol to knock out the glass of the window and put a towel over the jagged edge that was left.

A shot came from outside, through the empty window frame, missed Hugo, and shattered a plastic tile in the false ceiling of the bathroom. Hugo leapt through the window as, behind him, ICE officers burst in through what was left of the bathroom door.

As he leapt, Hugo saw that the incoming shot had come from one of the two officers behind the open doors of an ICE truck parked close to

Valentina's car. He landed behind one of the dumpsters, sprang up again, and ran back into the service bay as the officers shot down at him from the window. He was still in the sights of the officers in the car on the other side of the parking lot, but he dove behind another dumpster and fired a shot at them to make them think twice.

Carl was the senior ICE officer. He dragged Valentina by the neck, out of the room and into the corridor.

"That shiteater boyfriend of yours has made a run for it, but you'll do for now."

Valentina twisted under Carl's grip, managed to bite one of his fingers, and then carried on shouting for help.

"The *migra* will come for you next if you do nothing!"

A couple of hotel guests opened their doors and watched as another officer put a spit hood over Valentina's head, then dragged her down the corridor.

One of the guests, a middle-aged woman, started haranguing the ICE officers.

"Thugs! Leave the girl alone, fucking criminals." More guests came out into the corridor, and the woman called them out.

"Did you come out just to watch? Are you going to let the death squad take away whoever they want?"

The ICE officers were heading for the stairs, but some of the guests had started to warily track them down the corridor. When they got to the emergency doors onto the stairwell, two of the officers dragged Valentina through. The other two drew their weapons and faced down the hotel guests. One of the guests had called the elevators and he was waiting by the doors with some others. The last two ICE agents gave the other two a few seconds start, then went into the stairwell themselves, letting the doors slam behind them.

Around the back of the hotel, Hugo had no way out. One of the ICE officers took a shot at him from behind the open car door, then called on Hugo to give himself up. Hugo said nothing back. For now it was a standoff because he could pick them off if they came for him. But soon he'd be out of ammunition, or they would get reinforcements.

Inside the hotel, as the officers dragged Valentina down the stairs, they heard chanting come up from the first floor.

"*¡Chinga la migra!* Stop disappearing people!"

They pushed the levers on the double doors and left the stairwell. The check-in desk was unstaffed. A crowd of hotel residents had filled the lobby and was backed down the corridor to the first-floor rooms. They were shouting at the ICE officers, and some of them were recording the scene on their phones.

The ICE officers stopped in their tracks and took in the situation. At least they could see that, in the drop-off area outside the lobby doors, their truck was ready with the driver waiting.

Carl shouted at the others to press on. That was their only choice, and waiting wasn't going to make it any easier. They stepped forward, guns drawn, dragging Valentina with them. They reached the protesters, who didn't move, just shouted all the more closely into the officers' faces.

Suddenly a shot rang out and the crowd looked around, wavering. The driver had gotten out of the truck and, with the protesters' backs to him, had fired a shot into the lobby, over their heads and into the plaster ceiling above the reception desk.

The ICE officers inside the hotel took their chance and pushed through the newly hesitant protesters. But, as they stepped out of the hotel, still dragging Valentina with them, the roof of the truck was caved in by a wooden bed falling from a third-floor window. The agents reflexively looked up, only to see a flat-screen coming down at them. They stepped back inside the front door as the TV shattered on the ground between them and showered them with glass splinters.

The crowd behind them was jeering them now, and edging closer. The doors of the truck were too buckled to open. The senior officer spoke into his radio, then shouted to his men to make a break for it. As they ran, another television, then a sink, smashed into the ground behind them.

At the back of the hotel, Hugo was preparing himself to break cover and use another of his rounds to keep the ICE officers honest. He heard one of the car doors slam shut. Were they going to charge him in the car? Hugo dropped to his knees by the side of the dumpster. The second door slammed shut. Hugo looked round the side of the dumpster as the car tires screeched and it took off. Hugo shot at the driver's side of the windshield but hit the rear passenger window as the car swerved away. They weren't charging him: they were rushing for the exit of the parking lot. Hugo, drained and bemused, let his pistol arm drop to his side.

The officers dragged Valentina to the sidewalk in front of the hotel as their other vehicle pulled up. One officer vaulted over the rear passenger seat into the cargo space. Two others dragged Valentina inside, ignoring her blind struggles. The last officer got in the front passenger seat, and they took off again.

Hugo ran to the lobby in time to see the ICE truck turning onto Bell Avenue, then heading away westwards. He stopped, looked at the chaos around him, and scoffed at their other vehicle, mangled and abandoned outside the lobby. Then he gritted his teeth and ran back up to the room to get his clothes and wallet.

In the ICE truck, the driver asked, "So what now?" Carl thought for a few seconds.

"Better not have this tonk heifer on our hands in the city. Who knows what size rat pack she'd attract?"

Valentina shouted, but her words were muffled by the spit hood. Carl carried on, ignoring her.

"Head to the federal building and drop us off," he said, drawing an air arc that took in himself and the other two from the other truck. "Then you two take her to Medro."

"Jeez."

Valentina swung blindly at her captors till one of them grabbed her wrists and the other cuffed them with a zip tie.

"After what happened back there, you want to be driving her through the city tomorrow?"

The driver grunted, acquiescing.

Valentina wilted and sobbed into the polyester mesh of the spit hood.

51

Medro, California

HALF AN hour later, the ICE truck was to the east of Los Angeles, turning north on Interstate 15 and heading up through the San Gabriel Mountains.

Gradually Valentina started to tell herself what she tried to tell her patients' families, when they been through the first wave of grief. The stronger they were, the more they could help the person they were grieving for. And she tried to remember what she'd read and been told about the Medro detention center. It made her shudder, but she tried to tell it to herself in a matter-of-fact way, like she was telling someone else who was going to be sent there. She felt them come down from the mountain, then fell asleep as they headed slowly up again into the high desert.

Valentina woke up again as the truck pulled to a halt. The officer beside her pulled off the spit hood, and she could see that they were in Medro town, stopped at a red light.

Judging by the officer's monotone, he'd been readying the words in his head.

"Valentina Díaz, you have been detained for harboring a fugitive in violation of the conditions of your permanent resident status. Do you understand?"

She nodded. Almost a thousand meters up, the cold made her shiver. Beyond a fence, dozens of old airliners were lined up on an airport apron, their windshields and engines muzzled with aluminum foil.

The truck pulled up to the detention center, a collection of two-story beige concrete blocks. The ICE officers handed Valentina over to the staff of the private corporation that ran the center and were gone. They cut the cable tie around her wrists, and she rubbed the red welts. She had to change into orange pajamas, then she was taken to a cell on the second floor of one of the blocks, along a walkway that looked down onto a central area with metal tables and stools built into the floor. Something was rhythmically hitting the inside of one of the metal cell doors as they walked past.

"Someone's banging their head on the door!" said Valentina to the two guards.

One of them looked away, the other frowned.

"We'll medicate them when we get a doctor's report."

A few cells further on, the guards stopped, unlocked the door, and motioned Valentina inside. She stepped forward but flinched from the tang of urine-soaked mattresses. She stepped forward again, into the cell. There were two bunks against each side wall, with a slit window high on the wall facing the door. The detainee on one of the lower bunks gazed affectlessly at Valentina. Each upper bunk also had a motionless occupant, their faces hidden in the far corners of the room.

Valentina had the free lower bunk. She paused, not wanting to soil herself on the mattress. The door clanged shut behind her and was locked from the outside. She stood over the stained mattress and told herself that they weren't her own clothes she was going to taint. She told herself she was tired, which she was, having only dozed fitfully, bound up next to the rancorous ICE officer. She took off her shoes, lay down, closed her eyes, and imagined the smell was from a patient left overnight, who she was going to clean up as soon as she got on shift.

She was woken up by the woman from the opposite bunk poking her midriff with the point of her foot.

"Ey."

As Valentina opened her eyes, her cellmate was loping out of the door. Valentina put on her shoes, stepped out onto the walkway, and looked down on the ground-floor gallery. The detainees were lining up to get one of the styrofoam boxes that a CO was handing out from a black plastic cleaning cart. Some of the women had taken their meals to the tables and were sitting on the built-in metal stools. Others stood at the edge of the gallery, heads bent over the styrofoam as they ate with plastic cutlery.

After lining up, Valentina opened the disposable white box and retched at the lumpy black effluent inside. The styrofoam lid squeaked as she closed the box again, holding her breath.

She looked past the box at the dented metal of the table. She wasn't ready yet to accept all this. She looked around the cell block, stood up, picked up the styrofoam box, and headed over to one of the onlooking

COs. He was a young guy, didn't look so different from Daniel. His gaze flickered uneasily as Valentina approached him. Valentina knew that the COs in the private ICE prisons got little training and didn't tend to stay in the job for long.

As she reached the CO, she opened the styrofoam box and held it under his nose.

"You think it's legal to serve this rancid shit?"

The CO looked away from the box, grimacing and trying not to gag. "We don't make the food here."

"But you're giving it to people. If you're not responsible for what's going on here now, then who is?"

Some of the other women around the tables were looking at them now. Feeling cornered, the CO decided to push back and looked up into Valentina's eyes as he replied.

"Being an illegal isn't a good place to complain about things not being right."

"I'm not an 'illegal,' son," she replied, with air quotes. "Can't you answer my question? Doesn't that uniform imply some kind of responsibility?"

"Get your lawyer to file a complaint," he said dismissively.

Valentina scoffed at him before walking away. At least she hadn't just sucked it up.

She tossed the box into an overflowing bin at the side of the ground-floor gallery, keeping a plastic-wrapped piece of fruit-flavored gelatin. Back in her cell, she couldn't bear to lie on the foul mattress again, so she sat on the floor against the wall. She peeled back the foil on the gelatin and squeezed it out of the packaging and into her mouth. As she let the sugary blob dissolve on her tongue, she thought about Hugo and the legal center people trying to find her.

52

San Ysidro Border Crossing

VALENTINA WAS moved again sooner than she'd expected. A couple of guards came when she was still sitting against the wall. One of them was the same young guy she'd confronted in the gallery earlier that day. He looked at her with a mixture of hostility and respect. For the other, Valentina was just a commodity that needed to be shipped elsewhere. On stepping out into the high desert sun, she'd expected to be joining a line of dozens of people to get on a bus, but instead she was headed back south in the same kind of truck that she'd arrived in.

Beyond the San Gabriel Mountains, they carried straight on into San Bernardino rather than turning west to LA. They went through the suburbs for hours, until she wondered whether California was built up all the way to the border. But then there were a couple of stretches of green before they got to the outskirts of San Diego. Valentina dozed, then woke up when they were skirting the city to the east, a few miles in from the coast. Then they turned east on State Route 905, parallel to the border.

They left the green of San Diego behind them and climbed slowly towards the hills. They came off the SR 905 at a sprawling multilevel intersection, then through an industrial area with big open lots of warehouses and shipping containers, everything coated with fine beige dust.

By now Valentina knew where they were heading. They drove along the road outside the south perimeter of the Otay Mesa Detention Center, an agglomeration of off-white two-story utilitarian blocks. Once through the main gate, they were into a parking lot with hundreds of spaces, only half-full of cars now that it was early evening, plus a couple of buses parked at the far end. They carried on towards a gate in the double-razor-wire fence that surrounded the monolithic detention building.

The officer next to Valentina opened the door, picked up a cellophane-wrapped bundle off the floor of the truck, and gestured for her to follow him. He signed them through the gate and they entered the building, but instead of booking her in, the officer handed her the cellophane bundle and gestured to a passage that led off the reception area.

Valentina looked down at the bundle and realized that it was her own clothes.

She looked up at the officer, then at another behind the booking desk. They were looking her in the eye, waiting to see whether they'd need to subdue her physically.

She went into the restroom and changed into her clothes which were still wet with sweat and tears. She gave the orange pajamas to the Medro agent and followed him back out to the truck.

They drove the hundred yards to the far end of the lot, and pulled up under the windshield of one of the bare aluminum buses. The officer got out again and went around the front of the bus, towards the passenger door, and out of sight. A couple of minutes later, he was back, nodding at the driver.

"This is it. Let's go," said the officer as he opened the passenger door and motioned her out.

"What the hell's going on?"

"You'll find out soon enough," he said, gesturing at her again. She got out and walked around to the passenger entrance of the bus, still in the clothes they'd detained her in. She walked up the steps into the bus and saw it was already full of people who looked at her wearily, some with hostility, others with curiosity or just indifference. As soon as she sat down on one of the few spare seats, the driver started the engine.

At first they headed west, back the way Valentina had just come, looking into the setting sun. But when they got to the I-805 they turned south. The border was only a couple of miles away.

"They're deporting us?" she asked the woman sitting next to her, in Spanish.

The other woman raised her eyebrows as if to say: what else?

Valentina sighed silently. She didn't know what she was going to do. She didn't know anyone on the bus, nor in Mexico, never mind in Tijuana.

By now they were in the tide of traffic bearing down slowly on the San Ysidro border crossing point. One of the tens of thousands of vehicles that crossed each day, the bus edged westwards across the lanes and doubled back at a traffic circle within sight of the border. For a few seconds

Valentina let herself imagine that they weren't going to the border after all, but then the road swung back south again. They pulled up outside a Customs and Border Protection building. On the far side of the building was the border wall.

The passenger door of the bus opened and one of the officers stepped down to meet a couple of his colleagues who were sauntering out of the building towards them. Valentina watched them converse a few yards from the bus. After a minute, the officer got back into the bus.

"OK, folks, I need you to step out of the bus and into the building here."

As if they were in an airport. Valentina scanned the faces of the other detainees, looking for any signs of defiance to latch onto. Nothing. One of the others caught her eye and silently asked her not to make trouble. Valentina realized that, unlike her, most of them would've been in the system for months, even years. If they'd put up any resistance, then it evidently hadn't worked for them.

The bus was emptying from the front. Soon it was Valentina's turn and she followed the rest of them down onto the blacktop and towards the building. They were channeled through to the far side of the building, between floor-to-ceiling crowd barriers made of steel cylinders that were kept shiny on the inside by the people rubbing against them. After about twenty meters, the corridor opened out into a hall with a low ceiling of off-white polystyrene tiles, and railings that funneled the detainees into a line that folded back on itself. Every few minutes a light would go on over the door and a guard at the head of the line would usher another detainee through the door.

One of the men shouted out "Ice is illegal" in Spanish, and a murmur of approval went through the crowd.

"Silence," called out one of the ICE guards, who then, with a second officer, started to force himself between the detainees towards the dissenter. The man turned to face them but didn't struggle when they grabbed him by the arms. The guards dragged him towards the far end of the hall, hauling him over the barriers like a suitcase. They pushed open the exit door, pulled the man through, and let the door slam close behind them.

An hour later it was Valentina's turn. She went through the door and turned to the right, following a green line painted onto the floor. It led to a smaller door that opened abruptly as she approached it. Beyond it was a bare white room with a pale gray linoleum floor. A CBP officer in dark blue uniform sat behind a metal desk at a computer that looked more than five years old. Another officer stood by a door with a big old-fashioned keyhole, around which the white paint had been worn away to reveal the copper color of the metal underneath.

"Right hand, four fingers," said the officer, gesturing at a scanner on the desk beside the computer.

Valentina did as she was told. As the lights on the scanner took their time turning green, she looked around the room. The door through which she'd come had no handle inside the room.

She asked herself, what could she do? But no answer came.

The voice of the officer at the computer brought her back to reality.

"Valentina Diaz, you are being deported from the United States for violating the terms of your visa. Good luck."

The other officer took a key from his belt and opened the door. Behind it was another door. A second later, there was a sound of a key in its lock, and it opened away from Valentina, into Mexico. There was no room on the other side: the second door just opened into the outdoors. Late-afternoon light came into the room. As her eyes adjusted, she saw a chain fence, and beyond that an irrigation channel strewn with rubbish and with puddles of iridescent oil-stained water on its concrete floor. She caught the rancid smell in the back of her throat.

Someone called her through to the Mexican side. She stepped over the threshold and saw there was a booth to one side of the door.

"Document?" a Mexican immigration officer called out in Spanish to her.

"They grabbed me when I had nothing, just my clothes."

He nodded. "Miss, please fill in this form," he said, pushing a sheet of paper under the glass panel separating them.

A six-inch-deep counter projected from the booth, and a pen was hanging by a wire from it. Valentina completed the form and pushed it back under the glass. Then she had her photo taken by a USB camera. A printer on the officer's side of the glass spat out a card, which he passed to Valentina.

"Thirty days."

A few men had gathered by the gate in the chain fence and were sizing Valentina up. She looked down at herself. She had no purse, no money, no phone, nothing.

"Mister, what can I do?" she asked the immigration official.

"Miss, people like you are a business here. They reckon that if you got into the US, then you can find a way to pay them for their time."

Valentina took the card in her hand but kept standing at the booth. Without turning her head, she looked out of the corner of her eye at what lay beyond the wire fence. To one side lay the flood channel. On the other side was a row of buildings. They looked like the back sides of houses and small businesses facing an unseen street on the far side. Some of them had banners advertising their services, and one or two had service windows.

Valentina turned and walked towards the gate. The men started calling out to her. Valentina told herself to walk like she knew what she was doing. Like being dumped into an unknown country was nothing, was normal for her.

"We can get you back across the border," called out one of the men.

"Get your paperwork fixed."

"Need a hotel?" asked another, poking a rolled-up flyer through the wire mesh.

She reached the gate. An immigration officer opened it for her, and she was by herself in Mexico.

She ignored the men calling out to her and concentrated on walking up the access road and getting to the street. One of the men held a flyer out in front of her and wouldn't move his arm, so she walked on, pushing the arm to one side, but it pressed and lingered on her rib cage below her breast as she walked on. She looked towards the buildings and told herself that when she got there, she'd figure out how to call someone. Another man grabbed her upper arm and she yanked it away. She couldn't call Hugo. She'd call the legal center.

"Valentina!"

Whatever they were selling, she didn't want.

She shouldered past another man.

"Valentina!"

How did they know her name?

She looked up and it was Daniel. They embraced.

53

Downtown Los Angeles

By that morning, footage of the ICE raid on the Bell hotel had gone viral. Some TV and social media channels were raging at ICE for detaining a Green Card holder and then using her as a human shield. Other channels were raging at Latinos for obstructing law enforcement. The protesters outside the ICE offices in the federal building in Los Angeles had gone from a handful to a couple of hundred. Hugo joined the back of the crowd and caught the eye of a man in an AFL baseball cap. The man headed off and a couple of minutes later Hugo followed him.

At the side of Grand Park, the AFL man stopped at a cart selling refreshments. As Hugo approached, the man turned and asked him how he wanted his coffee. A minute later they were sipping from cardboard cups as they walked slowly around the park.

"I want back in. Last time I shot at those ICE fuckers that took my girlfriend. I only wish I'd tagged one of them."

The AFL man nodded.

"I'm not going to freeze in action again," Hugo continued.

"You're in. You were never out as far as we were concerned."

Hugo nodded gratefully. "What about my girlfriend?"

"We think she's in Medro."

Hugo turned away and looked beyond the trees that bordered the park.

"Someone matching her description was booked there a few hours after the incident last night."

"The legal center people know?"

"Yep. They're doing what they can."

Hugo snapped back to the present and turned to the AFL man. "So?"

"We want you to join the homeless in this area."

Hugo looked around and noticed a couple of homeless people that he hadn't before.

"Got it."

"A lot of them are veterans."

"Objectives?"

"For now, blend in, get to know the area, the routine."

"Don't get wasted."

Hugo didn't feel like laughing.

"For now that's all there is."

"OK." Hugo looked down at his ripped and dirty clothes. "I guess I won't need too much work to pass as a homeless person?"

The AFL man smiled. "Have you got what you need to survive, though?"

"I've still got my pistol, but it'd be good to have a knife."

"Alright, I can get you that."

"Thanks. I'll be fine. But are we talking about days, weeks, months…?"

"Can't you see how things are boiling up?"

Hugo nodded.

The AFL man shrugged and raised his eyebrows, inviting Hugo to come to his own conclusions.

"Like I said, a good percentage of the homeless around here are veterans. And, out of those, a good percentage are liable to be deported."

"And are with us."

The AFL man nodded.

They agreed to meet in a parking lot on Fifth Street an hour later, where the AFL man gave Hugo a knife. Then Hugo was on his own.

He saw some trash bags on the street, outside a restaurant that sold pizza by the slice. He went over, untied one of the bags and tipped pizza crusts, greasy tomato-stained cardboard and a stream of old soda on top of the remaining bags. He walked off as someone shouted angrily at him from inside the restaurant.

Hugo walked east till he found a trash bin on the sidewalk. He paused a couple of feet away, breathing in the fumes of fermented sugar and chemical flavoring. Then, telling himself he was just acting out a role, he bent over the bin and, holding his breath, used his hand to dig into the fast-food wrappers, chicken bones and paper cups with coffee dregs and wet tea bags. He burst open a plastic bag to find shitty wet wipes and a used diaper covered in vomited-up baby food. But not what he was looking for.

He stood up and walked on. When he got to the next bin, he dredged through it the same way, but this time he found a soda can, which went into the trash bag from the restaurant. After a few more he had a couple of plastic water bottles as well.

He carried on, working his way back to Pershing Square Park. But he walked right through it and out the far side, knowing that there were plenty of other homeless people there who would beat him to anything with a CRV deposit. He carried on to the bus station where he'd arrived a few weeks ago. He walked in as if he had just enough time to catch his bus. He stopped by a couple of bins and fished out half a dozen bottles and cans. By then a passenger had pointed him out to one of the security guards. As the guard walked over towards him, Hugo had to remind himself he was being a homeless person who had to obey, not a soldier who did the ordering around.

Hugo carried on south to the bus plaza outside the train station, then under the elevated section of Highway 101, and into the arts district, where he did well from what the lunchtime crowd had left scattered in and around the street bins.

By 5 p.m., he'd filled his bag and headed towards the recycling center on Alameda. Unable to stop himself from thinking of his work as a new business opportunity, he wondered about the pros and cons of getting a shopping cart to carry multiple bags, as he'd seen a couple of the other recyclers doing. He didn't reach a conclusion before reaching the recycling place. He got less than ten dollars for his work.

He headed back to Skid Row and picked his way through the rows of makeshift tents, sizing up those owners who were present. He got to the edge of the Toy District and retraced his steps. He stopped at one tent whose owner was squatting on a broken camping cooler.

"Hey," said Hugo.

The man looked up at him, then back down at the pavement.

"Know where I can get Ambien?"

The man jerked his head at some point further down the street. Hugo carried on walking till he got to the man in question. Hugo knew it was him because his tent was newer and cleaner, he was in a folding fishing chair, and his eyes were calm and critical, rather than jumpy and timorous.

"Zolpidem?"

The man just looked Hugo up and down.

"You look like a fucking cop."

Hugo squatted down next to the man. His hair was pulled back tight over his head, with gray streaks starting over the temples.

"Ex-Army. But they fucked me over. Look for the news from last night. I was getting shot at by the cops. I'm with the AFL."

"Politics," the man said dismissively, but Hugo had convinced him. "Ten bucks."

Hugo passed him the bill and waited.

"Under the corner of the tent here."

Hugo had to grope past the man's feet to find a single capsule that'd been cut out of a blister pack. He stood up, nodded at the dealer, and carried on. He found some cardboard that had been put out behind a store a couple of blocks away, then walked back to the tents. He found a space on the sidewalk, put down some cardboard, lay down on top of it, then patted the pocket where he'd put the zolpidem.

A few hours later, after midnight, the drone of traffic had been replaced by an occasional roar of someone enjoying the novelty of empty streets. Hugo was motionless, his body in a fetal position, facing away from the street, towards a chain-link fence that enclosed an empty lot.

Two other homeless people, a young man and a woman, sidled closer to Hugo. Hugo remained motionless. The couple carried on and stood by Hugo's head. When ready, the woman nodded at the man and they both jumped on Hugo. The man grabbed Hugo's exposed arm while the woman reached under his body for the other arm. Hugo used his arm to pull the man away from the street, overbalancing him so that he fell on top of Hugo himself and the woman assailant. Hugo scrambled out from under them and sprang up, pulling out his knife from the ankle holster. As the couple got to their feet, Hugo could see that the man was looking to the woman to take her lead, so Hugo faced off against her, holding his knife at the level of her heart.

"Want to get hurt?"

The woman held his gaze for a few seconds before nodding in sullen acquiescence.

"I don't want to see you around."

The woman turned to walk away and the man slunk after her.

A few others had woken up and were watching the show. Hugo reckoned he made his point. They'd tried to beat down the newcomer but he'd held up. The adrenaline started to fade. He took the zolpidem, at last, and lay back down, looking forward to sleep.

Hugo used the next few days to walk the areas next to downtown. He tried to work out the best times and places to pick up bottles and cans. He stole a shopping cart from the parking lot of a supermarket on Main Street, and used it for his trash bags of bottles and cans, plus a few possessions he'd picked up. Once a day he got food and water from a mission on Crocker Street.

He got to know the other homeless people on his street by sight. He learned that his zolpidem connection was named Scott. Having seen how he carried himself and organized his gear, Hugo asked Scott whether he'd been in the Army. He just scoffed and asked for ten bucks.

54

Los Angeles City Hall

MIKE GOT out of a pickup at the back of LA City Hall, part of a pest control team who were going to fumigate the upper floors. The mayor's office was trying to get ahead of the curve of an outbreak of typhus in the building. People got typhus from bites of rat fleas, and could end up in the hospital if not diagnosed promptly, which they usually weren't. Typhus wasn't something that the mayor wanted to be associated with.

The team started to get their gear out of the bed of the pickup, and they hefted and trundled it into the building and to the service elevator. A guard looked distastefully at the biohazard stickers on their pesticide tanks and waved them through. A second pickup rolled into the unloading bay with more operatives, including Jaime Gutierrez, and more fumigating gear. Jaime took the elevator up to the twenty-fifth floor with Mike. When they walked out into the front of the building, there were no City Hall workers, no computers, and the furniture was protected by dust covers.

Mike and Jaime zipped themselves out of their fumigation overalls to show dark blue security guard uniforms. They walked out of the office space and up one floor to the twenty-sixth, where they waited for the elevator to arrive. A couple of minutes later, the doors opened to show a batch of tourists who were trying to get to the Mayor Tom Bradley Room, the observation deck on the next floor up. But Mike told them that there'd been a security alert and they'd have to go back down the stairs to the twenty-second floor, which was where the express elevator from the street level had taken them. Mike and Jaime were used to ordering people around, so the tourists got the idea they were lucky to be avoiding something serious and headed down the stairs without complaining. Jaime stood in the doorway to stop the elevator from going down again. When the tourists were out of sight, Mike put a fire extinguisher against the open door to stop the elevator going anywhere.

Having seen the tourists go down, half a dozen more fumigators, all of them AFL members, came up from the twenty-fifth floor. One stayed on the twenty-sixth floor to deal with anything unexpected there, and the others went up the blue-gray granite steps and into the observation deck. The triple-height space with tall rectangular windows on all sides looked out over the city. The height of the room was accentuated by cast-iron light fittings dangling halfway to the floor from the red-and-gold checkered ceiling.

A couple of legit security guards were watching from opposite sides of the observation deck. Two of the AFL squad, still in their fumigator overalls, headed for one of the guards, grinning apologetically, as if about to pass on bad news about the progress of the pest control. When they reached her, one of the AFL squad drew a pistol while the other stood by, blocking her escape route.

"We're going to get everyone out of here, that's all we want to do. Understand?"

She nodded.

"Look at your partner over there."

The other guard was in the same situation on the other side of the room.

"Be cool."

The guard nodded across the room at her colleague.

The tourists were still unaware of anything going on. One of the kids was taking a photo op at the lectern while others looked out the windows.

An AFL man had taken off his overalls to reveal the fake security guard uniform. He spoke up to the four corners of the room.

"Ladies and gentlemen, it's time to start to go back down the stairs, making room for the next group of visitors."

Most of the tourists started to head for the exit. One bristled, saying that this wasn't how it'd been on a previous visit.

Jaime said something to the guard on the far side of the room. The guard nodded grimly, then spoke up.

"This is our change of shift, please head back down the stairs."

The bellyacher shrugged and went along with the rest.

The AFL members relaxed, knowing that there'd be no more pushback.

The crowd went down the granite steps, only to find the elevator out of action. The faux security guards explained that they just needed to walk down four more floors, to the twenty-second, and get the express elevator from there to the ground floor.

The real security guards realized that the situation didn't just have to do with the observation deck. They looked around again but saw themselves outnumbered by the AFL men.

The walkie-talkie of one of the guards beeped, then a static-laden voice came through.

"Hey, the upper elevator's out. Can you see what the deal is? I've got a bunch of visitors backed up here on the twenty-second floor."

The AFL man who had the guard at gunpoint made a wheeling motion with the index finger of his other hand, telling him to string the guy along. The guard nodded sullenly.

"Roger. While I do that, the current visitors are making their way down the stairs."

The AFL man nodded approvingly.

"Jeez. OK. Get back to me on the lift," came the voice from the twenty-second floor.

"Roger. Out."

"That's the way," the AFL man told the guard. "Now you're going to follow the tourists down the stairs and you'll be off your shift early."

The guard glowered back at the AFL man, and the gun he was still holding on him. But he did as he was told.

The AFL members shepherded the tourists and guards down the stairs as far as the twenty-third floor, then waited and told them to carry on down one floor more, to get the express elevator on the twenty-second. The real guards sized up the AFL men again but realized there was no percentage for them in taking them on, now that they were almost free anyway. The AFL men watched them all carry on down till they went out of sight around a turn in the staircase.

Then they hurried back up and went through the door from the stairwell to the twenty-fifth floor. There, another member of the squad was waiting with a welding unit, which had been disguised as an insecticide pump. He set to work sealing the door shut.

They went back up the stairwell to the twenty-sixth floor, then up the curved granite processional staircase to the viewing gallery.

They walked over to Devon, who was taking a circle cutter out of a flight case. As they approached, Devon stood up and looked at them inquisitively.

"The door's being welded up now."

"Good job," Devon replied. "Bring it over here," he continued, gesturing at the flight case and the window behind him.

Devon stepped towards the center of the room, taking a used cell phone from the pocket of his overalls.

He tapped on a saved number. As he waited for the call to go through, he looked up at the red circles within black squares on the art deco ceiling twenty feet above him.

"Mayor's Office."

"Devon Reid, leader of the American Foreign Legion."

After a pause, the staffer continued. "We need you to prove your identity."

"Check what's happening in the Mayor Bradley Room in City Hall. If you want I can describe the situation."

The line went silent as the staffer muted her microphone to speak with her colleagues.

Devon smiled. As he waited for a response, he watched Mike fix the circle cutter to the lower end of one of the corner windows.

It took a minute for a different voice to come over the phone.

"My name is Patricia, I'm from the city's Crisis Negotiation Team."

"Devon Reid. Good morning."

"You're occupying the Mayor Bradley Room?"

Devon didn't respond. He watched Mike score a circle into the glass with the tungsten carbide bit of the circle cutter.

"Do you have any hostages?"

"We don't detain people illegally. That's what we're trying to stop."

Patricia's voice was a touch more relaxed.

"You know this is going to end. You've made your point. The sooner you come down out of there, the better it will be for everyone."

"Thanks for your concern."

"Why did you call?"

"Our argument isn't with you. It's with the federal government agencies."

"We can't just sit back and watch your occupation on social media."

"We've secured our position and we're well prepared."

"So we're done?"

"Just one more thing."

Patricia waited.

"There's going to be a small amount of falling glass—better keep people away from the outside of the building for the next hour. It'll be better for everyone if no one gets hurt."

Devon hung up. Mike finished scoring the circle in the window and gently tapped out the glass inside. The fragments fell down towards the lower, broader section of the building. Some stayed on the horizontal step, others bounced off or were caught on the breeze and fell onwards into the paving stones around the building.

Mike took the circle cutter a few steps around the corner of the observation deck and started on the end window of that side.

From Hill Street, in the middle of Grand Park, Hugo noticed a difference in the flow of people in and out of City Hall. Looking again, he realized that people were still leaving, but no more were being allowed in. A couple of security guards came out, one going one way around the building and the other the other way. As they left, they glanced up occasionally. Hugo followed their eyes up a corner buttress to the top of the Art Deco tower. Nothing seemed untoward. He pushed his cart on towards the next pile of garbage.

On one side of the observation deck, holes had been made in the windows at both ends. At one end, one of the AFL men picked up a hooked metal rod and poked it through the hole. At the other end, another man hung a one-pound metal weight through the hole and paid out about fifty feet of rope. Then they started to swing it back and forth with greater and greater amplitude till the man at the other end could catch the weighted end in his hook. He drew it inside the building. Now the man at the other side of the room tied his end onto a roll of canvas and paid that out of the window as the other man pulled it towards him.

Hugo looped around to the northeast end of Grand Park and looked back to City Hall. People were still coming out, but some were hanging around the entrance without going in. As Hugo pushed his cart through the park, closer to City Hall, he could make out news crews with cameras among those pressing the security guards to let them nearer to the door. As he got closer still, he could hear the journalists shouting out to the city employees leaving the building, asking them what was going on.

Hugo turned aside, walked to the north side of the park, and carried on as far as the next trash can. But rather than looking inside, he looked up and down the building for anything untoward. After a few seconds, he caught sight of the rope outside the highest part of the building, swinging from one side to the other of the tower.

A minute later, Hugo saw a white banner being pulled across. When it reached the far side, it unfurled. It said "No more citizens deported" in English and Spanish. Hugo knew that this was why he'd been deployed here. He went back to picking up empty bottles and cans, but circling around City Hall. Half an hour later, a second banner hung across another side of the tower: "Prosecute ICE kidnappers."

Hugo kept at his work and looped back to Grand Park. Then he spotted the AFL man who'd asked him to go off-grid here. He caught his eye and the man followed Hugo as he pushed his cart under the shade of a tree towards the side of the park.

"It's happening," said Hugo as the man caught up with him. Hugo tipped his chin up towards the occupied top floors of City Hall.

"Yep."

"What's our role?"

"The situation is going to last a few days. Tonight, about seven p.m., I'll be on the street where you sleep, and I'll tell you more then."

Hugo nodded, and they parted company.

Hugo worked the area to the southwest of Grand Park, then headed east. The next banner atop City Hall said "Stop disappearing people."

He kept working on around, till he could see the back side of the tower: "End the American gulag."

Hugo smiled.

Carl was in the federal building downtown, digging up whatever he could find on Devon, Hugo and other AFL members.

His cell phone rang: his boss, Loy, from Sacramento.

"Which way are you facing?" Loy asked.

"Huh?"

Carl turned from his computer screen to look out of the window.

"I can see Union Station across Highway 101."

"Reid and his brazer army have taken over the Bradley Room at the top of City Hall. From the other side of your building, you'll be able to see their banners."

"Shit."

"We're putting together a task force with the FBI to clear them the hell out."

"What about the local cops?"

"Need-to-know basis. Put it that way."

Carl laughed. "Right. These days they're no better than the Tijuana chato."

In the Bradley Room, Devon was getting ready to go live on social media. Since the AFL had been declared a terrorist organization, it had lost its original channels, but he was going to livestream with a Mexican NGO, an ally of a US immigrants' rights group. The cell phone camera showed Devon at the lectern from which mayors were accustomed to make policy announcements and present awards. The shield of the City of Los Angeles had been replaced by the badge of the AFL. In the style of a military shoulder badge, it showed a flag with stripes like the American one, but with the rectangle of stars replaced by an oval globe, with the equator and curves of longitude. Behind him, a red velvet drape covered the window, going up, out of shot, as far as the ceiling.

The cell phone had been set up on a mini tripod on a table in front of the lectern. It was linked to a battery-powered wireless router blinking next to it on the table, from which a cable emerged and headed to the wall. An AFL member monitored the phone while another had logged in to the social media feed on a second phone, connected to the same router.

The presenter kicked off the session.

"Today we're glad to have with us Mr. Devon Reid, of the American Foreign Legion. Mr. Reid, please explain where you are and why."

"Thank you. I'm speaking from Los Angeles City Hall." He paused. "The American Foreign Legion has peacefully occupied the Bradley Room at the top of the building in order to protest against the illegal detentions and disappearances carried out by Immigration and Customs Enforcement and other federal agencies."

On the livestream, as Devon continued talking, the image cut away from him for a few seconds, to show still photos of the banners hanging from the building.

The AFL and its allies had put the word out to watch this NGO's channel, and the number of people in the stream was in the thousands.

Devon continued.

"Snatching people off the streets and deporting them without due process is against the laws and traditions of this country and is reminiscent of historic abuses that we thought would never happen again, such as the imprisonment of Japanese Americans in the 1940s, and the mass deportations from California in the 1930s."

More people were joining the livestream all the time, taking the number into the tens of thousands.

"Thank you," said the presenter. "And welcome to all those joining us in the livestream. Devon has agreed to reply to as many of your questions as we can fit in."

Downstairs, City Hall's IT people ran diagnostics and saw that Devon was physically connected into their network. But they couldn't immediately take him off-line without doing the same to themselves. It didn't help having to field angry calls from the city, state and federal authorities telling them to find a way.

The presenter started putting questions to Devon.

"Mr. Reid, your demands are expressed on the banners which you've hung from City Hall, is that right?"

"That's right. And please call me Devon, by the way."

"And to whom are you addressing those demands?"

"It's ICE that has been disappearing people, including citizens, off the streets and deporting them while pretending to their loved ones that they don't know where they are. That's where the change has got to start. ICE is a federal agency. It's the leadership of ICE and their bosses in Washington who must start acting lawfully."

"Have you and the AFL always been acting lawfully?"

"That's for a court to decide, but ICE bypasses courts and becomes judge, jury and executioner of people it targets."

The number on the livestream was into the hundreds of thousands.

Carl was still at work a couple of blocks away. He cursed at Devon on the livestream while he tried to call Loy in Sacramento. Loy had been in touch with the FBI, who'd told him that the FCC was working to shut down the livestream.

"Now I'm going to relay questions from those joining the livestream," said the presenter. "First, from Concerned Citizen in Houston, 'Why put yourself at risk by coming out of hiding into one of the most exposed locations imaginable?'"

"Our cause is just and deserves to be heard. That's what we're trying to achieve with the current action."

The presenter put in his own follow-up question. "But this can't end well for you, can it?"

"ICE doesn't have everything its own way anymore. They tried to kill me and I escaped. They tried to abduct Cheddi Maharaj and failed. They're on the defensive and we need to push them back further. They deport citizens, ignoring the courts, and it's our duty to stop that happening."

Devon was working up a head of steam.

"ICE has plainclothes snatch squads out there right now. We need to spot them and prevent them from illegally grabbing people off the streets and deporting them."

By now there were over a million on the livestream.

Downstairs, City Hall staff were homing in on how the AFL had spliced into their network. Now they were ignoring the mass of incoming calls and IMs, except those from their immediate bosses.

In the Brady Room, the presenter relayed another question to Devon.

"'What can people do to stop their friends and family being deported by ICE?'"

Counting off the steps to take, Devon raised his index finger.

"Prepare yourself. Look out for ICE surveillance vehicles."

Lifting his middle finger as well, making a V sign, he continued.

"Connect yourself. Keep your closest contacts up to date with where you are, and tell them if it seems that you're being followed."

Now he had three fingers lifted.

"Defend yourself. Know AFL members in your community. The AFL is the only group that is physically stopping illegal removals. ICE is end-running the courts by keeping prisoners incommunicado. ICE works in secret and is not accountable to anyone. We need the AFL to keep it in check."

Devon waited for the presenter to come back to him, but there was silence. Devon saw a movement at the edge of his field of view and glanced away from the camera to the AFL member with the second phone. He waved his fingers together horizontally in front of his throat, telling Hugo that the connection had been cut. Hugo raised his eyebrows at him quizzically.

"We got cut off just as you were finishing that last answer. Everyone will have understood you loud and clear."

55

Downtown Los Angeles

EARLY THAT evening, Hugo was waiting, sitting on his cardboard sheet, with his back against the chain-link fence.

Half an hour later, a panel van rolled slowly up the street. A speaker above the cab alternated between a choir singing snippets of hymns and a preacher declaiming how much Jesus loved sinners like himself.

The van pulled over. The driver and front passenger got out, walked around to the back and opened the doors. None of the homeless people moved, but Hugo recognized one of the evangelists as his AFL contact from Grand Park. The other took a sheaf of flyers from the back of the van and started up one side of the street, offering them to the residents, who ignored him. Hugo got up and walked over to the van. The AFL acknowledged him with a nod.

"Bring your cart over," he told Hugo.

56

Los Angeles City Hall

AT FIRST light, a squad of Humvees and Mine-Resistant Ambush Protected Vehicles, belonging to the FBI Counterterrorism Division and ICE Enforcement and Removal Operations, took the off-ramp from Route 101, swung back underneath it, and sped southwest on North Spring Street. Meanwhile, agents and officers of regular FBI and ICE units were blocking off streets around City Hall.

When he heard the vehicles and realized something was up, Hugo and the other veterans got inside the perimeter. The agents told them to get lost, but they just shuffled on a bit until the agents got fed up shouting at them. None of them wanted to be wrestling with a stink-infested homeless guy.

So Hugo had clear sight of the Humvees and MRAPs as they pulled up outside City Hall. A Bell helicopter flew low around the building, trying to spot any sniper lining up a shot from inside.

The federal agency vehicles pulled up at the bottom of the City Hall steps. Officers and agents poured out, carrying carbines and wearing helmets and body armor. A few of the men, including Carl Mack, stayed by the vehicles, alert to any attack from the ground or from the observation deck, where the AFL banners were still flying. The rest of the men walked warily up the steps and into the building. A couple of them hefted door-breaching rams and armored shields.

The ranking FBI agent outside the building swore as he saw a couple of camera crews taking up position just outside the perimeter. And a few other people seemed to have no better way to spend their morning than standing around pointing their cell phones at them and City Hall. Only now were the media being briefed by press officers back at HQ, but the news had already gotten out somehow.

Inside, City Hall was empty except for security guards. The others had been told not to come back till the occupation was over. The ranking agent spoke to the head security guard, who was waiting for them in the double-height Byzantine-style lobby. After a few words, the squad walked over to the elevators, black boots clicking on the circular floor mosaic, and went up to the express elevator to the twenty-second floor.

From Tijuana, the AFL started to livestream from the phones of people outside City Hall, alternating between shots of the federal agency vehicles parked outside, the helicopter circling, and the banners outside the observation deck.

On Temple Street, a couple of blocks from City Hall, Hugo was pushing his cart towards an ICE ERO officer standing by his black truck, which was marking a perimeter around City Hall. Hugo ignored the officer's call to stop. The officer drew his sidearm, but still Hugo walked on. Hugo held the officer's gaze rather than glancing to the side, where another homeless veteran was sidling up. As the officer raised his pistol and aimed it at Hugo, the other veteran tasered the officer's neck. The pistol clattered to the ground as its owner went into rigor and toppled over.

Hugo stepped over and cuffed the ICE officer's hands behind his back with a zip tie. He allowed himself half of a second to look down and enjoy the sight of the twitching officer. Then he fished out a walkie-talkie, body armor, and an M4 from his cart. He walked around to the front passenger door of the ICE truck, putting on the body armor as he went. He sat next to the other veteran, who was already behind the wheel. Hugo squeezed the bar on the side of the walkie-talkie.

"Unit three ready."

"Roger, unit three. Stand by," came the response.

Hugo looked over to the driver.

"All set?" he asked Hugo, who just smiled back.

They checked in with three other units over the ICE radio.

Then a pause.

"Go, go, go."

Hugo and the driver turned their heads to the right and waited silently. A second later, another ICE truck appeared from the next side street and headed towards them, gathering speed as it came. As it passed, Hugo's driver pulled out and fell in behind. A few seconds later, they turned right onto North Spring Street. They approached the cluster of vehicles that had brought in the task force.

From the far side, the southwest, another two ICE vehicles were also closing in fast. Beyond those were another two. Hugo looked in the side mirror and saw two more coming up behind their own trucks.

The FBI and ICE men watched their own vehicles approaching with puzzlement. An FBI agent radioed the field base to ask why ICE had left the perimeter. The helicopter told them what they already knew, that eight vehicles were closing in. By the time the field base came back to say that they had no idea, the first four captured trucks had slammed to a halt, their radiator grilles pointed at the assault team's vehicles.

Loy had come down to Los Angeles to join the task force. In the federal building, a couple of blocks from City Hall, he swore at the AFL livestream, and again when he saw the number of viewers.

Inside City Hall, the main assault group had come out of the elevator on the twenty-second floor. They found it deserted except for one security guard, who nodded nervously at the black-armored task force men. The lead officer barely acknowledged the guard as he led the team around towards the stairs. Outside the stairwell, those responsible for breaching doors got into formation and, on the signal from their leader, burst through behind the shield, weapons at the ready. Nothing. So much the better. They went up the stairs slowly, single file, some watching what was in front of them, others scanning the next sections of stairway for hostile intent. Via their radios, they heard the vehicle crews questioning what was going on, but there was no reason for them to slow down their ascent.

On the plaza outside the building, AFL men opened the driver and passenger doors of the first four vehicles and took up position behind the doors, aiming their carbines at the federal vehicles. On seeing the guns being pointed at him, Carl opened fire with his own M4 on one of the AFL vehicles. The men there returned fire and an ICE officer was hit in the chest by multiple rounds and knocked back onto the ground. Carl recognized Hugo and concentrated his fire on him.

Inside the building, the assault group was approaching the door to the twenty-fifth floor when they heard the shooting from the plaza over the radio, echoed as the sounds reached them directly. The ranking agent shouted over the radio.

"Vehicle one, do you copy?"

No answer.

"Base, what the hell?"

"The vehicles are taking fire," came the reply over the radio.

"Is our situation stable?"

"Negative."

The agent swore before replying.

"We're returning to the plaza."

"Roger."

He looked at the other men in the squad and spoke to them over the sound of gunfire, which continued to reach them.

"The men maintaining position by the vehicles are under heavy attack. That's obvious. We're going back down to the plaza to counterattack."

No one liked having to retreat when there was a single door separating them from their quarry, but defending their comrades took priority over everything else. They headed back down towards the main elevator on the twenty-second floor.

The livestream showed the firefight from different sides of the plaza and was adding thousands of viewers every minute.

The livestream chyron explained that ICE and FBI were trying to storm City Hall to end the AFL protest. It called on all citizens and noncitizens to converge on the area to stop the federal agencies capturing and disappearing Devon and other AFL members.

Outside the Spring Street entrance to the building, Hugo recognized Carl among the task force personnel, but told himself to keep taking the best shot he had at them, whether or not it was Carl.

Whenever an FBI agent or ICE officer showed from behind their vehicles to take a shot, they came under heavy return fire. After a few minutes, and a couple of casualties on each side, the gunfire stopped, with the task force pinned down.

The perimeter around City Hall now had huge gaps, and civilian cars and pedestrians started coming through, whether answering the call to activism from the livestream or just out of curiosity. The few ICE officers left on the perimeter were stranded and were told to concentrate in Grand Park outside City Hall, but the streets were jammed. The ICE officers asked for permission to use force to get through. In the federal building, Loy didn't want to make that call himself and told them to stand by. The officers had to hunker down and bite their tongues as their vehicles got buffeted and abused by the crowds heading to the City Hall.

Inside the building, the elevator reached the ground floor with the first group of the assault squad. As the doors opened, the men split, some running to the left and some to the right, to avoid any gunfire coming through the main door. They skirted around and approached the door from each side. Once there, they could see AFL outside in their captured agency trucks but didn't open fire. By now the rest of the assault squad had come down in the other elevator and were joining them.

The ranking agent sized up the situation. It was a standoff. The AFL had control of the street and park outside. If the federal forces tried to break out of the building, they'd be picked off. But, equally, the AFL wouldn't be able to take the building from the plaza. He briefly asked himself what would happen if the AFL men in the observation deck came down to simultaneously attack them from the other side, but he pushed that thought aside.

He spoke to his superiors over the radio.

"When can we expect reinforcements?"

"We're readying helos. Stand by."

"Roger."

On Loy's screen, he could see people still flowing into the City Hall area.

He'd been trying to get the police commissioner on the line, and finally he got through.

"Good morning, Commissioner."

"Morning."

"Our men are surrounded at City Hall, and we can't get reinforcements through as long as the streets are filled with people bent on obstructing us."

"So, you dove into this situation without consulting us and now you want us to fix it for you?"

"We can debrief later, but my concern now is the safety of our men."

"If the LAPD goes in with force now, it'll only inflame the situation and turn the population against us as well."

Loy waited for the commissioner to say more.

"We're sending officers to keep the demonstrators away from the disputed area. That should stabilize the situation and give you time to find a way out."

"Thank you, Commissioner."

They hung up.

Loy hadn't expected much more. The sooner the helicopters got there, the better.

His thoughts were interrupted by a distorted voice speaking over a bullhorn, coming over the livestreams.

"Hugo Ayala of the AFL. Tell your recon helicopter to pick you up in groups and take you to LAPD Hooper Heliport. Leave your weapons behind. You have one hour to complete the operation. Any other helicopter approaching City Hall will be shot down."

"Jesus," Loy said to himself.

He looked across the table at Hany Nader, the agent in charge of the FBI side of the task force.

"It's plausible. Plenty of MANPADS for sale out there."

"It'd be like Mogadishu trying to get ground reinforcements through." Nader frowned at him.

After a second, Loy continued. "Let's get our men out first."

Nader nodded.

Loy relayed the decision to the officer in command in the vehicles pinned down outside City Hall. In turn, he replied over his bullhorn to Hugo.

"The helicopter's going to land, like you said, to start taking us out."

"Roger. Remember, leave your weapons behind."

By now crowds had welled up to the edges of the plaza in front of City Hall. LAPD officers had squeezed their way through and stood between the crowd and the armed standoff.

The Bell helicopter, which had been circling the City Hall tower, landed on the plaza, and opened its side door. It kept its engines running while two pairs of men approached, each carrying an injured squad member. The crowds chanted anti-*migra* slogans as the ICE and FBI men climbed inside. The helicopter gingerly lifted off again and flew up and past the north side of City Hall, towards the police heliport, jeered by the crowd.

A few minutes later the helicopter was back to take the last of the men from the vehicles.

Now there was just the assault team, inside the ground floor of the building. Unlike the men outside in the vehicles, they hadn't yet come under fire and had no casualties.

Their agent in charge spoke to the task force base in the federal building over the radio.

"We don't want to lay down our weapons to these reject joes. We're in a good position. They can't touch us."

Nader tended to prefer persuasion over pulling rank.

"They can't touch you, but you can't get out. You saw that they let the rest of your team go with no catches. Those guys are already leaving the heliport on their way back to their units. We can't get any reinforcements to you now without a bloodbath. The risks of evacuating are much less than staying put."

"Roger, out," the field agent replied grudgingly.

The helicopter was audible again.

Out in front of City Hall, Hugo and the others waited as the pitch of the helicopter engine lowered and it settled down onto its metal runners. Hugo imagined himself in the position of the men inside the building. He wouldn't want to leave under conditions imposed by the enemy. He kept watching the entrance.

One of the doors opened. An FBI agent appeared and walked briskly towards the helicopter. He didn't have his hands up. But Hugo couldn't see any weapon either.

"Hold your fire," he said over the radio to the other AFL men.

By now, other FBI and ICE men were following the first one out of City Hall and towards the helicopter.

The crowd jeered as the last of the group boarded the helicopter, and it took off again.

From the federal building, Nader spoke on the radio to plainclothes agents mingling in the crowd.

"Keep your eyes on Ayala. He's the highest-value target."

The helicopter landed again. The last of the assault team came out of the building and boarded the helicopter.

A shout went up from the crowd.

"Occupy City Hall!"

The helicopter engines upped their pitch as they took the weight, and the metal runners twitched on the ground.

In the federal building, Loy and Nader saw the same message run along the ticker at the bottom of the livestreams: "Occupy City Hall!"

"What's going on?" Lay called over the radio.

"Some people are trying to push through the police cordon."

The helicopter put a foot of air between itself and the ground.

On the southeastern corner of Grand Park, the crowd squeezed down the side of the criminal justice center and past the end of the police line. Encouraged, the crowd surged forward in a couple of other places. Over the police radio, the chief told the LAPD officers to hold fire unless they were in personal danger.

Hugo and the others started to take off their body armor.

The helicopter was twenty feet into the air and turned to follow its course north of City Hall.

The crowd chanted "Occupy City Hall" and burst through the middle of the LAPD line. Seeing this directly, or on the livestreams, those demonstrators who were further away, in Grand Park and on Spring Street to the north and south, pushed forward.

Over his radio, Loy told his agents to move with the crowd and get to the AFL vehicles.

The LAPD stopped trying to hold their line and the crowd surged through towards City Hall. The demonstrators ran past Hugo and the other AFL men, who had shed all their military gear and were ordinary homeless men again.

The FBI plainclothes agents went with the flow of the crowd. They'd lost sight of Hugo and the others, but tried to edge towards the AFL vehicles.

The crowd reached City Hall, but the metal-paneled outer doors had already been shut. The demonstrators banged and yelled fruitlessly.

Pushed this way and that by the crowd, Hugo remembered what he'd learned in his scuba training. When the pull is strong, go with it. When it eases off for a second, inch yourself towards your goal.

As more and more people entered the plaza, those at the doors had to put their energy into pushing back against the crowd, rather than futile efforts to get in.

Around Hugo, the flow towards City Hall slackened, and he was able to take more steps the other way, heading south towards Spring Street.

Agents reached the ICE vehicle that Hugo had appropriated. A protester was on top of it, stomping dents in the roof. The agents looked inside and saw that it was empty except for body armor and weapons. They looked up and scanned the crowd in vain, looking for the AFL men.

57

Federal Building, Los Angeles

An hour later, Loy and Nader joined a conference call with their heads of department in Washington. After hearing the situation report, the secretary of Homeland Security was livid.

"So the lowlifes can stick around for days, hang up whatever slogans they want from City Hall, putting out whatever propaganda they want on social media, telling everyone how they kicked our asses. We can't just wait and watch while that happens. We're going to get ahead of the curve on this thing."

58

Inglewood, Los Angeles

THE NEXT morning, Joseph had just turned up for his shift at the ambulance depot when a couple of ICE vehicles swooped across the gate and blocked it. Officers got out of each vehicle and unholstered their sidearms, stopping any vehicle or staff member from leaving. Behind them, a minibus pulled up and let out a dozen more officers, some of them bleary-eyed from having flown in overnight.

The officers streamed in, shouting at the employees that it was a police operation and that everyone should stay where they were. The head of the office took out his phone and started livestreaming the raid, till an ICE officer knocked the phone out of his hand and smashed it under his foot.

Joseph had tried to prepare for this moment. He ran out the back door of the office and scrambled up onto the hood of an ambulance that was parked there, waiting to be taken for repairs. But the raid had too many officers. One of them saw Joseph and was after him immediately. Trying to jump onto the roof of the ambulance, he tripped over the wide pod of lights that stood out from the windshield. The officer grabbed Joseph's foot but was left holding just his shoe as he twisted it off and clambered up onto the roof. But the officer was right behind him now and tripped Joseph as he tried to vault over the fence and into the alley beyond. Joseph fell short and ended up grabbing razor wire with both hands. The officer jumped down and waited. Joseph tried to pull himself up and over the fence, but his feet couldn't get traction, and the razor wire just cut deeper into his hands. His body would do no more and Joseph started to weep. The ICE officer watched Joseph swinging by his hands from the razor wire and chuckled as he waited for him to fall.

Other ambulance depots were being raided simultaneously across Los Angeles. The FBI was joining ICE on the grounds that federal funds were involved via a scheme for deprived areas. All of the raids were livestreamed. Within a few hours, as the shortage of ambulances became felt, social media was thick with people desperate over family members who were comatose after strokes or in agony after accidents or shootings. Although the AFL had been skimming money charged for unnecessary ambulance trips, now the raids had also taken out of service those that did answer emergency calls.

Social media channels in California, and not just those favoring the AFL, railed against ICE and the FBI for causing unnecessary deaths.

Crowds grew around the federal buildings near downtown LA and in Wilshire, stopping employees from getting in or out.

There were louder and louder calls for the governor of California to step in. Vijay Jain was a billionaire thanks to the success of a health care fintech company he'd founded. He'd self-financed his campaign and, after his election, had gradually withdrawn behind a circle of advisers, mostly Silicon Valley cronies, as he lost patience with the glad-handing that was a customary requirement of political success. The day after the ICE raids, he called a press conference to announce actions that he hoped would bolster both sides of his centrist position.

First he reconstituted the California State Police, which had been absorbed into the California Highway Patrol back twenty years earlier. He signed it back into existence, with its old seven-point star badge, and gave a press conference in which she said its mission was to protect all Californians. That was code for citizens plus immigrants. The leadership team of the new state police was lifted from the CHP, but the governor planned for it to grow to thousands of officers. The ICE and the FBI spat blood when they heard about the new CSP, but there was nothing they could do except brief the press against it.

Then, for the benefit of his more conservative supporters, he fired Gabriel Rangel, the activist attorney general who'd forced ICE out of the courthouses where they were arresting people. In his place the governor appointed Micah Ovey, a former corporate lawyer who had helped him put together his tech corporation.

59

East Hollywood, Los Angeles

RAUL WAS driving away from the care home after a day at work when a call came in from an unknown number. He picked up.

"Raul?"

"What's up?"

"I'm calling from the AFL. At midnight tonight, recruitment is going to start for the new California State Police. We think you'd be an outstanding recruit. Why don't you get your resume and official documents together, ready to apply?"

"Thanks for the heads-up."

Even without any advertising, there were soon over a hundred applicants for each post in the new CSP. The governor restricted recruitment to US citizens, but a big proportion of the applicants had been born abroad or were children of immigrants. Those with firearms training could follow a fast track through training.

60

San Francisco Peninsula, California

THE CALIFORNIA National Guard Armory was across Highway 101 from the San Francisco International Airport. Raul was part of a California State Police team that rolled up there one Sunday morning. They left in a vehicle that looked like an old-fashioned articulated truck, carrying a giant steel wedge the size of a building.

The following day, the National Guard officer in charge of maintaining the vehicle access control log handed in his resignation, as did the officer in charge of maintaining inventory. The same day, the president of the United States activated Title 10 to put the California National Guard under the control of the Department of Defense. As the order was being signed, US Army officers were already driving from Camp Parks and up and over the foothills of the Diablo Range. They crossed the bay on the San Mateo–Hayward Bridge and took command of the Armory.

By then, the six-axle truck from the armory had reached San Diego and parked at a site that had been assigned from the Bureau of Land Management to the CSP.

The following morning, the truck fired up again and headed back towards the coast. After half an hour, half a dozen ex-Army Humvees, recently bought for the CSP, fell in behind the truck and followed it in formation, all of them rumbling at a steady fifty miles per hour.

As the convoy passed to the north of Chula Vista, a couple of minibuses joined. Following the truck, they all doubled back on Highway 5, and, short of the San Ysidro border crossing, turned south and stopped at the water treatment plant. The Tijuana River, the stinking channel that Valentina has passed on her entry to Mexico, carried on to here, and whenever it filled in a flash flood, the plant had to work to capacity, filtering out the detritus.

A CSP officer opened the passenger door of the truck, climbed down onto the road, and walked over to the control booth at the side of the treatment plant's entry gate. In his hand he had a clipboard with half a dozen sheets of paper that ruffled in the breeze. The officer spoke with the security guard, showed him some papers, waited while he phoned the main building, and joked with him while he waited for the call back. After twenty minutes, in which the CSP officer tried to avoid scanning the horizon and the skies for Border Patrol vehicles, the guard lifted the bar on the entry gate and the convoy went through into the water plant.

At the far side of the lot, the driver turned the truck and backed it up to the fence along the southern edge. Beyond the fence was the International Highway, which ran along the geographical border but which carried only Mexican traffic. The fence was effectively the border, because the south side of the highway was open to a northern suburb of Tijuana.

A couple of the CSP Humvees had stayed close to the entrance gate. Their officers got out, apparently to stretch their legs but really to size up the location. The other two Humvees, and the minibuses, had followed the truck and parked a hundred meters away.

By now the truck had been picked up on the CCTV monitoring screens in the Border Patrol building in Chula Vista, the headquarters of the CBP San Diego sector. They glanced curiously at the wedge-shaped load on the back, but their remit was people heading the other way, into the US from Mexico.

With the truck in position, instead of turning off the engine, the driver revved it harder as hydraulic feet extended down from the truck, met the ground, and took the truck's weight off its wheels, stabilizing it.

Then the enormous steel wedge started to lift off the bed of the trailer, pushed by a hydraulic ram.

Two CSP officers got out of one of the Humvees. Each took a coil of rope from the back of the vehicle, then they walked over to the back of the truck, by the pointed end of the steel wedge.

61

Tijuana, Mexico

VALENTINA WAS in a motel on the southern side of the border, opposite the water treatment plant. At least, it called itself a motel, but the only parking was on the street out front. Valentina knew from Daniel that something was going to happen today. When she'd first gotten to the motel in the early afternoon of the day before, she'd found herself waiting in line with others with the same fish-out-of-water body language.

After checking in, she'd gone back out onto the street and then north to the end of the block. The street led directly onto the International Highway that went to the San Ysidro crossing. Although legal, it would've been difficult to access the highway from the street, just because the asphalt ended in a step down of a couple of feet, strewn with trash and chunks of concrete.

Valentina had stood and looked across the road, which had two lanes in each direction, separated by a median with a few straggly bushes trying to sprout pale pink flowers. Beyond the traffic was the border fence, made up of parallel vertical steel cylinders.

Later that afternoon, an AFL man had come to the motel with a couple of technicians and they recorded her story on video in her room in the motel. They put a cell phone on a lightweight tripod and she told them what'd happened to her. How she'd been abducted illegally, how she'd been disappeared into the immigration gulag, and how she'd been forced across the border, to a country she didn't know, without being able to contact her family, a lawyer, or anyone else.

After they finished recording, the technicians left, and an AFL man asked her if she was willing to try to get back across the border into the US. Valentina asked some questions and found out that the AFL had identified a group of about twenty illegally deported people. They had worked out a way that wasn't risk-free but that had a good chance of getting her back, and humiliating ICE and other federal authorities. They had her at that point, but Valentina told herself to think it through clearly. It wasn't right that she'd been arbitrarily detained and deported without having done anything wrong. And Hugo was still in the US without anywhere else to go. She told the AFL man to count her in.

Now, the following morning, Daniel and another man came to her room and told her to go down to the lobby of the hotel. Not for the first time, he told her that she couldn't take any bags, that any documents and money she had should be in a money belt or otherwise concealed in her clothes, and that she shouldn't have any bag or scarf or anything that could get caught up or snagged.

Other guests had already come down. They filled the lobby and spilled out into the narrow corridor that led to the street entrance.

62

South Estuary Water Plant, California

THE METAL wedge on the trailer had been pushed vertical by the hydraulic ram. The thick end of the wedge was now thirty feet in the air. It carried on past the vertical and started to unhinge into two.

The truck was a mobile bridge, designed to get tanks and other military vehicles over rivers.

The narrow end of the wedge was still close to the ground and bifurcated as the bridge unfolded. Each CSP officer tied one end of their rope to a ring attachment point at the far side of the bridge. As the central hinge lowered again and the bridge flattened out, the men moved along its length, using carabiners to clip the rope to the rings.

By now, the CSP team had caught the attention of the Border Patrol officers a few miles away in the San Ysidro base. The officers watching the surveillance cameras didn't know what to make of it and kicked it up to their bosses in the Department of Homeland Security. Before long, the head of DHS in California was on the phone to the headquarters of the California State Police. There, the second-in-command said that the chief wasn't available but the CSP vehicles near the border were just doing an exercise. The DHS state head knew he was being stonewalled but kept his replies polite while he thought of other angles to get traction on whatever game the state police were playing.

Meanwhile, the bridge had reached halfway across the International Highway, stretching and reaching lower to the ground as it unfolded. Cars on the highway slowed down to rubberneck.

In the motel lobby, an AFL man read out half a dozen names, Valentina's among them. They made their way towards the front door, elated and grinning at each other. Another AFL man led them out onto the street, with the one from the lobby following up behind. When they turned north, they took a step back on seeing the mobile bridge silhouetted against the sky.

The head of DHS in California gave up trying to get answers from the CSP and called his own people back instead. Fifteen minutes later, a convoy of half a dozen light trucks rolled out of the Chula Vista base, carrying a team of armed Border Patrol agents.

The deportees walked as far as the International Highway, then turned and carried on alongside as far as an abandoned, derelict house.

The mobile bridge had reached all the way across the highway and was settling on top of the uneven parapet above the house's facade.

The lead AFL man showed the deportees through the empty doorway of the house, up the bare stairway, and through another empty doorway onto the flat roof. A few items of clothing remained from its time as a laundry zone, bleached and baked by the sun onto its unpainted cement. By now the roadway of the mobile bridge had come to rest, with one end projecting over the parapet into the footprint of the house, a couple of feet over the flat roof.

Valentina and the other deportees could see along the line of the bridge. A couple of CSP officers were coming from the American side towards them over the bridge, clipped to the ropes that they'd laid along the sides of the bridge.

The two AFL men on the Mexican side stepped up onto the bridge and, like the CSP men, clipped themselves to the ropes. One of them held out his hand to Valentina and the other to the next member of the group, a pudgy young man with a ponytail. He and Valentina stepped up onto the mobile bridge. Then another pair was handed up, so there were two with each AFL member. They started to walk along the bridge towards the American side. At first Valentina was just walking a few feet above the roof terrace of the house. When she stepped over the edge of the parapet, there was a fifteen-foot drop onto the International Highway.

Her legs weakened and she leaned against the AFL man who was guiding her over. She got her breath back and carried on. She tried not to look down but could sense that the traffic was backed up on each side of the mobile bridge.

When she was over the median line of the road, the AFL man handed her over to a CSP officer, who guided her in the same way over the last two lanes. She realized that she'd almost made it, and started to take in the situation. She looked down at the border fence and enjoyed a sense of revenge for the way ICE had abused her. She looked a bit further again, saw the cab of the truck, the Humvees parked beside it, and beyond them the hills inland from San Diego. She almost turned her head to look for the ocean but the idea made her feel faint again. Then she was at the end of the bridge and another CSP officer helped her down the side of the truck and onto American soil. She hugged the CSP officer then turned to look back towards Mexico. Another batch of four deportees were heading towards her.

She turned round to look north. She couldn't help flinching when she saw Border Patrol vehicles at the gate of the lot.

"Don't worry," said the state police officer. "You're Valentina Díaz, right?"

She nodded.

"Have you got photo ID?"

She shook her head.

"We're going to take your photo to check against California State databases, OK?"

She nodded, and the officer took her photo with a mobile phone app.

"You're good," he said, waving her towards one of the Humvees. When she got there, she saw that the man who'd come over the bridge with her was in the front passenger seat.

The side door was open. Valentina looked across and to the opposite seat, where another state police officer was sitting. On the panel between them was a portable printer. It spat out a laminated card, the officer asked her to confirm her name again, and then he gave her the card. It was her new ID for the State of California.

The federal officers were having a harder time negotiating entry to the water plant than the CSP had. The Border Patrol didn't have a warrant, and it didn't help to have the CSP staring them down from inside the fence.

After about ten minutes, the guard called over Raul and handed him the phone. It was the head of the CSP, the same guy who'd been too busy to speak to DHS half an hour earlier. The two of them spoke for a couple of minutes, then Raul came out of the booth, walked over to the gate, and gestured to the lead Border Patrol truck that they should talk.

It took Raul an effort to keep his game face when he saw Tyler, his ex-boss, get out of the passenger side of the truck and walk towards him. Tyler spoke first, pretending not to recognize Raul.

"We need you to hand over the illegals you've got there."

Raul didn't answer. Tyler gritted his teeth and carried on.

"You tried to sneak them back in and got caught. Let's wrap this up and get back to chasing bad guys, not each other."

"All the people in our care have the right to be in the US," replied Raul.

"So why did they need to scramble over a metal gangplank instead of the border crossing?"

"You know why. Because ICE snatch squads have been disappearing people illegally."

Tyler tried another tack.

"Your new state police has been patched together in the past couple of weeks. You can't win a face-off with Homeland Security and the FBI."

Raul pretended to ponder.

"Let's pick this back up in thirty minutes," he said, turning away from Tyler and heading back to his Humvee.

Tyler cursed under his breath at Raul's back.

In the Humvee, Raul closed the door and took out his cell phone. As he dialed CSP HQ in Sacramento, he turned to the driver and smirked confidently as he put the call on speaker. The chief picked up.

"Going to plan so far," said Raul. "The Border Patrol is blustering. With the force they have here, that's all they can do for now."

"But they can stop you from leaving?"

"On the main access road, yes. They've got six trucks outside the gate."

"How many have we repatriated?"

Raul looked over to the driver, who used his hands and fingers to show him the count.

"Sixteen, sir."

The driver stepped out and down of the Humvee and looked south.

"And the other four?" asked the chief.

Raul looked at the driver and translated his gestures.

"On the bridge with our men, sir, almost over."

"Roger. So far so good."

The chief hung up.

"I'm going to keep those idiots waiting," Raul told the driver, gesturing to the Border Patrol trucks on the other side of the fence.

On the south side of the lot, by the border fence, the last of the twenty had made it over and been repatriated. The mobile bridge was already starting to fold up again and had cleared the roof terrace on the other side of the highway.

Valentina and the others were divided into two groups and each boarded one of the minibuses parked by the mobile bridge.

On the far side of the fence, Tyler had reported back to base. The chain of command up to DHS realized that they were being stonewalled.

From the far side of the fence, the Border Patrol officers could see some of the state police approaching the wire mesh fence that divided the water treatment plant from a public road to the west. They called their base to get them to direct their cameras that way, and were told that the state police seemed to be preparing to cut through the fence.

Raul saw some civilian vehicles coming south towards the water treatment plant. He climbed down out of his Humvee and started walking back towards the Border Patrol trucks. Tyler did likewise and they met at the gate.

Raul waited for Tyler to speak.

"We can't let these people just disappear back into the crowd."

"Do you think that's what we want?" Raul replied. "The better documented they are, the harder it'll be for ICE to abduct them again."

This was more like what Tyler wanted to hear. He gestured at the state police officers by the far corner of the fence.

"Do you think we don't have other vehicles closing down other roads?"

Raul affected to let that sink in before he replied. "We want to take these repatriated people to the San Diego Central Courthouse."

Tyler tried not to show his relief. "Those people are wanted by federal agencies."

Now Raul acknowledged his history with Tyler. "Remember how we kept people out of courts because immigration was an administrative matter, not a crime?"

"What are you going to book them for, trespassing?" He reckoned that the CSP was trying to keep the deportees under their control, while hoping that something would turn up to stop the federal agencies from getting their shot at them down the road. But the Border Patrol would back themselves in a long game.

"Let's say that several of them are pursuing complaints related to their treatment."

"So, we leave peacefully, and go in convoy to the courthouse?"

Raul grimaced as if to say that maybe that could work. He turned and walked back towards his colleagues.

Ten minutes later the state police Humvees filed out of the water treatment plant. They'd agreed that a Border Patrol truck could lead the convoy, with the others at the rear. The truck with the mobile bridge stayed behind. The convoy headed north, past the civilians, who recorded them on their phones as they drove past.

In a few minutes the convoy turned onto Interstate 5, heading north. Ten minutes later the ocean came into view, and they drove the length of San Diego Bay, past the naval base, before taking the off-ramp towards downtown.

63

Downtown San Diego

THE SAN Diego Central Courthouse was more than twenty stories high, beige like its neighbors, but newer and shinier. Its footprint was more than doubled by an enormous soffit: a flat expanse of metal, sculpted into waves on the lower side, which projected out beyond the top floor, sloping rakishly down from one end to the other.

The convoy of state and federal vehicles pulled up at the street-level entrance at the southeast corner of the building. The state police officers escorted Valentina and the others up the concrete steps. Tyler and three other CBP officers got out of their trucks and followed. The state police ignored them, but the courthouse guards let them in.

It was another couple of floors up escalators to the reception level. The foyer opened onto a plaza that was exposed to the winds but shaded by the soffit twenty stories above.

Raul spoke to a clerk standing behind a desk, then stepped over to a state police colleague and had a few words in his ear. Then he walked over to Tyler, who was trying to look like he was doing something constructive rather than eavesdropping.

"In the public spaces you can follow us around like dogs, but you won't be allowed in the courtrooms."

"Like hell," his ex-boss reacted indignantly. "We've got a right to be in the gallery and see the proceedings."

"With certain exceptions. I'm just telling you as a courtesy, trying to avoid a confrontation outside the courtroom."

Raul turned on his heel and nodded at his colleague as he walked off.

Tyler spluttered as he reached for his phone and tagged along behind Raul and half of the repatriates, who included Valentina. The other half followed the state police that Raul had spoken to, and Tyler gesticulated at one of his subordinates to follow them. Tyler forced himself into the same elevator as Raul and the others, then cursed as he lost his cell phone signal on the way up.

They spilled out on the central corridor of the eighth floor. Raul led them to the main door of one of the courtrooms. One of the guards started to check their IDs against a list she had in a tablet computer. Valentina was nodded through, based on the new ID she'd been given in the Humvee.

Tyler jostled through the others up to the door, waved his Border Patrol ID at the guard, and tried to bluster his way past her.

"These people are wanted by the Department of Homeland Security—we need to keep tabs on them."

"Sir, the session is in camera," the guard replied without looking up from her tablet.

"Don't you understand that we're talking about the integrity of our border?"

But the guard was already checking the ID of the next repatriate.

Tyler told his deputy to note the names of the people going into the courtroom, then stepped back. He walked down the corridor to another courtroom where the same situation was being played out with the other half of the repatriates.

He walked to the end of the corridor, where he wouldn't be overheard, called his boss, and told him that the proceedings were being held in camera.

"The state police seem to be putting some token charges onto those deportees, but how can they be in camera?" his boss replied.

Tyler took it as a rhetorical question and didn't answer.

"I'll ask around the lawyers here," continued his boss. "And I'll see if I can get some FBI agents to tail the deportees when they come out."

"Yes, sir."

"Alright, keep me posted."

With about ten people to be heard in each courtroom, Tyler knew there wouldn't be news quickly.

It was late afternoon when Raul came back out of the courtroom with the other couple of state police officers.

Raul looked askance at Tyler as he walked past him towards the elevators.

Tyler ignored him and waited for the ex-deportees to follow the police out of the courtroom. But they didn't. Raul stepped into the courtroom, but there was no one but clerks, a stenographer and the guards.

Tyler cursed and turned on his heel. He ran down the corridor and caught up with Raul. "What the hell?"

"They went out through chambers," replied Raul innocently. "I'm going to save you some time by telling you what's going on."

They both knew that he was telling Tyler just to see him squirm.

"The State of California's case is that the people we repatriated today were the subject of illegal detention and deportation."

"Case against who?" asked Tyler warily.

"Against ICE and CBP."

Tyler was lost for words. Only after Raul had turned away to face the elevators did he answer.

"So if they're making cases against us, where the hell are they?"

"Do you think they're going to walk around openly, as long as you can pick them up, disappear them, and deport them again?"

Tyler glowered, as if answering that would be beneath him.

The elevator pinged as its doors opened.

"They're in witness protection."

Tyler didn't get it.

"*California* witness protection," continued Raul before turning away and entering the elevator.

Tyler watched the elevator doors close, not liking the feeling of being at a disadvantage.

He reached for his phone but this time dialed the compliance desk at CBP in Chula Vista. He asked to be informed of any Federal Tort Claims Act forms filed in California over the next few days against them or against ICE.

64

Lennox, Los Angeles

CALIFORNIA WITNESS Protection put Valentina in a cheap motel in Lennox, under the LAX inbound flight path. They told her not to go out of the motel or even to call anyone. They brought her three lukewarm meals a day in styrofoam boxes. For a couple of days it all suited Valentina just fine. She slept more and more hours each night, so she realized how stressed she'd been, and not just from the deportation itself. Even when the AFL had taken care of her on the Mexican side of the border, she'd still been on edge, from being somewhere she didn't belong. Now she could listen to the sounds of the city, to the voices of the other guests behind the door in the corridor, or through the wall in the next rooms, and she absorbed it all, imagining herself part of it again.

On the third day, the walked out onto Century Boulevard, got herself a burner phone, and caught up with the news. The governor hadn't been able to appoint his new attorney general because he'd been in the capitol in Sacramento at the time of the announcement, and the demonstrators had stopped him from leaving. Rangel was defying the governor and continuing to act as AG. The incoming AG, Jed Abad, was being painted as a stooge of the federal government who wanted to let ICE roam free in state and local courthouses again. More and more people were camping in State Capitol Park, and the demonstrators were controlling who entered and left the building.

65

Lennox, Los Angeles

NORTH SPRING Street and Grand Park were filled with crowds day and night. Hugo still slept each night on his cardboard mat a couple of blocks away. Every day he criss-crossed the territory that he'd established for himself, gradually pushing back the other homeless recyclers. A couple of days after the defeat of the FBI attempt to storm the City Hall observation deck, Luke found Hugo digging into a dumpster a couple of blocks from the park.

"You didn't give a sniff to the feebs."

Hugo nodded.

Before continuing, the AFL man sipped coffee from his cardboard cup.

"You can imagine, they've been getting ridiculed on social media, TV, everywhere."

Hugo still waited.

"One guy that has gone quiet is Cheddi Maharaj."

Hugo grunted. He didn't want to be reminded of his part in freeing Maharaj.

"That's going to change now."

Now Hugo met Luke's gaze skeptically.

"ICE can't operate freely everywhere anymore. Maharaj has been in a safe place, obviously, but we need to keep momentum, keep getting stronger relative to the federal agencies. Maharaj has been going stir-crazy not being able to speak out, says that it's worse than being holed up like before. Now we're going to grant him his wish.

"For now we're going to keep him east of downtown, between the Los Angeles River and Rio Hondo. No ICE or FBI are going in there anymore."

"At least, not overtly," Hugo added.

"Right. There's still a risk."

Hugo raised his eyebrows, as if to say that he didn't need to be told that.

"I know you're still a wanted man. It's up to you. Now we've got some kind of safe spaces. We thought you'd like to come out of hiding even if there is a chance you'll be snatched."

Hugo nodded, acquiescing.

"And, like I said, if we don't keep building every day, and keeping the federal agencies on the defensive, then they'll take back the initiative and crush us."

"I'm in."

"So, when he speaks publicly, Maharaj is going to need more security."

"A PSD," said Hugo doubtfully, thinking back to his time in Yemen. "Something like that," said Luke.

Luke drank the last of his coffee and tossed the cup into Hugo's cart. Hugo held back the impulse to deck him.

"There's enough there for a cheap hotel tonight in Boyle Heights. I guess it'll be good to shower again."

When the AFL man had gone, Hugo picked the coffee cup out of the cart. Between the sleeve and the cup were a couple of hundred-dollar bills.

66

East LA, Los Angeles

JUST AFTER nine the next morning, Hugo was waiting inside the entrance of El Mercadito. He wore nylon shorts and a T-shirt with a counterfeit sports logo, which he'd just bought in one of the small stores inside the mall, using the change from the hotel room. A few minutes later, Luke walked up the steps towards him, trying not to smile at the ill-fitting clothes. He gestured to Hugo that they should leave, and they walked to his car, down a couple of streets that were sparsely lined with single-story houses.

They got onto Whittier Boulevard, then under the Long Beach Freeway, and parked in East LA. They carried on east on foot, walking round piles of pallets, produce stalls, and a table of old men playing *dominó*.

"What the hell, man?" Luke asked Hugo, drawing to a halt.

Hugo looked at him and shrugged, not understanding.

"You need to recognize your principal."

Hugo stopped and looked around. A young woman opened the back door of her parked car and reached in for her baby. A man shouldered open the door of a bakery and walked off, eating a doughnut.

The AFL man slapped him on the back and moved off again.

"Don't look around, but Maharaj is one of those guys at the table."

Forcing himself not to look back, Hugo grasped for an explanation.

The AFL man laughed. "Yeah, porkpie hat, baggy clothes, mustache. Him."

Hugo grunted in admiration.

A couple of blocks later, Hugo followed Luke into Wolfsbane Tattoos. The place was narrow, and open to the back wall, where there was a large octagonal mirror in a wooden frame, a black-and-white Raiders poster, and dozens of tattoo designs in black ink on white paper. Sprawled on a hairdresser's chair was the owner, a man in his fifties with a graying Hell's Angels mustache, talking to a Rasta with dreadlocks in a red gold, green and black slinky beanie. They stopped talking as the two AFL men walked in. Hugo followed Luke to the back of the shop. The owner nodded at Luke and tipped his head to the door into the back office.

Hugo followed Luke into a windowless room that served as an office, stockroom and cafeteria.

Luke introduced the two men who were already there.

"Joriz, Linford. Hugo."

The other two nodded at Hugo and Luke without standing up.

Luke gestured Hugo towards a battered coffee machine. While Hugo poured himself a cup, Joriz dug into a cardboard box on an old desk in the corner of the room. Hugo sat down at the table with Linford. Joriz found what he was looking for and threw a transparent plastic bag of clothes towards Hugo, who just about caught it with one hand without scalding himself with the coffee.

"That's like our uniform," explained Linford.

"OK, guys," said Luke.

Then he started to describe how they were going to ride with Maharaj.

67

Los Angeles City Hall

IN THE Bradley Room at the top of LA City Hall, Devon was livestreaming an announcement, using a Wi-Fi signal from one of the protesters in the plaza below.

"ICE doesn't want you to know that they track all vehicles with a built-in GPS. That means more than ninety-nine percent of new cars."

"Unfortunately we can't stop that. Yet. But what we can do is turn that tool against them.

"Federal agencies aren't the only ones who can use AI."

Devon stood up and walked over to the east side of the observation deck. The livestreamed image swayed as the person transmitting the video from their cell phone followed Devon. Devon took a burner phone from his pocket and held it up to the camera.

"I'm going to zoom in on a car parked down on Spring Street."

Devon started the camera app on the burner phone and zoomed in on a sedan car parked on the street to the north of the protesters. He took a photo and held it up to the camera being used to livestream. The car roof had white painted on top with a license plate number.

"Now I'm going to put this photo into an app," continued Devon as he switched windows and pasted in the image. He tapped a green button on the app and held the screen up to the livestream camera again.

A warning message popped up: "This vehicle is used by ICE! Alert community networks of the risk of illegal detention and deportation."

Devon lowered the burner phone and faced the camera himself again.

"That's the license plate of one of the vehicles from the downtown shoot-out when ICE tried to detain me." He paused for a second, inviting the viewers to share that memory.

"We can all use this on photos of bumper license plates. If it's in the database as a federal agency vehicle, then you can share its location within the app.

"This is one of the ways that we can turn the tables on ICE. Rather than just jumping us and disappearing us over the border, they'll know that we're watching them and can take preemptive action.

"Thanks for watching."

He'd wrapped up the livestream before the FBI and FCC had been able to shut it down.

68

Leimert Park, Los Angeles

LATE THAT afternoon, the AFL detail set off in two battered sedan cars from outside the tattoo parlor. As in Yemen, Hugo was in the front passenger seat of the first vehicle, with Luke driving. Joriz and Linford were in the second vehicle, a few cars behind them in traffic. They were wearing guayaberas, white collarless cotton shirts with short sleeves, vertical pleats front and back, and dark blue stitched detailing. Their loose fit concealed pistols on their belts.

A few blocks to the west, they stopped outside a barbershop, while the second car proceeded. Maharaj stepped out of the barbershop and into the car. Although he was wearing the Nehru jacket that Hugo knew from media photos, his hairstyle and mustache made it difficult for Hugo to make him as the man he'd helped to rescue from ICE. A few blocks further to the west, Hugo saw in the side mirror that the second car had turned into traffic behind them. Luke had said that it'd be about half an hour's drive, without telling them the destination. They got onto the Santa Monica Freeway for about twenty minutes, then back south, then west again on Martin Luther King Boulevard into Leimert Park. They stopped in front of a storefront church. The sidewalks were covered with cars, but a couple of men standing in a gap in front of the door stepped aside to let Luke pull up and park there.

Hugo got out and held the rear passenger door open for Maharaj, scanning the surroundings for threats. Maharaj got out, looked confidently around, caught the eye of one of the men who'd stood aside to make way for the car, and acknowledged him with a nod before striding towards the door of the Haitian Church of the Nazarene. As Hugo turned to follow, he saw the second AFL car approaching and signaled to the driver that the situation was under control.

Inside, most of the floor space was taken up with neat rows of stackable white plastic chairs, about a quarter of which were occupied. Maharaj walked down the aisle that'd been left at one side. As he got closer to the far end, the rows of chairs were more fully occupied and he slowed down to turn his head and acknowledge the people who'd come to hear him. There were about fifty people in total.

The pastor had a few words with Maharaj and Luke before stepping up onto the dais. He walked over to the lectern pulpit, in front of red velvet drapes and a rolled-up projection screen. He introduced Maharaj as a brave man who had borne witness to the Bible's injunction to treat foreigners in the same way as the native-born.

"When a stranger resides with you in your land, you shall not wrong him," he said, quoting Leviticus. "The stranger who resides with you shall be to you as one of your citizens. You shall love him as yourself, for you were strangers in the land of Egypt."

The pastor stepped back and motioned Maharaj to the pulpit. As Maharaj was applauded, the pastor took a seat in the front row. Hugo and Luke stood behind Maharaj, each on one side of the red drapes. From behind their sunglasses, they scanned the people attending the meeting.

While Maharaj talked about setting up a rapid response team to counter the ICE snatch squads, Hugo looked for potential flashpoints in the room and listened on his earpiece to radio communications with the other two men in the AFL squad.

Maharaj was saying that they had ICE on the back foot now. That the rapid response teams were now more proactive, that they could put a brake on ICE before they even got close to their targets.

Hugo heard Joriz say over the radio that a couple of ICE vehicles were popping up on the app, heading southeast through Crenshaw on Martin Luther King Boulevard. He looked over at Luke on the other side of the dais, who caught his eye and nodded.

Maharaj was talking about the civil disobedience campaigns of Mahatma Gandhi. That as a boy he'd been bored hearing of them from his parents, that he'd thought they were all in the past, but that now he was proud to be using the same methods.

Luke caught the eye of the pastor in the front row and clasped his hands in front of his belt buckle, giving a signal that they'd agreed before Maharaj had stepped up. In turn, the pastor gave the nod to Maharaj, then stood up and walked back to the front door onto the street.

Maharaj didn't miss a beat. "Friends, tonight we can show the value of the teamwork I have been describing," said Maharaj. "The pastor has informed me that ICE agents are a few blocks away, heading towards us. Unfortunately we must bring this event to a close, on the assumption that ICE will try to detain and deport myself and anyone in my company."

The pastor stepped out of the front door, locked it behind him, and waited.

Joriz parked his car across the entrance to the back alley, at the end closer to the church. With Linford, he went inside via the back entrance and asked the people in the meeting to file out the back.

An ICE truck pulled up on the street outside the front of the church. The driver stayed inside as three officers got out and strode towards the front door of the church.

"Police. We have a warrant to search the premises," shouted the lead officer, waving the paper at the pastor.

"You're not police," the pastor replied disdainfully.

A couple of pedestrians walked calmly up to the confrontation, recording it on their phones.

The officer shouldered the pastor out of the way. The pastor steadied himself and started to chide the first two officers as they tested the door and found it locked. The third officer had hefted the breaching ram from the truck and started aiming it at the main door lock, starting with small swings and building up momentum. He was concentrating so hard on his target that he paid no heed to the metal canister hitting the wall and clattering to the ground.

As tear gas plumed out of the canister, the other two men swore, and one of them kicked it into the street. But they were already choking, and their eyes were swollen, so they didn't see the other canister that'd landed on the other side of the frontage and from which a cloud of gas was smothering them.

In her motel room in Lennox, Valentina was among those watching the livestream. The scene shook and shrank into the background as the cell phone camera operators sought refuge from the tear gas.

The ICE driver cracked open the door of the truck.

"Over here!" he shouted to his blinded colleagues, then slammed the door shut again, choking on the fumes. He pressed the ignition and revved the engine, trying to make the air conditioning filter the chemicals. Then he leaned on the horn to try to guide his colleagues back towards him.

Meanwhile, the other ICE element had been blocked from going into the back alley by the AFL vehicle, which was now empty. The last of the people who'd attended the meeting inside were approaching the far end of the alley. The rest had already turned the corner away from MLK Boulevard and out of sight. Three ICE officers opened the doors of the truck, intending to catch a few stragglers. There was still light from the low sun.

As the lead officer stepped out of the front passenger side, a rifle bullet smashed the windshield where he'd been sitting a second earlier. As they took cover behind the open doors of the vehicle, a tear gas canister clattered off the roof of their truck and onto the ground. By the time the ICE officers recovered and came out from their cover, their quarry was lost in the Los Angeles traffic.

69

Florence, Los Angeles

HUGO DROVE Maharaj to an AFL safe house between Compton Avenue and FDR Park. Over their radios, they were asking their controllers about any signs of federal helicopters. They drove up the driveway of the house and paused to check for any signs of trouble. Then Maharaj stepped out between two AFL men, who hurried him inside.

Hugo was last out of the vehicle with the driver. Inside the house they found the detail that was taking over the duty of guarding Maharaj. Hugo and the others were exhilarated by the fight with ICE.

Maharaj sat with Joriz and Linford at the kitchen table but declined a beer as long as the others were on duty and not going to join him.

"You guys had better have a plan, because there's only so much humiliation that the federal government is going to take."

When Hugo saw that the guys from the new detail had no response but laughter, he made his exit. Outside on the driveway, he looked up and scanned the sky for helicopters.

Luke snuck up behind him and slapped him on the back.

"Don't worry about the feebs, man. Whatever they do, we've got to hide in plain sight."

"Right," replied Hugo.

He wasn't convinced. But standing still in a garden and squinting up at the sky could get them noticed.

The four of them got back in the car and headed east.

Hugo had no possessions, beyond what he was carrying, and no idea where he was going to spend the night. On the other hand, having spent the last couple of months homeless downtown, that didn't faze him either. Luke seemed to read the way Hugo was gazing out the car window.

"You're going to be billeted in a hotel."

70

Downey, Los Angeles

HUGO WAS watching the nighttime streets when the car pulled up, across from a container park in Bellflower. Linford got out. Next was a subway station, and finally Luke pulled up outside a hotel on Firestone Boulevard near Lakewood Boulevard. Hugo got out and clasped hands with Luke through the open window before heading inside.

"Reservation for Rico, please," said Hugo to the clerk.

"Yes, sir," he said without looking up from the computer monitor. He reached under the desk and pulled out a key card for room 213, with Hugo's pseudonym written in marker on the paper sleeve.

Hugo walked up the stairs to the second floor, then pushed open the fire escape door onto the corridor. The odd numbers were opposite him, facing onto the street below. The door to 213 had a cheap bead bracelet hanging on the handle, striped blue, red and yellow. Hugo smiled. The lock whirred as he inserted and drew out the key card. He eased open the door, revealing a strip of blackness inside. He swung the hinges gradually, willing his eyes to accommodate.

He stepped into the room and looked around as one of his hands gradually closed the door behind him, darkening the grayness of the room. But a streetlight beyond the curtain enabled him to make out the outlines of the furniture. A queen-size bed pressed up against one wall, with a rail on the opposite wall serving as a closet. Next to the rail was the door into the bathroom.

Hugo padded past the corner of the bed and paused with his back to the bathroom door. Looking at the rumpled bedclothes, he pressed the palm of one hand against the plywood door and felt it give. He turned around, stepped into the bathroom and gently closed the door again.

Now he allowed himself to breathe deeply and turned on the bathroom light, using two fingers to slowly move the rocker switch without it clicking. He looked down at his clothes. The guayabera shirt was rumpled and must stink of tear gas, he thought to himself as he pulled it over his head. Looking around for somewhere to put his pistol, he caught himself in the mirror. The weeks living on the street had left him as thin as a whippet. *That's fine, I can bulk up again soon enough*, he thought as he took off the rest of his clothes and laid them on top of the toilet tank, the pistol grip just emerging between the trousers and guayabera.

He stepped into the shower, turned on the water, and squeezed out gel via the dispenser lever. He dipped his head into the cold stream and shuddered. As the water warmed, he lifted his head again and let the jet of water break against his chest and flow down over his groin. He heard a soft swish of the shower curtain behind him but carried on soaping himself. He sensed someone standing close behind him in the tight shower cubicle, and waited for them to make their move.

Valentina pressed her cheek against Hugo's back, in the concavity between his shoulder blades. She squeezed her hands and arms between his arms and his sides, then reached up and caressed the muscles of his chest. A citrus smell reached Hugo as he watched Valentina's hands massaging him.

"That hotel soap is not good for your skin, you know, Rico," she said, laughing.

"I guess I need help," he replied as he felt her press the length of her naked body against his.

"Let's see."

The fingers of one hand paused for a few seconds to explore his navel, then carried on down. Hugo arched backwards against Valentina as her soapy hand caressed the length of him. When he felt the point of no return approaching, he took her hand away and turned to face her. He wrapped his arms around her, and she looked up at him for a second before they kissed.

71

Downey, Los Angeles

THE NEXT morning, there was a message for Hugo that his shift would start at noon, so he went out to have breakfast with Valentina in a restaurant a few blocks away. They held hands across the table while their order came.

Only after they'd eaten and they were left sipping the bottom of their coffee cups did they start to speak about their plans.

Both of them had only found out about the hotel the day before.

"I don't know how long they'll billet me there for. It's inside the free area, so as good as anywhere else."

"Yeah."

"As long as Maharaj is doing his campaigning in and around LA."

"Right." Valentina paused. "Let's make the most of being together while we can."

Hugo smiled and they held hands across the table again.

He was still wearing the stinking T-shirt and shorts, so after breakfast, they went to buy some more presentable clothes.

A block from the hotel, Hugo stopped outside a café on the corner. Valentina pulled on his hand for them to go on, but he asked her to hold on for a minute. He looked into the café through the window, and out again through the far window. One of the cars parked outside caught his eye. It was in a no-man's land between the cheap sedan that mostly populated the neighborhood and a flashy statement car. Hugo gave it a second look. The windows were tinted as much as California law would allow, but he could see there was someone sitting waiting in the driver's seat.

He turned back to Valentina, and looked in her eyes while he squeezed her hand.

"My love, go back to where we had breakfast and wait for me there.

"Please," he added, when he saw that she was reluctant to leave him.

She nodded. They embraced before she went back the way they'd come.

Hugo looked at his watch, then went into the café and took a seat on the far window, from where he could see the hotel and a couple of sets of lights beyond.

Ten minutes later he darted out of the café, already having left the money for his order on the table. He dodged cars to cross the street and headed briskly for the hotel.

Both passenger doors opened on the sedan car in front of the hotel. Two men in their thirties got out. Each had one hand on their hip and, when they were within twenty yards of Hugo, they used their other hands to reach inside their button-down shirts.

The two men froze but Hugo kept walking and stopped just in front of them.

"Aren't you going to identify yourselves?" Hugo sneered.

The two of them had been told by the squad leader over their earpieces to hold back on the arrest.

Looking past the ICE officers, Hugo could see that Luke, arriving to pick him up from the hotel, had stopped alongside the undercover ICE car. Joriz, in the passenger seat of the double-cab pickup, had his window down, with his pistol trained on the ICE squad leader, while Luke leaned over and spoke to him.

"So, undercover, right?" Luke laughed.

"You think you can threaten federal agents with impunity?" replied the ICE squad leader.

Before replying, Luke raised his eyebrows, inviting the squad leader to believe his own eyes.

"A rental?" Luke continued, eyeing the car. "I guess the SafeStreets app is stopping you using your own cars."

The ICE officer didn't reply. The two officers facing Hugo were tensing up.

Luke continued. "If we raise the alarm, how far do you think you'd get before getting lynched?"

The officer still didn't reply. "If you get the fuck out of here, then we'll let it slide this time."

Acquiescing, the squad leader nodded to the driver, then spoke over the radio to the two officers who'd intended to arrest Hugo.

Hugo watched as they edged backwards to the car, keeping their eyes on him and their hands close to the pistols on their hips. They got back into the passenger seats and the car drove off slowly, followed by Luke and Joriz in the AFL pickup.

Hugo had nothing in the hotel room, so he just waited outside till they came back, having seen the ICE squad as far as the freeway.

Hugo got in the back without saying anything.

After setting off again, Luke voiced what was on their minds.

"You're a famous face from before. Anyone could've tipped ICE off about you."

"Just needs one," replied Hugo. "Thanks for getting that ICE squad out of the way."

"Rather ICE than the feebs."

"Yep."

"Luckily it didn't spoil your reunion." Joriz smirked expectantly. He waited a couple of seconds, but Hugo wasn't one to swap girlfriend stories with his buddies.

"Anyway," said Luke, "that was only going to be for one night, even before the mishap just now."

Hugo gritted his teeth and looked fixedly ahead out of the windshield. He'd been fooling himself, imagining that he could live with Valentina while working security for the AFL. But Luke was right. His face was known and, at least for now, being with Valentina was putting her in harm's way.

Luke gave Hugo a couple of minutes to chew that over before changing the subject.

"That operation with Maharaj last night sure got a lot of people's attention."

Hugo nodded. That was the idea, after all.

"The social media traffic is getting more and more heavily in our favor. In California at least."

Hugo grunted.

"Although the longer we keep this up, the crazier the *migra* and the feebs will be to recapture Maharaj."

They headed to the tattoo parlor again. From the following day, Hugo would have to make his own way there by noon. In the back of the parlor, they debriefed the operation last night and Luke put up some social media analysis that people in most neighborhoods of LA blamed the federal agencies for the violence.

Luke loaned Hugo a burner phone and gave him the number of a different hotel that the AFL had gotten for Valentina. He called her and told her he was fine, that he had to sleep elsewhere that night, and they agreed to meet for breakfast the following morning before he went on shift again. Maharaj wasn't due to appear in public again for a couple of days.

72

Downey, Los Angeles

THE NEXT morning, Hugo met Valentina outside a café, as they'd agreed. They embraced for so long that they started to turn heads. Once inside, after ordering, Hugo told her why they needed to stay apart for the time being.

Valentina didn't reply for a long time, and Hugo started to dread having to console her in the café. But she was already thinking ahead.

"I get it. We had another honeymoon but now you're back on the front line."

Hugo was surprised, in fact slightly affronted, that she was taking it so calmly.

"At least this time it's something worth fighting for."

She smiled, and Hugo squeezed her hand on the table.

"I need to play my own part as well," she continued. "I know the AFL is trying to expand the free area in LA, but right now it doesn't include any hospitals where I can do my job. Right when people are getting hurt and need orthopedic care, I want to be doing what I can to help them."

Hugo was surprised again, but he realised that he had no right to complain if Valentina wanted to follow her vocation.

"I've kept in touch with colleagues in Sacramento. Hospitals and clinics can hardly cope with all the people with fractures and gunshot wounds from the unrest there, especially around the capitol."

Hugo acquiesced.

"I'm in good standing in California again," she said, gesturing at her purse, where she had her new ID card. "They can't stop me from working."

"But why do you think you're in witness protection? Because the federal agencies were humiliated and they'll publicly take it out on you if they find you again."

"So? Do you want me to hide away?"

Hugo looked evenly at her, as if to say that she knew he didn't.

"That's why I don't have my own cell phone."

Hugo nodded.

"I'm going to get the bus to Sacramento and pay cash, alright?"

They both laughed. Hugo realized that she was making sense.

After their breakfast, as Hugo was taking money from his wallet for the check, he tried to look at the bigger picture.

"Let's hope the federal government realizes that we're not going away and that they need to make some kind of deal."

Valentina shrugged like her expectations weren't high.

On the street outside, they embraced again before parting.

73

Sacramento

THE BUS to Sacramento left at 7:30 that evening. For the first couple of hours, Valentina tried to stop herself from looking out of the window, because the bus was retracing the route she'd taken with Hugo, the day that ICE had abducted her. As they crested the pass into the Central Valley, she finally started to doze, and she was asleep by the time they reached Bakersfield.

When the bus stopped in Sacramento at about 4 a.m., she was still asleep. The bus was carrying on to Vancouver and she almost didn't get off in time. The driver had already closed the baggage doors but of course she had nothing there.

The new bus station was in an industrial area north of downtown, not far south of the American River. Luz had offered to meet her, but Valentina had told her not to worry. No need to mess up her sleep routine and struggle on her next shift.

But she had accepted the offer of a couch, so she got a rideshare to Luz's apartment. The driver headed west, then south on Interstate 5. As they approached the Capitol Mall, Valentina looked east. The encampment of besieging protesters extended a couple of blocks on her side of the capitol, and likewise to the north and south. She imagined that the park on the far side of the capitol must be overflowing.

Luz buzzed her in but then went back to her room. Valentina stood by the kitchen window, wondering how hard ICE would try to track her down. Yes, she was borrowing phones, using her new ID, and paying in cash, but they would surely find her if they wanted. Would they really devote resources to putting surveillance on someone like Luz? She started to imagine plainclothes ICE officers in the occasional car that was going past on the road outside at 5 a.m.

One of the things that ICE could easily do, Valentina thought, was flag any apparently new nurses starting at clinics where she had worked before. She didn't want to go back to an agency, and Luz helped her find vacancies at different clinics. She hadn't been exaggerating when she'd told Hugo that there was a shortage of orthopedic nurses, with so many gunshot injuries and other fractures presenting to clinics after confrontations with ICE and flareups all over Sacramento.

74

East LA, Los Angeles

OVER THE next couple of days, Hugo and the rest of the PSD kept close to Maharaj, whether he was planning his next public appearance in back offices, or hanging out on the street, playing *dominó* or chatting over food stalls. They told his political handlers how risky it was, as if they didn't know, but they replied that, after being in the church for months, he needed to spend time outside.

75

Federal Building, Los Angeles

Loy cursed out loud. His social media feed had just thrown up another map of Los Angeles showing a 'free area' centered on downtown. This 'free area' supposedly showed neighborhoods where ICE hadn't arrested anyone in the past two weeks. He looked through the channels which had posted different versions of the map. They weren't identical but must've come from the same source. The official AFL channel had been blocked, but there were plenty more which were sympathetic.

Loy cursed again.

It was true that they were having operational problems. In some areas now, as soon as they identified themselves to arrest someone, they'd have a crowd around them, blocking them in and threatening violence if they didn't retreat.

They weren't getting any more friends within the LAPD or county sheriffs either. Every night, some car carrying straight guys would get lost, get mistaken for undercover ICE officers, and end up getting beaten. The local police had to try to sort it out and blamed ICE for having riled people with their real undercover ops.

Anyway, the 'free area' map was exaggerating. They needed to get a different narrative going. But based on what? He pushed a speed dial button on his desk phone and Mack was in his office a couple of minutes later. Loy explained the situation to him.

"How do we push back on this treasonous bullshit?" asked Loy, gesturing at the map on the screen.

Mack just shrugged.

"Come on, let's just spitball it," insisted Loy.

"Right. OK, if we just say that the AFL data is false, that'll be weak."

"Or, at least, if we do say that, we'd better be able to back it up."

"We'd be saying that we *have* been operating inside that area recently. Then, how to deal with the questions?"

"Operational confidentiality?" Loy was stretching.

"Say we do come out with some times and places."

"Yeah. But remember the advantages that we get from keeping that information to ourselves."

"Right," agreed Carl.

"So maybe we should just ignore the 'free area' bullshit for now. Not give it any more oxygen."

"For now, while we wait for a chance to show how fake it is."

76

Griffith Park, Los Angeles

BY THE time they got within a couple of miles of Griffith Park, Hugo realized where they were taking Maharaj. Hugo and the rest of the PSD were in a ten-year-old Hyundai sedan edging up the Golden State Freeway. Sure enough, they got the word over the radio to take the off-ramp that led to the south side of the park, and then to the Argo Theater, an open-air concert venue with a capacity of over five thousand. Even though his social media browsing rarely got far from the AFL-friendly channels, and his online time was disrupted by having to change his phone every week, he'd seen plenty of mentions of the Parce concert there. Parce was a male Colombian singer, part of the latest iteration of reggae-rap-champeta urban music. It was a bit in-your-face for Hugo, but, when off-duty, he could get into it after a few beers.

As they crawled along on North Vermont Avenue, Hugo looked at the traffic ahead, then in the mirror, then out the side at the mimosa and ceiba trees in the golf course. On social media, the latest maps showed all of Griffith Park in the free area. That surprised Hugo, but ICE hadn't been pushing back much on the free area over the past couple of weeks. It seemed to have been gaining momentum, with neighborhoods on the edge of the area kicking the ass of anyone they thought looked half like an undercover ICE officer.

They parked in Los Feliz, half a mile south of the stadium. Not the best practice, but they hadn't come up with a better option that'd keep their cover. Maharaj's look was a small businessman acting the *patrón*, inviting his nephews to the concert to show them that he still had his mojo. Maharaj had used some of his ample free time to work up Maharaj's wardrobe from the bargain stores of East LA. The garish shirt was trying and failing, but not so outlandish as to make people look twice. Hugo and the rest of the PSD faded into the background next to Maharaj's would-be hotshot.

As they got closer to the stadium, they merged in with the crowds. Vendors sold Parce merch, fast food, and bottled drinks from styrofoam coolers. The occasional scalper called out his wares. Maharaj's Spanish was still heavily accented from his Caribbean English, so when someone called out to him, he affected to glare at one of the PSD, delegating the reply to them. He was enjoying himself, and that just fed more into his role. As Hugo joined in as one of the compliant nephews, he wasn't exactly happy with the security situation, but he thought they were making the best of it so far.

It took them about half hour to get to the tall fence that enclosed the open-air amphitheater. They edged their way round to the backstage access door, where, pretending to ogle the niche celebrities entering as guests, they looked out for any undercover ICE officers. After a few minutes, on the nod from Hugo, they pulled out passes from under their shirts and made their way in past the bouncers.

Being an outdoor amphitheater, backstage space was at a premium, and Maharaj and the others were directed to the side of a repurposed storage area. In the center of the room, aspiring personalities held forth, making themselves heard over the support act on stage. Maharaj was still in character but wanted to wind down and think through what was coming up.

A production assistant pushed her way through the packed room, announcing that the support act was going to wrap up soon. Unbeknownst to her, this was Hugo's cue. He gestured to the others to follow him, and they jostled their way to the side of the stage, where Hugo made himself known to the stage manager.

The band reached the crescendo of their last song, held the pose of the final chord till they felt the audience wavering, and were done. They walked off, passing Maharaj, who was swapping his loud shirt for a guayabera. The crowd had fallen quiet after the end of the set, but now a drone of conversation loaded the air, and roadies came on to prepare the stage for the headline act.

Maharaj looked over to the stage manager and got the nod. Maharaj looked out and up into the sky before walking on. He took a wireless microphone from a stand in the center of the stage.

"Hi, I hope you're enjoying this great show tonight. I'm Cheddi

Maharaj and I'm going to say a few words while the stage is being set for Parce."

The hubbub faded. Some people were surprised to see Maharaj, others didn't know or care who he was and started to jeer. Maharaj had attended enough rallies prior not to be fazed: better that than being ignored.

"Some of you know, for years I've been targeted by the *migra*"—pause for jeers from the crowd—"because of my support for undocumented people in America."

Some of the jeers were still for him. He knew that not every person in the audience would support him.

"A few weeks ago I was holed up in a church, unable to leave for fear of being kidnapped and deported to a country I'd never been to."

Shouts came back from the audience, ranging from "*¡Viva México!*" to "*¡Chinga la migra!*"

From where he stood to the side of the stage, Hugo noticed some of the security guys look at each other and nod, like they were planning something.

Maharaj carried on. "Thankfully the AFL released me and I can carry on with my work of defending those who are illegally targeted by ICE and other immigration agencies."

Hugo watched the security guys talk into their radios even though the situation with Maharaj and the crowd was well under control.

"Now I can travel around central LA because ICE is scared to go there, because they know that people have good cause to hate them."

A few security guys wouldn't act by themselves, Hugo reckoned. They would need to have backup close by. Hugo gestured to Luke that he was going to check out backstage. As he traced his steps back towards the stage door entrance, he heard Maharaj continue.

"The free area is expanding every week. For that to carry on, we need you, everyone, to stand up to ICE, and post to the app when you see them getting ready to snatch people."

Backstage, there was a new bunch of people whose clothes didn't sit well on them. They weren't talking to the others, and some of them had concealed weapons.

Maharaj was working up to the climax of his short speech.

"We need you to peacefully block ICE's way back out of your barrios, so they can't escape with the people they've kidnapped. So they have to face up to the people that they're supposedly serving."

Hugo ran back to the stage. As he got there, four of the stage security crew pulled out ICE ERO badges from under their shirts and headed for Maharaj. Two of them drew pistols while the squad leader shouted out that Maharaj was a fugitive and under arrest. The fourth officer circled behind Maharaj, handcuffs in his hand.

Maharaj stood his ground and appealed to the crowd.

"This is what we need to stop! Stop people from being snatched and disappeared in public, in front of their friends and family!"

Hugo spoke into his radio while gesturing to the other members of the detail to protect Maharaj.

The crowd erupted into a maelstrom of factions: some chanting against ICE, some for the AFL, some jeering Maharaj.

The ICE officers knocked the mic from Maharaj's hands, silencing him, and forced his hands into the cuffs. Then they turned their weapons against Hugo and the rest of the PSD who had surrounded them.

The crowd surged towards the stage. Some of those near the front, with phones in their hands recording, couldn't brace themselves and fell underfoot.

There was a standoff between Hugo's PSD and the ICE officers. Hugo knew that the backstage officers must be arriving any second, but he didn't take his eyes off those in his sights. He and his men were outnumbered and he had to act. He picked the mic off the floor and called out to the crowd in Spanish.

"Are you going to just watch like wusses while the *migra* disappears someone, just for criticizing them?"

The clamor upped a notch, divided between those acclaiming Hugo and those trying to shout him down. The momentum of the crowd pushed them past the remaining security men and onto the stage. Further back, a few spectators scrambled up lighting rigs to keep streaming the chaos.

Hugo called out to the PSD to keep close to Maharaj.

The other ICE squad appeared from backstage, weapons drawn, and shot into the air, trying to turn back the flood of angry people who were trying to rescue Maharaj or attack ICE or attack the AFL.

The ICE officers around Maharaj saw a crowd of mad foreigners out to kill them. The leader of the snatch squad shouted to them to join up with the backup squad that'd appeared from backstage. They tried to force their way through by shooting whoever was in their path. The crowd was rocked by people falling wounded among them, but then surged forward again, enraged.

Hugo shouted over the radio for his squad to seize back Maharaj. They used the force of the crowd to edge closer. The ICE officers started trying to shoot their way towards their colleagues who'd come out from backstage. This other squad was holding its own on the side of the stage, but not advancing.

Hugo's squad members stumbled over the bodies of those who'd been shot, trying not to slip on the blood. Maharaj was in the middle of a knot of the ICE squad, trying to stay calm despite being buffeted by the crowd and gagging on the smell of flesh burned by point-blank gunfire. Hugo got to within a couple of yards of Maharaj, and shouted over the radio to the others to make their move.

Two of them drew their guns on the ICE squad while Hugo and Luke tried to force their through to Maharaj. Both sides opened up with their semiautomatic pistols, and the combined gunfire rose above the baying of the crowd. Hugo felt the impact of a round against the Kevlar vest on his back, but managed to grab Maharaj's upper arm and start to drag him away from the snatch squad. Then he felt a warm slap on his cheek. He turned around and saw that Luke's brains had been blown out over the side of his face. He let go Maharaj took a two-handed grip on his pistol, and put a round through the neck of the ICE officer who'd killed Luke. He turned back to grab Maharaj again, but he was slumped against the back of one of the audience who'd stormed the stage. Maharaj's eyes were dull and he was only held upright by the throng. Hugo took him by both shoulders and Maharaj tipped forward onto his chest. Hugo saw that the back of Maharaj's skull was missing.

Hugo called down a blessing from God. Still holding Maharaj's body, Hugo looked around and found himself looking down the pistol barrel of one of the ICE snatch team. Despite his training, Hugo froze, still thinking of Maharaj. Hugo drank in the details of the SIG Sauer pistol pointed at him. A shot rang out, but Hugo found himself still standing. He looked around and saw Joriz lowering his pistol from its sight line to the dead ICE officer. Joriz looked at Hugo and jerked his head to one side. Hugo followed the gesture and came back to the reality of holding Maharaj's dead body. Dazed, he looked back at Joriz, who motioned for Hugo to let the body fall. He was right, Hugo realized: there was nothing more to be done for him.

As Maharaj's body slipped down, Hugo looked around and saw that

Linford was there as well, standing with his back to him. Joriz gestured that they should go. Hugo looked through the crowd for what was left of the ICE snatch squad. Now that Maharaj had been killed, they were concentrating on fighting their way to the other part of their team and not risking any more losses.

Hugo nodded in agreement at Joriz. There was still chaos around them on stage. Members of the audience were fighting, struggling to find their friends, howling over those they'd found dead on the floor, and searching for someone to avenge themselves on. The PSD formed themselves into a wedge, with Hugo in front of the other two, who were shoulder to shoulder. They headed to the side of the stage that was opposite the ICE squad.

When they made it offstage, they paused. The three men looked at each other, grateful to still be alive but also thinking of the way Luke and Maharaj had died. After a couple of seconds, the eyes of the other two rested on Hugo, wanting guidance.

"Our principal was killed. It's too late to change that, but we can still save what's left of the detail."

The other two nodded.

"We can't go back to our car, we have to assume that's under observation."

"We could make emergency contact with the leadership, but first we should know our own situation. We saw the ICE forces in here, but we won't know what kind of help we need till we see the situation outside the venue."

"People will be piling out onto the street any which way they can," offered Linford.

"Right," replied Hugo as he followed a train of thought.

Outdoors, there was a heaving mass of people heading downhill towards the exits. Hugo led the other two against the current, along the side of the building, back towards the amphitheater. They had holstered their guns and were acting like regular fans, trying to find their friends after getting separated during the riot.

The going got easier when they turned the corner of the building and the amphitheater opened up ahead of them. There was still fighting going on on the stage, but the ICE officers were just interested in getting the hell out.

The house lights hadn't been turned back on since the trouble started, so the amphitheater got darker and darker as it sloped up towards the back rows. The three AFL men strolled up one of the aisles as if looking for something. By the time they got to the top, the stage was almost empty except for half a dozen bodies. But now they could see flashing emergency lights cast on walls and trees beyond the main theater building. They could've been any mixture of ICE, FBI and other agencies, but there was no upside and plenty of downside in trying to get out past them.

Joriz kept his eye on the stage while Hugo and Linford turned to the back wall of the amphitheater. Linford gave Hugo a leg up to the top of the wall. There he hung on to the fence with one hand while his other hand took a multitool from a trouser pocket. He clambered up the fence, hung on again, and clipped away the razor wire with the wire cutters on the multitool. A twisted manzanita tree was silhouetted on the horizon. He looked down on the ground on the far side of the wall and gave his eyes a few seconds to adapt to the deeper darkness. Then he looked back, gave the all clear to the other two, scrambled to the far side of the fence as far as the wall, and let himself drop. A couple of minutes later, the three of them were heading west through the chaparral vegetation of the park, with the Griffith Observatory silhouetted against the night sky in front of them.

Without speaking, they carried on a few hundred yards, skirted the observatory to the south, and followed the access road down to Los Feliz. Not wanting to traipse through the upscale neighborhood in their ripped and bloody clothes, they stopped and called a rideshare to take them back to East LA.

77

East LA, Los Angeles

On arrival they waited grimly to be debriefed. Hugo watched the other two scrolling through the feeds on their phones.

Joriz raised his eyebrows at something and turned to Hugo.

"Hey, know a guy called Raul?"

Hugo pointed at the phone, asking to see. He read the message and gave Joriz his phone back. Then he stepped out of the room and into the tattoo parlor out front. The owner was still there, drawing new designs with a black Rotring pen on a pad of thick art paper.

Hugo asked him if he could borrow a phone.

The owner pulled open a desk drawer to show half a dozen secondhand phones in battered multicolored covers. Hugo thanked him, took out the nearest one, with a flaming basketball on the cover, and dialed Raul.

As it rang, the AFL debriefing officer walked past him, towards the back of the shop, gesturing at him to follow. Hugo looked up from the phone and nodded.

The debriefing officer reached the back room, and looked at Joriz and Linford like they were guilty of Maharaj's death till proven innocent. He sent Joriz out front to fetch Hugo.

In an instant, Joriz was back, saying that Hugo had gone.

78

East LA to the San Joaquin Valley

WHEN HUGO had gotten his call through, Raul had told him that his unit of the state police had been deployed to Sacramento. They'd been put onto a convoy of buses by their building in University Park that morning. They weren't told their destination, but the obvious one was the siege of the state capitol in Sacramento. With Valentina working as a nurse there, Raul thought that Hugo would want to know. Hugo thanked him and hung up. Raul was right. If the CSP was being deployed there from Los Angeles, then there was bigger trouble in the offing, and he wasn't going to leave Valentina there to face it by herself.

Hugo tossed the phone back into the drawer, then walked out onto Whittier Boulevard and headed west. He paused on the corner to listen to sporadic gunfire coming from different directions. He carried on till he found what he was looking for, a Korean-made sedan parked on the boulevard, more than five years old. He looked through the window and saw that the owner had left a USB charging cable. Hugo took out his knife and felt for the small pyramid of metal on its end. He smashed the driver's-side window with the glass breaker. Ignoring the car alarm, he opened the driver's-side door, sat behind the wheel and closed the door behind him. With the knife, he snapped off the plastic cover of the steering column, then pried open the ignition cylinder. He yanked the USB cable out of the center console and jammed the connector down onto one of the exposed tines of the cylinder. He turned the connector, and the engine started.

When Hugo got up onto the Pomona Freeway, he scanned the horizon, looking for signs of disturbances. Ahead of him, nothing seemed amiss in downtown. That was to be expected, because the AFL had been keeping ICE out of there for weeks. At the East LA Interchange, just short of the LA River, he swung north. The interstate turned slowly left to run towards the northwest. To the right, across the river, was Cypress Park. Hugo could see smoke rising in a couple of places, from burning cars, he imagined. That was still a disputed area, and he could hear sporadic gunshots through the broken driver's-side window.

A couple of kilometers further on, he could see Griffith Park coming up on the left side of the interstate. He looked over towards the Argo Theater, where he'd been a couple of hours earlier, and saw that there were still blue and red flashing lights from emergency vehicles. As he went through Burbank, Hugo tried to make out the malls that he knew were on both sides of the elevated freeway. As he was looking to the west, he was dazzled by a fireball that erupted a couple of hundred yards away. He turned back to the road ahead and gripped the steering wheel as hard as he could. A second later, the car was buffeted by the blast of the explosion. He realized that the blast had come from Burbank Airport and imagined that a fuel tank had been blown up by people trying to stop deportation flights.

A couple of miles further up, the interstate got closer to the end of one of the runways. Hugo turned the rearview mirror and could see flames rising over the roofs of the houses in between. He realized that he was coming up to the Hollywood Freeway intersection, and had to concentrate on finding the route out of LA without crashing his stolen car.

When he started to climb into the Transverse Ranges, Hugo felt like the flames and explosions were wind on his back, pushing him northwards. By the time he'd descended again into the Central Valley, tension was draining from him and sleep starting to well up. He knew from experience that it'd be folly to resist for long.

He was tempted to go back to McClure and sleep in the parking lot where Valentina had rescued him. But to get there, he'd have to go through Bakersfield. That wasn't friendly territory and he didn't want to be stopped by the local police. He looked over to the east, across the fields of citrus and olives, and saw a couple of the town's taller downtown buildings reflect orange from nearby fires.

At the next intersection he turned west, towards the Coast Ranges. He kept on for about ten miles, through fields of kiwi fruit vines whose green seemed black in the night. Suddenly the irrigation ran out and Hugo's car emerged into a bare moonscape. He hung a U-turn, headed back into the fields and turned into the next farm track to his right. He curled up on the back seat, imagined he was back in the dorm room, tired after a day picking grapes, and was asleep in a couple of minutes.

79

Fresno, California

THE SUN woke Hugo up the next morning. He started the car and saw that the tank was almost empty. Any gas station was a vulnerable spot. Even on the open highway, his smashed side window would be a magnet for any kind of cop or federal agent. As he set off, he was still weighing up the different options. He got back on the I-5, then the next state highway to the right. Inside an hour, he was passing through the southern suburbs of Fresno. He drove under a highway, then over two sets of rail lines. Up ahead on the left was downtown Fresno, dominated by a tower of yellow concrete and black glass. He came down off the highway and looped back towards downtown, passing just north of the rail station. Then he took a right and parked on a side street because of debris and abandoned cars on the road ahead. He wiped down the surfaces he would've handled and left the car behind. He walked towards the yellow and black building from another side street.

It was a federal building and courthouse and had been attacked and set on fire the previous night. Hugo guessed that demonstrators had been trying to free ICE detainees from the building. Some of the abandoned cars had been trashed or burned out. There were a few police but hardly any pedestrians. Hugo stood under a tree a few meters back on the side road. He spotted an old SUV parked on the side of the main road but not quite straight, and with one of the windows partly down, like it had been ditched in a hurry. He walked straight to it, nodding at a policeman on the way, and pulled the door handle like he was expecting it to open. Luckily it did. He closed the door behind him and checked in the mirrors that the policeman wasn't still watching. He took his time, hot-wired the car and was off. The tank was about half-full.

80

Sacramento

WHEN THE third gunshot wound patient was admitted inside an hour, Valentina realized that something was going on. The EMT records showed that all three calls had come from near the state capitol. The patients had been sedated by the time they got to the orthopedic ward and didn't tell her much. The next one in was a CSP officer in his uniform of tan shirt and green trousers. The gunshot had fractured his pelvis. He'd been transfused and had his fracture stabilized. Valentina put him on intravenous antibiotics as wound infection prophylaxis. He had to stay on his gurney in the corridor, with no hope of his own room for at least twenty-four hours.

A couple of hours later when her shift finished at 7 a.m., she knew she couldn't just go home when there were more wounded in State Capitol Park. The governor had declared a state of emergency and put all clinical personnel on call. But she wasn't going to wait for an order to come via the hospital.

She had a stash of modafinil that she used when her shift time changed. The drug helped her stay awake while her body clock caught up. She'd been on the night shift for the past week, so she knew that she'd be falling asleep within a couple of hours if she did nothing. She popped one of the white tablets out of the foil strip and downed it with some water.

She headed west on the El Dorado freeway, then north on Sixteenth Street. She parked on a side street and opened the trunk. On the floor, next to the scissor jack, was a tan backpack with a red cross badge: an individual first aid kit. Valentina shouldered it and headed west towards the State Capitol Park.

She crossed Fifteenth Street and carried on in the direction of the capitol dome, between the World Peace Rose Garden and the Desert

Garden. In the early days of the demonstration, the protesters had set up a first aid post in the Civil War Memorial Grove, about a hundred meters east of the capitol.

As Valentina approached, she could hear screams of pain, punctuated by calls from the emergency response personnel who were trying to help the casualties. She walked into a ten-foot-by-ten-foot canopy tent that was the original aid post. Two people in CSP uniforms were bending over a patient on a folding bed. Valentina walked up to a CSP officer who was speaking, grim-faced, into her cell phone via earbuds. Valentina spoke when the officer caught her eye.

"I'm a military nurse. How can I help?"

While continuing her phone conversation, the officer looked expectantly at Valentina.

"IFAK," Valentina added, shrugging the backpack off one shoulder to show her.

The CSP officer nodded gratefully, still holding her cell phone in one hand. With her free hand, she gave Valentina the OK sign, then gestured back out of the tent in a way that implied there were more casualties than she'd be able to deal with.

Under the trees, about twenty casualties were lying in a row on the ground. Medical personnel were working on a couple of those nearest to the tent. Most of the casualties were accompanied by at least one other person, squatting on the ground next to them, often holding their hands and bending down, their heads close together.

Valentina walked to the far end of the row, going over the military triage categories in her head.

She squatted down next to the farthest casualty, a young man in his twenties. His chest was wounded and his clothes were soaked with blood, which was turning black. His eyes were glazed and his lips pale. A woman his own age was holding his hand and crying softly.

"I'm a nurse," Valentina said to her. "I'm going to check for a pulse," she added as she put on a pair of disposable gloves. The young woman nodded, but she kept looking at her boyfriend and the rhythm of her sobbing didn't change.

Valentina pressed her index finger into the top of the young man's neck, and felt a faint and irregular pulse. In the triage categories, he was expectant. A euphemism meaning that medical personnel would be better off trying to save those with a chance of survival.

She looked at the girlfriend again. "Stay with him for the time he's got left."

The woman nodded. She didn't lift her eyes but the sobbing deepened and she tightened her grip on his hand.

Valentina waited a couple of seconds. She wanted to hug the woman but, instead, vicariously squeezed the dying young man's other hand. Even through her gloves, it felt clammy.

The next casualty was a woman in her forties. Her eyes were shut tight, her body tense, and she was whimpering from the pain of her wounds. Most of her right hand had been shot off. Most likely from reflexively putting up her hands as she was about to be shot. The round had carried on and hit her in the shoulder. Maybe the bones in her hand had deflected the bullet enough to save her life. Like the previous casualty, she'd lost a lot of blood, but her pulse was stronger and regular. In the triage categories, she was immediate.

Valentina started to give the woman a commentary on what she was doing.

"You've lost a lot of blood, but you've got a good chance of survival."

Valentina asked the woman's name but she just groaned through gritted teeth.

"I'm going to apply a tourniquet to your lower arm."

She'd taken the nylon webbing strap from the IFAK. She gently lifted the wounded arm to get the strap underneath, then put the end of it through the buckle. As Valentina cinched the tourniquet tight, the woman howled.

That was when Valentina heard the shooting start. First from the east, on the capitol side of the park, she heard what she thought was rifle fire, interspersed with handgun shots. She looked up for a second but could see nothing through the trees. Then she looked back down at the casualty she was treating. She was going to do the job that she'd come to do.

There was limited bleeding from the shoulder wound, but the casualty was waving the arm from side to side as if trying to cast off the tourniquet.

Now she heard gunfire from further away, from the west side of the park. It seemed like a coordinated attack on the park. The state police had had the situation under control, so Valentina assumed it was an attack by federal forces.

"I'm going to give you something for the pain."

Valentina took a morphine autoinjector from the backpack and ripped off the gray cuff around the top, priming the mechanism.

"You're going to feel a jab in your leg."

Valentina squatted on the woman's ankles, trying to steady her legs against her writhing, then thrust the business end of the injector against her sweatpants, at the midpoint of her thigh, towards the side. The needle plunged through the textile and delivered its sweet morphine payload.

The shooting from the west side was getting closer and was now dominated by rifle fire. Through the trees, she got a glimpse of an armored vehicle approaching.

Valentina looked back down to her patient, who was now sighing with relief as the morphine took effect.

"I'm going to turn you over slightly."

The bullet had gone through the woman's back. The exit wound had some splinters of bone from her shattered shoulder blade.

Valentina gently laid the casualty down on her back. She noticed the two CSP officers come out of the tent with their sidearms drawn. The armored vehicle rolled towards the tent. A rifle shot exploded through the chest of one of the officers, who was thrown backwards and lay on the ground, twitching.

81

Sacramento

Hugo mostly kept to sixty-five miles per hour, and three hours later he was in Sacramento. He abandoned the SUV in midtown, went into a convenience store and bought a burner phone. It was a risk, but he had the feeling that soon it'd be more than a phone putting him on the federal radar. He called one of the numbers that Valentina had given him, for an orthopedics department. He asked for her by her witness protection name, left a message for her to call Rico, and left his new number.

As he walked west, the few people on the streets were coming the other way, towards him from State Capitol Park. Young adults in sweatpants, T-shirts and hoodies, looking dazed and confused, some of them with fresh cuts on their faces and hands. As Hugo upped his pace, he heard gunfire up ahead, from the direction of the park. He got to Fifteenth Street, facing the park. He paused, put his head quickly around the corner, taking a look at the main entrance to the park, a block to the north, before ducking back out of view.

An FBI MRAP armored vehicle was on the next corner of Fifteenth Street, guarding the main entrance to the park on its east side. Gunfire from inside the park drew Hugo's attention and he found himself looking towards the top of the capitol dome over the tops of the intervening trees.

If he knew Valentina, she would be helping the casualties inside the park. He needed to get in, but the FBI was surely guarding all the entrances. Getting picked up, or worse, before getting inside would be no use to anyone.

As Hugo stood looking straight across into the park, hunched into the corner, pondering his next move, an old-model black-and-silver Bronco with an American flag on the back bumper turned the corner a block behind him and headed his way.

"Get in here!"

Valentina finished applying a chest seal to another casualty and looked up.

A CSP officer was crouching in the doorway of the canopy tent, aiming his pistol towards the FBI armored vehicle. He glanced back over towards Valentina and shouted at her again.

"Come on!"

An ICE officer showed momentarily from behind the armored vehicle and fired a round from his M4 carbine that would've killed the CSP officer had he not hit the deck a second before.

Valentina was enraged at the federal agents. Then she realized that they had a clear line of sight to her, and that maybe the CSP officer had been right to tell her to take cover.

She looked again and realised that the CSP officer was Raul.

"They need you alive," Raul shouted at her again. Valentina looked over the line of casualties on the ground. Some of them had passed out and some of them were groaning or crying. But Raul was right.

"OK," she shouted back.

"When I move again, then run."

Raul sprang up off the ground and back into his crouch position, aiming at the MRAP.

Valentina looked at the the MRAP, then at the row of supine gunshot wound victims.

"Hey!" Raul called out.

Valentina realized that she'd frozen. She told herself it was anxiety from the modafinil.

"Again!" she called back.

Once more, Raul took aim, and this time Valentina sprinted towards the tent.

As the ICE officer appeared again, Raul fired, and the round ricocheted off the hood of the vehicle.

Valentina reached the tent and lay on the ground, face up, gasping for air, more from fear than tiredness.

"Stay there!" Raul shouted to her as he crawled along the ground to the back corner of the tent. Through the crack between the two tent panels, he took a shot at a federal agent as he appeared from behind the MRAP. The agent cried out and staggered back behind the vehicle. As Raul scrambled towards Valentina, another agent stepped out and put an M4 burst through the tent where he'd just been.

A federal agent ran from behind the MRAP, seeking cover behind a tree. Raul kneeled and aimed his pistol through one of the bullet holes in the canvas. He hit the agent who was providing covering fire from the side of the armored vehicle, but took a bullet in the chest himself. He was thrown back and his head hit the corner of a black polypropylene case of medical equipment.

Valentina caught her breath, then crawled over to Raul. She ripped open his shirt where the bullet had struck. There was no blood. Raul's body armor had stopped the M4 round, but he was dazed from the impact of the rifle round, and concussed from the blow to the head. He tried to tell Valentina something, but she concentrated on her physical assessment. Only when she saw Raul grimace with contempt, his eyes trying to focus above and beyond her, did she realize that someone was there, looking down at them.

She gathered her thoughts for a split second, then leaned back, away from Raul, and started to stand up. She got as far as looking into the face of the assailant: Carl Mack. He gave her a heavy slap with the back of his hand that sent her sprawling back down on top of Raul's body.

Valentina started to scramble to her feet again but was knocked down again by a kick in the chest from Carl.

"You keep coming back like a stray dog," he said, aiming his M4 at her.

Valentina knocked away the rifle barrel, but Carl let it hang in one hand while he drew his pistol with the other, then kicked her down again as she tried to stand.

"You won't be whelping any more of your kind in this country," he said as he drew his pistol down on the center of Valentina's chest.

Two FBI SWAT agents stepped from the park gate into the road as the Bronco approached. One held his M4 carbine with both hands, the other had one arm raised, telling the driver to stop.

The Bronco drew up ten yards short of the FBI MRAP armored vehicle. The lead FBI agent now took his own M4 in both hands and approached the driver's-side window. The driver showed both his hands to the agent through the glass, then lowered the left one and gradually wound down the window. He was in his forties, going gray over the temples.

"Better turn around and leave the area, sir."

Slowly lifting his left hand onto the steering wheel, the driver nodded in agreement before replying.

"We thought we'd better hand over this fugitive. We apprehended the brazer trying to make his way into the park."

The man in the front passenger seat, his hands on the dashboard, twitched his head towards the back seat, where Hugo was lying on his back, his legs twisted with the knees doubled up and hanging over the foot well. He sneered at his captors.

The lead FBI agent smiled as he recognized Hugo from the most-wanted lists.

He looked across the hood of the Bronco at the other agent and gestured for him to go to the rear passenger door. As he started to obey, sounds of more gunfire came from the park. At the same time, he heard something in his earphone and turned to see another car approaching from the other side.

The lead agent hesitated.

"We're off-duty cops," said the driver. "From Dixon."

The FBI agent nodded. Clearly Dixon was a conservative city, where the police wouldn't betray their country like the Sacramento ones.

"Want to stash this wet in your MRAP, or should we take him somewhere else?"

The agent looked at the driver for a second. Wanting the credit for arresting Hugo, he tipped his head towards the MRAP.

The Bronco passenger got out immediately. The driver looked at the FBI agent, who took a second to realize he was in the way before he stepped back.

The Bronco passenger hauled their captive out of the car. Hugo struggled, but his wrists were bound behind his back with a cable tie. Each captor took hold of one of Hugo's shoulders, and they dragged him towards the MRAP. The other FBI agent patted them down cursorily, then opened the back door.

The men tossed Hugo in the back of the MRAP and headed back towards their Bronco. One of the FBI agents climbed into the back of the

MRAP. The other kept watching Hugo for a second too long. When he turned back to survey the street again, he found himself facing two Ruger EC9 pistols, which the men in civvies had drawn from ankle holsters. He raised his M4 but was shot in the head before he could train it on either of the supposed off-duty cops.

Inside the MRAP, Hugo already had his hands free, because his AFL colleagues had cut the cable tie as they'd slung him inside. Hugo wrestled the other FBI agent for his M4. One of the AFL men was helping Hugo subdue the agent when the MRAP driver turned round from his seat and looked back towards the rear door. He had his pistol raised but was shot in the head by the other AFL man. They overcame the last FBI agent and left him bound and gagged out of sight, behind a recycling point.

The Bronco driver took over behind the wheel of the MRAP, with Hugo alongside him. The other AFL man headed back to the Bronco. The armored vehicle lurched forward as the driver got used to handling its fifteen tons. He took it past the World Peace Rose Garden and parked under trees.

"Thanks, man," Hugo grinned.

"You were the one trussed up like a pig," smirked the driver. He was Scott, Hugo's zolpidem connection from downtown LA. they embraced.

"That's Darnell," said Scott, gesturing at the Bronco, which was pulling up behind them.

Darnell jumped out, ran to the driver's side of the MRAP, tossed a two-way radio to Scott, then headed back to the Bronco. Hugo waited for Scott to bring him up to speed.

"The FBI can't accept that their ICE buddies got sent packing by a state police full of immigrants."

Hugo nodded.

"So they surrounded the park, and they're trying to take prisoner anyone they can, and shooting anyone who objects."

He looked away from Hugo and lifted the walkie-talkie.

"Unit three. We've acquired the vehicle from the Fifteenth Street entrance, over."

"Roger, unit three. All units, proceed to the objective, out."

The back door of the MRAP opened, and Darnell heaved a black polypropylene rifle case up onto the floor before climbing in himself.

Scott turned to Hugo.

"The CSP is operating out of the Civil War Grove at the other end of the park," he continued, tipping his head towards the capitol dome.

"The feebs are trying to encircle them there."

As the driver started the engine, Darnell made his way in a crouch towards the front of the vehicle.

"Still got your pistol?"

Hugo nodded. "Plus one of the M4s we just acquired."

"Thanks."

As they headed west, an FBI voice came over the vehicle radio.

"Tango Three, this is Tango One, request status, over."

"They don't know yet," smirked Scott.

The MRAP accelerated towards the capitol, passing between the slender cypress trees on each side, and pulled up fifty meters short of the grove where the CSP was treating casualties.

On the far side of the grove was another MRAP. FBI agents were crouched down behind it, exchanging fire with CSP officers. It was an unequal fight, between the FBI's carbines and the CSP's pistols. If the officers in the other MRAP were suspicious of the arriving vehicle, they gave no sign.

Hugo looked across at Scott, expecting the sign to join the fight.

"Let Darnell do his thing first," replied Scott. Hugo followed his eyes and saw that Darnell was unpacking a Barrett M82 .50-caliber rifle. Hugo looked back at Scott and nodded appreciatively.

Darnell opened the gunner's hatch, settled the rifle with its stand on the roof, and took aim. The first round smashed through the engine grill of the FBI MRAP, and the sound of the radiator being ripped apart shrieked out across the park.

As the FBI officers shrank back behind their armored vehicle, trying to locate the source of the fire, Hugo and Scott scrambled to the back of their own vehicle. Darnell sent another .50-caliber round through the radiator and into the engine block of the FBI MRAP. In response, the agents showered the captured vehicle with carbine fire, but the lighter rounds made no impression on its laminated windshield and composite armor. Now it was the FBI agents' turn to take cover, surprised at being outmuscled by the enemy.

Scott jumped down onto the ground behind the MRAP. Hugo followed him, ready to head towards the state police position, but Scott indicated to stand with him by the rear passenger side. After a few seconds, as Hugo fidgeted impatiently, Scott gestured for Hugo to listen. They could hear the growl of a seven-liter turbodiesel engine as another MRAP approached.

Hugo looked quizzically at Scott, who pushed the flat palm of his hand down towards the ground, indicating for him to be patient.

The third MRAP emerged from the north and halted about fifty yards from the state police position, the same distance as the other two.

A couple of men emerged around the side of the latest MRAP. Scott grinned because they were in civilian clothes like he and Hugo were, not the olive-green FBI SWAT uniform.

"The feebs will be wondering as well. We need to provide cover while they set up their fifty-cal on the roof."

Hugo and Scott ran along one side of their MRAP. Scott opened the passenger door and started to shoot his M4 from the angle of the door and windshield. Hugo crouched down, advanced a few steps, put his M4 on burst, then stood up behind the engine compartment and aimed the three rounds at the FBI MRAP. Scott gestured for Hugo to follow him. They went back behind their MRAP and around to the other side and surveilled the state police position again.

Hugo looked expectantly at Scott, who thought for a couple of seconds before replying.

"OK. But I can't fire left-handed. Wait here and be ready to cover me."

Hugo nodded and set his weapon to single-shot mode as Scott went back around into the front compartment from the passenger side and cracked open the driver's door so that Hugo would know he was there.

Although there were no FBI agents visible, Hugo leaned out from behind the MRAP and squeezed off a couple of rounds, aiming for the tires of the FBI vehicle.

He called out "Go," and Scott opened the driver's door, jumped down ground behind it, and aimed his weapon in the angle between the door and the windshield. Without looking back, he waved at Hugo to advance.

Hugo ran past the open door, crouching slightly but keeping an eye on the FBI MRAP as he headed towards it. To reach the Civil War Grove, he had to cross the line between the two armored vehicles, getting in the way of the covering fire that was supposed to protect him. Sure enough, he saw an agent who appeared from behind the FBI MRAP, but as he prepared his shot, Hugo changed the angle of his run and the shot went a few inches to one side Then Scott was able to fire again, and by then Hugo was reaching the white park benches that lay round the quarter circle that bound the grove. He vaulted over and was hidden from FBI and AFL fighters alike by the shrubs. Hugo straightened up and lengthened his stride as he reached the center of the grove.

Beyond the gray stone monument, he saw the CSP canopy tent. Beyond that was an FBI MRAP, without any personnel in evidence. Hugo saw movement on the canvas wall of the tent and realized it was the shadow of someone inside. He approached the tent, both hands on his M4 but almost broke his step when he recognized the voice coming from inside the tent: Carl. Hugo couldn't make out his words, but Carl's sneering tone made Hugo grit his teeth. He slowed his pace and started to head towards the back of the tent, hoping for a way to take Carl by surprise. But then he heard another voice, challenging Carl but tense and fearful. It was Valentina. The sound of her voice overrode all he'd been taught about protecting himself in a firefight. He raised his weapon and his aim zeroed in on what he judged Carl's position to be, based on his shadow on the wall of the tent and the angle of the light from the door. He squeezed off a single round. He thought he heard it hit Carl's chest, but he knew that was impossible above the discharge. Hugo crouch-ran to the door and into the tent.

First he saw Valentina, lying on the ground next to someone that, at the back of his mind, he realized was Raul. Then he saw that Carl had been thrown by the impact of the rifle shot across the tent. He was dazed and immobile, his head and torso leaning against the fabric wall. There was no visible blood or organ spatter: his body armor had saved him. Hugo rolled him onto his front, causing him to scream out in pain and twitch spasmodically. Maybe broken ribs, thought Hugo as he bound Carl's hands behind his back with a cable tie.

"You and your mongrel bitch are still going to be taken out," sneered Carl.

Enraged, Hugo rolled Carl over and raised his rifle butt to crush his face, but Valentina shouted at him.

"Not in cold blood!"

Hugo paused, then swung his rifle over his shoulder. He rolled Carl facedown again and used more cable ties to hog-tie him.

Valentina rushed over to Hugo and they embraced.

"You're going to see why you couldn't make it in the Army," Carl taunted Hugo.

Still with one arm around Valentina's waist as she hugged him, Hugo looked over at Raul. Neither of them liked what Carl seemed to be suggesting. They held each other's gaze while they paused, listening. They heard the clattering of helicopter blades.

"We should get out of here," said Hugo as he looked back down at Carl, making sure he was securely bound.

Hugo took his knife from his pocket and cut a slit in the wall of the tent that faced the FBI MRAP that Carl had come in. There was no sign of life there. Still, rather than risk being shot at should they leave by the tent door, Hugo cut a new door in the opposite wall of the tent and gestured to the other two to follow him.

A couple of minutes later they were approaching the MRAP that Hugo had arrived in.

"Hey," called out Scott when Hugo and the others were about fifty meters away.

Hugo gestured to the other two that they should halt. Scott was right: he needed to know what was going on.

"I rescued a CSP officer and a civilian who were under fire from the FBI," Hugo called back.

"Proceed."

Seconds later, the three of them were inside the vehicle.

"Darnell is with the others, trying to outflank," added Scott, seeing Hugo look around.

Hugo grunted in acknowledgment.

"The feeb tried to needle me by saying the cavalry was coming," Hugo continued.

"We've got people watching the Collins base to the east of downtown, and there's no movement."

Hugo didn't want to let it go, but didn't have an answer either.

The helicopter sound filled the gap in conversation.

"It's not overhead anymore, it's to the west, near to the Sacramento River."

Hugo scrambled out of the back and round the side of the MRAP, then stepped away till he could get a clear sight of the helicopter through the trees, then ran back into the vehicle.

"It's a Bell 412, probably FBI."

The others looked at him blankly.

"Can you use that thing?" he asked Scott, pointing to the .50-cal rifle on the floor.

A couple of minutes later they were heading back towards the state capitol. Hugo stuck his head and shoulders out of the roof hatch, trying not to let the helicopter crew see that he wasn't wearing the black uniform of FBI SWAT. He lifted his arm, palm open, giving them the all OK signal.

"Is there any green space with trees, closer to the helicopter?"

Valentina thought of what Hugo might have in mind and hesitated to reply, but then thought of Carl.

"The closest would be Plaza de California, on the far side of the capitol."

The MRAP accelerated. Although Valentina yelled at Scott, there was no way for him to avoid running over some of the civilian bodies that remained from the assault by ICE and the FBI. He headed south and went along the side of the park, to be able to get around the capitol building. Then he swung the MRAP north again, in front of the rotunda. Hugo jumped out and headed up the steps, while Scott kept on west towards the river, and the helicopter.

In the plaza, Scott parked MRAP pointing at one of the cedar trees, and the roof hatch under only the smallest branches. Then he went into the rear compartment and hefted the .50-cal rifle up through the hatch and onto the roof.

Hugo caught them up, running.

"I can see armored vehicles approaching. On the far side of Tower Bridge."

"Taking out that helo might give them pause," said Raul.

Hugo nodded.

"Better stay inside," Scott told them, as he clambered from the driving compartment towards the back of the vehicle, then up through the roof hatch. A few seconds later, he took his first shot at the helicopter.

Nothing seemed to happen.

He shot again and debris blew up and off the rear fuselage of the helicopter before gently floating down again. The helicopter climbed. Scott took another shot with no apparent effect.

Smoke started to come out of the helicopter and it lost height again, then headed towards the MRAP. Before Scott could shoot again, the helicopter turned side on, and the MRAP was pocked with rifle fire. Scott got off his last shot, which hit the rotor mechanism and sent the helicopter heading down, northwards, towards the Southern Pacific district. Scott yelled and slumped against the back of the roof hatch.

Valentina went to ease him down inside the vehicle, shouting at Hugo to help her. A rifle bullet had ricocheted off the roof of the MRAP and hit Scott in the face, smashing through his cheekbone and taking off his left ear.

"We need to get him to hospital."

"How bad is he?"

Raul could tell what Hugo was thinking.

"I saw how Scott was driving this thing. I'll take it a few blocks further west, you jump out, and we'll take him to the hospital."

"You're concussed, remember?" said Valentina.

Hugo and Raul avoided her gaze.

"How different is this thing to drive than a normal car?"

The two men didn't answer.

"Do you even know the streets of Sacramento?

"I don't want those army bastards taking over the city after how they've treated you," she said, looking at Hugo. "Don't worry, I don't have a problem with Raul's plan, just let me drive."

Seconds later they were heading west on L Street, parallel to Capitol Mall but less visible, they hoped. There was no traffic, and the only pedestrians looked like they were hurrying to get home. When they came to the end of the street, with the West Side Freeway in front of them, Valentina turned south on Third Street, then stopped again at the next corner. Hugo leaned forward to kiss her, then jumped out of the back of the vehicle onto Capitol Mall. The MRAP speeded across the mall and turned back east at the next corner, heading to Valentina's hospital in Elmhurst.

Hugo looked towards the bridge from the corner of Third Street and Capitol Mall. There was no moving traffic, just a yellow light reconnaissance vehicle parked at the near end of the bridge, in the middle of the four lanes. There was no sign of any opposing forces coming from the side of the capitol, either from the CSP or the AFL. Hugo looked back at the LRV. It usually had a crew of four. Hugo needed a way to get onto the bridge without being seen.

A bus had been abandoned between the bridge and the Capitol. Hugo climbed the fence into the empty corner lot, walked over to the other side and climbed back out again. From his backpack he took out a thermite grenade and ducked through the bus's open door. He pulled the pin on the grenade and was back out and over the fence before it started sparking.

Over his shoulder, Hugo had an M4 carbine with an M203 grenade launcher under the barrel. When he was back on Third Street, he opened the barrel of the launcher and snapped in an olive-and-gold 40mm round. He walked a block to the north and took aim at the clouds reflected in the facade of the California State Controller's building on the far side of Capitol Mall. The high-explosive round punched through the glass, exploded inside and blew out windows across half the width of the building. By the time the glass hit the ground, Hugo was running north.

One of the LRV crew trained their binoculars on the building, then noticed the bus on the other side of Capitol Mall. The thermite grenade had burned through the floor of the bus, and flames were licking up the aluminum bodywork.

Hugo turned west and ran under the West Side Freeway on K Street.

The LRV left its position at the end of the bridge, trying to ascertain the cause of the fires a couple of blocks east.

Hugo reached the deserted tourist piers and restaurants on the bank of the Sacramento River. He was tempted to turn back south and run along the pier, which went as far as the bridge, but for all he knew the LRV crew would have him in their sights. So he carried straight on and dove into the river. He let the slow current do the work as he stayed close to the pier. No sign of the LRV.

The base of each tower of the bridge was shielded with diagonally sloping wooden boards, to absorb the impact of flood debris. Hugo climbed up the boards to the top. He pulled himself and took a glance along the level of the pedestrian walkway before letting himself back down. Having seen that the LRV had left its location, he pulled himself up again, rolled over the fence onto the walkway, then ran west, towards the middle of the bridge. Then he left the walkway again, climbed onto the bottom of a metal staircase, and kept on up.

The staircase led to the control room on top of the bridge's middle section, between the two towers. From the other side of the control room's glass door, the operator looked back at Hugo in a daze, as if he'd already seen too much that day. Hugo gestured at him to open the door. Having clocked Hugo's rifle, the operator complied reluctantly.

"I'm not going to hurt you. I'm not going to blow anything up. I just want to raise the bridge."

The operator just looked at Hugo blankly. Something caught Hugo's eye on the road below, and they both looked west. A column of tanks on Tower Bridge Gateway was heading towards them. As things stood, they'd be over the bridge in a couple of minutes and would take the capitol area unopposed.

The operator was still acting dumb. Hugo wanted to knock him down but told himself to remember what he'd just said about not hurting him.

"Do you want those cowboys turning Sacramento into Baghdad?"

"I don't want to be on the wrong side of them either."

"Turn around."

As the operator did so, Hugo took a zip tie from a pocket, then used it to cuff the operator's hands behind his back.

The control board was pretty simple. Hugo pointed to where it said "BRIDGE RAISE," between a gearstick-style lever and a couple of chunky push buttons.

"This is how you do it?"

The operator raised his eyebrows, as if asking what else.

The first tank was past the first pair of limestone pillars on the far side of the bridge, going about thirty miles per hour.

The first button was labeled "Engage pawls." Hugo pressed it, and it lit up green inside. Same with the next one, labeled "Raise."

The first tank had passed the second pair of limestone pillars and was inside the box girder frame of the bridge proper. Behind it, the second tank was passing the pillars, followed by a couple of Stryker armored vehicles and more tanks.

Hugo pushed the lever. Buzzers sounded and Hugo felt the floor tremble as the center section started to lift under them.

The first tank was also on the center section now, oblivious to the few centimeters that it had lifted.

Hugo jammed the lever up to its limit, willing the bridge to lift faster.

The first tank went under the control room and disappeared from Hugo's view. The second one slowed down as it approached the center section but easily mounted the step up. But it didn't speed up again. Hugo imagined its commander speaking to his comrade up ahead. With his hand still on the lifting lever, Hugo turned round to look out the windows on the east side. The first tank hadn't yet come out from under the control room. But the central section was getting ever higher, and closer to the lowest of the east tower's horizontal girders.

The first Stryker armored vehicle had reached the west end of the center section. As Hugo turned back to watch it, clouds of exhaust fumes plumed from the side of the vehicle as the driver revved the engine and the wheels spun against the exposed vertical end of the center section. By now, the step up was too high to climb. Worse for him, the driver hadn't noticed that the center section had reached the nose of his Stryker, and had started to lift it. Now the front wheels were spinning off the ground, and the front of the vehicle was getting hoisted higher and higher. As the second set of wheels left the ground, the infantry squad started to leave the vehicle via the rear ramp.

The second tank had stopped while it was still in Hugo's line of sight. Conversely, he was in the line of fire for its machine gun, which turned towards him in the control room. It took aim, but instead of firing, it held its position. The center section was still lifting both the tanks and the control room. Hugo imagined the soldiers on the radio, doubting whether to shoot at the machinery that was holding them up above the Sacramento River.

Half a dozen infantry from the Stryker had climbed up over the top of their immobilized vehicle, which was now forty-five degrees to the road. The infantry jumped off the nose of their vehicle, down onto the center section, and ran east, towards Hugo and the control room. He kept the lever up to its maximum position and they carried on lifting. He looked to the east again. The first tank was coming to the end of the center section. Its gun projected over the end and it looked like the tank commander was going to take his chances diving over the edge and onto the east section. But as he went ahead, the top of the turret jammed against the lowest horizontal girders of the east tower. The driver revved the engine and the tank jerked forward a couple more feet, but at the cost of jamming itself more firmly between the center section and the tower.

In the control room, a warning light flashed red and Hugo heard the gear wheels of the mechanism groan as they worked vainly against the tank hull. On the east side of the bridge, he could see the Army LRV was targeting its .50-caliber machine gun on a pickup truck further up Capitol Mall. The control room was twenty feet above the road level now. A movement on top of the multistory parking garage caught Hugo's eye, to the north of the Mall. Before Hugo could focus, he saw a weapon discharged from the top floor. A split second later the LRV was blown to pieces. Another high-explosive round from a grenade launcher. As bright yellow shards of LRV bodywork continued to fall back down into the bridge off-ramp, Hugo looked to its south side, where windows were being knocked out of the top floor of the hotel.

Hugo realized that he'd bought enough time for his mission to be successful. Even if tanks got through now, they'd be targeted from above. The tanks' main guns couldn't elevate high enough to fire on the defenders, who could them themselves fire down on the tanks' weakest spot: the upper surface of their gun turrets.

Hugo looked back down and saw the soldiers from the Stryker approaching the center of the elevated section. Hugo nodded to the bridge operator trussed up on the floor, who glared back at him. Hugo stepped out of the door and aimed his weapon at the soldiers, but he was too late: they were out of sight, under the control room. The first of them would be starting up the metal staircase towards him. Hugo looked down again, and his eyes took a split second to focus on the smooth surface of the Sacramento River. Although the center section had been jammed before reaching its maximum height, Hugo reckoned he was still fifty feet above the water.

Hugo tried to remember his training in the Colombian military. He stepped one leg over the handrail and put his heel back on the edge of the step. Then the other leg, hooking his ankles together. He heard the American soldiers' feet pounding up the metal steps. He used his arms to lift himself off the ladder and let himself drop feet first.

82

Sacramento Capitol

VALENTINA GUNNED the MRAP's engine, barrelled it round the plaza, then out and left at the corner of Capitol park. As she turned the mammoth vehicle, she looked in vain, up and to the north, for any clue about Hugo. She accelerated along the wide-open N Street, Capitol Park to their left, with smoke rising from a couple of burnt-out vehicles.

"Ambulance," said Raul, pointing to the side of the street, a block ahead.

"Right," replied Valentina as she saw it parked on the left, with a few walking wounded around it.

"Stop!" shouted Raul.

Reflexively, Valentina jumped on the brake and wrestled the wheel of the AMRAP as it slewed to a halt.

Only then did she realise that a garbage truck up ahead wasn't going their way but was reversing towards them, fast. And AFL men were aiming rifles at them from behind parked vehicles on both sides of the street. She remembered that they were in an FBI vehicle, and looked across at Raul. He was already slowly opening his door. She followed his cue, and they both climbed down to the ground and walked slowly forwards, hands on heads.

One of the AFL men approached them. Valentina and Raul didn't look like FBI and they soon convinced the AFL men. They showed them Scott in the back of the AMRAP, groaning in pain and with a bloody chunk missing from the side of his face. The AFL men gestured to the ambulance and a couple of paramedics ran over. As they attended Scott, Raul saw Valentina looking across Capitol Park to the north. One of the paramedics brought a gurney from the ambulance and they helped Scott onto it.

As the paramedics trundled scott back to the ambulance, Valentina gestured at Raul to get back in the MRAP. She turned it around as quickly as she could, smashing a couple of parked cars in the process, and headed back.

From the Plaza de California they had a clear view up Capitol Mall to Tower Bridge. Smoke was rising from the remains of the LRV on the ramp. The center section of the bridge was partly raised, with the turret of a tank jammed against the horizontal girders of the nearer tower. An FBI helicopter was hovering over the near end of the bridge. As they watched, the center section shuddered and started to lower.

"Hugo," Valentina and Raul said together.

"We need to get closer," said Valentina.

"That way we'll be sitting ducks for everyone," said Raul, gesturing up Capitol Mall, "and we can't even shoot back."

So Valentina turned back south, then west, parallel to Capitol Mall, swerving round the uneven grid of city blocks. She had a clear run at the overpass above I-5, and she and Raul floated for a second as the MRAP lifted off. They thumped back down, and Valentina's eyes refocused on the Sacramento River in front of them.

Valentina had a flashback to what Hugo had told her, of passing out from hypoxia in the Atrato River, of the dismembered bodies of people who, if they were lucky, would be renamed and buried by campesinos downstream.

"He's in the river," she told Raul.

She tried to keep the MRAP straight as they ran out of road and bounded over railway tracks. The engine almost stalled as they hit concrete steps, but Valentina revved the engine till the vehicle jolted up onto the riverside walkway. To their right, armored vehicles were backed up on the west side of Tower Bridge, stranded by the center section which was still on its way down to their level.

Leaving the engine running, Valentina climbed down out of the cab of the MRAP and looked down on the river.

The vehicle radio came to life again.

"Tango Three, this is Raven Two, request status, over."

"They sound more serious," Raul called out to Valentina, who just continued to scan the river haphazardly. She told herself to reconstruct what Hugo would have done.

"Tango Three, this is Raven Two, identify yourselves, over."

Raul looked out the right side window and saw that the FBI helicopter left its station over the bridge off-ramp and was headed towards them.

"They know their vehicle's been captured," shouted Raul, as he headed out the cab on the left side, away from the helicopter.

Valentina let her eyes follow the water currents in the river, trying not to get ahead of the flow. Then she looked back upstream to the east tower of the bridge, the one which Hugo had blocked. She followed the current, imagining Hugo trying to use it to get away from the bridge, but avoiding the full force of the center of the river. The eddies led her past their point on the bank. She turned left to follow them, further downstream than she wanted Hugo to be.

She saw a white fleck on their side of the river, a couple of hundred yards downstream.

Raul grabbed her shoulder.

"They're coming for their vehicle," he shouted, gesturing at the helicopter, which was almost above them.

The white fleck moved downstream, then stopped again.

"There," Valentina pointed.

She and Raul clambered over the walkway and down to the riverbank.

Epilogue

Hugo was waiting in a pickup outside City Hall with Darnell. They were relaxed, knowing that, to avoid all-out urban warfare around the Sacramento capitol, the president had ordered the federal forces back to their bases. ICE detentions and deportations had been paused in California. Thanks to Hugo, the Army column had lost the element of surprise in their attempt to seize the capitol in Sacramento, and the president had agreed to a cease-fire with the governor. Federal warrants against Hugo and the other AFL men had been withdrawn, although they would be reinstated if they entered other states.

Hugo looked up towards the top of City Hall. The banners had been taken down from the Bradley Room, but there were a few small knots of people with anti-ICE messages written on old cardboard boxes.

The main doors opened. A couple of CSP officers came out and stood guard on either side. Devon emerged, speaking on his cell phone over a wireless headset. He strode confidently over to the pickup and got in the back seat. He nodded at Darnell in the rearview mirror, and they set off.

Devon seemed to be speaking with Gabriel Rangel. The governor had not pursued his plan to swear in a successor to Rangel as attorney general. As the pickup climbed the up ramp to the Harbor Freeway, the AG brought the call to a close.

Devon hung up and turned to look at Hugo in the seat in front of him.

"So you going AWOL to Sacramento turned out good," said Devon, needling him amicably.

"Yes, sir."

"Up to a point. When are they taking those things off?" asked Devon, nodding at the casts round Hugo's calves. He was a purely honorary part of Devon's PSD today. Despite his precautions, he'd broken both his legs on jumping into the Sacramento River. He would have been swept downstream if not for Valentina and Raul.

"A couple of months, sir."

Devon continued in a more serious tone.

"I heard you were disappointed with the AFL funding model."

"Yes, sir."

"High standards."

Devon paused before continuing.

"I'm going to tell you something that's going to come out now, with the peace talks. But I want you to hear it from me."

"Yes, sir?"

"You know the big lie from INS about my false Jamaican passport?"

"Yes, sir."

"It's not a lie."

Hugo was jolted but didn't say anything.

"But it's not the whole truth either. They were happy enough with my passport when I wanted to sign up for the Army. When I wanted to become a citizen, then they had another look and decided it wasn't right."

Devon looked over the concrete wall bordering the freeway, at the heads of palm trees in Westmont.

"My mother was an Apostle, you know that?"

"No, sir."

Devon laughed.

"Not the church kind. She was a guerrilla in the New Jewel Movement in Grenada. She was the only woman in a squad of twelve that got trained in Guyana. The so-called Apostles. Soon enough they led the revolution in Grenada. That lasted four years before America invaded. My mother fled to Cuba with the Cuban forces that had been based in Grenada. I was born in Cuba, man."

He laughed again.

"And my parents were communist guerrillas. You can see why I went with that fake passport.

"My mother couldn't stomach Cuba for long. She took her chances with me in a boat to Jamaica as a—what d'you call it?—*balsera*. We made it just before they started turning people back."

Hugo was staggered and it took him a second to think of a comeback.

"So you're doubly illegal, man. Just who we need at these peace talks."

"Yeah, regular man of the world, I am."

By now they were off the freeway, driving south across the eastern end of the runway of Hawthorne Municipal Airport. The peace talks were going to be in Puerto Rico, outside the jurisdiction of any US state. Darnell turned off the road and up to the terminal, a two-story building partly covered with wooden cladding.

"You know, there's one thing I wish the peace deal could say," said Hugo.

"Yeah?"

"Service guarantees citizenship."

"You got it."

Devon was already stepping out of the door. He headed towards a couple of California State Police officers. Hugo watched the three of them go inside the building, then turned to Darnell. They clasped hands, then Darnell helped him out of the truck.

Valentina was there to hand him his crutches. She embraced him, then they headed slowly towards her car, for the short drive to Mrs. Torres's place.

Enjoyed the book? Spread the word!

Please take a moment to leave a review online.

Your thoughts help other readers discover and enjoy this story.

Thank you for your support!

About the Author

Neal Alexander was born in Newcastle upon Tyne in England. He has lived and worked in Nigeria, Papua New Guinea and Colombia. He has co-written multiple scripts for short and feature films, and this is his first novel.

About the Publisher

Extraliminal Producciones was established in Cali, Colombia, in 2007, and has produced multiple short films, some scripted by its members and others developed in youth workshops.

Made in the USA
Middletown, DE
30 July 2024

58225488R00189